BAD NEWS BRIEFING

Pacino outlined the operation. "Our only way out of the bay is through a six-mile-wide channel. That choke point will be patrolled heavily by the Northern Fleet. Force strength of the fleet includes three missile cruisers, fourteen destroyers, sixteen frigates, thirty-four torpedo patrol boats and their new aircraft carrier, the one they got from the Russians, the *Shaoguan*. There are some two dozen minor coastal patrol craft but none of them can hurt us unless we surface. The skimmer forces are most formidable because of the helicopters they carry. I expect to see over forty seaborne choppers. There could be more, a lot more, in the form of aircraft based on land. Plus, the *Shaoguan* will be putting up vertical takeoff/landing aircraft. Plus, there are three Han-class nuclear-powered attack subs and two Ming-class diesel subs, both of them new." Pacino paused and looked at his men. "Now, how do we get out of the bay once we get in?"

After a moment of silence, Pacino frowned. "Oh, hell, maybe we just worry about that when the time comes. Dismissed."

ATTACK OF THE SEAWOLF

"Nail-biting excitment . . . a must for techno-thriller fans!"   —*Publishers Weekly*

"Gobs of exciting
supervillain who gi
'torture.' "

ATTACK OF THE SEAWOLF

Michael DiMercurio

AN ONYX BOOK

ONYX
Published by the Penguin Group
Penguin Books USA Inc., 375 Hudson Street,
New York, New York 10014, U.S.A.
Penguin Books Ltd, 27 Wrights Lane,
London W8 5TZ, England
Penguin Books Australia Ltd, Ringwood,
Victoria, Australia
Penguin Books Canada Ltd, 10 Alcorn Avenue,
Toronto, Ontario, Canada M4V 3B2
Penguin Books (N.Z.) Ltd, 182–190 Wairau Road,
Auckland 10, New Zealand

Penguin Books Ltd, Registered Offices:
Harmondsworth, Middlesex, England

Published by Onyx, an imprint of Dutton Signet,
a division of Penguin Books USA Inc. This is an authorized
reprint of a hardcover edition published by Donald I. Fine, Inc.
For information address Donald I. Fine, Inc. 19 West 21st Street
New York, NY 10010

First Onyx Printing, June, 1994
10 9 8 7 6 5 4 3 2 1

PUBLISHER'S NOTE
This is a work of fiction. Names, characters, places, and incidents either are
the product of the author's imagination or are used fictitiously, and any resem-
blance to actual persons, living or dead, events, or locales is entirely
coincidental.

To Theresa Lynn,
Matthew Robert,
and
Marla Dean

ACKNOWLEDGMENTS

This book, and an entire writing career, is the result of a long chain of people, all of them extraordinary. The line certainly begins with parents and extends through teachers and mentors, commanding officers and colleagues. To those who have helped on the way, I offer my thanks:

To Donald I. Fine, the giant of publishing who taught me the hard parts and was patient with me when I might not have deserved it.

To Natasha Kern, my agent, the first to see something in the words I wrote.

To Alice Price, who convinced Natasha that what she saw was not a mirage.

To Adam Levison, an editor who listened and explained.

To Barbara Field for her superb illustrations, and for her willingness to learn the insides of a nuclear submarine to make them.

To Andrew Hoffer, production manager, who made it seem easy.

To Richard Marcinko, the venerable commander and founder of SEAL Team Six, a daring and creative Navy SEAL who revolutionized modern special warfare commando techniques, whose life stories came to me not only from his excellent book *Rogue Warrior* but from Bique family folklore and the girl who used to babysit his kids.

To Lieutenant Commander David DeLonga, Ph.D., my old roommate from MIT, Scuba School, and the USS *Hammerhead,* who opened up the world of deep-diving submersibles and showed me exactly how one goes about flying a helicopter.

To the officers and men of the U.S. Submarine Force, especially the alumni of the USS *Hammerhead*, SSN-663, and especially to Commander Tim Mulcare, now executive officer of the *Norfolk*, who showed me the workings of a 688 class.

To every teacher who cared, particularly those at Ballard H.S. in Louisville, KY., and at Annapolis.

And, of course, to Mom and Dad.

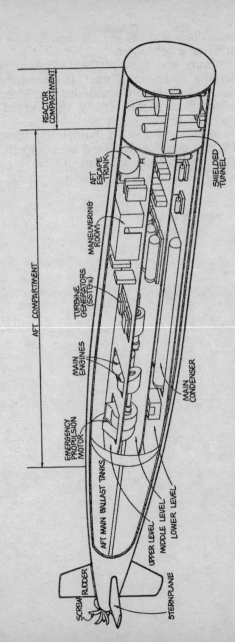

USS Tampa (Los Angeles-Class)
SSN-774 (Aft Section)

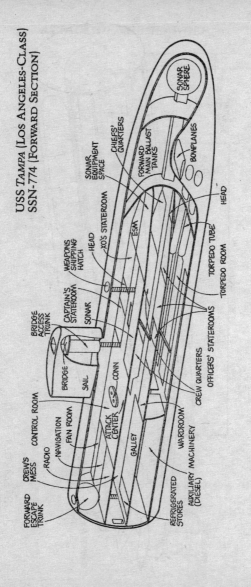

USS *Tampa* (Los Angeles-Class)
SSN-774 (Forward Section)

SONAR SPHERE

BOWPLANES

CHIEFS' QUARTERS

FORWARD MAIN BALLAST TANKS

SONAR EQUIPMENT SPACE

HEAD

XO'S STATEROOM

TORPEDO TUBE

ESM

TORPEDO ROOM

HEAD

WEAPONS SHIPPING HATCH

CAPTAIN'S STATEROOM

SONAR

BRIDGE ACCESS TRUNK

OFFICERS' STATEROOMS

CREW QUARTERS

BRIDGE

SAIL

CONN

CONTROL ROOM

ATTACK CENTER

WARDROOM

NAVIGATION

FAN ROOM

GALLEY

RADIO

CREW'S MESS

AUXILIARY MACHINERY (DIESEL)

FORWARD ESCAPE TRUNK

REFRIGERATED STORES

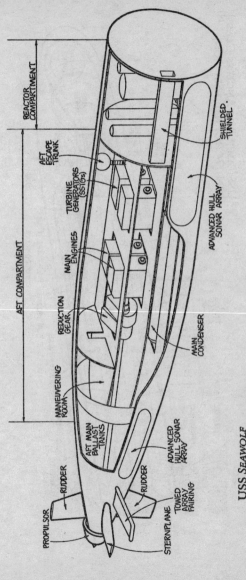

REACTOR COMPARTMENT

AFT COMPARTMENT

SHIELDED TUNNEL

AFT ESCAPE TRUNK

TURBINE GENERATORS (SSTGs)

MAIN ENGINES

REDUCTION GEAR

MANEUVERING ROOM

ADVANCED HULL SONAR ARRAY

MAIN CONDENSER

AFT MAIN BALLAST TANKS

ADVANCED HULL SONAR ARRAY

PROPULSOR

RUDDER

RUDDER

STERNPLANE

TOWED ARRAY FAIRING

USS *Seawolf*
SSN-21 (AFT SECTION)

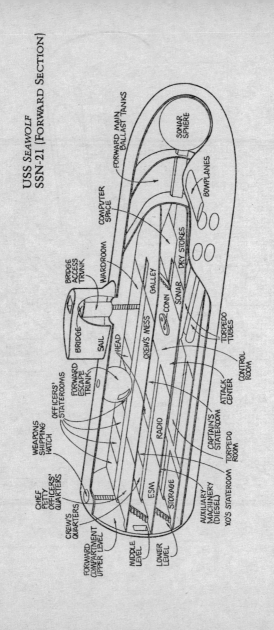

USS *Seawolf*
SSN-21 (FORWARD SECTION)

SONAR SPHERE

FORWARD MAIN BALLAST TANKS

BOWPLANES

COMPUTER SPACE

DRY STORES

WARDROOM

BRIDGE ACCESS TRUNK

GALLEY

SONAR

CONN

BRIDGE

SAIL

HEAD

CREW'S MESS

TORPEDO TUBES

FORWARD ESCAPE TRUNK

CONTROL ROOM

OFFICERS' STATEROOMS

RADIO

ATTACK CENTER

CAPTAIN'S STATEROOM

WEAPONS SHIPPING HATCH

ESM

STORAGE

TORPEDO ROOM

AUXILIARY MACHINERY (DIESEL)

XO'S STATEROOM

CHIEF PETTY OFFICERS' QUARTERS

CREW'S QUARTERS

FORWARD COMPARTMENT UPPER LEVEL

MIDDLE LEVEL

LOWER LEVEL

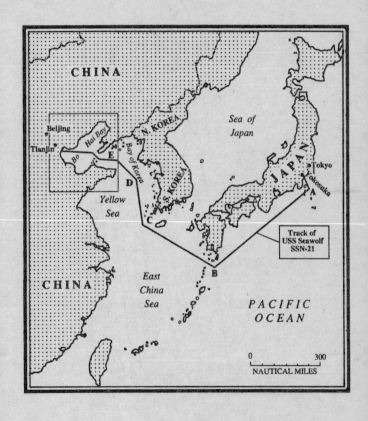

CHINA

N. KOREA

Beijing

Tianjin

Bo

Hai Bay

E

Bay of Korea

D

S. KOREA

Yellow
Sea

C

CHINA

East
China
Sea

Sea of
Japan

JAPAN

Tokyo

Yokosuka

A

Track of
USS Seawolf
SSN-21

B

PACIFIC
OCEAN

0   300

NAUTICAL MILES

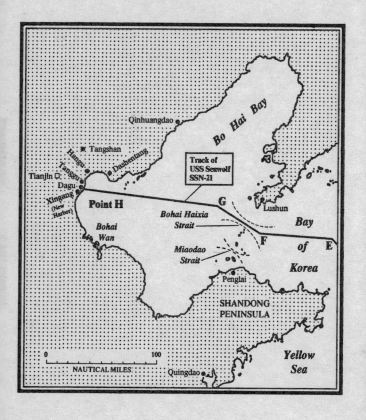

He who will not risk cannot win.
  —JOHN PAUL JONES

Pick out the biggest and commence firing.
  —CAPTAIN MIKE MORAN, USS *Boise.*

Fight her till she sinks and don't give up the ship.
  —CAPTAIN JAMES LAWRENCE OF THE USS
    Chesapeake, as he was carried below,
    mortally wounded, in his losing fight with the
    HMS *Shannon.*

The colors must never be struck.
  —LIEUTENANT WILLIAM BURROWS, USS
    Enterprise, 1813.

Take her down.
  —COMMANDER HOWARD GILMORE, aboard the
    World War II submarine USS *Growler,*
    ordering his crew to leave him on deck,
    wounded as he was, and submerge
    to save the ship.

CODE OF CONDUCT FOR MEMBERS
OF THE ARMED FORCES
OF THE UNITED STATES

I. I am an American fighting man. I serve in the forces which guard my country and our way of life. I am prepared to give my life in their defense.

II. I will never surrender of my own free will. If in command I will never surrender my men while they still have the means to resist.

III. If I am captured I will continue to resist by all means available. I will make every effort to escape and aid others to escape. I will accept neither parole nor special favors from the enemy.

IV. If I become a prisoner of war, I will keep faith with my fellow prisoners. I will give no information or take part in any action which might be harmful to my comrades. If I am senior, I will take command. If not, I will obey the lawful orders of those appointed over me and will back them up in every way.

V. When questioned, should I become a prisoner of war, I am bound to give only name, rank, service number, and date of birth. I will evade answering further questions to the utmost of my ability. I will make no oral or written statements disloyal to my country and its allies or harmful to their cause.

VI. I will never forget that I am an American fighting man, responsible for my actions, and dedicated to the principles which made my country free. I will trust in my God and in the United States of America.

ATTACK OF THE SEAWOLF

PROLOGUE

WEDNESDAY, 1 MAY

Loyang, Honan Province
People's Republic of China

Even in the moonless night, the KL-87's digital infra-red camera captured the endless rows of crudely cam-ouflaged People's Liberation Army tanks, the Main Force Battalion that was waiting to ambush the oppo-sition White Army brigade advancing from the west.

Su Lee snapped off the images, the photos captured on the camera's computer memory, satisfied that she had gotten it all. After one last glance at the huge armored force in the valley below, she climbed back onto the rickety bicycle for the trip back to the village, to her room in the women's dormitory of the farming cooperative. Although it was risky to be out in the middle of the night, her situation gave her an implied cover—as a former prostitute under rehabilitation, her nocturnal activities would immediately be assumed to do with her original crime. No one would suspect her of espionage. Unless they found the KL-87's digital camera in her bag. And who would want to search a prostitute's handbag?

She pedaled through the moonlit night back to the village, past the sleepy and shabby buildings of the farm cooperative, until she reached the hut of her own co-op. She parked the bicycle against the building and slowly climbed the creaking stairs to her tiny room. She shut the door behind her, set the digital imager on the bed, and pulled the remainder of the KL-87 set from its hiding place in her beat-up suitcase, wrapped securely in old clothes.

The KL-87 was a three-module secure communications system, newly developed in the United States by DynaCorp International. The first module was the digital imager, a camera that took photographs recorded not on film but on a computer hard disk for later uplink by the transmitter module. The second piece was a small computer keyboard and tilting screen, used for typing in a message and encoding it. The third module was the transmitter/antenna assembly, which took the encrypted messages and digital camera images and uplinked them on a time-varying secure UHF frequency to an orbiting U.S. communications satellite in a geosynchronous orbit over the western Pacific. The entire kit, when stowed, took up no more room than two shoe boxes, but weighed a solid ten pounds.

Su Lee checked the door and the window, then sat on the bed to begin her typing, the message introducing the uplink of the photos with a brief verbal description of the PLA force strength. She typed in the instructions for encoding the message, plugged in the digital imager, tied in the transmitter, and hit the two-key combination ordering the unit to transmit. Satisfied, she watched as the unit transmitted the signals to the satellite above. It was unfortunate that the photographs contained so much data—the transmission would take almost fifteen minutes to uplink all the bits from the photos. Su was about to cover the KL-87 with a bundle of clothing from the suitcase when the door crashed open.

Su Lee stared down the barrels of three AK-47 automatic rifles held by three Red Guards. She felt a burst of adrenaline, a flash of raw fear, soaking her armpits, nauseating her stomach. In reflex, she plunged her hands under the KL-87, getting under its weight, and threw the connected modules at the first of the Red Guards. As the unit flew through the air, Su turned and plunged through the window, falling the twenty feet to the street below. Pain shot through her chest as ribs punctured lungs. Blood spurted from her neck, her flesh ripped apart by the fall through the window's thick glass. Su pressed a hand to her neck, the slick warm liquid soaking her arm. Above her, rifle fire sounded in the room, blowing the remainder of the glass from the window, showering her with fragments. One guardsman appeared at the window while footprints sounded on the street coming from the direction of the door.

By now blood surrounded Su. She couldn't move her legs, and the boots of the guards were thumping closer. Agony flooded her, more at being caught than at her injuries. In a savage movement of her free arm she pulled out the hem of her tunic, and with it, two tiny white pills she had carried with her since her arrival at Loyang. She bit both of them and swallowed, an almond bitterness filling her mouth.

By the time the guardsmen arrived to drag her up by her arms, Su Lee was dead.

LANGLEY, VIRGINIA
HEADQUARTERS, CENTRAL INTELLIGENCE AGENCY
OFFICE OF THE DIRECTOR OF CENTRAL INTELLIGENCE

Director Robert M. Kent frowned as he put the coffee mug down on his desk. The brew had gone cold and bitter. He looked up at Steve Jaspers, the Deputy Director of Operations, and accepted the briefing folders Jaspers handed over.

"The China penetration operation has derailed, sir," Jaspers said without preamble, sinking into a couch in front of Kent's large desk. "Six penetration agents were sent in. Two were lost on insertion, the other four reported they were set up and in position, but as of now the final four are compromised."

"Details," Kent said, opening the folder to the first page, showing a passport photo of an attractive young oriental woman and beneath it a summary of her background.

"The first was a contractor, operational name, Su Lee. She was dropped into Loyang in the Province of Honan south of the Yellow River. The territory is still in Communist hands, but only miles from forces of the White Army, which we believed were massing for an attack. Su was given identity papers as a relocating Beijing resident. The relocation was for political reasons—she was listed as a convicted prostitute, sent out to a farm co-op as 'rehabilitation.' We got her initial report on the KL-87 that she had picked up on rumors of White Army forces preparing for an attack from the west with the People's Liberation Army forces waiting for a counterattack to the east. She intended taking the digital imaging camera to the PLA troop encampment first. Apparently she was successful. The images had just started to come in on her second KL-87 transmission, which ended suddenly. Nothing more was heard from her.

"The second was another contractor, operational name, Chu Cheng. Chu parachuted into the village of Ganyu near the seacoast in northern Kiangsu province, again very near the border of White Army occupation, but still on territory controlled by the People's Republic. For the last two weeks his identity was working. He was set up as a teacher in a vocational school, with political relocation orders from Beijing. His cover story cast him as a former manufacturing engineer being rehabilitated for falsification of factory production statistics. We got his initial report that he was in place and intended to scout out the PLA positions in the vicinity, perhaps make a weekend trip over the line to the frontier. We haven't heard from him since. He's missed four scheduled reports. I have to presume he's captured or dead."

"The third?" Director Kent asked, a sour look

crossing his face as he shut Chu's file and opened the next in the stack.

"Third was Sung Yu-shu," Jaspers continued. "He was dropped into the village of Kangba, about one hundred and eighty miles north of Beijing. We had suspected this to be an area of future attacks by the White forces to the north. A week after Sung was inserted, we got his set-up transmission, but he reported that there was no White or PLA activity as we had suspected from the satellite photographs."

"Damned satellites," Kent grumbled. "We're getting less information from them than I'd have ever guessed. And they cost a half a billion each ..."

"They only show things, sir, not intentions or trends. Anyway, Sung intended to head further north and find out if he could sniff out any activity. We never heard from him again."

"The fourth?"

"Operational name, Hu To-pin. We set him up in Beijing after bringing him in by ship from the port of Tianjin and from there by rail to the capital. He took a job as a stock boy in a state-run store for party officials, which was conveniently located on Chang'An Avenue, not far from the Great Hall of the People. In addition to the KL-87, he was given some sophisticated eavesdropping gear for reception of UHF communications and microwave transmissions. The former to listen to orders from Beijing to PLA unit commanders, the latter for possible phone intercepts. He wasn't going to listen or interpret, just record the intercepts for compressed burst relay to the COMMSAT using the KL-87. The western Pacific COMMSAT yesterday afternoon logged that it was being addressed by Hu's KL-87, but after just a few seconds the transmission stopped. We haven't heard anything more. Hu has missed three check-in transmissions since. I'm listing him as compromised."

Kent glanced at the map of China that now occupied an entire wall of his office across from his desk. The Chinese Civil War remained the main priority of the CIA as well as Kent's chief personal frustration. The map showed the Japanese-supported insurgents of the White Army occupying a wide swath of the mainland from the southern coast to the north central region, cutting Communist China in half. The Communist Chinese still held the far west and the northeast, including the vicinity within three hundred miles of Beijing. The White Army was rumored to be preparing a massive assault on Beijing, but the rumors also held that Beijing was planning a counterattack that could wipe out the White Army and take back central China.

This bloody war had the potential to torch all of Asia, Kent thought, perhaps even spread further. There was still the question of China's old nuclear weapons, supposedly destroyed over the last five years, but perhaps only stockpiled in a PLA weapons depot. If China could sever the link between the White Army of the New Kuomintang and Japan by attacking Japan itself, this struggle, a mere Shanghai rebellion just the year before, could break out into world war, which was never supposed to happen again after the end of the Cold War. With the linking of the world's economic markets, a single air raid on Tokyo might well wipe out the computers of the world banking system, and with them start the worst depression of the century. If the Communists won, China would be sent back fifty years to the Mao era, perhaps starting another cold war, this time with the Chinese. If the democratic forces of the White Army won, China would likely be a future ally and trading partner.

America had to act, but Congress and the President had ruled out direct military intervention. The best Kent could hope to do was keep an eye on the war and make sure the White Army at least had the benefit of knowing what Beijing was doing. But how could he do that? Since diplomatic relations had been severed with Communist China, the CIA no longer had embassies or consulates to allow the operations of the station chiefs, which meant they had no way to collect intelligence from Chinese local agents. The progress of the Civil War was a complete mystery to the CIA and the administration. With Jaspers telling him that the penetration agents had failed, intelligence on the Civil War would be solely by satellite photographs, which were nearly useless without human reports from the ground. Without hard intelligence, the White Army would not have the benefit of intelligence and U.S. foreign policy would have to be made in the dark. And the President wanted answers. Now.

Kent shut the last of the four files and looked up at Jaspers.

"So now we brief the President that we haven't got a single idea what's going on in goddamned China." Kent stood, handing back the briefing folders to Jaspers. He pulled on his suit jacket from a hanger near the door and walked into the anteroom, Jaspers trailing.

"Your car's waiting," the receptionist said to Kent, who nodded, continuing out the door, Deputy Director Jaspers still following.

"Sir, just a thought," Jaspers said, "the commander of the Navy's Pacific Fleet, Admiral Richard Donchez, is in Washington visiting the Pentagon. I can have him at the briefing at the White House by the time you get there."

Kent looked at his deputy from under the ridge formed by his bushy gray eyebrows.

"The Navy? What are you getting at, Steve?"

"Sir," Jaspers said, "I think maybe it's time we sent a submarine into the Bo Hai Bay to listen to Beijing."

Kent shook his head. "That'd be like sailing a sub up to Chesapeake Bay to the Potomac River to eavesdrop on Washington. Too dangerous."

"But that's all we have left."

After a moment Kent stepped into the limo, shut the door, and lowered the window. Jaspers crouched over to listen to Kent's decision.

"You're right." Kent said. "Get Admiral Donchez to the briefing."

CHAPTER 1

WEDNESDAY, 1 MAY
2125 GREENWICH MEAN TIME

WESTERN PACIFIC OCEAN
300 NAUTICAL MILES SOUTH OF TOKYO BAY
0625 LOCAL TIME

The sun climbed above the horizon, its glare shimmering over the calm water of the western Pacific. The water was a tranquil deep blue, mirroring the sky above. No land was visible; there were no ships. Only the vast stretches of ocean stretching from horizon to horizon. Beneath the calm surface the underside of the waves appeared silvery, reflecting some of the light back deep. The water was so clear that the surface could be seen down to a hundred feet. Below that, there was diffuse light enough to see fifty feet in any direction, but the underside of the gentle waves above could no longer be made out.

At a depth of two hundred and ten feet, the temperature of the water suddenly changed from the lukewarm water of the Pacific in spring to the frigid cold of the sea below, the deep water unaffected by sun or waves. At three hundred feet the light was barely enough to equal that of a flickering candle. Deeper, at four hundred feet, all light from the surface was blocked and the sea was darker than a coal mine. At five hundred feet, the water temperature was a fraction of a degree above freezing, the sun above no longer a factor. At a thousand feet, the weight of the water above caused the pressure to be thirty times atmospheric pressure, enough to crush all but the most primitive life forms. Here the water was undisturbed by currents, fish, sound or light. It was a world more dead, more hostile than the surface of the moon.

The nuclear submarine cruising at this depth was invisible, no light to show the three-hundred-sixty-foot length of her hull, the thirty-three-foot diameter cylindrical black pipe narrowing to a cone at the rear and to a bullet-nose at the bow. No light showed the conning tower presiding over the cylinder of the hull. The conning tower, the "sail," was a fin of black steel that afforded visibility for navigating the vessel on the surface and housed the periscopes and antennae—her vital sensors that could scan the world on the surface from the protection of the deep.

Inside the cylindrical pressure hull of the ship, beneath the sail, the forward compartment's upper deck was subdivided into rooms, most of which were full of watchstanders doing the routine duty of driving the huge nuclear ship deep below the surface. In the control room, the Officer of the Deck stared at the fire-control screens and the sonar repeater monitor, bored now that no surface or submerged contacts were being tracked. Forward of the control room, the sonar room was quiet, filled with consoles and screens and enlisted sonarmen, one with headsets scanning the passive towed array narrow-frequency display. The radio room and ESM room were empty, both of them unused unless the ship was at periscope depth.

One deck below, in the middle level, the crews' mess was half-filled with enlisted men eating traditional bacon-and-eggs breakfasts, their eyes heavy from six hours of watchstanding through the middle of the night, the midwatch. In the neighboring galley cooks were finishing the last servings of breakfast, cleaning up and preparing for a lunch of "sliders," hamburgers so greasy they were known to slide down the throat. On the starboard side of the middle level, officers' country was quiet. The staterooms were empty. The officers' wardroom, which doubled as a conference room, office, movie screening room and dining room, was crowded with men, some officers, some senior enlisted chiefs and petty officers. Most were dressed in blue cotton coveralls, their silver or gold submariner's dolphin pins above their left breast pockets, all of them wearing sneakers or crepe-soled shoes for ship silence.

The seat at the head of the table was empty. The man in the seat just to the right of the end seat counted heads, stood up and lifted a phone by the starboard bulkhead communication/ship status console.

"Captain, Engineer here," he said into the phone. "We're ready."

One deck above, in the captain's stateroom adjacent to the control room, Commander Sean Murphy smiled as he acknowledged and hung up the phone. Murphy was forty, of medium height with the muscular build he had had at the Naval Academy. Since then, of all his classmates, he had probably changed the least. He had yet to lose a single hair to baldness, although gray seemed to be appearing with regularity in his wavy blond hair. He had fought off the weight gain of middle age and was still able to fit into the dress-white uniform he had worn to his graduation eighteen years before. His only wrinkles were the laugh lines around his dark blue eyes, accentuated by hours of squinting out of a type-20 periscope. Murphy was almost always cheerful, his smile softening the planes of an otherwise harsh-looking face. His leadership style had always featured encouragement and reward, rarely threat or admonishment, and it had taken him up the Navy's ladder quickly, giving him command of the second newest submarine in the entire fleet, the last Los Angeles-class nuclear submarine built before Electric Boat retooled for the new but already canceled Seawolf-class ships.

Here at sea, Murphy was in his element, in the role that he had trained for for nearly three decades— command at sea. Although he could not walk onto the bridge, smell the sea air and scan the horizon with binoculars and see dolphins and seagulls, like his surface-warfare classmates, the smells and sounds of the submarine deep under the Pacific were compensation enough for him. His only regret was that one year hence he would have to turn the boat over to her next skipper and give up the sea for an endless series of desk jobs. The thought filled him with a momentary sadness, and again he found a foreign thought entering his head, to resign his commission and leave the Navy, but then he would be trading a desk job at squadron for a desk job in civilian industry. What was the difference? He made an effort to put the matter out of his mind, picking up the drill briefing sheets and scanning them before affixing his signature on the bottom. As he considered the schedule for the day—nuclear reactor emergency drills in the morning, tactical drills in the afternoon, perhaps some approach-and-attack runs against surface ships with some simulated torpedo shots—he found his mood improving. Another day of play deep beneath the Pacific with this brand new billion-dollar toy.

Murphy closed the spiral notebook he had been writing in before the call from the wardroom. The notebook was a long letter to his wife Katrina, whom he hadn't seen in ten weeks since *Tampa* deployed to WESTPAC; in the next six weeks the book would be filled with his daily notes to her, the only way he knew to ease the ache of being away from her and nine-year-old Sean Junior and two-year-old Emily. Murphy tucked the photo of Sean and Emily into the notebook and put it in a cubbyhole on the aft wall of his ten-by-ten stateroom, grabbed a red baseball cap from a hook near the door and walked out to the passageway, down the ladder, and into officers' country and the crowded wardroom.

As he entered the wardroom, a familiar feeling took over as he saw the collection of his officers and men, waiting for him at the table and on the bulkhead sofa seats, some standing, leaning against the bulkheads. The feeling was an odd mix of affection, gratitude, and obligation. These men had given up their lives and families to go to sea with him, to submerge for months in a steel pipe hundreds of feet underwater, all to drive a nuclear submarine, to poke holes in the ocean in the name of service, the defense of America, in a time of peace, when few if any at home noticed or cared. It was more an honor to be their commander than to command the magnificent machinery of the *Tampa* itself. As wonderful as the hardware was, it was nothing next to these men. Centuries before John Paul Jones had said, "Men mean more than guns in the rating of a ship." That was as true in the space age as it had been in the era of wooden sailing ships.

Near the head of the table the Engineer, Lieutenant Commander Jackson "Lube Oil" Vaughn, stood and nodded to Murphy. Vaughn was Murphy's age, his career delayed by leaving the Navy for several years after his first submarine sea tour. Finding something missing in civilian industry, Vaughn had volunteered to go back to sea. Vaughn's nickname had survived from a decade before, from his first submarine, *Detroit*, when he had repaired a DC main lube oil pump himself after the Mechanic Division chief had given up on it. But in the process Vaughn had also flooded engineroom lower level with lube oil, requiring a complete main engine shutdown and twenty-four hours with the entire ship's company to clean up the oily mess. The incident's survival in his name had always irked Vaughn, but Murphy knew that aboard *Detroit* he had been much more a hero than a goat from the incident, and the *Detroit* crew had affectionately called him Lube Oil ever since. Now that he was chief engineer on *Tampa,* he was rarely called anything other than "Eng," unless one of his division officers was kidding him on liberty or at a ship's party.

Vaughn was a solidly built and tall Texan with graying hair and a cowboy drawl. His at-sea beard was fully grown in, since he had quit shaving the day they had left San Diego ten weeks before. Vaughn was a serious officer, which was an advantage when entrusted with the sleeping giant of the ship's powerful and potentially dangerous nuclear reactor system. Still, Vaughn was capable of sudden bursts of humor and a grin that took over his entire face. But when things went wrong Back Aft, Vaughn was as likely to raise his voice, a stern frown clouding his face, preaching to his officers and men, sometimes even lecturing broken equipment. Ship's folklore held that more than one stubborn repair problem had been solved shortly after one of Vaughn's episodes of "counseling" the offending machinery.

"Morning, Skipper," Vaughn said as Murphy took his seat at the table and Vaughn sat down beside him on the right side.

"How're you doing, Eng?" Murphy said in his gravelly voice, a signature hoarseness left over from his days as a two-pack-a-day smoker. "Ready to break the plant?"

"No, sir, just test it a little," Vaughn drawled, turning to address the men in the room. "This drill session will start with a reactor scram initiated by the Captain." When he finished his briefing, the men grabbed their red caps and left the room for the engineering spaces aft.

Murphy took his place in the forward part of engineroom upper level, where the electronic cabinets were jammed forward of maneuvering. Maneuvering was the nuclear-control room, a cubicle twenty feet square where three enlisted nuclear-qualified men operated the reactor under the supervision of a nuclear-trained officer. Vaughn walked up to Murphy in the red cap, the red indicating that the wearer was part of the drill team and was to be ignored by the watchstanders.

"We're ready, sir," Vaughn reported.

Murphy nodded and reached into the cabinet next to them, pulled the Plexiglas cover off a switch marked MANUAL SCRAM, and turned the rotary switch lever to the position marked GROUP SCRAM.

All hell broke loose.

The switch Murphy had operated had done an emergency shutdown of the nuclear reactor, which until that moment had provided steam for the four huge turbines that powered the ship's screw and electrical grid. The turbines aft of maneuvering, so loud before, like jet engines screaming mere feet away, spun down, their steam gone. As they came to a stop they howled mournfully, their cry deeper in pitch as the rotors slowed, until the room grew eerily quiet. The lights overhead flickered as the battery picked up the ship's loads. The fans wound down to a stop, the air-conditioning shut down, and the compartment's temperature almost instantly climbed twenty degrees at a hundred percent humidity. Murphy broke into a sweat, his face and hands and body soaked—the room had become a sauna.

The Circuit One P.A. system crackled through the unnaturally quiet space.

"REACTOR SCRAM. RIG SHIP FOR REDUCED ELECTRICAL."

The deck tilted up, barely perceptible at first, then becoming as steep as a stairway. Like a scuba diver whose air is suddenly cut off, the ship was no longer able to survive deep and had to fight to get to the surface.

Murphy walked aft to look into the maneuvering room to see how the Engineering Officer of the Watch was handling the frantic actions required during a reactor scram. As Murphy leaned over the chain at the door of the cubicle the reply of the control room came over the overhead speaker above the EOOW's head.

"REACTOR SCRAM, MANEUVERING, CONN AYE."

The Circuit One speakers again boomed through the space, this time the voice of the Officer of the Deck up forward.

"PREPARE TO SNORKEL."

Murphy waved at Vaughn, who was now in maneuvering watching Lieutenant Roger Sutherland, the EOOW, trying to control the reactor and steam plants as the men tried to troubleshoot the drill's simulated problem. As the deck became steeper, Murphy pointed forward, and Vaughn nodded, returning his attention to the reactor-control panel. The panel blinked with alarm lights, showing the failing health of the suddenly paralyzed reactor core.

Murphy walked forward through the reactor compartment shielded tunnel and through the massive watertight hatch to the forward compartment. As he made his way down the narrow passageway the angle came off the deck, the ship leveling out. In the control room the Officer of the Deck was on a phone waiting impatiently. A speaker over the periscope stand crackled as maneuvering reported, "PROPULSION SHIFTED TO EMERGENCY PROPULSION MOTOR."

The control room was the nerve center of the ship, controlling its speed and depth, the deployment of its weapons and sensors. A visitor to the room would find it ugly, cramped, but to Murphy it was more comfortable than his den at home. It gave Murphy the same familiar feeling that a pilot has for his cockpit, a driver for his steering wheel, a preacher for his pulpit. It was where the captain of a submarine belonged.

For just a moment Murphy let his eyes take in the room. It was about twenty-five feet long by thirty feet wide, its center dominated by the periscope stand, the conn, an oval-shaped elevated platform, the long axis of the oval going from port to starboard. The platform surrounded the twin periscope wells and gave the conning officer a view of the entire room. The high-tech type-20 periscope was on the port side, the World War II-era backup scope was on the starboard side. The conn platform was surrounded by brushed stainless steel handrails on the forward end, allowing the conning officer to hold on and look majestically down on the deck of the control room below. Nestled into the crowded overhead above the periscope stand were the UWT underwater telephone console and the NESTOR UHF secure voice radio panel. The room was arched overhead since it was on the uppermost deck beneath the sail, the curve of the cylindrical hull's steel hoop frames forming an arch ten feet tall at the centerline. But the room still seemed cramped from all the pipes, valves, cables and equipment cabinets set below the frames. A tall man would have to duck to avoid cracking his skull on a protruding valve or pipe.

On the forward port side of the room was the ship control console, a station that looked like the cockpit of a large aircraft, complete with two pilots' seats on either side of a central console, each panel with a control yoke, and a supervisor's seat behind the console. The men controlling the yokes were the helmsman/bowplanesman, who controlled the ship's course and depth, and the sternplanesman, who controlled the ship's angle. The aft seat was for the Diving Officer, a chief petty officer who was responsible for ship's depth. To port of the ship control station was the wraparound ballast control panel, a complex console of lights and switches and television screens.

On the starboard side of the control room, starting at the forward starboard bulkhead and wrapping around aft, was the attack center, a group of firecontrol consoles and seats for the officers manning them. The CCS-Mark I firecontrol system consisted of four main consoles, Positions One through Three and the weapons control console, each console containing a large television computer screen and keyboard, each set configured for a different purpose. Above the Pos One console was a sonar display repeater screen, showing the control room officers one of the displays of the sonar system. Aft of the periscope stand were twin plotting tables, one set up as the navigation table, the second used to plot manual firecontrol solutions to targets, as a check on the computers, and also as a backup in the case of a central computer failure. The port wall of the room was taken up with the fathometer and under-ice sonar consoles. On the aft port corner wall, a door led to the navigation room, where the ESGN inertial navigation equipment was housed. At the forward starboard corner, between Pos One and Pos Two, a sliding door opened to the sonar display room, where the sonar computer consoles held the eight television monitors of the BQQ-5D BATEARS sonar suite. An opening in the forward bulkhead led out of the room to a narrow passageway leading forward to Murphy's stateroom and further on to the Executive Officer's stateroom and the sonar/firecontrol computer room.

After decades of building cramped and dysfunctional control rooms, DynaCorp's Submarine Boat Division had finally gotten it right with the Late Flight Los Angeles-class submarines. For a moment Murphy felt pure contentment at the shipshape look of his control room. It was the shout of the officer on the periscope stand that brought Murphy from his reverie.

"Where's the captain?" he barked into his phone, his back to Murphy.

The officer, Lieutenant Commander Gregory Lee Tarkowski, was the Officer of the Deck for the morning's drill session. Tarkowski had brown curly hair and a thick red mustache that had swallowed his upper lip, the cause of constant orders to shave it off. He was as lean as he had been when he pitched for the varsity baseball squad at Yale, and tall enough that his head was in constant danger of knocking into the NESTOR UHF radiotelephone console hanging from the overhead of the periscope stand. Considered an officer on the Navy's fast track, Tarkowski was both the Navigator and Combat Systems Officer, jobs that were usually given to two separate mid-grade second tour officers. But for Tarkowski, the assignment was not unusual. Although a modest man by nature, it was common knowledge among the crew that Tarkowski had graduated at the top of his Yale class with a degree in international relations and a second one in electrical engineering, while still managing to be the baseball team's star pitcher. He had sustained the same level of energy after graduating—skydiving, scuba diving and flying any aircraft he could get his hands on, including gliders, hang gliders, ultralights and an aerobatic biplane. The married officers' wives, apparently believing that as a bachelor he was having entirely too much fun for his own good, had conspired to fix him up with one San Diego beauty after another, and two of them habitually jammed the ship's phones when *Tampa* was in port.

On this run Tarkowski was also acting Executive Officer, since Commander Kurt Lennox, the ship's XO, was taking leave in Japan with his wife for the next month. At first Murphy had been hesitant to add the additional duties of XO to Tarkowski's already heavy load of being the officer responsible for the ship's weapons and tactical systems as well as navigation. Unfortunately, the choice for acting XO was only between Lube Oil Vaughn, the Engineer, traditionally the busiest man aboard, and Greg Tarkowski. Murphy had decided to give the job to Tarkowski, and was pleased to see the way the young lieutenant commander had taken to it. Tarkowski seemed to be loving the responsibility of the executive officer, the second-in-command. Murphy began to believe that Tarkowski would be sorry to give the job back to Lennox four weeks from now. It was more than any captain deserved, Murphy thought, to have two department heads, Tarkowski and Vaughn, who were probably the best officers at their level in the entire squadron, perhaps in the entire fleet. To have both of them working under him, *and* the newest submarine in the fleet, was a Navy miracle.

Murphy stepped up to the conn and tapped Tarkowski on the shoulder.

"Glad we found you, Captain. We're at depth one five zero feet, no contacts, course zero seven zero, speed five knots. Request to come up to periscope depth and snorkel, sir."

Murphy glanced at the sonar repeater console above the Pos One firecontrol console. The waterfall display was clean, no telltale streaks showing noise of surface ships. Murphy nodded.

"Off'sa'deck, proceed to periscope depth and snorkel when you're ready."

"Aye, sir," Tarkowski replied. "Dive, make your depth six zero feet. Lookaround number-two scope."

The ship again took on an up-angle as Tarkowski drove to the surface. Murphy watched as the young lieutenant commander raised the type-20 periscope and began rotating it in furious circles, looking above for surface contacts. On the forward bulkhead of the room a television monitor showed the view out the periscope, complete with crosshairs and range divisions. Murphy watched, seeing only the underside of the waves high above as the ship ascended.

"Eight zero feet, sir," the Diving Officer called from a seat behind the airplane-style controls of the ship control panel. The underside of the waves in the television screen grew closer. Tarkowski continued circling at the periscope, trying to avoid colliding with any surface ships.

"No shapes or shadows," Tarkowski said, his words muffled by his face being pressed against the periscope. "Scope's breaking ... scope's breaking ..."

On the television, the view was white as waves broke against the periscope lens, the foamy water blocking vision.

"Scope's clear."

Suddenly the foam vanished, and the view showed the crisp blue waves of the Pacific spinning by as the periscope was rotated in three full circles.

"No close contacts," Tarkowski called out, slowing his periscope search to find more distant contacts or aircraft. "Raise the snorkel mast," he said to the Chief of the Watch.

The sound of hydraulics clunked as the snorkel mast came up. The forward part of control was hectic for a few moments as the ship control team lined up the system to suck air into the ship from the surface above so that the emergency diesel generator could sustain the ship's survival electrical loads while the nuclear reactor was down.

"Commence snorkeling," Tarkowski ordered.

"COMMENCE ... SNORKELING!" rang out over the shipwide P.A. circuit, just prior to an earsplitting roar from the decks below as the massive emergency diesel engine came up to full revolutions.

"Let me look," Murphy said to Tarkowski, who was still doing slow circles on the number-two periscope. Murphy took the periscope, putting his right eye on the rubber eyepiece, the sharp blue of the Pacific coming into sharp focus, the gentle waves coming toward the crosshaired view, the sky and clouds above a beautiful seascape. Murphy smiled, wondering what could be better than command at sea, command of one of the most remarkable nuclear submarines ever built.

CHAPTER 2

WEDNESDAY, 1 MAY
2230 GREENWICH MEAN TIME

WASHINGTON, D.C.
THE WHITE HOUSE
1730 EASTERN DAYLIGHT TIME

The Cabinet room was frigid in spite of the broiling May afternoon sun streaming in through the tall windows facing south to the White House lawn. Admiral Richard Donchez suppressed a shiver as he crossed his arms over his ribbon-covered chest. Donchez was in his mid-fifties, young to hold the rank of full admiral. He was slim as a midshipman but completely bald, his head shining in the bright lights of the room's chandeliers. As if to compensate for his lack of hair, his eyebrows had grown bushy with age, gray mingling with black. His dark eyes were set between rows of smile-wrinkles from years of squinting out a periscope. Donchez's submariner's dolphins sparkled above his ribbons—solid gold, a present from a family friend when he had received his fourth star.

Donchez was the Commander in Chief of the U.S. Pacific Forces, CINCPAC, and as such had three main subordinates—the commanders of the Pacific Fleet's surface, air and submarine forces. Vice Admiral Martin Steuber, the man on Donchez's right, was Commander Submarines Pacific Fleet, COMSUBPAC. In Donchez's opinion Steuber was underqualified for the job; he could name a dozen men more suited to commanding the Pacific Fleet's submarines, but at that level the Navy, Congress and the Department of De-

42

fense had more say in promotions than the Navy's officers. Politics. The way things were.

Steuber was thin and balding, with large brown-rimmed glasses perpetually perched on the tip of his nose. In Donchez's memory Steuber had never worn any expression except a tight-lipped frown. Donchez was tired of the man. When they had flown together from Pearl Harbor the night before, Steuber had tried to chat the whole damn flight, repeating his theories about the Chinese Civil War and how the Communists were going to win the struggle against the insurgent White Army. He didn't say why and Donchez didn't ask. He realized, though, that the Chinese crisis undoubtedly was the reason President Dawson had called them to Washington.

As Donchez waited for the President to arrive, he stared out over the lawn at the row of helicopters parked on the grass. Finally the room's north door opened and Dawson and the Secretary of Defense and Secretary of State entered. Newly elected, President Bill Dawson was a big man with a distinct paunch. Known for his casual style, Dawson wore no jacket and his tie was drawn to half mast below an open shirt collar. His sleeves were rolled up and slight traces of sweat began to show under his arms in spite of the cool of the refrigerated room. He plopped down now into a seat in the middle of the table on the side facing the windows, smiled and opened a briefing file.

On Dawson's right was Secretary of Defense Napoleon Ferguson, an ex-Navy aviator admiral who had been a POW in Vietnam. Fergy, as he had been called during his days as a pilot, was arguably the best Secretary of Defense in the last half-century, Donchez thought, well known for his devotion to the troops, the grunts who did the military's real work.

On Dawson's left was a unique hybrid—Secretary of State *and* National Security Advisor Eve Trachea, the most powerful of the three female members of the Cabinet. The Secretary was in her late forties, attractive and model-thin, with a striking high-cheekboned

face. The wife of a former House of Representatives
Majority Leader, Eve Trachea had begun her rise to
Cabinet level only two years earlier during the cam-
paign, when her effort had been viewed as the reason
for winning states assumed to be opposition strong-
holds. President Dawson had given her the job at State
partly out of political obligation, but also out of re-
spect for her organizational abilities, and after a few
months at State, named her to the position of National
Security Advisor.

For Donchez, Eve Trachea was a worrisome pacifist
who seemed to pride herself on the conviction that
war was, finally, obsolete and that all of mankind's
conflicts could be solved by diplomacy. Well, Donchez
thought, the China crisis might give her reason to re-
think that notion. Trachea seemed to have Dawson's
ear in a way Napoleon Ferguson did not and her abilities made her pacifist views especially dangerous.

Across from President Dawson sat Director of Central Intelligence Robert M. Kent. Kent, fifty-three
years old, was short and wrinkled beyond his years,
his neck too thin to touch his shirt collar, his voice
tremulous and high-pitched. But in spite of his small
physical presence, he cast a long shadow. He was so
highly regarded in the intelligence community that he
was held over from the previous administration. Kent
was rare for Washington, a highly placed official who
cared nothing of partisan politics. In all the Kent
briefings Donchez had ever attended the analyses had
never contained any political spin. Kent was known
for insisting that the President and policy makers see
both sides of any issue. He never gave his personal
opinion unless asked for it—he usually was asked—
and his opinion was usually dead on. Kent and Dawson exchanged pleasantries for a few moments. Then
Kent got up and the dozen men in the room turned
their attention to the end of the room near the fire-
place where Kent stood. Kent worked keys on the
podium, shutting the room's heavy curtains, dimming
the lights and drawing the curtains on a screen behind

him. He clicked on a slide, a map of China flashing up on the screen. He opened a file on the podium, checked his notes.

"Good afternoon, Mr. President, gentlemen," he started, then added, "Ms. Trachea. This brief concerns the situation in China, at least what we know if it." He turned to look at the projected image of the Asian continent, dominated by the area of China. The map was multicolored. Much of the southwest and east coast of China was colored white, with the Beijing area and northeast provinces colored red. Donchez glanced at President Dawson, whose smile was gone, replaced by a frown now that the room was shrouded in darkness.

"As you can see by our extrapolation here," Kent went on, "the Nationalist White Army of the New Kuomintang, the NKMT, now seems to be closing in on Communist Beijing. Unfortunately, this evaluation is little more than a guess, since intelligence out of China has slowed to a trickle ever since the White Army broke out of Xi'an. Ever since the early days of the Civil War journalists have been expelled by both Communist and rebel forces. The Communists have their normal allergy to open reporting. The NKMT is probably worried that news reports would give Beijing free intelligence. Most of you have heard this, but this morning Maria DeLavelle of the 'Good Morning USA' show was executed by the Red Guards outside of Beijing. She was charged with violating the Western Media Expulsion Order."

Donchez had *not* heard the news. Maria DeLavelle had been the leading morning-show anchor woman for almost three years. It seemed inconceivable that she could be executed.

"In the meantime our human intelligence out of China, our HUMINT, has come to a dead halt. Our network of local agents dried up when we lost the embassy and the consulates. Many of them are rumored to have been taken by the Red Guards and executed. Six penetration agents were sent into China last month after we failed to hear from the foreign-national agents we had previously placed in the Communist forces. All six of the penetration agents have disappeared. Intelligence, military and political, is nonexistent.''

"Mr. President," Napoleon Ferguson said, his voice a grumbling growl, "I know I've said it before but one more time—isn't this the time to come in on the side of the Kuomintang? They're pro-democracy, they're mostly financed by Japan, our ally. Both the Japanese and the NKMT are doing *our* work on the Asian continent, restoring a government with a human face. A democratic China would be an ally and trading partner. How can we sit out this war? History will condemn us. We already lost China once this century. It's unthinkable for us to lose it again. With a small push from our forces the White Army could march into Beijing, neutralize the Communists and have free elections in a month . . .''

Dawson glanced at Eve Trachea.

"I can't agree with you on this, Napoleon," she said, using the first name Ferguson hated. "Are we going to spill American blood again interfering in Asian self-determination? We made that mistake in Vietnam. Iraq was not exactly a great victory. The new Kuomintang, the NKMT, *look* like they're pro-democracy, but after they seize power they could become a dictatorship too. And as for making China a trading partner—are you *sure* you're not more worried about money than, say, morality, Napoleon? Mr. President, I say don't get dragged into a war in China just to change the name of the government. Reestablishing our relations with the government should be the main item on this agenda, *not* going to war against it.''

President Dawson looked from Ferguson to Trachea, as if they were trial attorneys approaching the bench.

"As far as committing U.S. troops to a ground battle in China, I have to go with Eve on this one, Fergy," he said. "When it's clear who the NKMT *are*, and that they truly are the good guys, then things might be different. Until I get a different picture from Bob Kent we should stay out of this thing. I also don't want to do anything now that would say to the world that we're tilting in the direction of the Communists. I say we stay neutral, or at least look that way. For now let's just stay focused on the immediate problem, which, if I read Bobby right, is that there's no proper intelligence coming out of China. It seems like a powder keg behind a locked door, and, Bobby, I have to tell you, that's just unacceptable. We can't run foreign policy in a vacuum. We have to do *something* to get reliable information out of the area."

"Sir, there are some additional things we can be doing to get intelligence out—" Kent began. Dawson cut him off.

"Wait a second, Bobby. I have a few questions for you. First, the Japanese are bankrolling the Kuomintang, presumably to eliminate a Communist presence on the continent and free up future markets for goods and a supply for raw materials. Right? Okay, so if the White Army is the agent of Japan, why don't the Japanese just tell us what's going down in this war?"

"Because they don't *know,* sir. They're supporting the White Army, but the NKMT generals are an independent lot. They take yen but not orders. There's no real-time communication between Shanghai and Tokyo. I'd guess that most of Tokyo's intelligence came from us in the first place."

"So what about the U.N.? Why can't a U.N. peacekeeping force be mounted, and the western contingent can get out eyewitness accounts?"

"That would never happen with the Communists on the Security Council, sir. They don't want 'peacekeeping,' they want to fight for their sovereignty. They'd veto a peacekeeping force immediately."

"Eve?"

"Bob's right. The Chinese have veto power over any resolution brought before the Security Council. And I agree they want to win the war, not stop it."

"Bobby, any chance of this thing, you know, going nuclear? Where are the nuclear warheads the Chinese were destroying for the treaty? And do the White Army forces have any nukes?"

Kent turned to the chart. "Here in the northern provinces of Kansu, Sinkiang and Heilungkiang are the principal locations of the ICBMs China used to have aimed at Soviet Russia. These were partially dismantled after the collapse of the Soviet Union and the rest were supposedly being disassembled per the provisions of the nuclear arms-reductions treaty. Unfortunately the process was not complete before the White Army's arrival on the continent. There could be some remaining stockpiled warheads, but we are fairly certain that the delivery missiles are destroyed. We were hoping one of our penetration agents could tell us if there was any truth to the report that a Communist weapons depot had been sabotaged. That would have shown us whether the White Army is targeting any residual nuclear capability of the Communists. That's the long answer, sir. The short answer is, again, we really don't know."

"What about the Kuomintang? Any nukes there?"

"The NKMT has publicly forsworn any use, first or retaliatory, of any kind of nuclear weapon, sir. This may be more than a play for world opinion—they expect to gain the support of the people in the countryside, and that promise will earn them the loyalty of both the peasants and the urbanites. Besides, nuking territory they hope to occupy makes no sense. But I can't confirm any of this."

"So what about all our KH-17 spy satellites, Bobby? Half a billion dollars a copy. What do they show?"

"Mr. President, we've used the KH-17s to the limit of their abilities, and all they've revealed are battlefields and ruins where the People's Liberation Army, the Communist troops, have clashed with the White Army. The images don't show who won. They don't show troop strength. They give us enough data to be able to show you this," Kent said, pointing to the slide showing NKMT occupation of roughly half of China, "but they can't read the minds of the leaders of both sides."

"What about the NSA outposts in Korea? Aren't they intercepting radio transmissions?" The President was referring to the National Security Agency's eavesdropping stations on the west coast of South Korea, Donchez knew. He himself had visited one of the complexes the year before; it was impressive, but Korea was too far away from China to receive the critical communications.

"Sir, not to go into the physics of radio transmissions, but if you'll bear with me . . . most tactical transmissions are made on UHF. It's for short-range secure communications, because it's line-of-sight just like light waves. The radio waves go in straight lines. If you're trying to listen over the horizon you don't get it."

"But the satellites would," President Dawson said.

"Yessir, but only for the few minutes the spacecraft is over the territory, which means we can't intercept Chinese communications without using the military."

"What about flying reconnaissance planes outside of China's borders?" Dawson asked.

Kent seemed ready for the question.

"The PLA air alert radars would detect the planes and they'd deduce the reason for them. The result would be only that they'd get careful about their communications security. We'd gain nothing."

"What about the recon Stealth fighters?"

"We only have one outfitted for eavesdropping and it has been having mechanical problems. We can get it up but we can't keep it up, and that risks losing it over Communist territory. That leaves us the Navy."

Donchez sat up straight in his chair, suddenly realizing why he had been asked to attend a top secret National Security Council meeting. *What Kent wants is a submarine,* he thought. A nuclear sub could hide in the Bo Hai Bay just outside Beijing and intercept UHF radio transmissions from anywhere on the north-

eastern mainland while sitting there invisible underwater.

"Admiral Donchez can explain this next slide, Mr.
President." Kent looked at Donchez, who rose and
walked to the front of the room. Kent clicked the
slide to a close-up view of the northern Yellow Sea
and the Korea Bay, the sea between the peninsula of
Korea and mainland China. At the northern end of
the Yellow Sea a finger of land pointing south and
one pointing north enclosed the Bo Hai Bay. The Bo
Hai was a triangle of water three hundred miles tall
and two hundred miles wide at its base to the south.
At the western point of the triangle's base was the
port of Tianjin, which was a mere seventy miles from
Beijing. Donchez looked at the slide, the geography
familiar to him from the hours of briefings he had
given.

"Mr. President, I believe the director is proposing
putting a nuclear-powered fast-attack submarine in the
territorial waters of Communist China about right
here, a few miles off Tianjin. A patrolling sub here is
ideally positioned to perform multifrequency surveillance—eavesdropping, in a word—on Beijing, which
from the sea side is less than a hundred miles to the
northwest. From this point our submarine will be able
to intercept UHF, VHF, HF and other frequencies of
radio transmissions from the Red Chinese as well as
the White Army. It will know as soon as there is an
imminent attack. It will know if Beijing is going to
fold. All in real time."

Dawson looked at Donchez.

"Real time? Don't you need to decode the
transmissions?"

"We use spooks, sir. NSA intelligence specialists.
They ride the sub and translate the Chinese transmissions. Decoding may or may not be required. Most of
the time they transmit UHF battle comms in the clear
without any encryption. The spooks just pick it up and
write it all down."

"But how does the sub do that without surfacing?"

"Sticks the periscope up, sir. All the antennae are in the periscope."

"Couldn't it be seen?"

"We stay away from traffic and watch the length of time the scope's up, sir. Generally it's not a problem. We do this a lot, sir."

"What about radar? Wouldn't a radar see a periscope?"

Donchez was impressed. Not many laymen could come up with that question.

"Sir, ninety-five percent of all radars are trying to find surface ships or aircraft or missiles. A periscope is usually too small. Any return from a periscope would look like a return from a wave. Besides, the new type-20 periscope is packed with RAM, radar absorptive material, the same stuff in the Stealth bombers and fighters. It's practically invisible." Unless the Chinese were operating orthogonal-polarization radars, Donchez thought, radars built to find periscopes. They usually found them quickly, too, but certainly that technology wasn't in Chinese hands ...

"Well, then," Dawson said, "it sounds like a nobrainer. We need intelligence, and our allies and spies and satellites aren't getting it. Time to send in the submarine. All right, let's do it."

"Sir," Donchez said, realizing Dawson had never done this before, "you realize you have to sign the Penetration Order."

"Penetration Order?"

"Yessir, the authorization for a submarine commander to penetrate the twelve-nautical-mile territorial limit of another sovereign nation. It's a violation of international law, sir. You're the only one authorized to order it."

"I thought you said you do this all the time."

"We do, sir," Donchez said. "And the President always signs the order to penetrate."

Donchez watched Eve Trachea. If she didn't object, the mission would soon be underway.

"We can't," she said, "violate territorial limits or

international law, Admiral. The CIA does this, but now you want to send a shipload of American soldiers into a bathtub outside Beijing and spy on a civil war. If your people get caught it would ruin our integrity internationally. Not to mention what might happen to them. Mr. President," she said, turning to Dawson, "the State Department opposes this idea. And so I do. I know you're concerned about a so-called tilting toward the Communists, but reestablishing diplomatic relations with Beijing would at least get this country back into reality."

"Bobby?" Dawson said, his face a mask.

"We've tried everything," Kent said. "All we've done is get our agents killed. I don't recommend continuing that. I also urge you to allow us to do what we can to gather crucial intelligence. We can't have surprises coming out of China. This situation is *dangerous*." He looked at Trachea. "Let me spell out a scenario ... Japan is financing the Kuomintang so the Communists decide to dry up the river of yen by launching an air strike on Tokyo. The financial center of Japan is gutted, the computers and banks are destroyed, and because of the connectivity of world markets, the world stock markets plunge overnight. Meanwhile the Communists plow through the White Army, plunging Asia into totalitarian darkness and beginning a new cold war that will make the last one look tame. It would be the worst of 1929 and 1939 all in a day."

Evidently the President was impressed, holding up a palm to hold back Kent.

"Okay, Bobby, okay, I understand the need for intelligence, but let me ask the admiral—can't the sub just stay outside the twelve-mile territorial limit?"

Donchez shook his head. "No, Mr. President. Navigation in a tactical situation like that is difficult enough without having to worry about stepping over an arbitrary line twelve miles from the beach. You would take away maneuvering room should surface traffic come by. And twelve miles further out means fewer intercepted communications. Besides, the submarine is still *inside* their goddamned bay and besides, the Chinese claim the whole bay as their territorial waters anyway. If they detect us, it won't matter if we're one mile out or fifty—we're still spying in a Chinese lake. Sir, it's a risk, but the risk of no intelligence seems worse. It's your decision, but not one of your predecessors had any trouble signing penetration orders."

Clearly, Dawson was not happy with the decision. For several moments he sat there, staring at the screen. Finally he spoke.

"Admiral Donchez, send a submarine into the Bo Hai Bay. Have the order to penetrate on my desk within the hour. I'll sign it."

Steuber and Donchez stood at the base of the large east China chart in the Pentagon, the map towering almost twenty-five feet over their heads. The chart showed the East China Sea, north to the Yellow Sea and on to the Bo Hai Bay. To the east the island of Japan had a blue dot flashing into the Pacific, three hundred miles south and east of Tokyo. The blue dot was labeled USS TAMPA SSN-774 SUBMERGED OPERATIONS.

Steuber pointed to the flashing blue dot. "I'm planning on sending the *Tampa*. She's a Los Angeles-class, one of the last built before the Seawolf-class started construction. She'll do okay on this mission. I just need to get the NSA spooks out to her—maybe a helicopter rendezvous—and in she goes."

"I don't know, Marty," Donchez said, using the name Steuber hated. "*Tampa*'s nearly brand new. I'd hate to risk losing a hightech sub if something went wrong. Why not send in one of the old Piranha-class boats? It could do the job."

"Sir, the old broken-down Piranha-class boats are rust buckets. No way would I want to trust a stealth mission to an old Piranha-class."

Donchez had once commanded the USS *Piranha,* lead ship of the class that Steuber was dismissing.

"Who's in command of *Tampa*?" Donchez asked.

"Commander Sean Murphy."

"Murphy's good. Okay, Marty, you just sold me. Draft the message, get the spooks and send in the *Tampa*. We've got some spying to do."

A half-hour later a UHF satellite burst communication was relayed to the COMMSAT in the western Pacific, a message for the USS *Tampa,* while an extremely low frequency ELF signal was transmitted through the depths of the sea, calling *Tampa* up to periscope depth to receive the satellite's message.

CHAPTER 3

WEDNESDAY, 8 MAY
2000 GREENWICH MEAN TIME

Bo Hai Bay
Point Hotel: Two Miles Southeast
  of Xingang Piers
USS *Tampa*
0400 Beijing Time

Tampa cruised slowly north at 1.5 knots at a keel depth of sixty-eight feet, the top of her sail ten feet below the surface of the dark water of the Bohai Wan.

The ship was rigged for ultraquiet. All off-watch personnel were confined to their bunks. One of the turbine generators and one of the main engines aft was shut down to minimize radiated noise. Reactor main circulation pumps were in slow speed. Ventilation fans were turned to low speed. All lights were rigged for red to remind the watchstanders of the need for silence. The P.A. circuit speakers were disabled so that a transmission on them would not be heard outside the hull. Watchstanders in each compartment wore headsets and boom microphones to take the place of the P.A. circuits. The control room was rigged for black, all lights extinguished except for the backlit gage-faces and the dim green light from the firecontrol console screens. A heavy dark curtain was drawn around the periscope stand to screen out the low level of light from the rest of the room. The precautions were designed to protect the night vision of the Captain and Officer of the Deck.

Commander Sean Murphy was pressed up against

the hot surface of the deck-to-overhead length of the number-two periscope optic-module. His right eye was tight against the wet rubber of the eyepiece, now drenched with sweat and skin oil. He gripped the periscope with a grasp as familiar as a motocross racer's on his motorcycle's handlebars.

The view through the scope revealed the floodlit piers of New Harbor, Xingang, a mere four thousand yards away. The nearest pier was occupied by two rusty tankers and an old freighter. The pier further to the north was not so well lit but the backwash of the first pier's lights showed a half-dozen warships of the PLA navy tied up, looking deserted and forlorn. Two were Luda-class guided-missile destroyers; the third was a Russian-designed Udaloy antisubmarine destroyer. Further aft were several Huchuan and P-4 fast torpedo patrol craft. Properly manned and alerted, the surface vessels could pose a threat, but it looked like the PLA navy might have abandoned their ships to lend troops to fight off the land attack of the White Army. That suited Murphy just fine.

The piers of Xingang slowly passed by as the ship proceeded north, dead slow, keeping up just enough flow over the bowplanes and sternplanes to provide sufficient depth-control to keep the sail from broaching. Should the sail become exposed, standing orders called for the captain to assume he had been seen and quickly withdraw at maximum speed while attempting to remain undetected. The first commandment of the Silent Service—remain undetected.

The number-two periscope, the type-20, was more than a collection of lenses and mirrors. Viewed from the surface, the periscope would look like a telephone pole with an oval window in it. The top of the pole had two large spheres on it, one atop the other, called "elephant balls" for obvious reasons. The elephant balls were highly sophisticated radio receivers able to receive UHF, VHF and HF radio signals and to perform rough direction-finding to the source of a radio transmission. Below the elephant balls was a highly sensitive UHF antenna designed for receiving communications from the COMMSAT communications satellite in orbit above the western Pacific as well as from the NAVSAT geopositioning navigation satellite that enabled them to get a fix to within yards of their actual position. The oval window contained television optics, low-light infrared capability and the laser-range finder, a system designed to beam a narrow laser beam at a surface target to determine the range. For decades before the laser-range finder, submariners had prided themselves on being able to call a vessel's range by using the division marks on the crosshairs and knowing the masthead heights of various ships. Not only was the laser device considered unneeded, it was unpopular because preliminary reports by U.S. Navy research ships showed that properly equipped warships could detect the laser beam. Being detected robbed a submarine of her one natural advantage—stealth. On the *Tampa,* and on most other fast-attack submarines, the laser range-finder was disabled, its fuses removed and its breakers locked open to prevent an inadvertent transmission. The whole package of the type-20 scope was shrouded in radar absorptive material, RAM, to lessen the chance of radar detecting them. That left two ways to detect a submarine's periscope—by sighting the periscope's vertical wing-shaped fairing that rose to the level of the water, or by an orthogonal-polarized radar that so far as the United States knew was beyond the reach of the Chinese.

Aft of control in the cramped radio and ESM rooms four Chinese-speaking NSA cryptologists listened through headsets to communications from the Chinese mainland surrounding the ship. Wide-band tape recorders captured every word from the dozens of frequencies being scanned and intercepted. Their computers alerted the spooks to the reception of any of the hundreds of key words programmed in, such as *missile* or *nuclear* or *attack.* In the hour since *Tampa* had arrived on station at Point Hotel, the harvest of communications intelligence had been rich. A fifth spook collected quick summaries from the other four, writing his situation report that would be transmitted within two hours, assuming no urgent communications were intercepted.

On the surface, the telephone pole of the ship's number-two periscope protruded four feet above the calm water of the Bo Hai, moving north at almost a yard per second, a small foamy wake trailing behind it. It was barely visible in the overcast blackness of the night. No one on shore saw it. No one in a patrol boat or fishing vessel noticed it.

But at 0430 local time, the orthogonal-polarized radar waves began washing over the exposed length of periscope.

DASHENTANG, TIANJIN MUNICIPALITY,
   BEIJING MILITARY REGION
DASHENTANG PLA RADAR SURVEILLANCE POST
0435 LOCAL TIME/2035 GREENWICH MEAN TIME

Fighter Sai Fu-Ting sat at the console of the orthogonal-polarization radar set in the crude block building in the Dashentang compound housing the PLA radar-surveillance corps. Sai was a senior enlisted technician in the PLA's radar corps, but in the theoretically rankless military structure of the PLA he was called "fighter," like any other enlisted man. His uniform also did not indicate his seniority, his olive drab Mao suit jacket buttoned to the top, the red tabs on his collars the only insignia other than the red star on his liberty cap. Sai Fu-Ting was one of the best radar technicians in the platoon. He had taken over the watch on the radar console at 0400 after a night of tossing and turning. With the White Army closing in on Beijing, the radar outpost could be overrun in a matter of weeks. An electronics technician, Sai wondered how he would be in a real fight. Hand-to-hand combat was not something he looked forward to, nor was looking down the barrel of a Kuomintang rifle.

He tried to concentrate now on the screen of the DynaCorp International AN/SPY-45 console, the top-of-line equipment acquired through an intermediary in the Middle East. At the time of its purchase two years before, the leaders in Beijing had been worried about an invasion of Beijing from the sea, but now that the main worry was a land assault from the White Army, Sai wondered what use the SPY-45 would be. His orders were to scan the Bo Hai Bay for ships, patrol craft, divers or evidence of a shipborne amphibious assault by White Army forces. Unlikely, he thought, but those were the orders, and he watched the radar screen and sipped his tea, trying to shake the heaviness from his eyes ...

The blip on the screen two miles offshore from Dagu flashed as it was first registered by the SPY-45 system. A small contact, no bigger than a piece of driftwood. Sai logged it in and called for more tea. The blip could be nothing more than a piece of garbage or a drifting fishing boat, perhaps even a loose dinghy.

Twenty minutes later Sai frowned at the small contact. It had not disappeared like a chunk of garbage or driftwood. It seemed to be moving northward at a slow steady pace, only a few clicks, walking speed. But it had regularity. When the blip continued on north, Sai decided it was just some sort of detritus drifting in the current.

At 0500 exactly, at a position two kilometers east of Qingtuozi, the blip reversed itself and began moving to the south.

No piece of driftwood or castaway dinghy could do *that* if it were merely drifting in the current. And a fishing boat would not be trolling so close to shore. It might be some kind of White Army spy boat or a raft of White Army divers. Sai called the officer in charge of the platoon, Leader Peng Chung, who no doubt would have something to say about the mysterious contact. Perhaps they needed to get a patrol boat out on the bay to identify the contact.

At 0510 Leader Peng squinted at the blip on the SPY-45 screen. The contact was continuing south at its creeping slow speed. For the next ten minutes Peng monitored the contact and its motion, then reached over Sai to the console and adjusted a knob, changing the scale of the projection so that the contact's detection was at the bottom and its furthest north penetration was at the top.

The computer-generated curve drawn through the contact's previous positions was a straight line north, a curving turn some fifty meters in diameter, then a straight line to the south.

Peng stood up abruptly and reached for a phone. While he waited, he caught sight of Sai's inquiring look.

"It's a submarine," Peng said quietly.

The phone to the control-room periscope stand buzzed. Murphy grabbed it. "Captain."

"Radio, sir. The SITREP is ready to send. Request the Bigmouth antenna."

"Captain, aye, wait." Murphy tapped the shoulder of the officer on the periscope, Lieutenant Commander Greg Tarkowski. "Let me look."

The world outside was getting lighter with dawn only fifteen minutes away. The situation report needed to get out before the sun rose or the antenna exposure during daylight could risk detection. Murphy did a quick circle in low power, seeing the world at a distance, then engaged high power with the right periscope grip. The shore, only a few thousand yards away, jumped suddenly close, as if he were standing, wading in the water. Not a soul was visible in the shabby buildings crowded together along the shoreline. Murphy turned the scope over to Tarkowski.

"Radio, Captain," Murphy said, tilting his head toward the overhead where the Conn Open Mike microphone was nestled among the valves and pipes and cables. "Prepare to transmit." Murphy looked at Tar-

kowski pressed up against the scope. "Raise the Bigmouth and transmit the SITREP."

Tarkowski acknowledged. Twenty-five feet above
them, from the aft part of the sail, the Bigmouth antenna raised steadily upward, the top of the mast
breaking the surface. The pole continued rising out of
the sail, rising steadily higher until it towered ten feet
above the top of the periscope, fat as well as tall, over
a foot in diameter.

The transmission began, a ten-second burst to the
satellite overhead, the text of the message a summary
of all the Chinese communications received since the
Tampa had arrived on-station. As the Bigmouth antenna was lowered back into the sail, Murphy felt at
once relieved and apprehensive. Relieved because the
SITREP was out and the antenna was down. Apprehensive because the sun was rising, exposing the ship
to a greater chance of detection, and because the
transmission might have given them away to an alert
surveillance crew ashore. But for the next four weeks,
or until called back by the Pentagon, this SPEC-OP
would continue, and *Tampa* would remain at risk, spying on the Chinese.

HANGU, TIANJIN MUNICIPALITY,
  BEIJING MILITARY REGION
HANGU PLA NAVAL AIR FORCE STATION
0530 LOCAL TIME/2130 GREENWICH MEAN TIME

Commander Yen Chi-tzu maneuvered the heavy airplane to the end of the runway and coaxed the old
turbines to full power, his eye on the number-three
engine tachometer and oil-pressure indicator. That engine would fall off the airplane someday, he was convinced, if the maintenance technicians continued to
neglect it. Still, other than some vibrations, it came
uncomplainingly up to twenty-four thousand RPM.
The big four-engined jet, an ancient British-built Nim-

rod antisubmarine patrol craft, lifted off the runway and headed south toward the point the Dashentang radar station had detected a suspicious contact. It was undoubtedly a false contact, Yen thought, but he didn't mind. Better to be flying than cooped up in the ready building, trying to sleep, waiting for word about the encroaching White Army.

It did not take long to maneuver the plane over the water east of Beitang and cruise over the supposed path of the radar contact. The sun was rising as Yen approached the point in the bay where the spy boat or submarine was suspected. Yen, as he was trained, flew east of the intercept point so that he would be upsun of the contact. As he approached the intercept point, still a mile away, he thought he saw something. He flew toward it, keeping it down-sun, and now as the plane closed the contact he blinked hard, not quite believing.

It was a periscope. No doubt. Yen keyed the radio button on the control yoke and called the contact report back to Dashentang, then flew back around, alerting the crew to prepare the load he was about to drop into the sea.

USS *TAMPA*

"Conn, Sonar," Murphy's earphone crackled, "we're getting aircraft engines, close contact."

"Air search!" Murphy called to Officer of the Deck Tarkowski. Tarkowski flipped his left wrist down, scanning his view upward, rotating the scope rapidly.

"Goddamn," Tarkowski said. "Mark on top! Looks like a P-3. Dipping scope."

Tarkowski snapped up the grips and rotated the hydraulic control ring, and the periscope dropped into the well, coming down slowly, slowly.

"Conn, Sonar, the aircraft is still close, high-bearing rate. It's circling us."

"Get us out of here, course east," Murphy ordered. "Ten knots."

"Helm, all ahead two thirds," Tarkowski called to the helmsman at the control panel. "Left fifteen degrees rudder, steady course east."

"Station the section tracking team, OOD, and restart the port turbine generator. Start up the port main engine and shift propulsion to both mains."

"Aye, sir, station the section tracking team and restart the port engineroom." The OOD reached for a phone and began barking into it.

"Conn, Sonar," Murphy's headset intoned, "splashes in the water up our port side. Sonobuoys, sir . . . confirmed. Sonobuoys, bearing zero four zero."

The aircraft was dropping buoys into the water, each one a listening device with a portable radio, listening for them to drive by and nailing their position. Prelude to a possible torpedo attack, Murphy thought. The standard way of dealing with a sonobuoy volley was to get away from it and change course and speed, to zig, so that the aircraft above couldn't predict his next position. He figured if the next round of buoys found nothing the aircraft would have lost them.

"I have the conn," Murphy said. "All ahead standard. OOD, plot the splash, mark range fifteen hundred yards."

"Sonar, Conn, we have another volley of sonobuoys, this time to starboard. He's trying to box us in."

The eerie sound of sonar pulses came through the hull, louder than the background noises of the ventilation fans and the gyro. Sean Murphy's stomach filled with bile as an ugly thought filled his head.

We're caught.

CHAPTER 4

WEDNESDAY, 8 MAY
2155 GREENWICH MEAN TIME

Bo Hai Bay
Eight Miles East of Dagu Point
USS *Tampa* 0555 Beijing Time

Commander Sean Murphy stood on the periscope stand looking at the traces on the sonar-repeater monitor, covered now with the streaks of broadband noise from the aircraft above, the curling lines showing that the plane was orbiting the *Tampa*'s position, keeping up with it. They were deeper now, as deep as the forty fathom channel depth allowed, making the top of the sail over a hundred feet beneath the surface. Still, it felt to Murphy like he was trapped in a tiny bathtub.

Murphy glanced aft of the periscope stand to the navigation chart, which showed their past track. The pencil line leading to their present position was a serpentine path, the result of Murphy's speed changes and rudder orders, his attempt to wiggle on the way out of the bay to make the aircraft's firecontrol solution more difficult. But the zig-zagging was costing them precious time. Murphy longed to order up maximum speed, all ahead flank, which would give them forty knots, if they could control the ship in the shallow water at that speed. But at flank the ship's wake in the shallow flat-bottomed bay would be so violent that the rooster tail from it would give their position away. Even so, despite Murphy's evasive maneuvers, the plane stayed with them, never seeming to run out of sonobuoys, whose odd wailing noise in the water sent shivers down Murphy's spine. At least the bastard hadn't let loose with a torpedo, he thought, as his headset clicked, prelude to another report from the chief sonarman.

"Conn, Sonar, we have multiple diesel engine startups, one probable gas turbine engine startup and what sound like surface-ship screws bearing two seven eight. At least four contacts. Designate Sierra One through Four."

"Sonar, Captain," Murphy said into his boom microphone, "do you have a classification on the contacts?"

"Yessir. Contacts are all surface vessels. Warships."

"Damnit," Murphy muttered. The three destroyers and one of the patrol boats at Xingang must have gotten underway after a radio call from the aircraft, which meant the mainland knew he was here. "Sonar, designate Sierra One through Four as Targets One through Four respectively."

"Sir, the surface vessels are now making way at maximum revolutions, estimated speed, thirty-five knots."

"Starting from Xingang, how long until they intercept our track?"

Tarkowski crouched over the aft end of the conn at the navigation plot table, grabbing the table's dividers and a time-motion slide rule. "Wait one, Captain," he said, manipulating the circular slide rule in three rapid motions. "Eighteen minutes, sir."

"Conn, Sonar," the chief in sonar called over the control room circuit, "we're getting active sonar from Target Two, bearing two eight four. The pulse rate is set for long range."

Murphy felt Tarkowski's expectant gaze. What are you going to do now? it said. And what are you going to do to safeguard the one hundred and forty men aboard ...

Murphy stepped off the conn and leaned over the Pos One console at the attack center, where the Junior Officer of the Deck, Lieutenant John Colson, sat ad-

justing the computer's assumed target-parameters—
the distance to the targets and their speed and course,
which together formed the target "solution." Colson's
solution showed the contacts on an intercept course,
still closing at thirty-five knots. Murphy looked over
at Tarkowski who stood at his right shoulder, likewise
fixed on the console.

"Looks like they've got a lock on our position,"
Murphy said.

"The aircraft, sir, that bastard had us dead-on with
his sonobuoys."

"He'll run out sooner or later, then we can move
off to the north or south—"

"No layer to hide under here, sir. I'd guess if the
airplane runs out of buoys another will replace him
on station."

"How long to intercept, Colson?"

"Fourteen minutes, sir."

Obviously running for the bay entrance would not
work—at their present speed, or even at maximum
speed, the Lushun/Penglai Gap, the entrance to the
Korean Bay, was hours away, Murphy realized. Getting detected was bad enough. Letting the PLA navy
direct weapons at them would not happen, not while
he was in command. He turned to Tarkowski.

"XO," Murphy said, using his acting title intentionally, "we're going to try something ... We'll maintain
this course and speed until the next pass by the aircraft. When he drops the sonobuoys we'll clear datum
from the buoys with the same course and as soon as
we're outside fifteen hundred yards we'll turn to the
northeast and head up toward Qinhuangdao. They
won't expect us to diverge that far away from a base
course leading out of the bay." He hoped. "With luck
the plane'll continue east and try to drop his next load
of sonobuoys at our next expected position. If it works
he'll run out of sonobuoys and we get out with our
necks. We keep going to the north of the bay and
hide until the surface force gives up and goes home.
If that doesn't work and the plane keeps us nailed

down with sonobuoys we'll try to keep him guessing with course changes. The key is that airplane. The surface force alone, active sonar or not, is never going to get us. Once we ditch that plane we're out of here. What do you think, XO?"

"I think, sir, he's on us like white on rice. I wonder if he's tracking us on magnetic anomaly between sonobuoy drops. He's just too damned dead-on with those things. And if he runs out of sonobuoys he might just decide to drop a few torpedoes on us."

"He'd have done that already if he had them onboard." Murphy sounded more certain than he was.

Tarkowski nodded and peered at the sonar-repeater console. The plane was nowhere to be seen. Murphy and Tarkowski waited, neither speaking until finally Tarkowski glanced at the Pos One display.

"Eight minutes to intercept, Captain. If the plane doesn't drop a load in another sixty seconds we should be turning to the north to evade the surface task force."

The chronometer's minutes clicked by. In spite of the three air conditioners aft blowing frigid air into the room to help cool the electronics, the space had grown airless and hot. Finally, Murphy's headset clicked.

"Conn, Sonar, aircraft approaching from the port side ... we've got a splash bearing three five five ... sonobuoys going active now."

Sonar's report was redundant with the splashes audible through the hull. Now the active sonar from the buoys began, the wailing whistles an eerie reminder that the *Tampa* might soon be under attack.

"XO, plot the distance to the splash and mark range one-five-hundred."

"Aye, sir," Tarkowski said, leaning over the tactical geographic plot board. Three minutes later Tarkowski called the range at fifteen hundred.

"Helm, all ahead full, left full rudder, steady course zero four zero. Mark speed twenty."

The deck canted into a starboard roll as the ship

came around with full rudder and turns for full speed. Murphy could feel the vibrations from his feet as the main engines aft began to accelerate them through the water of the shallow bay, moving them away from the sonobuoys.

"Captain, steady course zero four zero, ship's speed twenty knots," the helmsman called from the ship-control panel.

"Helm, all stop, mark speed six," Murphy called. "Downshift reactor coolant pumps to reduced frequency." Murphy looked over to Tarkowski at the geo plot. "That'll be the last sonobuoy that guy finds us with." He hoped. Tarkowski said nothing.

"Captain, speed six knots, sir," the helmsman said.

"All ahead one third, turns for six knots."

"One third, turns for six, helm aye, sir."

Murphy joined Tarkowski at the plotting table, seeing the plot of their drastic maneuver since the last splash. For several minutes nothing happened, the team in the control room silent as a funeral, waiting to see if their attempt to fool the aircraft above had succeeded. Murphy's attention switched back and forth from the plot to the sonar display. Each minute without contact on the airplane was a plus.

"Seven minutes since the maneuver, Captain," Tarkowski said.

"Sonar, Captain, any sign of the aircraft?"

"Conn, Sonar, we're not getting him at all. No sign of him, sir."

Murphy allowed a smile. Tarkowski's frown stayed in place. Murphy turned to look at the display on Pos One.

"Colson, any speed or course changes by the surface force?"

"No, Captain. The previous intercept-solution is tracking." As Murphy watched, a new dot in the dot stack on Colson's screen veered off to the left, away from the neat rows of vertical dots that Colson had lined up by dialing in his solution course, speed and range. "Sorry, sir, now I've got a possible target zig,

Target Two." Colson began lining up to find the new solution to the surface forces. Murphy chewed his lip, wondering if the skimmers had found out their new course and position.

"Conn, Sonar, the surface force is slowing down, turn-count dropping fast. Sounds like they're doing a large-sector sonar search."

"Captain, JOOD," Colson said, "I'm getting a solution with the surface force at fifteen knots."

Murphy nodded, pleased.

"Sonar, Conn," Tarkowski said to his lip mike, "any detects on aircraft engines?"

"Conn, Sonar, no."

Only then did a smile break out on Tarkowski's face. "We ditched them, Skipper."

"Conn, Sonar, we're getting a faint detect on ... helicopter rotors."

"Helm, all stop!" Murphy said. "XO, line up to hover."

"Conn, Sonar, chopper's getting closer."

"Ship's speed, a half knot and slowing, sir," Tarkowski reported, "ready to hover."

"Chief of the Watch, hover on the trim pump," Murphy ordered, feeling the sweat on his forehead and under his arms.

"Ship is hovering, Captain," Tarkowski reported. "You think that's an ASW chopper?"

"That's exactly what I think it is. That son of a bitch is about to drop a dipping sonar set. If he does, when he does, we'd damned well better not be showing any speed through the water or his Doppler will snap us up."

Murphy and his crew were well aware that helicopters were a lethal enemy to the submarine when they were equipped with a dipping sonar—the chopper could cover hundreds of square miles of ocean an hour with the dipper. It could dip and listen and move to another spot, dip and listen and go on until it located the submarine. All a good ASW chopper pilot needed was a sniff from a surface ship or an aircraft, just the slightest hint that a submarine was there, and after a few dips, get the target's position down to within a hundred yards. Murphy silently prayed it wasn't an ASW helicopter.

Pwiiiiiing! The sound of a dipping sonar pulse coming through the hull, a whistling sound, very prolonged, perhaps four seconds.

"Conn, Sonar, that's a dipping sonar, bearing one five five. Fairly distant ..."

Tarkowski plotted the bearing to the dipper.

"Sir, if he sees us we've had it," Tarkowski said.

"Range to the surface force?" Murphy, tight-lipped, directed at Colson.

"Thirty-five hundred yards, bearing two two zero, sir."

"Damned close, if that chopper catches us, Captain," Tarkowski said.

Murphy nodded. Still, he thought, hovering dead in the water should make it tough for the dipping sonar to find them. With no ship's speed, the hull would not upshift the sonar's frequency when it was reflected, and the sensor would have trouble distinguishing the return-ping from the water's reverberations of the original ping.

"Conn, Sonar," the sonar chief said, his voice distorted and loud in the earpiece, "we've got helicopter-rotor noises, close aboard to starboard! Contact is hovering overhead!"

Murphy looked up at the sonar display above Colson's panel. A broad, ugly, loud streak was forming on the red television monitor, the noise of the helicopter. *PWIIIIING!* The sonar ping seemed impossibly loud. This close, Murphy thought, the dipper shouldn't be able to pick out their ping from the return off the bottom. Right on top of them, and they'd be just so much bottom clutter—

"Conn, Sonar, the surface force is speeding up. Sounds like max revolutions again."

"Colson?"

"Can't tell without own-ship speed, sir, but when I

dial in an intercept course the dots are stacking ... I think that chopper just nailed down our position ..."

"Conn, Sonar, up-Doppler on the surface force, thirty-five knots approach speed."

Murphy leaned over Colson's Pos One console and dialed in other solutions for the surface force. The only one that worked showed them coming on a direct intercept course.

"Time to intercept?"

"Two minutes, sir," from Colson.

"Let's clear datum, sir," Tarkowski said, the urgency distorting his voice. "They've got us pinned."

PWIIING!

"Helm, all ahead flank and cavitate!" Murphy ordered. "XO, man battlestations and spin up the torpedoes in tubes one through four." They were going to have to fight their way out of this.

As Tarkowski prepared to arm the torpedoes, the deck began to vibrate with the ship coming up to thirty-five knots. Murphy looked over at the ship-control team. The Diving Officer and bowplanesman were struggling to maintain depth control in spite of the odd effects of their rooster-tail wake aft and the shallow-bottom venturi force amidships. It was possible that depth control would get so difficult that the ship would leap from the water like a whale or dive into the bottom.

The control room began to get crowded as watchstanders filled the room for battlestations. The geo plot that had been manned by Tarkowski was now taken over by two plotters and an officer. Another officer now sat at each console of the firecontrol system where only Colson had sat before. Other manual plots were manned along the aft bulkhead of the room. Within a minute of the initial call to battlestations the room's population had grown from eight to twenty-one.

"Attention in the firecontrol team," Murphy said to the assembled battlestations watchstanders. "It's clear that the surface force is alerted and prosecuting us at maximum speed, close range. The ASW helicopter above has gotten our position down so there's no longer any benefit to stealth. We're trying to withdraw at maximum speed and I don't care that we're putting up a hell of a wake topside. We're only a few moments away from being attacked. It's my intention to put four wake-homing torpedoes out astern of our track to target the surface force and to act as evasion devices. If they connect with one of the surface ships, that may distract them long enough for us to make good our escape. If the skimmers detect our launch from the transient noises of the torpedo shots, that alone may make them break off their approach. Any questions?"

At first there was nothing but shocked silence in the control room, broken by the sonar chief calling them over the phone circuit.

"Conn, Sonar, we've got a *rocket*-launch transient from the bearing to Target Two—"

"What the hell?" Tarkowski mumbled, looking over at Murphy.

"Right fifteen degrees rudder! Steady course one four zero!" Murphy ordered, realizing too well what the report from sonar meant—a rocket-launched depth charge.

A tremendous splash sounded from above on the port side followed by a momentary silence. The deck rolled to port as the ship turned, the snap-roll robbing them of some of their speed but getting them away from the depth-charge splash. Murphy looked up at the chronometer. Four seconds since the splash, and nothing. He could feel his heart beating hard in his chest. The chronometer seemed to have frozen, as did the watchstanders in the control room, time somehow oddly slowing down to a crawl as Murphy waited for the explosion, the crashing roar that would breach *Tampa*'s hull and send them to the bottom of the bay. And the worst of it was that the ship was helpless. Once a depth charge was in the water beside them, there was nothing he could do except hope it was a dud and buried itself in the sand of the bottom.

When the violent explosion did come the deck jumped several feet upward, throwing the men in the room into the overhead, twenty-one pancakes flipped by a huge skillet. As Murphy lost his footing and was hurled into the periscope pole of the number-two scope he wondered whether the depth charge had broken the ship in half. He slid down the pole of the type-20 periscope, his chin crashing into the curb around the periscope well. A lump was rising from his jaw, the pain momentarily clouding his mind. He pulled himself to his feet, surprised he was still whole, and felt a moment of hope that the ship had likewise survived the explosion. But as the watchstanders around him picked themselves up from the deck, something seemed very wrong ... the deck wasn't vibrating the way it should for an ahead-flank speed order.

Murphy looked over at the ship control console to the starboard display panel. The ship's speed-indicator showed fifteen knots and slowing—they must have sustained a casualty in the propulsion plant. Murphy was turning and reaching for the P.A. Circuit Seven microphone when he heard the Seven's speaker rasp out Lube Oil Vaughn's voice, harsh in the quiet of the room.

"CONN, MANEUVERING, REACTOR SCRAM, REACTOR SCRAM."

Murphy clicked the button on top of the microphone and shouted into it. "Engineer, Captain, what's the cause?"

"SCRAM BREAKERS TRIPPED FROM THE SHOCK."

"Engineer, take the battleshort switch to battleshort and restart the reactor and main engines with emergency heat-up rates and *give me propulsion now*."

"CAPTAIN, ENGINEER, COMMENCING FAST RECOVERY STARTUP WITH EMERGENCY HEAT-UP RATES, BATTLESHORT SWITCH IN

BATTLESHORT. ESTIMATE FULL PROPUL-
SION CAPABILITY IN TWO MINUTES."

Murphy tossed the microphone to the deck and
moved over to the Pos One console. The ship was
drifting without propulsion power, at least for the next
two minutes, but the battery would still allow them to
get some weapons into the water. And by the time he
had some torpedoes on the way to the skimmers, the
reactor would be back in the power range and with
luck he could get the hell out of here.

"Weps," Murphy said to the officer at the Pos Three
panel, Lieutenant Chuck Griffin, the Torpedo/Cruise
Missile Systems Officer, "report weapon status."

"Sir, tubes one through four loaded with warshot
Mark 50 torpedoes, all tubes flooded and equalized,
all weapons spun up and warm. No indications of
problems from the shock of the depth charge. I reini-
tiated the self-checks. Self-rechecks are all complete,
all torpedoes nominal."

"Good. Open the outer doors on tubes one and
two. Select active circler mode, surface-wake homing
enabled. Set the astern-default solution for Targets
One, Two, Three, Four, high-to-medium passive
snake-search pattern." And into his lip mike: "Sonar,
opening outer doors, tubes one and two."

"Outer doors open, tubes one and two," from
Griffin.

"Solution status, Pos One?" Murphy to Colson, the
Pos One console operator.

"All four contacts are within a thousand yards of
each other, sir, on the edge of the port baffles, range
twenty-three hundred yards, solution quality fair from
our course change."

Murphy looked at the faces of the men surrounding
him on the control-room floor below. "Attention in
the firecontrol team. Firing Point Procedures, tubes
one and two, horizontal salvo, Targets One, Two,
Three and Four."

"Ship ready, sir," Tarkowski reported from the aft
part of the conn.

"Solution ready, sir," Colson said.

"Weapons ready, sir," Griffin called.

"Tube one, shoot on generated bearing," Murphy ordered, full of the realization that he was about to shoot the first torpedoes in a combat situation since 1945.

"Set," Colson called, pressing a variable-function key on the Pos One panel, locking in the latest fire-control solution to the surface warships astern.

"Standby," Griffin said, pulling the trigger to the STANDBY position. The torpedo in tube one was now seconds away from launch.

"Shoot!" Murphy ordered.

"Fire," Griffin replied, rotating the trigger to the FIRE position.

A loud thunk sounded from two decks below, followed by a violent crash. The air-driven pneumatic/hydraulic ram had just pressurized the water tank around the tube, blasting the weapon from the steel cylinder with a burst of water pressure. The first torpedo was on its way.

"Tube one fired," Griffin reported. "Lined up for tube two."

"Conn, Sonar, own-ship's unit, normal launch."

"Tube two," Murphy commanded, "shoot on generated bearing."

Again the combat litany sounded in the control room. When Griffin pulled the trigger the second time the crash of the torpedo ejection sounded again, so loud that Murphy's eardrums ached. He grabbed his nose, closed off his nostrils and blew until the pressure equalized. In the control room the men were doing the same.

"Conn, Sonar, own-ship's second-fired unit, normal launch."

"CONN, MANEUVERING, REACTOR's CRITICAL, READY TO ANSWER ALL BELLS!" the Circuit-Seven speaker blared.

"Helm, all ahead flank, steer course one two zero," Murphy ordered. The deck began to tremble as the

huge twin steam propulsion turbines aft came up to
full revolutions, blasting the *Tampa* through the water
at one hundred percent reactor power. The needle on
the speed indicator climbed off the zero peg and rotated upward, fifteen, twenty, twenty-five, thirty knots.
A few moments later the ship was doing forty knots
and heading toward the mouth of the bay and away
from the surface task force.

"Cut the wires on tubes one and two and shut the
outer doors," Murphy ordered Griffin. "Line up for
tubes three and four."

A distant rumbling explosion sounded, coming from
astern. A second explosion.

"Conn, Sonar, we have two explosions from the
bearing to Target One. Also secondary explosions . . .
hull break-up noises, Target One."

Tarkowski said, grinning, "We got two hits,
Captain."

"Sonar, Captain, any other activity out of the surface force?"

"No."

"Maybe they'll break off the attack, Skipper."

"We'll see." Murphy addressed the entire room:
"Attention in the firecontrol party. Firing Point Proce-
dures, tubes three and four, horizontal salvo, Targets
Two, Three and Four."

"Ship ready."

"Solution ready."

"Weapon ready."

"Tube three, shoot on generated—"

"Conn, Sonar, we've got two—no, *three*—rocket-
launch transients from Target Two . . . correction, four
launches, sir. Probable SS-N-14 depth charges."

Murphy's jaw clenched. With four depth charges
coming in by solid-rocket booster there was nothing
he could do to evade, at least not until sonar reported
the bearings to the splashes. After the last impacts
four of the depth charges were sure to do greater damage, particularly if they all got close.

"Tube three, shoot on generated bearing!" Murphy

ordered, his voice loud to overcome the inertia of the near-paralyzed watchstanders.

"Set."

"Standby."

"Shoot."

"Fire."

The crash of the torpedo leaving tube three slammed the eardrums of the crew a half-second before a violent splash sounded in the water above, followed by three more. Murphy waited for the report to come from sonar on the bearings. No report. Either sonar was slow to report or time had again slowed to an adrenaline-induced crawl.

"Sonar, Captain, report bearings to the splashes!"

"Splashes in the water bear zero one five, one two zero, two six five, and one astern in the baffles." The sonar chief's voice sounded distorted by stress. The depth charges had entered the water in a perfect pattern, surrounding the ship. The worst was the one at bearing one two zero dead ahead.

"Left five degrees rudder," Murphy ordered, "steady course zero seven zero."

At least that course, he figured, would bring the ship between the splash to the north and the one ahead. Not that that was much comfort.

With the first detonation the ship rolled hard to starboard, throwing Murphy into the conn handrail. The second explosion came a fraction of a second later, blowing the ship back over to port. The lights in the overhead flickered, the firecontrol console screens winked out, the green glow replaced by dull-dark glass. The sonar repeater likewise blacked out. Murphy looked over at the ship-control panel, where the bowplanesman, sternplanesman and Diving Officer struggled with depth-control, fighting to keep the ship level. The speed-indicator needle was dropping fast. Maybe the damn reactor had scrammed again.

And the third explosion came, a ripping sound following.

"CONN, MANEUVERING," the Engineer's tight

voice said, the speaker of the P.A. Circuit Seven
crackling in the overhead. "MAJOR STEAM LEAK
... REACTOR SCRAM ..." Vaughn's voice faded
for a moment, the circuit clicking. The connection returned but Vaughn was no longer talking to the control room. Murphy strained to hear Vaughn's voice
shouting an order with a rushing sound coming over
in the background. "Shut MS-Two ... load the TG's
and depressurize the steam headers ..."

Jesus, Murphy thought, not just a reactor scram but
a *fucking* steam leak—a ruptured main steam line had
enough energy to roast everyone in the aft compartment. It was probably a miracle that Vaughn had survived long enough to try to isolate the steam-headers.

But a steam leak meant more than just the possibility of roasting the crew—it meant the reactor, their
ticket out of the Chinese bay, was dying. Murphy's
worries over the engineering compartment were interrupted by the fourth explosion, which seemed to come
from the very deck beneath his feet, launching him
and the other watchstanders into the room's overhead
piping and valves and cables and hoop frames. This
time the lights went out completely, all except the
gages on the ship-control panel, which continued to
glow eerily in the cavernlike darkness of the room.
Murphy had been tossed up into the periscope
hydraulic-control ring. He collapsed to the deck of the
periscope stand.

Murphy realized that his face was touching something cool and hard. The room looked odd in the
darkness lit only by the light of the ship-control panel
gages. Someone turned on a battle lantern. Murphy
could hear voices around him but couldn't make out
any of the words, just pieces of phrases:

... *loss of depth control* ...

... *can't keep her down* ...

... *jam rise on the bowplanes* ...

... losing speed, you can hold ...

... coming up ...

... broach depth, our sail's coming ...

... ballast tank vents are jammed shut ...

... Captain? ...

... must have blown gases into the ballast tanks ...

... flooding in the forward ...

... who's reporting ...

... goddamnit ...

... can't get the vents open ...

... manual override the ...

... steam leak isolation ...

... fuck the bowplanes, shift to emergency on the stern ...

... we're on the goddamned surface ...

... Captain? ...

CHAPTER 5

WEDNESDAY, 8 MAY
2216 GREENWICH MEAN TIME

Bo Hai Bay
Twenty-Six Miles South of Shaleitian Dao
USS *Tampa*
0616 Beijing Time

Murphy found a handrail on the periscope stand, pulled himself to his feet, ears ringing, vision receding into a black-edged tunnel. He stood up, dropping his head low to keep from passing out, felt Tarkowski's arm pulling him up. The lights in the room came back on. The room was rocking gently and it wasn't Murphy's shaky condition, it was actually rolling to port and coming back to starboard.

Which could happen only if they were on the surface.

"What happened?" Murphy asked Tarkowski.

"You were out of it for a minute or so, Captain. The last blast caused a jam rise on the bowplanes, maybe blew some gases into the aft ballast tanks. Plus, the damned vents jammed in the shut position. We still can't vent aft. All that blew us up to the surface. With no reactor or steam plant, jammed bowplanes and stuck vents, I don't think we can get deep. Not to mention, firecontrol and sonar are dead. Likewise the nav systems."

"Colson, check radio," Murphy snapped to the Pos One officer, who was still at his dead firecontrol console. "Get out a transmission that we're under hostile fire by a Chinese surface force. Send it as an OPREP-3 PINNACLE, straight to the White House. And tell them I intend to do a ship self-destruct if we're boarded. When you've got that out, get back here."

"Aye aye, sir," Colson replied, ripping off his headset and running aft.

"XO, get on the line to maneuvering. See if we can shift propulsion to the EPM and check battery discharge rate. And check if we lost any cells. Get the engineer to report on the steam leak—if we can restart on one side of the engineroom."

Tarkowski pulled off his headset and grabbed the phone handset to call maneuvering.

"Griffin, get down to the torpedo room and see if we can still manually program and launch a Mark 50. I want to use as many of those fish as I can."

Griffin hurried forward and down the ladder.

"Diving Officer, try to resubmerge the ship. Chief of the Watch, get an auxiliaryman working those damned vents. Get the vents open as soon as you can. Lookaround number-two scope," Murphy said, rotating the periscope control ring in the overhead, the same ring his head had connected with moments before. Slowly the periscope came out of the well, thunking to a halt as the six-foot-tall optic-module came out of the well. Murphy snapped the grips down and rotated the scope, finding the surface vessels almost immediately. They were close, within five hundred yards, closing quickly, all three of them headed directly for the *Tampa*.

Murphy saw Tarkowski hang up the phone to maneuvering.

"Sir, the Eng can't find the leak but he's still looking. We've got propulsion on the emergency-propulsion motor but at one-third speed, there'll only be twenty minutes on the battery."

"Helm, all ahead one third, course east," Murphy ordered. "XO, the Eng has got to find that damned leak, it's our only chance to get out of here."

"If anyone can get this plant back, Lube Oil Vaughn can."

"It may be too late," Murphy said. "Greg, I'm putting you in charge of doing a classified-material destruct.

Burn it all, everything." Murphy pulled a key off a chain around his neck and held it out to Tarkowski.

"This is the key to the small-arms safe. Get the classified material bonfire going, break out and distribute the pistols and M-16s, then station a team of armed men at each hatch."

Tarkowski turned and left the room.

"Captain," the Diving Officer said, "we can't get down at this speed with the vents stuck. We're still on the surface."

"Get those vents open, Chief of the Watch."

"Stanton's working on it, Captain."

Murphy turned back to the periscope. The first Chinese destroyer, the Luda-class, was gliding to a halt only a few yards away, pulling up on the port side. Sailors were manning her rails, heavy manila ropes in their hands. On the starboard side a Udaloy had pulled up close and had her own lines ready. The *Tampa* was to be taken into port—a hostage.

Too bad NAVSEA had banned ship-destruct explosives on U.S. submarines, Murphy thought. At least it would keep *Tampa* out of Chinese hands.

Murphy ordered the engineer from aft, and in a few moments Jackson Vaughn appeared, hair soaked with sweat, coveralls stained with dirt, a Beretta 9-mm automatic stuffed into his belt.

"Any luck finding the leak?"

"We need more time, sir. I bypassed Main-Steam-Two and pressurized the header, and we had at least three-dozen leaks, impossible to say which were minor and which were major pipe breaks. The steam-header insulation is broken in a half-dozen places. The major leak could be anywhere. Without a proper hydro test I can't be sure. And I risk the crew if I open Main-Steam-One or Two. A double-ended pipe shear would kill every man aft, maybe you guys too."

"Start patching the lines with seawater pipe patches if you have to, and bypass the cutout-valve again. We've got to get that system back. It doesn't look good topside. The Chinese want to take us home with them. If they make a mistake and if you can get steam back in the engineroom we could still make a break for it."

Lieutenant Chuck Griffin, the torpedo/missile officer, came into the room, out of breath from running up the ladder. "Sir, the torpedo-room firing-panel is a wreck. And the tubes are leaking, all of them. The hydraulic rams are both out. Most of the weapons took a hell of a beating from the shock of the last explosion. There's nothing to shoot with. Holt is working on the panel and Norall is looking at the tubes. And Watson is crawling on the racks looking for a working weapon, but it'll be hours before we can give you anything. Without that firing panel, it's ... useless."

Murphy and Vaughn exchanged looks.

"Keep working on it, Mr. Griffin," Murphy said in a monotone, and turned back to the engineer.

"Eng, split off a few of your men from the steam-leak isolation and have them get ready to scuttle the ship. Find some seawater valves aft that we can open. When I give the word have them opened. It'll be better to put this ship on the bottom than give it to the Chinese without a fight. Have a team standing by under the aft-hatch. Make sure they're armed. We'll try to hold off a boarding party as long as we can, but when I give the word on Circuit One melt down the reactor and flood the ship. Meanwhile we'll try to rig some Mark 50 warheads for an in-hull detonation."

"Goddamned shame, Skipper, to sink our own ship."

"I'll only give the order if there's no other way."

Vaughn stood there for a moment, as if he wanted to say something. "Good luck, Captain," he finally said, nodded at Murphy, then disappeared from the room, headed for the ladder to the middle-deck.

Murphy looked back out the periscope. The Chinese warships had tied up tight on both sides. They were being towed to the Xingang piers. For a moment Murphy looked around at the crew, wondering if he were really capable of destroying his own ship. A rush of guilt overwhelmed him, guilt that he had failed them, first by getting caught, second by failing to escape once the Chinese were alerted. At least he had put one of the surface ships on the bottom. If the steam leak could be isolated before the Chinese got into the hull, if the ballast-tank vents could be repaired, if the ship had enough power to break the lines to the towing vessels, then maybe it was not over yet ... except the entire Chinese Northern Fleet would be waiting for him at the Penglai/Lushun Gap, the choke-point at the entrance to the bay. Still, there had to be a better way out of this than scuttling his ship and sacrificing his crew.

Could he even consider surrendering the men to the Chinese, hoping they might release the Americans? The thought went against two decades of military training. What had the Code of Conduct said, the Code they had all committed to memory the first week as plebes at Annapolis—*I will never surrender of my own free will. If in command I will never surrender my men while they still have the means to resist.* No, he would not give up the *Tampa* without a struggle, even if it were a death-struggle.

Tarkowski returned to the control room. "Sir, the classified material burn is just about finished. But we've got bad news from the forward hatch. Chinese boarding party. There are flames from an acetylene torch around the upper hatch. The Chinese will get through that hatch within twenty minutes."

"And if they burn through the lower hatch we'll never be able to rig the ship for dive."

"That's right, sir. If they burn through the upper and lower hatches we'll have a bunch of permanent holes to the outside."

"Have all the lower hatches on all access points opened. Have the fire teams ready. As soon as the upper hatches are opened and troops are coming in, open fire. If we can keep them out long enough to get propulsion we might still be able to break away ..."

Tarkowski pointed to the television monitor of the periscope view. The Chinese crews were doubling, tripling, quadrupling the thick lines coming over the *Tampa*'s hull. It would take more than *Tampa*'s 35,000-shaft horsepower to break through all that.

"Look at all the lines, sir. Even at flank I don't think we'd break away."

"We've got to do what we can, until there's no longer hope. I'll order the Eng to flood the aft compartment and melt down the reactor. I'll order you to flood Auxiliary Machinery and detonate one of the Mark 50 warheads or some of the torpedo fuel. At least they won't be taking us alive."

Tarkowski said nothing.

"Greg, lay below and wait for my order to emergency destruct. Then flood the Auxiliary Machinery and detonate the weapons."

"Aye aye, Captain."

When he had gone, Murphy felt alone, even surrounded by the men remaining in the control room. It was not long before he could hear the loud reports of shots coming from the forward escape trunk, the pathetic short blips of the Beretta pistols, the roaring of the Chinese assault weapons that soon drowned out the sound of the Berettas. All was silent again except for the sound of a dozen Chinese voices, the odd tones of their syllables causing a rush of bile to Murphy's stomach.

He had already hoisted the P.A. Circuit One microphone to his mouth and clicked the top button to allow him to speak, to allow him to pass word to Vaughn and Tarkowski to do the unthinkable—to destroy the ship. He had even heard his own voice blaring out of the ship's speakers—"THIS IS THE CAPTAIN"—when the Chinese bullet hit him in his right shoulder, spinning him around and dashing his head against the pole of the number-one periscope.

The deck seemed to rise toward his face in slow motion, ready to strike him.

His world went black before the deck had a chance to come up.

CHAPTER 6

THURSDAY, 9 MAY
0020 GREENWICH MEAN TIME

ANDREWS AIR FORCE BASE
SUITLAND, MARYLAND, OUTSIDE WASHINGTON, D.C.
1920 EASTERN DAYLIGHT TIME

The Gulfstream SS-9 swept-wing twelve-passenger jet touched down on the south runway, the rain on the asphalt forming a cloud behind the swift jet as it reversed its engine thrust, making its way to a halt on the diamond-cut pavement. At the mid-point of the 8,000-foot runway the jet turned off to a taxiway and headed for the hangar building, where the green Marine Corps SH-3 Sea King helicopter idled. The jet braked to a halt, its engines whining as they spun down. Almost immediately the forward port door opened, a stairway unfolded and Admiral Richard Donchez climbed out and jogged into the helicopter. The deck canted forward as the aircraft lifted off and climbed from the wet asphalt, heading north toward the Pentagon's helipad. Donchez turned to the other man in the chopper, Vice-Admiral Martin Steuber, who held his glance for a moment, then looked away out the rain-streaked window.

Donchez wasn't happy to be pulled off the podium as he was in the middle of a speech at the launching of the SSN-22, the second of the controversial Seawolf-class submarines built by Electric Boat in Groton, Connecticut. Donchez's speech was calculated to condemn cancellation of the Seawolf program in favor of the inferior follow-on class of fast-attack submarines, the Centurion-class.

Steuber leaned over to Donchez. "Sir, I'm sorry, but it seems something went wrong with the China operation. The SPEC-OP boat's in trouble. That's all I heard, but after we get the word in NMCC we've got a date at the White House to brief the President."

Donchez looked hard at Steuber, suddenly mindful of what could go wrong with a nuclear submarine sent into China's restricted territorial waters.

WASHINGTON, D.C.
WHITE HOUSE BASEMENT—SITUATION ROOM
2000 EASTERN DAYLIGHT TIME

Admiral Richard Donchez would give the briefing, since he had been responsible for the China operation. Steuber handed him the transparencies.

President Bill Dawson sat on the side of the large table against the curtained wall. He wore a golf shirt and khaki cotton pants, looking as if he had been pulled from a golf course. If Donchez had to guess his mood, it was one of impatience, but an impatience that was a prelude to anger. Secretary of Defense Napoleon Ferguson sat beside Dawson, looking uncomfortable in his rumpled gray pinstriped suit, his collar unbuttoned, his patterned tie at half-mast. Ferguson could be relied on to support military operations even when they went as badly as this one had. Ferguson was solid, Donchez thought. As if reading his mind, the SecDef gave him a nod. Donchez returned it, his face grim.

On Dawson's right sat Secretary of State and National Security Advisor Eve Trachea, impeccable in a blue suit, her face serene, her eyes on Dawson, giving him the odd feeling of being sized up. He had predicted that Trachea would be ready to say I-told-you-so when the operation's failure was reported, but now he was not so sure. Eve Trachea was unpredictable.

On the other side of the table CIA Director Robert

M. Kent sat with his deputy director and the deputies of the operations and analysis divisions. Kent looked like he had a migraine headache.

At the end of the table, the end opposite from Donchez, sat Chairman of the Joint Chiefs of Staff, Air Force General Brian Bevin, who had been promoted to Chairman when Dawson was inaugurated only months earlier. The general was a big man, athletic, tough-looking—a linebacker's jaw, a broken nose, sunken eyes beneath a pronounced brow under tightly trimmed blond hair. Donchez's only contact with Bevin had been at a Pentagon staff cocktail party four months ago, the last time he had been in D.C. He'd seemed an amiable sort, known to his staff as "Uncle Brian." Bevin took pleasure in his nickname, it was said, but he did not seem his jolly smiling self now— his wide face impassive, tight. Donchez suspected the Chairman was not fond of evening meetings in which his military was in a position of reporting failure. For that, Donchez could hardly blame him.

Next to Bevin were President Dawson's military aides, one from each service. Near Bevin, Martin Steuber had taken a seat, his eyes unreadable, staring through Donchez as if he weren't there.

"Gentlemen," Donchez began, "we're here because of a problem with the China intelligence operation, with our SPEC-OP boat, the USS *Tampa*, in the Chinese Bo Hai Bay. About two hours ago *Tampa* transmitted an emergency message that she'd been caught in the bay by units of the Chinese navy and was being taken captive after a battle in which she sank one Chinese surface vessel. The message also indicated that the captain was planning to initiate a ship self-destruct if he was unable to repel a Chinese boarding party. That was the last transmission we had from her."

Donchez paused, scanning the faces for reaction. No one moved. The contents of the messages had apparently already been known to most of them. Donchez turned on the overhead projector and parted the curtains.

"At 1645 our time, shortly after sunrise Beijing time, we had a KH-17 satellite pass over the Bo Hai in the vicinity of Tianjin. That was before we got the distress call from the *Tampa*. But we did pick this up." Donchez dropped a transparency on the top of the projector and stepped away from the picture.

The scene was a black-and-white high-elevation view of the western bay, obviously a satellite photo from the faint appearance of the scan lines running diagonally across the picture. At the bottom of the picture three large surface warships and one small patrol craft were heading east. The wakes of the ships were white streaks across the blank darkness of the bay water. At the top of the picture two helicopters were taking off, heading in the same direction as the surface ships.

"The satellite shot showed the three destroyers you see here and one patrol boat heading on course zero eight five. In the direction of the estimated position of the *Tampa* at that time. As you can see from the wakes of the ships, they are moving out at maximum speed."

Donchez let the image sink in for a moment before he pulled it off and went on to the next. "The next satellite pass was not due for another ninety minutes, and it was not going to overfly the Tianjin area. We decided to retask the satellite, to use the KH-17's onboard fuel reserves to maneuver the unit into a new orbit that would place her over the western shore of the Bo Hai Bay. In the maneuver, almost all of the unit's fuel was expended." Donchez paused, taking in the glares of the men at the table. He had just admitted to ruining a half-billion-dollar surveillance satellite by using all the fuel that had been intended to last five years. "But we did get this," Donchez said, lifting the cover off the projector's lens.

The photo on the screen showed the piers of New Harbor, Xingang, China. One large finger of concrete, the seaward pier, extended horizontally across the picture. Near the pier a strange assembly, looking like three ships lined up alongside each other, was maneuvering toward the pier. Donchez looked at the photo for a moment, feeling sick to his stomach. That photo had engraved itself in his mind. He pulled it off and replaced it with a blowup showing only the three ships together, the image becoming grainy from the magnification. The shape between the destroyers was the cigar shape of the topside portion of a nuclear submarine, her paint blown off in patches to reveal bare metal, perhaps scars from the battle that had resulted in her capture.

"I regret to tell you that *Tampa* has been taken captive by the Communist Chinese. As you can see, there is a destroyer tied up on both *Tampa*'s port and starboard sides, and she's being pushed in toward the pier."

Donchez turned off the projector, not wanting to look at the image of one of his fleet's finest submarines captured by the Chinese.

"That's all I have," Donchez concluded. "I requested an overflight by an RF-117E, the reconnaissance aircraft that's equivalent to the Stealth fighter. So far we haven't heard from the Air Force."

He sat down on Kent's side of the table, opposite Dawson, Trachea, Ferguson and Steuber.

"What about the Stealth?" Dawson asked, frowning at General Bevin. "Did you do an overflight?"

Bevin nodded at Dawson, then pointed to the Air Force aide, a colonel who vanished from the room and came back with a sealed enveloped marked TOP SECRET that he handed to Bevin. Three glossy black-and-white photographs that Bevin handed to the President. Dawson frowned at them, then passed them around the table. It seemed to take forever for the shots to reach Donchez.

The photographs were high-altitude shots of the Xingang pier where the *Tampa* was held. The destroyers were still tied up to her port and starboard sides, but now the starboard destroyer was tied up to the pier. A frigate was tied up to the pier forward of the *Tampa,* another one aft. The three hatches were open on the deck of the submarine, all of them guarded by PLA soldiers or sailors with large weapons in their hands. The second photograph was a similar shot from a different perspective. The third photograph was an infrared shot of the pier and the ships.

Heat was shown in orange or white, cool spots in blue, cold in black. The middle of the *Tampa* was a large white spot. Orange lines and spots continued aft in splotches. The reactor and steam plants, Donchez thought. Her reactor was critical and the steam plant was hot. Maybe she could still get out of this ...

"Mr. President," he began uneasily, "I'd like to propose a rescue mission. I have a tentative plan—"

"Well, Admiral," Eve Trachea broke in, "I hate to say this, and correct me if I'm wrong, but it seems the ship's self-destruct didn't exactly work out. If it had, there would be no need for a rescue, which will be much more hazardous than the original mission."

Donchez bit his lip.

CIA Director Kent looked up from his notes. "Mr. President, the Chinese have made no mention of this. No diplomatic protests, no demands. Nothing."

"How do you read that?"

"The facts just aren't in yet—"

"Bobby, just give me your best guess."

"Well, maybe the Chinese PLA will try to use the submarine against the White Army, and so want to keep it quiet."

"How could they make use of a sub against the White *Army*? And don't the Chinese already have nuclear subs?"

"Five of them, sir, the Han class. Roughly equivalent to the old Russian Victor's. All useless in a fight with the White Army—"

"Sir," Donchez interrupted, "the *Tampa* has ten Javelin conventional cruise missiles on board. Those missiles are accurate enough so that if one were to be

launched at me from Wyoming it would be able to hit
my end of the room rather than yours. *That* well might
be something that could help the Chinese against the
Whites, but I feel the real issue is that the Communist
Chinese are holding Americans, and an American vessel, a top-of-the-line nuclear sub with the latest weapons and firecontrol. We *have* to get her *and* the crew
out of this."

"Well, Admiral, I agree, but how the hell are we
going to do it, short of landing the Marines? I don't
want a damned war."

Ferguson spoke up: "Mr. President, it's clear that
diplomatic channels can't be used to free the ship. If
we ask for the boat back it's an admission we sent her
in there to spy, and that just might be the move the
Chinese are waiting for. They could claim we sent her
there covertly to fire missiles on Beijing. They'd get
international sympathy, maybe they'd even get the
U.N. in there to fight the White Army."

"Sir," Eve Trachea said, her tone one of sweet rea-
sonableness. "We were spying on the Chinese and got
caught. We sank one of their navy's ships trying to
escape and they've captured and neutralized our sub.
Now they will probably hold the ship as a bargaining
tool to keep us from entering this conflict on the
White Army side. Since we aren't planning to do that
anyway, we should be able to send an envoy to Beijing
who can convince them to release the sub and its crew.
We may need to admit what we were doing in their
waters, however."

Donchez fought down his anger. "Sir, the submarine's reactor is critical. The third photo shows it. Her
crew is probably on board to run the reactor for
power—maybe they can't bring on shorepower, the
voltage may be different. So, with the crew aboard,
the reactor critical, what we need to do is put another
submarine in there, sink the destroyers at the pier and
Tampa sails out on her own steam."

"Admiral," Eve Trachea said, "*how* would you propose to get a submarine there now? The Chinese will

be waiting for you. All you'll have are *two* hostage subs. Or, if you do get in, your ship will kill a lot of their troops and probably sink the *Tampa* too. And then the rescue ship wouldn't get out of the bay. Remember Carter's failure in Iran, Desert One? A black eye for the Dawson Administration, contempt at home and hatred from the international community."

"I like Donchez's plan," Defense Secretary Ferguson said. "What's your plan again, Eve? *Apologize* for the incident?"

Donchez spoke up before she could answer. This sort of wrangling was getting them nowhere. The main issue was losing out. He looked directly at President Dawson.

"What if I get the ship out in complete secrecy, sir?"

"If you could do it fast enough I'd consider it. What's your plan?"

"Insert a submarine right next to the pier where *Tampa*'s held. It'll be no problem getting her in. I'll send the *Seawolf,* the quietest, most stealthy submarine there is. When she's there we'll insert a team of SEAL commandos to board and liberate *Tampa.* The sub will break away from the pier using her own power, which is more than enough to part those lines holding her, and out she goes, the *Seawolf* escorting her."

"What about the fleet piers at Lushun," Kent asked, "where the PLA has its Northern Fleet Headquarters, including antisubmarine surface ships and choppers? They'll be waiting for your subs at the Lushun/Penglai Gap. You could lose both submarines."

"*Seawolf* will get through," Donchez said quietly, intensely. "She's so quiet, our *own* surface ASW ships can't detect her. She'll get through and in the process create a diversion—perhaps even surface and resubmerge. The Chinese fleet goes after her, and meanwhile the *Tampa* goes right by. Net result—we get the submarines back, *with* all their intelligence, with no American loss of life and only a few Chinese. And the media, with luck, may never hear about it."

"What if the SEALs fail, Admiral?" President Dawson asked.

"Then, sir, you authorize the fleet's firepower to ... give the Chinese something more to think about."

"General Bevin?" Dawson looked hard at the general.

"I agree, sir. And suggest giving the Navy first crack."

"Eve?" Dawson said to Trachea.

Her answer reflected her dual role as National Security Advisor and Secretary of State. "I'll go along, sir, but if the SEALs fail, the *Seawolf* must withdraw. And no shooting. I also suggest this affair should be a lesson for future adventures of this kind, Mr. President."

Dawson noted her skating on both sides of the ice.

"Okay, Admiral Donchez," he said, rising from the table, "get the *Tampa* out using the SEALs. Tell your sub commander to avoid shooting and explosions, if at all possible. I can't tell you not to shoot if you absolutely have to, but minimize it. If the mission goes sour, and you can't get the *Tampa* out of there, for God's sake, get the *Seawolf* out of the bay."

Donchez stood. "I'll keep you informed of our timing. My aide will bring over the Penetration Order request for the *Seawolf* in an hour."

WASHINGTON, D.C.
PENTAGON E-RING—U.S. NAVY FLAG PLOT
2110 EASTERN DAYLIGHT TIME/0210 GREENWICH
   MEAN TIME

Admiral Donchez unwrapped a Havana and fished in his tropical white uniform trousers for his USS *Piranha* lighter. With three efficient puffs, the cigar's tip glowed red, the smoke creating a cloud around the admiral. Captain Fred Rummel, Donchez's aide, a heavyset officer in his fifties, coughed in the smoke. Over their last decade together, since Rummel was a lieutenant commander and Donchez a rear admiral, the men had worked together, and Donchez had always smoked and Rummel had always coughed. It made the relationship comfortable, familiar, Donchez thought.

Donchez looked up at the electronic wall chart of the western Pacific, showing the blue dot in the Bo Hai Bay labeled USS TAMPA SSN-774. The usual status indicator, either SUBMERGED OPERATIONS or SURFACED TRANSIT, was missing, there being no protocol for a status line when a submarine asset was held captive. The position of the dot was not just Top Secret, it was special compartmented information, and was shown only when Donchez and Rummel were in Flag Plot. At the moment, they were the only people in the room other than a crypto-technician and a senior chief radioman. But the *Tampa* was not the blue dot they were looking at. It was a second blue dot that concerned them, a dot a hundred miles south of the island of Japan in an area of the Pacific marked YOKOSUKA OPAREA.

The dot was labeled USS SEAWOLF SSN-21 SUB-MERGED OPERATIONS (SEA TRIALS).

"Take a message to the *Seawolf,* Fred," Donchez said, the cigar still clenched in his teeth. "Classification Top Secret, personal for commanding officer. Priority immediate."

"Who's the captain, sir?"

"Duckett, Hank Duckett," Donchez said. "You ready? Paragraph one: USS *Seawolf* to make port at Yokosuka Naval Station immediately. Paragraph two: commanding officer and executive officer will be flown to Washington, D.C., by Navy transport for conference. Paragraph three: Purpose of trip is to testify before the Armed Services Committee about the value of the Seawolf submarine class. Be prepared to discuss ship capabilities in detail. Trip duration, approximately three weeks. Paragraph four: Admiral R. Donchez sends. That's it."

"Sir, before this goes out, may I ask what you're doing? Isn't *Seawolf* going to do the rescue mission?"

"She's the one."

"So . . . why are you recalling her skipper?"

"We're giving *Seawolf* a new captain for this operation, someone who's been in combat before, the best sub driver we've got."

"Combat, sir? Our best? The only U.S. sub skipper in the last few decades to launch a torpedo in anger is Michael Pacino, and not only did he lose the *Devilfish* under the polar icecap, he left the Navy for medical reasons. And maybe personal reasons, too, if I remember. So who have you got in mind?"

"Right on the first time, Fred. We're bringing Mikey Pacino out of retirement for this OP. He's got the guts to do it, plus the brains and experience. The other captains, they're okay, but like our friend Marty Steuber, they seem allergic to risk. We need someone who isn't afraid to take chances. That's the only reason he had *Devilfish* shot out from under him. And let's not forget what happened to the other submarine in that incident—anyone other than Pacino would have come back dead or not at all."

"So, how are you going to convince him to go back to sea?"

"I'll personally order him. Get out a message to NAVPERS transferring Pacino back to active duty."

"I don't know, Admiral. We're talking about the most sensitive mission in maybe forty years. Even if Pacino comes back, he's a Piranha-class sailor—he won't know the first thing about the *Seawolf*. And as a civilian, he's under no obligation to go back to active duty to do this—"

"Leave all that to me," Donchez said. "Just get those messages on the wire."

CHAPTER 7

THURSDAY, 9 MAY
1150 GREENWICH MEAN TIME

Severn River Inlet
Annapolis, Maryland
0650 Eastern Daylight Time

Michael Pacino finished his morning run with a sprint to the back of the waterfront property, stopping in the middle of the yard to rest with Max, his big golden retriever. The sun was already turning the morning into a humid furnace. Legs aching, Pacino climbed the steps to the deck, leaned on the railing and stared across the river at the Naval Academy complex.

For a long time he stood there, staring at the copper roofs of the 150-year-old granite buildings, but seeing instead his own past. Himself as a midshipman two and a half decades earlier. The Academy had always been a time machine, taking him back to his youth, the years that were the best and worst of his life. He had chosen the house for its water view, but not just the view of the water, but the spectacular vista of the harbor of Annapolis, teeming with sailboats, the Capitol dome in the background dueling for grandeur with the Academy's copper-domed chapel. It was not the only way he brought back the past.

For a moment he looked down at the baseball cap he had been wearing on the run. Dark blue, soaked with sweat, the brim white where the accumulated salt had stained the cap. The cap's bill had an emblem, the golden embroidery thread forming twin-fish facing a submarine conning tower—submariner's dolphins.

Above the dolphins, block embroidery letters spelled USS TAMPA; below, the letters read SSN-774. A gift from Sean Murphy, his best friend and former Annapolis roommate who now commanded the *Tampa*, a new Los Angeles-class nuclear fast-attack submarine out of San Diego.

But when Pacino looked at the cap's letters they reformed into the name USS DEVILFISH, SSN-666, the name and number of the ship he had lost two years before. The *Devilfish* was now a crumpled wreck at the bottom of the ocean, the bodies of the men he had lost trapped aboard. Pacino looked away at the water, unaware that his wife Hillary was looking at him from inside the house.

Hillary walked out onto the deck, a glass of ice water in her hand. She set the glass on the deck railing in front of him. He ignored it.

"Michael. You okay?"

There was no answer. She tried again.

"Honey, isn't it time you got ready for work?"

"I guess," he mumbled, passing her on the way inside, the glass door sliding shut behind him and the dog.

Hillary looked back at him for a moment, then out at the sun-drenched harbor and the quaint village, the boats getting underway one by one for a day of pleasure sailing. She had hoped the setting and the Academy would help Michael heal, but the truth was, it was making him worse. She and their son missed the man he had been two years before, a confident man, a nuclear submarine commander. Maybe they needed to move inland, get away from the bay and the water and the Academy and all the reminders of his past. Or maybe what he really needed was to go back to sea, exorcise the beast that haunted him. *If* the Navy would take him, and *if* he would go back, and *if* there were another submarine for him ...

Finally she too went inside, the ice water still on the deck rail, forgotten.

U.S. Naval Academy
Annapolis, Maryland
0830 Eastern Daylight Time

Admiral Richard Donchez followed a midshipman into a cavernous high-bay dimly lit room. Donchez craned his neck looking up at the heavy steel rafters of the room, holding up another set of steel rails above the concrete walls of a large oblong pool. The midshipman led Donchez up steel stairs to a platform overlooking the edge of the tank. The models used for this tank were huge, some of them fifteen or twenty feet long. Below the tow platform with its trailer was a large model submerged below the surface. Not much of it was visible, but from what Donchez could see, it was a submarine.

"What is this thing?" Donchez asked.

"Tow tank," the midshipman replied. "The platform there can move along the rails above the water, dragging a ship model. The computer systems collect the data and use it to evaluate the ship design."

The sound of the wave generator startled Donchez for a moment. The angled plates at the end of the tank began pulsing, undulating back and forth, the waves building up in the tank until they were some five feet high.

The platform, with its office trailer on top, suddenly accelerated away from them, the drive mechanism whirring loudly. Donchez had to shout over the noise to be heard.

"Like I said," Donchez reminded his guide, "I need to find Dr. Pacino."

"He's either in the control room or on the platform."

Seconds after it had started, the model test run was over, the wake of the model and the waves in the tank splashing the surface below. Slowly, the model platform began to return to its starting position.

"I think I see someone in the platform control

space," Donchez said as the model platform drew up to them and slowed. "Thanks for your help."

The midshipman nodded and walked back down the stairs and disappeared through the double doors.

The model platform's trailer door opened on the other side from Donchez. Through the trailer's windows a man could be seen walking out of the trailer and toward the catwalk between the platform and the observation deck. It was Michael Pacino, who momentarily froze when he spotted Donchez.

"Admiral Donchez?"

"Mikey," Donchez said, his face crinkling into a smile. "Been a long time. How's life as a professor?"

As the younger Pacino approached, Donchez looked him over, inspecting him as if Pacino were a subordinate in the ranks. Or maybe more, as if he were Donchez's own son, seen for the first time after a long absence. In fact, young Pacino had been the son of Donchez's Academy roommate, Anthony "Patch" Pacino, who had died in a submarine incident years before. Since his birth Michael Pacino had been as close to a son as Donchez would ever have, and after the father's death, Donchez's feelings had intensified. Still, the younger Pacino had never exactly seen Donchez as his mentor, perhaps still too full of the memory of the day that Donchez had told him of the sinking of his father's submarine.

Pacino, over six feet tall and thin as ever, had just turned forty, his thick hair no longer jet black but graying. His lean face was tan, unlike the days he had commanded *Devilfish*, when he wore a pallor from being almost constantly submerged. He was dressed in khaki trousers, a starched white shirt, and a sport jacket, his striped tie cinched up tight to his neck.

Donchez looked for a moment into the younger man's eyes, measuring him. Pacino's green eyes at first stared back, then looked away. When Pacino held out his hand to Donchez his grip was strong and steady but moist with nervous sweat.

"What are you doing here, sir? And what's with the civies? You're still CINCPAC, aren't you?"

"I came to see you, Mikey. And easy on that CINC-PAC. I don't want the Superintendent finding out I came out here without notifying him."

"You're what, the number-three admiral in the Navy and you didn't tell Admiral Phillips you were coming to spy on his little empire?"

"What would I be doing right now if I had told him?"

"Probably reviewing a dress parade after a long tour of the facilities."

"Right. I don't have time for that stuff, Mikey. We've got a problem, I need you to help fix it."

Pacino laughed uneasily. "What's a professor of fluid mechanics going to be able to do to fix an admiral's problems? Come on, let's get out of this cave."

Pacino led Donchez down the stairs to the end of the tow tank room and out a door in the far wall to the door that opened outside to a small parking lot fronting a waterfront soccer field.

"So what really brings you all this way from Pearl Harbor, Admiral?"

"I had a stop at the Pentagon . . ."

They stopped at the midpoint of an arched bridge, looking down on the creek where it flowed past the athletic fields and into the Severn River. To the left, in the distance, the drawbridge of Highway 2 was up while a sailboat plodded slowly through. In front of them majestic houses overlooked the water from the far bank. To the right, the academic buildings gleamed in the sunshine, the black-uniformed midshipmen walking briskly in the few moments between classes.

"You ever miss going to sea, Mikey?"

"No," Pacino said, his voice flat. "What's going on, Admiral . . . You tell me you came to see me about a problem, you have no time for tours or dress parades, then you ask me whether I miss going to sea. You trying to recruit me back to the service? And if so, why? Hell, the Cold War's over. The Navy's got more hotshot young officers than it has submarines to command, and I'd never even consider coming back to the fleet without a sub of my own. *And* after I lost *Devilfish* no squadron commander would ever give me my own submarine again."

"Okay, Mikey, enough fencing. I did come here to offer you command of a fast-attack sub, the hottest one we've got. The *Seawolf.* If you're not interested, okay. You've got your family. You've got midshipmen to teach, research to do, toys to play with ..."

"Admiral, why would you want me to take over the *Seawolf*? Henry Duckett's in command of her."

"He is, but I've got other plans for Hank. We have an urgent SPEC-OP for the *Seawolf* and I need the best skipper for the job. You happen to be the only sub driver in recent history who knows how to handle himself in combat. So, you lost that rustbucket *Devilfish*? Don't forget that I ordered you on that mission, and I bear more guilt for it than you do. The point of all this is that you are the best there is for what I need. The commander of this OP will report directly to me, I'll report directly to the President. That's all I can tell you unless you take the mission."

The two were silent for a moment; finally Pacino spoke up.

"Let me understand this, Admiral. You're willing to give command of the *Seawolf* to an old Piranha-class sailor who's been out of the fleet for two years, who knows nothing about the Seawolf class. To a man whose last submarine sank, never mind who was most at fault. The mission is so sensitive that you and the President are running it yourselves, and you can't tell me what it's about."

Donchez said nothing.

"This wouldn't have to do with the Chinese Civil War, would it? Except what would the Navy be doing with ... unless you sent a sub into the waters close to Beijing ... what's the name of that bay ... the Gulf of China?"

"Chihli, Gulf of Chihli. The Chinese call it the Bo Hai Bay—"

"And something went wrong with the boat you sent in?"

"Bingo."

Pacino shook his head.

"This must be a rescue mission."

"You're close enough, Mikey. I need to know if you'll change your mind? This is no academic discussion."

Pacino let the dig at his current academic career go by.

"I've been away from the submarine navy too long, Admiral. There are a dozen skippers out there who could handle this mission. Sean Murphy, for one. His *Tampa* is one of the newest boats in the fleet and Murphy's damned good. I ought to know, I roomed with that guy for four years here and almost five years after graduation. I'd say *Tampa* could do this better than the untested *Seawolf*. Sean's boat is trained and ready."

"Only one problem, Mikey. Sean Murphy and the *Tampa* are the ones being held captive." Donchez decided he had to gamble in spite of his own rules of security. The risk had obviously been worth it, judging by Pacino's shocked expression. "The Chinese have had *Tampa* tied up at the Xingang piers outside of Tianjin for about sixteen hours. Intel indicates that the crew are being held onboard. The *Seawolf* made port in Yokosuka last night. Her captain and XO are on the way to D.C. now. I told them they'd be briefing Congress. I have a fast transport jet standing by at Andrews. I figure if you can get packed in an hour we can get *Seawolf* underway within twelve. What do you say, Mikey?"

For a moment Pacino said nothing. He no longer was registering Donchez's words, nor seeing the vista of the Severn River in front of him. He was traveling a corridor of time, back to the moments he and Sean Murphy had shared as roommates, struggling against the hazing of their firstclassmen. Back to the time that Murphy had risked dismissal from the Academy to go AWOL to see Pacino at the memorial service for Pacino's father, when only a plea from the senior ranks of the Navy had been between Sean Murphy and life as a civilian. Back to happier times, the double-dates in town, Murphy crashing his car and Pacino picking him up in D.C., Pacino speeding back to Annapolis to avoid having them both placed on report. Back to the moment before graduation when Pacino had had to pour Murphy into his dress whites, Sean being too hungover to stand on his own from the celebrating they'd done the night before. Back to the following year in Boston when the two of them had been at MIT, getting master's degrees in mechanical engineering, but also prowling the bars of Boston in search of action. Back to the times of frustration and triumph in the nuclear power pipeline, the prototype nuclearplant training that had them working shiftwork twelve hours a day, seven days a week until they were qualified as reactor supervisors. Back to the three years they had spent on the USS *Hawkbill* during their division officer tours. Back to the day Pacino had been Murphy's best man when he married Katrina, and to the day months later when the roles were reversed as Pacino married Hillary.

And now Murphy was a hemisphere away looking down the barrel of a Chinese rifle, and Sean Murphy's wife might soon be a widow and his children fatherless. After a moment Pacino realized Donchez was looking at him, waiting.

"What are we waiting for, Admiral?"

Donchez pulled a document from his pants pocket, sheets stapled together, the large stamp in black letters reading "ORIGINAL." He handed it to Pacino. Buried in the official message were the words "REPORT FOR TEMPORARY DUTY AS COMMANDING OFFICER USS SEAWOLF SSN-21."

"These are your orders. I've already talked to Hillary. Get home and say good-by to her. I've had Tony pulled from school—he'll be waiting for you. I've got uniforms on the jet for you. Just pack your shaving kit, maybe see if you can dig up your old dolphins. We'll have some poopy suits waiting for you on the boat. I'll meet you at your place and take you to the airport. I'll brief you in detail on the jet. I've had the Pentagon take care of your boss here. As of zero nine hundred this morning you no longer work here. You're back in the Navy now."

Pacino nodded, held out his hand to Donchez, then turned and walked quickly to the row of cars parked near the soccer field.

Donchez watched Pacino drive away, thinking about Pacino's handshake. There could be no mistake about it. The handshake he had given Donchez before he left was just as firm, but this time it had been dry as a bone.

Donchez threw the stub of his cigar into the creek and walked to the rental car, for the first time feeling that the *Tampa* was now much closer to freedom than she had been just an hour before.

CHAPTER 8

THURSDAY, 9 MAY
1845 GREENWICH MEAN TIME

WESTERN PENNSYLVANIA
ALTITUDE: THIRTY-EIGHT THOUSAND FEET

Captain Michael Pacino sat in the deep upholstery of
the Gulfstream's wide seat staring out the window at
the clouds below, thinking back to the scene at the
house when he had told Hillary he was going back to
sea. He had expected anger or tears from her, but she
had looked at him with deep understanding. Her
words still rang in his ears ... *"I'm scared to death of
losing you, Michael, but I've seen what happens to you
when you're not at sea. You haven't really been the
same, not since—"* Not since *Devilfish* sank, he had
thought—*"—and there's something you need to finish
out there, isn't there?"* She had seen right into him,
past his eyes to the rusting wreck of his last submarine.
She had held their son Tony as Donchez's staff car
had pulled away, young Tony still crying, trembling in
his mother's arms. The only thing that had kept Pacino
from turning the car around was the thought of Sean
Junior crying in Katrina Murphy's arms at the word
of his father's death, just as Pacino had when told that
his father had gone down in the *Stingray* so many
years ago.

Pacino's jaw clenched. Suddenly he couldn't wait to
get to Yokosuka and take command of *Seawolf*. His
hands seemed to itch for the feel of periscope grips,
his ears for the sounds of torpedo launches. He stared
out the jet's window, not seeing the rolling countryside

outside, but the blue waves of the endless stretches of the Pacific. It had been too damned long.

In front of him was a table with a half-dozen large three-ring notebooks scattered on top of nautical charts of the Bo Hai Bay. The interior of the new jet was cold, the air conditioning system improperly adjusted. The cool air had raised goosebumps on Pacino's exposed arms. He scarcely noticed.

As promised, Admiral Donchez had provided the new khaki uniforms in Pacino's size. Pacino had ransacked a steamer trunk full of old uniforms in the basement of the house, but the old garments still stank of the *Devilfish*. He had found the velvet display case holding his Navy Cross earned "in classified action under the polar icecap onboard the USS *Devilfish*." He had tossed the case back to the bottom of the trunk in disgust ... over one hundred and thirty men had died in the *Devilfish* incident, he had gotten a damned medal ...

He had salvaged his old submariner's dolphin pin, the brass emblem solid and heavy in his hands, the scaly fish facing toward the center where an old-fashioned diesel boat plowed through the waves. The pin had once belonged to his father, "Patch" Pacino. Donchez had given it to him years before when he had first qualified in submarines. After the *Devilfish* incident, the dolphins were practically all that he had left from his old submarine. Everything else had gone down with her to the bottom.

Donchez's voice brought Pacino back from his thoughts. "Mikey, this trip is the only chance I'll have to brief you. After that you're on your own. The first thing we've got to get through is the weapons loadout. The base is standing by to load the *Seawolf* with weapons and it'll take at least five, six hours to get that done. I don't want the mission delayed to load weapons. So let's go over the mission, commit to the loadout and I'll radio the request to Yokosuka. When we're done with that we'll go over the capabilities of the *Seawolf* and brief you on the crew."

"Fine," Pacino said, his voice wooden, suddenly wondering if he was really up to taking over command of the world's most advanced submarine and, within an hour, submerging it to sail into hostile waters to rescue another submarine.

"Okay, the mission first. Of course, you can tailor this to suit yourself. First you'll get into the Bo Hai as quietly as possible. At Point Hotel, off Tianjin's Xingang harbor, you'll come up to periscope depth and take a look at the situation. If nothing has changed since the last KH-17 flyover, the plan goes forward. *Seawolf* will hover at periscope depth and put the three platoons of the SEAL team out the escape trunk. When the SEALs are locked out they'll swim over to the *Tampa*, taking with them Kurt Lennox—"

"Who's he?"

"Murphy's exec. He was on leave in Japan when *Tampa* got the word to insert into the Bo Hai. He's integral to the plan. He'll be the one who will know the details of how we plan to get *Tampa* out, and he'll coordinate your escape plan with Murphy. He's also our insurance in case they've removed the officers and crew from the ship. In which case he'll be the only one who will be able to drive the ship out—the SEAL team sure as hell won't know the first thing about conning a nuke sub out of the bay. Then we at least get the ship back, and we'll try to figure out something else to get the crew back.

"The SEAL team's job will be to knock out the pier guards and get aboard the *Tampa*, overpower the Chinese inside and get the crew on-station for the underway, then lay topside to cut the lines to the Chinese ships. Here's where you may need to improvise. Somehow the Chinese destroyers will need to be distracted so *Tampa* has time to warm up her engines and get underway."

"Improvise?" Pacino said. "Distract the destroyers? My ideas on distracting the Chinese will involve some large-bore weapons, Admiral. I hope you're ready for that."

"Up to you. Once *Tampa* is underway you'll have to escort her out. I'm guessing she'll still be able to start up, get underway and submerge. If she can't, the backup plan is to get as many men out of the hull as possible and get them aboard *Seawolf*, then get out of there. I'm hoping that won't be the case—the mission has almost zero chance of success if that happens, plus we'll probably lose you and *Seawolf* too. I'm tempted to order you to get the hell out of there without Murphy and his crew if the *Tampa* is disabled. I won't order you to do anything specific. You'll be the guy up-close. You've got a free hand. Your only requirements are to get *Tampa* away from the Chinese with minimal loss of American lives and American equipment."

"Okay, so let's say *Tampa* gets down and I'm escorting her out. The Chinese will be waiting for us at the entrance to the bay ..."

"Yes. I expect the entire Chinese Northern Fleet to be waiting for you at Lushun. Including their new aircraft carrier, the *Shaoguan,* the Kiev-class carrier they bought from the Russians. Anyway, *Tampa*'ll be a lot louder underwater than you are, so once again you'll have to create another diversion to allow *Tampa* to get out of the Lushun/Penglai Gap. I'm assuming *Tampa* won't be able to shoot any weapons, that her systems are disabled. If she can fire, so much the better, but worst-case, you'll be the only one with firepower."

"This will be like stealing the crown jewels while they're under heavy guard."

"So, what weapons do you want?" Donchez pushed one of the thick binders in front of Pacino. Inside, each page had a laminated photo of a weapon with its capabilities summarized beneath. Pacino thumbed through the volume as Donchez went on. "I can't give you nukes, Mikey. We don't have any, and the President wouldn't authorize it even if we did. But you've got your choice of conventional Javelin cruise missiles, ship attack or land attack, the new ASWSOW standoff missiles, and Mark 50 torpedoes. You can carry up to fifty weapons. You'll also be outfitted with fifteen Mark 80 SLAAMs."

Pacino was looking at the photograph of one of the Javelin cruise missiles. Beneath the title were the words BLOCK III JAVELIN—DELAYED ENCAP-SULATION. "What's this, Admiral?"

"The Block III Javelin ... They came up with the idea of having the waterproof capsule of the cruise missile float just beneath the water's surface for a certain time-delay before the missile launches itself out of the capsule."

Pacino liked that. "Before, when you'd launch a cruise missile, a plume of smoke would point to your launching position. With this weapon you could eject it and get out of the area by the time the missile launched, all without giving away your position."

"In theory, yes, Mikey. In practice, it's a piece of meat. The test units all flooded and sank just before liftoff. Plus, the capsule needs a ballasting system to keep it submerged and then to broach the unit when it's time to light off the solid rocket motor. The ballast system takes up room that could be better used for the fuel and warhead. Like they say, you don't get something for nothing. They had to reduce the fuel load and warhead size on those missiles. I'd advise against using them."

Pacino's enthusiasm ebbed. "So what's an ASW-SOW?" he asked, turning the page.

"Antisubmarine Warfare Standoff Weapon, built by DynaCorp. Brand new. Nice unit. A solid rocket booster fires the warhead away from you, with a range of about forty miles. Its name says ASW, but it can be used for surface targets too. Very powerful warhead, enough to sink a cruiser with one shot."

"What about the Mark 80 SLAAM?"

"Beautiful, and only the *Seawolf* has it ... Have you ever been detected by a P-3 Orion patrol aircraft?"

"I played rabbit for one a few times."

"You never got snapped up by one in the VA-CAPES OP AREA? Never once been surprised?"

"Not that I'll admit to."

"Well, I have," Donchez said, "and I always thought, goddamn, why can't the sub force have something to launch at those damned ASW patrol planes? Those things are too damned good. In fact, the evidence suggests that's how Sean Murphy got detected. An old Nimrod aircraft picked up on his periscope."

"You were telling me about the Mark 80."

"Mark 80 SLAAM, Submarine Launched Anti-Air Missile. The *Seawolf* has fifteen units tucked into the top of the sail. If you see an aircraft or helicopter, anything that flies, and it's within ten thousand yards, you push a button on the periscope grip and one of those babies pops out of the water and flies right up the airplane's tailpipe."

"If the 688-class subs had these the *Tampa* wouldn't be tied up at Xingang now," Pacino said.

"So, Mikey, what'll it be?"

"I want some decoys, Admiral. You have any of the old Mark 36s?"

"Decoys? What the hell do you want with decoys? Those things just take up torpedo-room space. You'll be too quiet for the things to do you any good anyway."

"Admiral. I'm supposed to get a rattling, battle-damaged submarine out of restricted waters, with a motivated enemy chasing her. At least with decoys I might confuse even a large surface force. Give me twenty Mark 36s and program them for the Los Angeles-class subs. And make them loud."

"We don't even have the Mark 36s anymore, Mikey. But the Mark 38 is an improvement. Longer range. Has tonals at the same frequencies as a real 688-class, plus it can be programmed to make transient noises, like weapon launches, slamming hatches, rattles. It can drive a set-pattern, even wiggle like it's doing Target Motion Analysis. But like I said, every decoy you take is one less torpedo you can carry. Not one ship has ever been sunk by a decoy. I suggest you fill up with Ow-sows and Mark 50s, not wimpy decoys."

"I don't see it that way, Admiral," Pacino said, shutting the binder. "You said it's my ass, my call. Give me twenty Mark 38 decoys, fifteen Mark 50 torpedoes, fourteen Block III Javelins, all of them ship-attack units, and one Ow-sow. And of course the fifteen Mark 80 SLAAMs."

"It's your mission. I'll radio ahead."

Donchez didn't look pleased, Pacino thought, as he went forward to have the pilot radio Japan with the weapon loadout. Well, the OP was his, it would have to go by his plan. He was beginning to feel the self-confidence of command returning to him. It felt damn good.

YOKOSUKA, JAPAN, THIRTY MILES SOUTH OF TOKYO
YOKOSUKA NAVAL STATION, PIER 4
USS *SEAWOLF*
0305 LOCAL TIME

Lieutenant Commander Greg Keebes woke up with a start. The sound of the curtain of his coffin-sized bunk being opened never failed to bring him crashing back to the reality of the submarine. In his year aboard the *Seawolf,* Keebes had yet to sleep through an entire night aboard, whether in-port as duty officer or at sea.

"What is it?" he asked, rubbing his eyes. A petty officer in dungarees held out a radio-message board. Behind the enlisted sailor Keebes could see the chief torpedoman, who was also the duty chief for the evening, standing in the dimly lit passageway.

Keebes pushed back the message board, climbed out of the coffin and put on his khaki pants and shirt, feeling desperately in need of a shower. As he buttoned his shirt he nodded at the petty officer to turn on the stateroom's overhead lights. The bright white fluorescents flickered, then clicked to life. Keebes checked his watch—after three in the morning.

"What is it, Deitzler?" Keebes asked the chief, a salty hovering, forty-five plus, his hair already gray, his face lined. What was it that made men get old so fast in the sub force? Had to be the atmosphere, the nuclear radiation, the food, or the stress. Or maybe the months at sea without a woman. Whatever, the fleet was full of old youngsters.

"Sir, the base weapons officer is topside. He's asking for you, and get this—there's a crane and a lowboy loaded with cruise missiles and torpedoes waiting to be loaded. He wants to know why we're not ready to load weapons. Did I miss something, sir?"

Keebes ran his hands through his hair, wondering if the Navy bureaucracy had failed them again. Sea trials had been interrupted by the emergency orders to get the CO and XO stateside. But even so, the weapons tests weren't scheduled for another month. And when the weapons tests did begin they were only to shoot dummies of torpedoes to test the torpedo-tube ejection-mechanisms. The plan didn't have them launching cruise missiles for months.

"A little early to be loading dummies, if you ask me, Chief," Keebes said, taking the message board from the radioman.

"Sir, these are *warshots,* not dummies. Not even exercise shots. What the hell's up?"

Keebes held up a finger as he read the message on the board, which had the answer to the chief's questions:

091857ZMAY
IMMEDIATE

FM   CINCPAC

TO   USS SEAWOLF SSN-21

SUBJ   EMERGENCY SPEC-OP

SCI/TOP SECRET—JAILBREAK

*PERSONAL FOR COMMANDING OFFICER//PERSONAL FOR
COMMANDING OFFICER*

//BT//
1. *PREPARE TO GET UNDERWAY FOR EMERGENCY
   SPECIAL OPERATION.*
2. *NEW COMMANDING OFFICER EN ROUTE YOKOSUKA.*
3. *EXECUTE WEAPONS LOADOUT IMMEDIATELY TO
   SUPPORT TIMELY UNDERWAY.*
4. *UNDERWAY TO COMMENCE IMMEDIATELY UPON
   ARRIVAL OF NEW COMMANDING OFFICER, APPROX
   1000 LOCAL TIME TODAY.*
5. *ADMIRAL R. DONCHEZ SENDS.*
//BT//

Keebes looked up at Deitzler, handed the message
board over to the chief and waited for him to finish
reading it. Then: "Get on the Circuit One, Chief, and
get the crew up. Station the weapons loading detail.
Muster the officers in the wardroom and the chiefs in
the crew's mess. Whatever's going on, we'll know soon
enough. In the meantime you brief the chiefs and get
working on the loadout and the pre-underway
checklist."

Keebes hurried into the wardroom and called for
one of the cooks to stoke up the coffee machine. A
new captain, Keebes thought. An untested submarine.
An emergency special operation. Terrific.

CHAPTER 9

FRIDAY, 10 MAY
0047 GREENWICH MEAN TIME

Yokosuka Naval Station, Pier 4
USS *Seawolf*
0947 Local Time

Pacino knew he'd be too tense to sleep at his body's normal time. His submarine would be long submerged in the darkness of the local evening before he slept again. Besides, he thought, it wouldn't feel like he was an official submariner again until he had skipped a few nights of sleep. The feeling of fatigue had been as familiar and as comfortable as the deck shoes he used to wear at sea.

Pacino couldn't help feeling excited as he craned his neck to see the large dark shape ahead in the water next to the pier. When the car stopped, Pacino opened his door and stepped out, seeing the breathtaking size of the monstrous submarine lying in the water, waiting for him. The ship lay tied up at the end of the pier, her bow toward Pacino, her stern pointing away toward the waters of the channel.

Donchez joined him on the pier. "What do you think of her, Mikey?"

The ship was similar in lines to a 688 Los Angeles-class submarine, but the scale seemed blown up. Her diameter was so big that the deck appeared almost flat at the crown instead of curving and cylindrical. The sheer sides of the sail jutted straight out of the deck, unadorned by fairwater planes. The ship seemed to extend to the vanishing point; it had to be nearly three hundred and fifty feet long, Pacino thought. The fairing for the towed array extended longitudinally aft from the leading edge of the sail to the stern. The sail had a triangular fillet at the forward edge where it attached to the hull. The rudder protruded from the water far aft of the point where the water lapped the aft hull. Forward of the sail a large hatch was open, and further forward the hull sloped more steeply to the water, the bulbous bow rounder and broader than *Devilfish*'s. Eight doubled-up lines held the ship to the pier. Amidships, a gangway connected the ship to the concrete jetty. There were no shorepower cables on the ship but a heavy gantry with thick cables had been retracted aft near the rudder. They must be steaming the engineroom, Pacino figured.

Pacino realized Donchez had been waiting for an answer. "She'll do, Admiral," he said, trying to keep his voice flat. But Donchez must have seen through him.

"Come on, Mikey. I'll give you the rundown up here. I think you'll find this crew will be motivated to support you, Mikey. I had my aide call the acting captain from the airport while we were on the way in—he gave him a few stories about you."

"Great. All I need is for this crew to know I got my last command shot out from under me."

"All he told them was what happened to the other guy, and that you got the Navy Cross."

"Whatever. Tell me about this ship, Admiral. Give me her secrets."

Donchez smiled. "*Seawolf* displaces 9,150 tons submerged. She's forty-two feet in diameter—that's why the pier is new. Her draft is so deep they had to dredge the channel so she could get out."

"Forty-two feet. Unbelievable."

"She's 326 feet long from her sonar sphere to her propulsor. No screw, by the way. She's got a water-turbine propulsor. Much quieter. Very fast, although her acceleration is just a bit off, but that propulsor doesn't cavitate like a screw, so you can give her full throttle and she'll come up to speed quiet as a church mouse. Her test depth is 2,000 feet. Her hull has an anechoic coating, tiles made of foam that absorb active sonar pulses, kind of like a Stealth fighter's radar-absorptive material. She'll do forty-five knots at one hundred percent power, more if you take her into the red. She has 52,000 shaft horsepower, and get this— this boat is quieter going full out than a Los Angeles sub at all-stop."

"Fifty-two-thousand shaft horsepower, and you're telling me I'll be quieter at all-ahead flank than Sean's boat is hovering?"

"Right. Did I tell you the story of her acoustic tests? She was supposed to run through the instrumented sonar array at the Bahamas acoustic test site, and the DynaCorp crew radioed her asking what she was waiting for, that she was behind schedule. *Seawolf* radioed back that she had *already* gone through the test area. DynaCorp called back and said that was impossible— they hadn't *heard* anything. Fact is, when they analyzed the tapes, the only way they could determine that the ship had passed through the sonar range was that a hole of quietness went by—during her run the ocean's noise actually disappeared for a moment to be replaced by total quiet. When the boat moved on, the ocean noise returned. This ship is so damned quiet it is actually an acoustic hole in the ocean. And that ain't all. Her reactor's coolant system uses natural circulation up to fifty percent power, no circulation pumps. That'll get you up to thirty-three knots with no pumps. The loudest machinery aboard, and we don't need it until we go over thirty-three knots. Not only that, but we've completely rethought the engineroom layout. The maneuvering reactor control room is aft at the shaft seals, where it's nice and cool. It's in a special compartment so that even if there's a major steam leak, the maneuvering crew has a full thirty seconds to isolate it remotely. Makes more sense than having the crew roasted."

"What else? You're a regular encyclopedia, Admiral."

"About this baby, I am. Okay, you don't see any fairwater planes on the sail. This boat uses bow planes up forward for better depth control. The sonar system is the BQQ-5E advanced BATEARS suite, with the advanced hull array and the supersensitive spherical array forward. There's even a baffle-viewing sonar in the lower rudder, although so far it doesn't work. The combat-control system is the AN/BSY-2 Mark II advanced firecontrol system, a master computer that links sonar and navigation and keeps records of everything you do at sea. The control room is in the middle-level deck so you have the ship's full width for the room. Still a bit cramped, though. You've got the type-20 periscope. The forward escape trunk is set up to lock out ten men at a time, more if they squeeze together. That will come in very handy when you're locking out the SEALs. And as I already told you, you've got fifty room-loaded weapons and eight torpedo tubes. Well, that's about it. You ready to meet your crew and take a look inside?"

"Hell, Admiral, lead on."

Donchez stepped onto the gangway and saluted the American flag flying aft on the deck, then saluted the sentry.

"Request permission to come aboard," Donchez barked.

"Granted, sir. Welcome aboard, Admiral."

Pacino repeated the ritual. As he stepped off the gangway onto the spongy anechoic-tiled deck of the *Seawolf* he felt like he'd come home again. He followed Donchez toward the amidships hatch, the weapon-shipping hatch. As Donchez lowered himself down the ladder and disappeared Pacino took a look around the harbor, a habit from the old days, when he would look one last time at the world before vanishing into a steel pipe that would take the world away. When he found the rungs of the ladder and stepped into the massive hull, he smelled the smell, the unique smell of a submarine. He shut his eyes for a moment and drew the air in, savoring the smell like a wine expert lingering over the bouquet of a familiar vintage. The smell defied description, but Hillary had once tried to analyze it during one of her rare visits to his old boat—she had correctly identified diesel oil, lubrication oil, cooking grease, cigarette smoke and sweat. But she also had said there was something else there that she couldn't identify. Pacino hadn't told her, but what she couldn't label was the smell of raw sewage from the sanitary tank vents, flavored with ozone from the high-voltage electrical equipment.

As Pacino's feet hit the deck the Public Address Circuit One system crackled with the voice of the topside sentry:

"COMMANDER IN CHIEF, UNITED STATES PACIFIC FLEET, ARRIVING! CAPTAIN, UNITED STATES NAVY ... ARRIVING."

Pacino and Donchez were standing at the base of the ladder to the amidships hatch, which was in a narrow passageway. The walls, the bulkheads, were paneled in dark grain wood. Pacino reached out and touched it—it wasn't imitation Formica paneling but honest-to-god mahogany wood. The passageway extended forward for about seventy or eighty feet. A few feet down the passageway Donchez stood talking to an officer who wore starched cotton khakis and the emblems of a lieutenant commander on his collars, with gold dolphins over his left pocket and a key with a braided chain around his neck. The duty officer. The man's nametag read KEEBES; of medium height, in his mid-thirties, the most prominent thing about him his severe crewcut and horn-rimmed glasses. Pacino, thinking back to Donchez's briefing, recalled that Keebes was the navigator and acting captain.

"Mikey, this is Lieutenant Commander Greg Keebes. Mr. Keebes is a *Seawolf* plankowner. Mr. Keebes, this is Captain Mike Pacino, the man we've been telling you about. He'll be taking command as soon as you're ready."

Keebes said he had a course plotted but only to point Alpha. "Our track past the dive point isn't on the clearance message. Too highly classified."

"I'll brief the officers once we're underway, Nav," Pacino said. "You'll be able to plot the track as soon as we're at sea. Now I'd like to take a look around at this boat before I take command."

Keebes led the way forward. "This whole deck is devoted to crew living," Keebes said. "Officers' country is on the port side. Four large staterooms and a head, and the wardroom. Starboard is the chiefs' quarters aft and the crew's mess and galley forward."

At the end of the passageway, Pacino found himself standing next to a curving metal bulkhead. The shape of the surface seemed spherical. A round hatch was set into the side of the sphere.

"Forward escape trunk," Keebes said. "It can lock out a dozen men at a shot. We use it for commando insertions, diver ops, that kind of thing."

Keebes proceeded to a ladder leading down to the next level, lowered himself down the ladder and Pacino followed.

"Sonar and firecontrol computer room," Keebes said. He opened a door on a starboard bulkhead. "Sonar display room. Sonar's come a long way since the original Q-5. We've got two towed arrays; the hull one has six bulges isolated from internal noise, the spherical array is bigger, with more hydrophones, more sensitivity."

Keebes pushed through the door leading aft into a room the full forty-two-foot width of the submarine. Pacino whistled. The room looked absurdly open and comfortable to Pacino's eyes, accustomed as they had been to the old Piranha-class's cramped control spaces. The center of the room was taken up with the periscope stand, the conn, an elevated platform built around the wells for two periscopes set side-by-side. At the aft end of the conn was a display console housing repeater panels for the sonar set and the firecontrol computer as well as the red handset of a

NESTOR satellite secure-voice radio system. Beside the radio gear was the underwater telephone console.

In the port forward corner of the room were the ballast-control panel wrapping around from port to forward, and next to it the ship-control panel, a set of three control seats situated around airplane-style controls. The panels performed similar functions to their ancestors on previous ship classes, but the level of computerization had progressed enormously—the panels had almost no hardware instruments, only computer videoscreens, where the ship's combat computer displayed the faces of the instruments the crew would configure.

"Looks like something out of a sci-fi flick," Pacino said, staring at the ship-control console.

"We still haven't gone all the way to computer ship-control—the planes and rudder and ballast systems are still controlled manually by the four-man ship-control team instead of by the computer," Keebes said. "NAVSEA still isn't comfortable with computers driving the boat. Their mentality is still in the 1940s. Why pay for all these computers if it still takes four men to take the ship from periscope depth to test depth? But one step at a time, I suppose."

Keebes moved to the starboard side of the room, where a long row of firecontrol computer consoles were set up. Instead of three displays, there were five.

"The combat control system is the BSY-2/Mark II. A lot like the old CCS Mark I of the 688 and 637 classes, just more capabilities. Ties into the nav computers, so it automatically writes records of any combat encounters. The input from the hull, spherical, and towed arrays is integrated pretty well into this beast. Target acquisition and tracking are simplified. Weapons can be programmed from any of the panels. Works well."

"Let's get to the lower level," Pacino said.

They went down the aft-stairs to the lower level.

"Aux Machinery," Keebes said. "Emergency diesel lives here."

Pacino tried not to look too impressed by the sheer size of the diesel engine. It dwarfed the engine he'd had on *Devilfish*.

"Torpedo room has space for fifty weapons. We've got eight torpedo tubes. Like earlier classes the tubes are amidships. These are canted outward ten degrees."

Pacino followed Keebes through the torpedo room, walking the narrow aisle beside the tall racks of the weapons. He looked back at the room from the forward end, impressed by the huge size of the ship. The Mark 50 torpedoes and the Javelin cruise missiles were twenty-one inches in diameter and twenty-one feet long, graceful, sleek weapons.

"Want to see the engineering spaces, sir?"

Pacino looked at his watch, conscious that every moment that passed was another chance for Sean Murphy and his crew to die. Still, as commander of the rescue mission, he'd better have a mental picture of every aspect of the *Seawolf*, no matter how abbreviated.

"Let's go."

"Better put on your TLD, sir," Keebes said, reaching into a pocket and producing a black plastic cylinder the size of a cigarette lighter. The thermoluminescent dosimeter would measure Pacino's radiation dose from the reactor. As Pacino took the dosimeter he recalled the radiation sickness he had battled two years before, his strongest memory of that time being the hours he had spent vomiting and dry heaving. Pacino fastened it on his belt and gestured to Keebes to continue on.

Keebes led the way up the ladder to the middle level and aft, to a large watertight hatch that led through a long tunnel.

"Shielded tunnel, sir. This door here leads to the reactor compartment. Take a look through the lead window. We're in the power range and steaming, natural circulation mode, normal full power lineup, divorced from shorepower, with the main engines warm."

Pacino put his face next to the thick leaded glass of the reactor compartment viewing port while rotating the viewing mirror. That gave him a view into the compartment, to which entry was prohibited while the reactor was critical. The equipment was huge. No wonder the ship could produce such horsepower.

Keebes waited until Pacino was ready, then continued aft through the tunnel to another massive hatch and into the engineroom. "Aft compartment. This ship is built with the mechanics in mind—we can rig out virtually any piece of equipment without cutting open the hull, with the exception of the turbines and reduction gear. The motor control room is forward with the reactor control electronics. Those forward turbines are the SSTGs and the aft ones are the main engines."

The turbines were also big, but Pacino was getting used to the ship's scale. Still, the main engines, their counterparts only five feet in diameter on *Devilfish*, were fully a deck-and-a half tall, and the reduction gear casing was even larger. The room was hot and humid from the steam plant but not nearly as humid as on Pacino's previous boats.

Aft of the reduction gear was the enclosed maneuvering room. Pacino was interrogating Keebes on the procedure to shift from natural circulation to forced-flow when the maneuvering phone rang. Keebes answered, listened, hung up.

"Admiral Donchez wants us in the wardroom, sir. Time for the change-of-command."

Pacino nodded and followed Keebes forward, wondering how long it would take to get used to this new giant. And then, just for a moment, he felt dwarfed by her. Better get over *that,* he told himself.

CHAPTER 10

FRIDAY, 10 MAY
0125 GREENWICH MEAN TIME

Yokosuka Naval Station, Pier 4
USS *Seawolf*
1025 Local Time

"Attention on deck!"

The officers and chief petty officers in the wardroom came to attention.

"At ease," Pacino said, surprised at how confident his voice sounded. He had worried about this moment, wondering how the men would see him, and how he would see them ... how he could take men he had never met or trained and take them covertly into enemy territory on a combat mission.

Keebes stopped in front of the first man near the door, a slightly overweight lieutenant commander with an intense expression on his face, dark bags under his eyes, the odor of cigarette smoke strong in the air around him. Pacino had the impression of a man on a collision course with a heart attack.

"This is the engineer, Captain, Lieutenant Commander Ray Linden. With us since we laid down the keel. He knows every valve, cable, pump, pipe and switch of the propulsion plant."

"Hi, Eng. I hear you've got some serious horses under the hood back there."

"Yessir," Linden said, squinting up into Pacino's eyes, "and they're ready to gallop."

"Good. You'll need to make sure they gallop damned quietly."

"No problem, sir."

Keebes led Pacino to the next man, a heavyset lieutenant commander with a tightly trimmed beard covering his fleshy jaw, an open expression set into the lines of his face.

"Lieutenant Commander Bill Feyley, our weapons and combat systems officer."

"Weps," Pacino said, shaking Feyley's hand. "How did the loadout go?"

"We did it in record time, given we started in the early hours of the morning with a burned-out weapons-loading crew. But we've got what you wanted."

"Good. Sonar and firecontrol ready?"

"The best, sir."

Pacino was about to move on, when something struck him as wrong.

"Weps, about the beard ... maybe you should wait till we're underway before you grow that thing."

Keebes looked at Pacino. "They changed that regulation two years ago, Captain Pacino," Keebes said after a moment. "Submarine officers rate beards now."

Pacino nodded quickly ... He'd been away too long, he thought.

Pacino had memorized key portions of each man's service jacket, along with a confidential briefing prepared by Donchez's staff, including things that would never find their way into the official service records but items that Pacino would need to know in tight situations. Such as that Greg Keebes's wife had recently left him for a neighbor down the street; that Bill Feyley, the ship's gentleman bachelor, tended to drink and carouse, habitually waking up in port in the arms of nameless women; that Tim Turner, the sonar/firecontrol officer, an amiable man with a fashionable haircut, had recently fought with his live-in girlfriend over spending too much time with the *Seawolf* and not enough with her. It seemed that in a white-hot moment Turner had taken the keys to the

new Trans Am he had given her for her birthday and
smashed the car into a dumpster, then tossed the keys
back to her saying "Happy birthday, babe." And there
was Rick Brackovic, the reactor-controls officer, who
had missed the birth of his second boy the week before, not having been granted emergency leave for it,
after missing the birth of his first child just fifteen
months earlier. His wife was nearly fed up and
contemplating divorce. Each briefing sheet listed the
pain these men had suffered on account of their com-
mitment to the submarine force, leaving home for
months at a time to take a steel pipe to the bottom
of the ocean for reasons that often made no sense to
their families. And many of the stories seemed familiar to Pacino, whose own personal life had suffered in
his climb to command, at one point nearly forcing him
to choose between his submarine and his family.

After Pacino had met the officers and chiefs, he
went to the end of the table and pulled a set of papers
from his shirt pocket.

"Gentlemen, I'll read my orders: 'From NAVPERS-
COM, Washington, D.C., to Captain Michael A. Pacino, U.S. Navy (Retired). You are hereby reactivated
to active duty at the rank of Captain and ordered to
report for temporary duty as commanding officer of
USS *Seawolf*, SSN-21. You will relieve the acting commanding officer and retain command for an undeter-
mined period for execution of a classified operation.
Upon completion of said operation you will stand by
to be relieved of command, at which point you will
return to your previous assignment.' "

Pacino looked up from the papers, turned to the
navigator, Greg Keebes.

"Lieutenant Commander Keebes, I am ready to relieve you, sir."

"I am ready to be relieved."

"I relieve you, sir," Pacino said, saluting, the staged
ceremony signaling that he had just assumed the burden of command, the mantle of total responsibility for
the USS *Seawolf*. Keebes saluted back.

"I stand relieved."

Pacino looked at the men in the room for a moment.

"Nav," he said to Keebes, "as of now you are the acting executive officer."

"Aye aye, sir."

"Very well, then, XO. Station the maneuvering watch."

Pacino found Admiral Donchez waiting for him in his stateroom.

"Well, sir, what have you got for me?"

"SEALs will be here any minute, Mikey. Commander Lennox, the *Tampa*'s XO, will be coming on with them. As soon as they're aboard, get underway and make max speed to Point Hotel."

"Aye, sir."

"And, Mikey, listen to me. I picked you for this mission because you're a damned good captain. And because you know Murphy and I know you'll give this rescue OP everything you can to make it succeed. Now, I know you want to get Sean Murphy out of there. But remember, this ship and her crew are as important to us as the *Tampa*. If anything happens that threatens the survivability of *this* ship, get the hell out. Murphy would understand, so will I. I don't want to have to pull your broken hull off the bottom of the bay because you got pissed off at the Chinese. Am I clear?"

"Yessir," Pacino said, annoyed in spite of himself.

Donchez stared at him for a moment, and reassumed an easy smile. "Well, I've gotta run, Mikey. Good luck. Good hunting. I can find my way out. Get your ass to the bridge and get this sewer pipe out of here."

Pacino stretched out his hand to the admiral, who took it and gripped it, nearly crushing Pacino's hand.

"Thanks, sir. For everything."

Donchez nodded, then vanished out the door and up the ladder, the bridge communication box soon sputtering over the ship's Circuit One P.A. system:

"COMMANDER IN CHIEF, UNITED STATES PACIFIC FLEET ... DEPARTING!"

Pacino took up the blue baseball cap on the stateroom's table, the one Keebes had left for him. The brim had the scrambled eggs for the captain, the gold submariner's dolphins, and the block letters reading USS SEAWOLF SSN-21. Pacino put on the cap, shut the door of the cabin and headed forward to the bridge-access trunk, ready to drive the submarine, *his* submarine, to the open ocean.

CHAPTER 11

FRIDAY, 10 MAY
0145 GREENWICH MEAN TIME

YOKOSUKA NAVAL STATION, PIER 4
USS *SEAWOLF*
1045 LOCAL TIME

Captain Michael Pacino climbed the rungs of the bridge-access tunnel ladder, the light from the bridge above shining down from a distance. The tunnel was almost twenty feet tall, going from the upper level passageway outside the crew's mess to the cockpit at the top of the sail. At the top of the ladder Pacino's passage was obstructed by the metal grating that formed the deck of the bridge cockpit. The officer of the deck swung the grating open. Pacino grabbed a handhold and lifted himself up to the cockpit. Once he was on his feet, the grating was dropped down.

"Good morning, Captain," Bill Feyley said. Like Pacino, Feyley wore cotton working khakis and a khaki jacket, binoculars around his neck, a *Seawolf* blue ballcap and aviator's wirerimmed sunglasses.

"You'll be conning us out, Weps?"

"I'm the OOD," Feyley said. "But Mr. Joseph will take the conn as Junior Officer of the Deck."

"Where is he?"

"Topside talking to the linehandlers."

Pacino looked up and saw the tall, skinny youth walking topside. Jeff Joseph, the communications officer, was an oddball, Pacino thought. Smart, personable, funny, also maybe the ugliest officer he'd ever seen, bug eyes and buck teeth. Still, according to the

129

reports Pacino had read, the kid was showing himself
to be a champion ship driver even though he had been
aboard only a few months.

Pacino looked at the cockpit. It was just a cubbyhole
in the metal of the sail, formed by lowering clamshell
doors down to expose an unused volume at the top
of the bridge trunk. A small communication box was
fastened to the forward lip of the sail. Beside it
was a gyrocompass repeater. Above the lip of the sail
was a Plexiglas windshield. Pacino leaned out over the
starboard side of the bridge and looked at the pier
below. The view from the top of the sail gave him
the kind of perspective an oldtime square-rigger sailor
would have from a masthead's crow's nest. Pacino
looked forward down the length of the concrete pier,
the water in the slip empty except for *Seawolf*. At the
end of the pier a lone figure walked, a heavyset man
in a khaki officer's uniform. Pacino picked up his binoculars. The man was carrying a duffel bag, was non-
descript except for a thick mustache. He was bald, his
khaki garrison cap barely covering the skin of his
head. He was built like a cylinder.

"Captain," Feyley said, putting down a phone handset, "Commander Lennox is on the way. Pier guard
said he has orders to come aboard."

"I'll meet him on the pier," Pacino said, lifting his
leg over the bridge coaming and finding the ladder
rungs set into the flank of the sail. He lowered himself
down the two stories to the topside deck and saluted
the aft flag and the topside sentry, then walked over
the gangway to the pier.

"*SEAWOLF* ... DEPARTING!" rang out the Circuit One deck loudspeaker. It took a moment for Pacino to realize the sentry's announcement was talking
about him.

Pacino walked down the pier to the commander,
who stopped and saluted.

"Kurt Lennox, reporting as ordered, Captain."

Pacino waved a salute and shook Lennox's hand.

"I'm Captain Pacino. Come on down, Commander."

Pacino pointed to the ship and the two men began walking toward the gangway.

"Were you briefed on the *Tampa* situation?"

"Situation? I was just pulled off leave and told to report aboard. I figured something happened to your XO and you needed an emergency replacement. What happened to my ship, Captain?"

"Typical Navy not to tell you. Security too tight, I guess. Kurt, I can't tell you specifics until we shove off, but I can say now that your boat is in big trouble. *Seawolf* is going to help out, and you'll be part of that. That is, if you want to be."

Lennox's face hardened. "So am I your XO sir?"

"I've got something else in mind. Let's get you below and settled in. Once we've cleared restricted waters I'll brief you and the officers."

As the men neared the gangway, Lennox pointed down the pier.

"What the hell is that?"

Pacino turned. A half-ton truck was bouncing down the pier, two dozen rough-looking men hanging out the open sides of the bed, stuffed in with piles of equipment—diver's tanks, packaged weapons, pallets of explosives, and crates of ammunition. The truck drew up to the gangway and the truck's cab door opened. A man emerged and stepped down to the pier, walked up to Pacino and stopped. He had long black hair peppered with gray and drawn back into a ponytail. A handlebar mustache was over a beard that extended halfway down his huge chest. His biceps bulged out of a leather jacket cut off at the shoulders, numerous tattoos on each arm. At his wrists he wore leather spiked-dog collars. He sported dirty faded jeans and cracked and dusty cowboy boots. Behind him in the truck several men hooted and shouted at each other, all dressed like bikers. The character in front of Pacino took out a wrinkled pack of brown cigarettes, flipped one out and lit it with a wooden match struck into a flame on his zipper. After puffing smoke toward Lennox, he flipped the match to the pier.

"You the captain?" he asked in a throaty drawl. Pacino spoke up.

"I'm Captain Pacino, USS *Seawolf.* Who the *hell* are you?"

The man puffed the cigarette as he looked over the hull of the submarine like someone about to rent an apartment who wasn't too sure he liked what he saw.

"I was hoping this'd be an old missile boat refitted for divers. It will take us all day to get out of the hull of this bitch." He looked at Pacino, sizing him up. "Name's Morris. Jack Morris, Commander, SEAL Team Seven. Those are my shooters. Get some of your boys up here and help us load this shit in your boat there, Captain."

Pacino ignored the order.

"What in hell are you dressed for?"

Morris laughed. "They didn't brief you too well. This outfit is a counterterrorist unit, Captain, flown in special from Virginia Beach. My unit is using 'modified grooming standards,' which means we need to look just like terrorists. And we do a pretty good job, if I can judge by the look on the pier guard's face."

Pacino smiled, waving over Lieutenant (j.g.) Joseph.

"Mr. Joseph, get these SEALs and their gear loaded below. The linehandlers can help out—we're not going anywhere till the stuff is aboard. Put the equipment in the sonar equipment space, and make sure it's rigged for sea. The SEALs will bunk in the torpedo room, and Commander Morris will share the XO's stateroom with Commander Lennox. You've only got a few minutes, so move it." As Joseph motioned to the linehandlers, Pacino turned to Morris. "Welcome aboard, Commander."

"Thanks," Morris said, lighting another cigarette. "One thing, though, Cap'n. I won't be bunking with you pinky-in-the-air gentlemen in officers' country. At SEAL Team Seven I preach unit integrity, which means I sleep where my men sleep. You got a problem with that?"

"Mr. Joseph, you heard the man. Put the commander in the torpedo room with the other SEALs."

Joseph led the SEALs, some twenty of them, down the forward compartment access hatch and into the submarine. Pacino looked over at Morris, who was leaning against a pier bollard.

"Are you guys as good as they say you are?"

Morris took a last puff off the cigarette and tossed it into the brackish water of the slip.

"Captain, SEAL Team Seven is the best there is."

"Good. You'll need to be."

Pacino's Rolex showed 11:30 A.M. local time. He had wanted to be underway a half hour before, but stowing the gear of the SEALs had delayed them. Almost a ton of high explosives could not just be tossed into the hull.

Pacino stood on the flying bridge, a ring of steel handrails on the top of the sail behind the bridge cockpit. Beside him stood Lieutenant (j.g.) Joseph, connected to the bridge communication box below by a long microphone cord. Down in the cockpit were Lieutenant Commander Feyley, the OOD, and an enlisted phonetalker, there to relay communications in parallel with the speaker circuits in case of a failure of the bridge box. Below on deck two dozen linehandlers waited, facing a half-dozen of the bases' men on the pier. The lines were singled up and two tugboats were tied up outboard to help the mammoth craft pull away from the pier.

Pacino looked at the tugboats. Somehow, having to get underway with tugs had always annoyed him. It seemed to announce to the world that the submariners were less than capable shiphandlers in restricted waters. In truth, they were terrible shiphandlers. Single screw submarines handled like ungainly pigs on the surface, especially at slow speeds. And tied up bow-in as they were, they would have to back down to get away from the slip, and subs did unpredictable things when backing down, sometimes obeying the rudder, sometimes turning the opposite way from the rudder order. If he were honest with himself, he thought, he would admit that the prudent course of action would be to go with the tugs, let them pull him away from the pier, let them help him avoid embarrassment from banging the sonar dome into the pier or backing down in a complete circle to get into the channel. After all, he had been in combat before—why would he have to prove himself at the pier with cowboy showmanship?

Besides, the crew would expect him to do the safe thing with an untested submarine. No one would want him to maneuver out into the channel without tugs. But a thought nagged at him—if he did the cowboy method, and it came off, the crew would immediately know the sort of commander they were dealing with. He expected to return from this OP with the torpedo room empty and a few Chinese ships on the bottom of the bay. The crew might as well get used to the fact that this would be no milk run. Sea trials were over. The mission, the *combat* mission, started now.

"Mr. Joseph," Pacino barked. "What are we waiting for?"

"The pilot's still late, sir. A tug is bringing him in now. He should be here in about forty-five minutes."

A pilot was someone who knew the channel like his own home, who knew the currents and the tides, the depth of each sandbar, each treacherous rock. Another safe course would be to wait for him. Pacino thought of the *Tampa*. If his ship were held by an enemy, would Sean Murphy wait for a pilot?

"Mr. Joseph, tell the tugs to shove off."

"Excuse me sir?"

"Cut the tugs loose. We're going to get underway without them. And without the pilot. Prepare to get underway."

"But, sir—"

"I have the conn," Pacino said, taking the bullhorn

from Jeff Joseph's grasp. "ON DECK, PASS THE TUG LINES OVER TO THE TUGS."

A walkie-talkie in Joseph's hand squawked: "U.S. NAVY SUBMARINE, THIS IS TUG *MASSAPE-QUA.* SAY AGAIN YOUR INTENTIONS REGARDING TUG FORCES, OVER."

Pacino took the radio, seeing Joseph's surprised eyes on him.

"Tug *Massapequa,* this is Captain, U.S. Navy Submarine. Take in your lines and clear the slip, over."

"ROGER, CAPTAIN. ARE YOU SURE ABOUT THIS, OVER?"

"Affirmative. Clear the slip now. U.S. Navy Submarine, out."

Pacino handed the radio back to Joseph as the roar of the tug's diesels sounded over the water of the slip. A foaming wake boiled up around the bows of the tugs as they backed down and entered the channel, standing by in case the *Seawolf* found herself in trouble.

Pacino clicked the microphone attached by the long cord to the bridge box: "Control, Captain, I have the conn, Lieutenant Commander Feyley retains the deck. We are getting underway. Navigator, log that we have cast off the tugs and are going without the pilot."

The navigator's voice came up from the speaker in the cockpit, confusion plain in his acknowledgement. Pacino nodded. He had gotten the crew's attention.

"ON DECK," Pacino said into the bullhorn. "TAKE IN ALL LINES."

He watched as the linehandlers on the pier passed the heavy lines over, freeing the submarine from the pier. As the last line came over, the USS *Seawolf* was officially underway, no longer pierbound. Pacino smiled.

"Shift colors," he commanded. Bill Feyley pulled a lever sounding the ship's horn, loud and deep enough to be worthy of the *Queen Elizabeth,* the earsplitting blast sounding for a full ten seconds. At the same time the phonetalker hoisted a large American flag on a temporary flagpole aft of the flying bridge, the wind from the north flapping the fabric.

Pacino watched the ship from his vantage point on the flying bridge. The current from the channel was pushing the stern away from the pier, the distance between the ship and pier opening slowly, now perhaps ten yards. Pacino clicked his microphone.

"Helm, Bridge, all back full."

"ALL BACK FULL, HELM AYE, MANEUVERING ANSWERS ALL BACK FULL."

The pier faded away from the bow as the ship's main engines pulled the massive ship backward into the channel. The channel current pulled the stern further away from the pier.

"Helm, Bridge, right full rudder," Pacino ordered as the ship was halfway sticking into the channel, half into the slip beside the pier.

The helmsman acknowledged and the rudder, far aft, turned in the white wake of the stern. Slowly the ship's stern came into the channel. The ship was again parallel with the pier and still turning so that the stern was pulling upstream into the channel current. Finally the ship's bow, the sonar dome, was clear of the pier.

"Helm bridge, left full rudder, all ahead full!"

The helmsman answered, and the ship shuddered as it made the transition from full turns aft to full turns forward. *Seawolf* responded to the rudder, the nosecone avoiding the pier to the south of Pier 4 as the vessel moved into the channel and a violent white foamy wake boiled up aft at the rudder. Out of the corner of his eye Pacino could see Feyley and Joseph staring at him as if he had gone around the bend. The piers to the west slid by as the *Seawolf* picked up speed. The tugs soon vanished astern.

Seawolf was on the way.

Pacino picked up the bullhorn. "ON DECK, LINEHANDLERS RIG FOR DIVE AND LAY BELOW!" Below, the linehandlers scrambled for the forward compartment hatch, seeing the water of the bow wave climbing the hull. The last one shut the hatch behind him, clearing the deck.

"Helm, Bridge, steady course one six five," Pacino ordered. "Navigator, recommend course to bring us to the center of the channel."

The ship continued to accelerate, the water climbing up the sonar dome until the deck forward of the sail vanished, the water beginning to spray up the leading edge of the sail.

"BRIDGE, NAVIGATOR," Keebes's voice announced from the bridge communication box, his tone sounding nervous, "RECOMMEND COURSE ONE SEVEN TWO TO REGAIN TRACK. DISTANCE TO NEXT TURN, FIVE THOUSAND YARDS, NEW COURSE ONE SEVEN FIVE."

"Helm, Bridge, right two degrees rudder, steady course one seven two."

Pacino handed the microphone to Lieutenant (j.g.) Joseph, who still looked shocked.

"Mr. Joseph, you have the conn."

Ahead of the ship, in the wide channel that opened south of the naval station, several dozen small sailboats sailed back and forth, as if intentionally blocking their passage.

"Helm, Bridge, all ahead one third," Joseph ordered. The ship began to slow, the bow wave receding.

"What are you doing?" Pacino asked.

"Sir, look at the sampans. We have to slow down, we don't want to collide with them."

Pacino frowned. "Order up all ahead full. They'll get out of the way."

"Helm, Bridge, all ahead full," Joseph ordered.

The sail beneath Pacino's feet began to shudder as the ship's main engines again surged forward, the bow wave again roaring forward of the sail, the wake again boiling white aft. The noise of the bow wave became so loud that the officers would have to shout at each other to be heard.

Ahead of them, in the channel, dozens of boats, jamming the seaway ahead, caught sight of *Seawolf*'s bow wave and scurried out of the way in panic. A hole opened in the seaway, and the submarine moved through it, the boats bobbing violently in her wake.

"JOOD, shift the reactor to forced circulation."

"Sir, we're at fifty percent power. Shall I reduce speed to ahead two-thirds while maneuvering energizes the pumps?" The Reactor Plant Manual required a power reduction before starting the pumps, or the power surge from the cold water *could* cause a reactor accident, overpowering the core and melting the fuel. The only situation that allowed the requirement to be ignored was a tactical emergency under the orders of the captain.

What the hell, Pacino thought. It was a tactical emergency of sorts.

"No power reduction, Joseph. Shift to forced circulation and order all ahead flank."

"Aye, sir." He clicked the microphone. "Maneuvering, Bridge, shift to forced circ, remain at all ahead full."

The bridge box sputtered with the Engineer's astonished voice.

"SHIFT TO FORCED CIRC, BRIDGE, MANEUVERING, AYE, COMMENCING FAST INSERTION ... BRIDGE, MANEUVERING, REACTOR IS IN FORCED CIRCULATION, ANSWERING AHEAD FULL."

"Helm, Bridge, all ahead flank!"

"ALL AHEAD FLANK, BRIDGE, HELM, AYE ... BRIDGE, HELM, MANEUVERING ANSWERS ALL AHEAD FLANK."

The deck shuddered. The roaring bow wave climbed even higher up the sail, spraying salt and foam on the bridge crew. The flags flapped on the pole aft. The periscopes spun as the navigator took visual fixes on the way out. The scenery slipped by as *Seawolf*'s main engines propelled her out at flank speed.

Pacino's spirits seemed to skim the waves with the wind and the bow wave. Damn, he was at sea again, and in command. Hold on, Sean, he thought, we're on the way.

Pacino climbed down from the flying bridge into the cockpit, scanned the horizon for contacts, drank a mug of coffee passed up from the galley and watched as the coast of Japan faded away astern. Soon the ship reached Point Alpha, the dive point, and Pacino climbed back down the bridge-access trunk after one last look at the world above, one last breath of fresh sea air, knowing, as always, it might well be his last.

CHAPTER 12

FRIDAY, 10 MAY
0705 GREENWICH MEAN TIME

WESTERN PACIFIC OCEAN
DIVE POINT, 150 NAUTICAL MILES
  SOUTHWEST OF YOKOSUKA
USS SEAWOLF
1605 LOCAL TIME

The control room crew seemed tense, the room buzzing with the murmured voices of the watchstanders. Pacino stood in the forward starboard corner of the room, near the attack center, and watched the periscope video monitor, the television that showed the view out the number-two periscope. The sea was empty of traffic. The officer on the periscope, Jeff Joseph, was the Contact Coordinator, responsible for keeping them from colliding with a careless supertanker. Standing on the periscope stand, the conn, was Officer of the Deck Lieutenant Tim Turner. Turner, an affable young officer, was of medium height and build. His hair was moussed straight up from his forehead, mimicking the style of a current rap star. His eyes conveyed both joviality and confidence. It was hard to imagine him smashing his girlfriend's new gift sportscar into a dumpster, the way the CINCPAC gossip sheet reported it. Still, he would bear watching—a man who could lose control in an argument with a girlfriend could crack in combat—but then, Pacino reminded himself, he himself had not always been Mr. Tranquility at home.

"Captain," Turner now said, "we're ready to submerge. Sounding is seven hundred fathoms. No contacts. Ship is rigged for dive. Ship's position is three miles southeast of the dive point by GPS NAVSAT, ESGN agrees. Ship's course is two four two, all ahead two thirds. Request permission to dive."

"Off'sa'deck, submerge the ship," Pacino ordered, feeling excited to be giving the order for the first time in years.

"Diving Officer," Turner called, "submerge the ship to one five zero feet."

The diving alarm sounded—still the *OOH-GAH OOH-GAH* of Hollywood, but electronically generated and distorted. Then on the Circuit One: "DIVE, DIVE." The Chief of the Watch opened the main ballast tank vents by selecting one of the electronic options on the computer control system displays of the ballast control panel. Other than a slight hiss, there was no sensation that the ship was submerging.

Pacino looked at the periscope television monitor. Turner had taken over the number-two periscope, now the only mast raised, and had trained the instrument forward to the bow. On the screen, centered in the periscope view's crosshairs, an angry plume of vapor flew into the sky as the forward main ballast tanks gave up their trapped air and admitted water, making the ship heavier.

"Venting forward," Turner called, training the scope aft.

The aft view showed the same plumes of vapor coming from the cylindrical deck just forward of the rudder. As the venting continued, the deck settled into the waves, the white foam climbing steadily higher up the curving deck until the surface of the hull peeked through only every third or fourth wave. Finally, the deck aft vanished in the wake, which slowly calmed from its violent white foam to a light blue.

"Venting aft. Decks awash," Turner announced, returning to a slow periscope search, the water's surface slowly climbing higher in the television monitor's view.

142   *Michael DiMercurio*

"Five five feet, sir," Chief Deitzler called from the diving officer's seat.

"Very well, Dive, get us down."

"Six zero . . . six five feet, sir, sail's under."

At the call of "sail under," the ship was no longer visible on the surface. Only her periscope protruded above the waves. *Seawolf* was now officially submerged.

"Eight three feet, Off'sa'deck," the Diving Officer called.

"Scope's awash," Turner sang out as the foam covered the periscope view, the lens hitting the waves. "Scope's under."

Turner trained the periscope view upward with the left scope grip. The undersides of the waves were silvery, reflecting the light from the deep back down. The waves receded, until finally they were obscured by a dark blue haze. The surface high above had vanished. As if to acknowledge this Turner snapped the control grips up and rotated the periscope's hydraulic control ring, lowering the scope into the well. The optic module disappeared and the stainless steel pole of the scope came down and clunked to a halt.

For ten minutes the Diving Officer and Chief of the Watch pumped and flooded tanks with sea water and transferred the water to variable ballast tanks. Finally the ship had achieved a neutral trim, perfectly balanced, neither heavier nor lighter than the surrounding water.

"Sir, the ship is submerged to one five zero feet with a good one-third trim. Request permission to take her deep and increase speed."

"Off'sa'deck, take her down to eight hundred feet, course two four five, all ahead flank. And rig ship for patrol quiet."

"Aye, sir, eight hundred feet, course two four five, ahead flank, and patrol quiet."

The deck became steep as Diving Officer Deitzler ordered a twenty-five-degree down angle to take the ship to eight hundred feet. The hull creaked and popped, responding to the increased sea pressure at the deeper depth. For a moment Pacino missed the clicking of the old bulletproof digital depth indicator of the rustbucket Piranha-class submarines, the ships he had cut his teeth on, but then realized the progress was for the better. After all, hadn't they happily ditched diesel power for nuclear and moved forward? Sure, except Pacino couldn't help wondering what would happen to the delicate computer systems in battle—would one depth charge make them all useless?

"Helm, all ahead flank," Turner commanded.

The Circuit One announcing system blasted Turner's voice throughout the ship: "RIG SHIP FOR PATROL QUIET."

The ship leveled out, now at eight hundred feet beneath the waves, the speed indicator on the ship control panel showing ship's speed increasing. Pacino waited for the deck to vibrate with the energy of 52,000-shaft horsepower back aft pushing them through the ocean. But there was no vibration. He watched as the speed numerals steadily increased—36 knots, 39, 41, finally steadying at 44.8 knots. Forty-four point eight, in the inscrutable digital accuracy of the computer, and the deck was as steady as if the ship were hovering, smooth as a Rolls. Amazing.

Pacino realized Turner was looking at him, realized he was no longer needed in the control room and to stay any longer would violate Turner's turf as Officer of the Deck.

"I'll be in my stateroom," Pacino said to Turner. "Give me fifteen minutes, then send in Commander Lennox, Commander Morris, and Mr. Keebes." Now that the ship was on her way to Bo Hai Bay, Point Hotel, it was time to lay out the mission.

Even running at flank speed, they would not arrive on station at Point Hotel for another two days, but Pacino wanted his men to be mentally ready for the mission and think about it for the entire two days. That meant two days of intensive periscope-recognition training,

in which the officers would learn to tell each class of
Chinese ship with just a half-second glimpse from a
water-level periscope view, and know by memory each
ship's armament and threat level.

Pacino rolled the tall-backed swivel chair up to the
head of the conference table, the end facing the view
of the television monitors. A row of buttons set into
the table controlled the televisions on the centerline
bulkhead. Pacino changed the aft monitor's setting
from TY-20 to NAV and the end TV screen on the
left came to life, a color-coded chart of the sea lighting
up the screen, with their track and their estimated
position illuminated on the chart, the flashing position
showing them skirting the southeast coast of Japan.
Their future track was also shown, heading around the
peninsula of Korea and north into the Korea Bay.

A knock sounded from the centerline passageway
door and Morris, Keebes and Lennox came in. Keebes
and Lennox had changed into blue submarine poopy
suits. Morris, still unshaven and ponytailed, was in
green fatigues and shiny black combat boots.

Pacino waved them to seats at his conference table,
and Lennox poured coffee for himself and offered
some to Morris.

"Never touch the stuff," the SEAL officer said.
"Unless you've got some whisky to throw in."

As Pacino looked at the officers he felt a moment
of doubt. The mission was extremely complex and yet
it depended on Lennox, an emotionally involved and
unknown senior officer; on Morris, the headstrong
commando; and on young Keebes, the acting Executive Officer who already was overloaded with the duties of Navigator and Operations Officer. The mission
would be risky even with a crack crew that had trained
together for months—with these men who had never
worked together, with an untried submarine, the odds
on success seemed long.

But they were better than the ones for Sean Murphy
and the *Tampa*.

Pacino reached into the duffel bag on his bunk and

pulled out a black zippered briefcase. He unzipped
the case and withdrew a bundle of papers. The first
was a large-area plot of the western Pacific and the
east coast of China. The ship's track was laid out in
straight black lines, each turn marked by a letter.
South from Yokosuka to Point Alpha, southwest to
Point Bravo, the dive point Alpha-Prime in between.
At Point Bravo the track turned northwest to the Yellow Sea opposite the southern tip of Korea, where at
Point Charlie it extended north into the Korea Bay.
The track turned steadily west at Points Delta and
Echo, where it headed due west to the Lushun/Penglai
Gap, the entrance to the Bo Hai Bay. After jogging
northward of Point Foxtrot and Golf, the track contin-
ued west to Point Hotel at Tianjin on the western
coast of the bay.

"As you can see, we're headed for Point Hotel off
the Chinese coast at Tianjin in the Bo Hai Bay. Our
ETA at Point Hotel is seventeen hundred zulu time
Sunday. That will be zero one hundred local time,
nicely in the middle of the night."

The next paper was a large blowup of an overhead
photograph, either a satellite view or a shot from an
RF-117A Stealth. It showed the concrete pier at Xingang with the American submarine secured between
two surface warships, the pierside ship tied to the pier,
another warship astern of the submarine, a fourth
ahead of it. The submarine looked wounded, her paint
blown off in large patches, her sail damaged, the
hatches on deck guarded by several men wielding
weapons. Pacino spread the photo out on the table
and let the men look at it.

"This is the *Tampa,* now under the control of the
Chinese Communists at the PLA Northern Fleet piers
at Xingang. As you've all guessed by now, our mission
is to get the *Tampa* and her crew out of the bay in
one piece."

Pacino told the men that the *Tampa* crew were
likely held aboard, that the engineroom was probably
still steaming, and that the surface forces of Lushun

would be waiting for them at the mouth of the bay, at the Lushun/Penglai Gap.

"So, gentlemen, it's your turn. How the hell do we get this boat out of here?"

Morris had pulled a cigarette from his fatigue uniform pocket and was searching the room for an ash tray. Finding none, he shrugged and lit the cigarette, blowing the smoke to the ceiling. The room's quiet ventilation system sucked the smoke away almost immediately. Morris tapped an ash into his unused coffee mug and squinted through the smoke at Pacino.

"I say we dive under the inboard and outboard destroyers and blow them. Meanwhile we'll sneak aboard the sub, kill the guards, turn it over to the crew and get the hell out."

"You make it sound real simple," Lennox said. "What does 'blow the destroyers' mean? You got a couple girls from Subic in your unit?"

"Up yours," Morris said, hands balled into fists.

"*Hold* it," Pacino said, steel in his voice. "Let's understand each other. This is a mission to rescue the *Tampa,* not to play interservice rivalries. Commander Morris, you SEALs are always bitching that no one in the rest of the Navy knows or cares how to use your forces. Well, this is your chance to define the mission *your* way. I'm open to anything you want to try. Just don't insult our intelligence with macho crap about 'blowing the destroyers and taking the boat.' How, where, why, damnit . . ."

Morris looked into his cup, now filling with ashes. "Okay, Cap'n," he said, his voice calm. "This is how it goes down. SEAL Team Seven's first, second and third platoons are aboard. Each platoon has six enlisted men and an officer in command. You get us close to the pier and lock us out a platoon at a time. When we're all out, we'll put a series of high explosive satchel charges under the keels of the inboard and outboard destroyers. First and second platoons knock out the topside guards, as quiet as possible, and board the sub. While they are taking care of the guards

aboard, third platoon keeps watch to make sure no
reinforcements board from the other ships or the pier.
They'll get aboard the sub just before the charges
blow. If the crew is aboard, they can get the engines
going. At time zero, the charges under the surface-
ship keels go off. The sub is freed, it backs up and
gets out of there. The rest is up to the crew."

"Blowing up the inboard and outboard destroyers
will *also* sink the *Tampa*," Lennox said. "She'll be
dragged under by the lines to the destroyers. Once
her hatches are underwater, you'll drown every man
aboard."

"So we'll cut the lines or detonate some C-4 explosive ropes—that would be even quicker. With the lines
cut, the sub will stay afloat. Better yet, she'll stay
afloat with no gangway or connection to the pier. The
only way the Chinese can get to her from the land
side is by swimming, and the third platoon will take
care of anyone who enters the water. Of course, the
problem is a patrol boat or another destroyer coming—that could really screw things up."

"We'll keep the sea side clean," Pacino said.

"What if the crew has been taken off?" Lennox
asked.

"Then you're up the old creek," said Morris.

"So are you. You'll be trapped in a submarine with
no one to sail it. You'll be dead meat."

"Then maybe we'll need to extract and lock back
into this ship and get out."

"Commander, I could take care of the destroyers
with cruise missiles," Pacino said. "You and your men
could save some time and exposure and all get aboard
the *Tampa* at once. When you're in I put a cruise into
each surface warship at the piers. *Tampa* only has to
start up and clear the wreckage, then follow us out of
the bay."

Keebes frowned. "The smoke and rocket-exhaust
trail would give away our position and alert the Chinese that we're there. We'd never make it out of the
bay. Every ASW asset in the north and east fleets

would be hunting for us. And even if they couldn't hear us, they'd sure hear the *Tampa*."

"They'll know we're there anyway, with the take-over of the boat—"

"For all they'd know," Keebes pressed, "the SEALs could have parachuted in. Launching cruise missiles would eliminate all doubt about how they got in. It would be better to use torpedoes. That would get the surface ships without exposing us to detection."

"Torpedoes are no good," Pacino said flatly. "A small bearing-error could lead to the *Tampa* taking a torpedo hit from us. If we use fire from the *Seawolf* I think it will have to be a salvo of Javelin cruise missiles. What do you think, Commander Morris?"

"I don't like it, Cap'n. If I place the satchel charges under the destroyers, at least then I know they'll be put on the bottom. A cruise missile could go any-where, get lost on the way to the target, or blast into us. Plus it tells the whole wide world you're there, like your XO says."

"But it would also get your forces in-hull sooner with more force. Correct?"

"Yeah. But that does me no good if those Javelins fuck up."

"The time delays on the charges are fixed. If things go sour on the rescue I can launch the missiles at any time—"

"Not true. I have radio-controlled detonators," Morris said.

"How would that work with the explosives under-water?" Pacino challenged. "Radio signals don't pene-trate water very well."

"Each train of satchel charges will have a float with a radio trigger. When I hit the key, the floats receive the signal and detonate the fuses, which are wired in parallel to the float."

"Someone could see the float. Or the guy carrying the trigger radio could get hit," Pacino said.

Morris shot back: "If the satchel charges screw up, you can go ahead and fire your catch-me-fuck-me missiles. Plus, I'll put all the swimmers on the satchel-charge operation. That'll make it quicker. When we're ready we'll board *Tampa,* get topside and blow the charges."

"Your guys will be worn out by the time it comes to board," Pacino said.

"Cap'n, my men do this shit all day, every day. You leave them to me."

"Fine," Pacino said, reasonably satisfied. "Then we're decided. The SEALs will lock out, lay the satchel charges, board the *Tampa* and take her over. As soon as your guys are out of the water, blow the satchel charges. I'll be the backup with the Javelins. Have you got radios for signaling us if you need the missiles?"

"Scrambled VHF voice units," Morris said. "I'll give your radiomen the freaks."

Pacino pulled a large roll of papers from his bunk and spread them across the table. "These are the plans for the *Tampa.* In the next two days I suggest you walk this ship with me and find out what you can shoot at and what needs to be spared damage."

"Taking the sub won't be a problem, Cap'n. We've practiced this before with 688-class subs in New London. Last month we captured the *Augusta*—man, was her captain pissed." Morris looked at Pacino. "So once we take the sub, what then?"

Pacino looked at Kurt Lennox, who until then had mostly frowned at the exchanges. "That's where Commander Lennox comes in. Kurt is the XO of the *Tampa.* He knows her inside out. He'll relay the escape plan to Captain Murphy and coordinate with us to get out of the bay. If the captain or other officers are injured, dead, missing, he'll take command to get the boat out."

"Excuse me," Morris said, "but just how is Lennox getting to the *Tampa?*"

"He'll swim out with your men."

"Bull-fucking-shit he will. We don't take noncombatants on SEAL operations. Sir."

Pacino gave it back: "What is it you guys say? 'You don't have to like it, you just have to do it.' Or if that won't serve, try the Coast Guard motto: 'You have to go out. You don't have to come back.' Besides, Commander Lennox, if I recall rightly from his file, is a qualified Navy diver."

"I took the four-week SCUBA course years ago but I haven't done anything other than a security swim since then," Lennox admitted. "My qualifications lapsed some years ago. And I didn't use the kind of stuff these guys have. I don't know, Captain, tell you the truth, this is kinda shaky . . ."

"You've got two days to learn the gear and the operation. Morris, you and Lennox will be twins for the next two days, and you and your XO will have to know everything Lennox does in case he gets hit on the way in. I don't want Captain Murphy to take command of his ship and not know our plan to get him out."

Morris nodded but obviously was unhappy with the order.

"Next topic," Pacino said, spreading out a chart of the Bo Hai Bay. "The escape. Tianjin's here on the west, about one hundred and seventy miles from the bay entrance here at the Lushun/Penglai Gap. The mouth of the bay is only sixty miles wide, and the navigable channel is much tighter. With our draft, for us to stay submerged, the channel is only six miles wide, up here north of the Miaodao Islands. That choke point will be patrolled heavily by the Northern Fleet, based out of Lushun.

"Force strength in the fleet is formidable. We'll brief this in detail to the wardroom, but for now I expect to see up to three task forces. The total surface forces include three missile cruisers, fourteen destroyers, sixteen frigates, thirty-four torpedo patrol boats and their new aircraft carrier, the one they got from the Russians, the *Shaoguan*. There are some two dozen minor coastal patrol craft but none of them can hurt us unless we surface. The skimmer forces are most formidable because of the helicopters they carry. Between the carrier, the cruisers, destroyers and frigates I expect to see over forty seaborne choppers. There could be more, a lot more, in the form of aircraft based on land out of Lushun, maybe another two dozen. Plus, the *Shaoguan* will be putting up vertical takeoff/landing aircraft like the Yak-36, except they have a VTOL Yak that hovers on top and drops depth charges. That puts our two submarines up against sixty-seven major combatants and sixty-four helicopters. Not to mention three Han-class nuclear-powered attack subs and two Ming-class diesel subs, both of them new. The exit has to be planned assuming the *Tampa* has no weapons-firing ability. If she can, that's great, but I'm not counting on it. So that's us against seventy-three ships and six dozen helicopters . . . Now, how do we get out of the bay?"

After a moment of silence, Pacino frowned.

"Oh, hell, maybe we just worry about that when the time comes. Dismissed."

The officers filed out of the room. The expressions on their faces were all somber.

CHAPTER 13

SUNDAY, 12 MAY
0530 GREENWICH MEAN TIME

Bo Hai Bay
Sixty Miles East of Point Hotel
USS *Seawolf*
1330 Beijing Time

Pacino watched from the galley door to the darkened wardroom as the officers concentrated on the large projection screen on the aft wall. Lieutenant Commander Greg Keebes stood at the outboard corner of the room, holding the control to the digital image console. The picture on the far wall was a periscope photograph of a sleek new destroyer, the crosshairs of the periscope centered on the large central funnel. On the aft deck a helicopter's rotors spun as it prepared to lift off the deck.

"Turner," Keebes barked. "Identification."

"Luhu-class DDG," Turner said from somewhere in the darkened room.

"Weps. ASW armament."

"Two triple tubes of thirty-two-centimeter ASW Whiteheads," Feyley said. "Just aft of the funnel—"

"Joseph, what else?" Keebes broke in.

"ASW mortars, up forward, twelve-tube fixed launcher."

"Parsons. Sonars, go."

"It's got a hull-mounted active-search medium-frequency Laihai and a variable-depth dipper, also active in the medium freaks."

"Mr. Vale, chopper, go."

"Carries two Harbin Dauphins. They've got dipping sonars, the HS-12. Also a magnetic anomaly detector. Has Whitehead torpedoes and up to four anti-ship missiles."

Keebes clicked the controller. Another destroyer flashed on the screen, another periscope shot.

"Brackovic. Identify!"

"Udaloy-class DDG. Baddest destroyer in the bay."

"Turner. ASW weapons."

"Eight fifty-three-centimeter tubes with the Type 53 with active or passive homing. RBU 6000 mortar launcher."

Keebes clicked the control and a periscope photo of a huge aircraft carrier came up, taken from such a low angle that it seemed as if the sub taking the picture would have to have been run over moments after snapping the picture.

"Schrader. What is it?"

"Kiev-class CV, obtained from Russia last year, formerly the *Novorossiysk,* renamed the *Shaoguan.*"

"What's she got?"

"Hell, XO, what hasn't she got?"

And so it went, Keebes clicking periscope shots and firing questions at the officers. The sheer number of Chinese surface ships was staggering. And nearly all of them could hurt a submarine. Hurt? They could blow the *Seawolf* into scrap metal between breakfast and lunch.

Especially the *Shaoguan,* the massive aircraft carrier out of Lushun, bristling with radars, sonars, missiles, torpedoes, ASW rocket-launched depth charges and, worst of all, helicopters and VTOL jets, nearly all of them sporting dipping sonars and depth charges and torpedoes. That one ship could fill the Bo Hai Bay with enough ordinance to wipe them out. Add on the new Luhu and Udaloy destroyers, with some first-rate Ludas, seasoned with nearly twenty frigates, all built for speed and for killing submarines. Toss in thirty or thirty-five torpedo fast-attack patrol boats, a few dozen coastal patrol vessels, three nuclear-powered attack subs and two ultra-quiet diesel-electric subs, and the Chinese Northern Fleet was a formidable force, indeed.

Seawolf had two major assets. She was *quiet* and she was *invisible*. But if that surface force got a sniff of her, she'd be just another shipwreck.

Pacino checked his watch. In less than twelve hours they would be on station at Point Hotel. It was time the officers and men got some sleep.

"Mr. Keebes, let's wrap it up. Gentlemen, remember it's one thing to look at a slide, another to get a half-second look out of the real scope when the sucker's bearing down on you with a zero angle-on-the-bow RBU. We'll be manning battlestations at midnight so get out of here and get some rack."

As the officers moved out, Pacino phoned the conn.

"Off'sa'deck, sir." Ray Linden's voice sounded calm.

"OOD, Captain. What's our ETA at Point Hotel?"

"Sir, we're showing about zero one ten."

"Very well. Rig ship for ultraquiet. And pass on to your relief that we'll man battlestations at midnight."

As Pacino put down the phone the Circuit One blared through the ship:

"RIG SHIP FOR ULTRAQUIET. ALL PERSONNEL NOT ACTUALLY ON WATCH, LAY TO YOUR RACKS."

Pacino made his way to the control room.

"Captain's in control," Linden announced as Pacino entered.

"Hello, Off'sa'deck. Where does the ESGN have us?" He was asking about the inertial navigation system that kept their position updated between fixes from the NAVSAT.

Linden leaned over the aft rail of the conn, over the chart table, and pointed with his finger to their estimated position. Pacino looked down at the chart. They had come halfway across the bay. If they could proceed at flank, Point Hotel would be less than two hours away, but crawling like this would take them all day. Still, any faster in the shallow water of the bay might well raise a telltale wake and make excessive noise. Stealth was their only friend, surrounded as they were by the hostile PLA Chinese forces on all four points of the compass.

Pacino pulled out the next chart, the small-area large-scale chart of the piers at Xingang. The *Seawolf* would be able to sail the channel without detection, but the channel narrowed near the pier to a width of a mere four hundred yards, barely enough to turn a supertanker around with eight tugboats. Further from the pier, where less maneuvering would normally be required, the width shrank even further to one hundred yards. Which meant, Pacino realized, he would have to drive *Seawolf* in an underwater roadway barely a ship-length wide. It would take only one ship to go by to ruin the entire operation. Could he drive the *Seawolf* that accurately, and maintain stealth, in that narrow a channel? Could he avoid colliding with a tanker above or a silty bottom below? And once he neared the tanker pier, then what?

He pulled the chart lamp closer to the chart. The deep channel ended at the twin-tanker piers and did not extend further north to the PLA piers, where *Tampa* was tied up. It was perhaps two hundred yards from the northern boundary of the supertanker channel to the PLA pier, a long underwater swim for the SEALs. How would his visibility be from that position, would he even be able to see the *Tampa*? Would the type-20 periscope be detected from the PLA side? Or worse, from the tanker pier? Someone standing on the tanker pier would be only a few hundred feet from the scope. *Seawolf* would be a sitting duck if the scope were discovered, and then *Tampa* would have some company.

Pacino folded the chart. Nobody said it would be easy.

Pacino climbed into his bunk and shut his eyes. When sleep finally came he saw the chart of the piers change from the gold-and-blue coloring of the chart to the brown-and-gray of a bird's-eye-view of the pier, and he saw the *Tampa,* and his friend Sean Murphy, a revolver being held to his head— When the wake-up phone from the conn rang at 2300, he had blanked out the dream.

CHAPTER 14

SUNDAY, 12 MAY
0605 GREENWICH MEAN TIME

Bo Hai Bay, Xingang Harbor
PLA Navy Pier 1A, USS *Tampa*
1405 Beijing Time

How long, Sean Murphy wondered, could a man go without sleep? It had been days since the ship had been taken by the Chinese, maybe over a week. Since he had regained consciousness after being shot in the control room, he had been kept awake by one of two bodyguards. He had been confined to the tight quarters of his stateroom with the guards, not allowed to sit in a chair or lie on the bunk. He was kept sitting on the hard deck, the thin carpeting giving little cushion to the carbon-steel decking beneath. When his buttocks and back could no longer bear the pain of sitting or lying on the deck, he was allowed to stand, limping in the small stateroom. Even though his right arm was paralyzed from the bullet he had taken when the Chinese came aboard, his hands were cuffed behind his back. It had been painful from the first, but after endless hours jolting pains shot up his arms to his chest from the awkward position of the cuffs. That was before the numbness mercifully set in. A Chinese medic had bandaged the bullet wound, stopping the bleeding, but the round was still inside him, and he was convinced the wound had become infected. His skin felt hot, feverish.

No one had yet spoken to him in English. The tor-

ture so far had been relatively low-level—no one had
beaten him or threatened him or interrogated him. He
had felt an undercurrent of fear, fear that he would
not hold up under questioning, fear of the torture,
fear that he would break and tell them everything.

He had not been allowed to speak to his men or
officers. The ship was oppressively hot and stuffy.
The fans were off but the ship's lights were on. Either
the battery was running, supplying only the lights,
or the PLA had brought on shorepower. Were their
voltage and current the same as the Americans'? No,
improbable. Maybe the steam lines had been repaired
enough for Lube Oil Vaughn's turbine generators to
be steaming, supplying the ship's distribution with
power. But if they were, the air-conditioning and ventilation systems would be working. Which left the
question—if the only electricity they had was the battery, how long could it last? Supplying only the lights,
maybe a week, ten days max. Which meant that they
soon would be out of power.

Murphy felt his eyes get heavy for the hundredth
time. He let them shut, and in spite of his numb arms,
he felt himself sinking into sleep. And just as he saw
the first drowsy sleep images he felt the butt of the
AK-47 rifle jabbing him in the ribs, in the spot sore
from having been jabbed there before. He came awake
with a feeling like a severe hangover, head heavy,
stomach churning. God, how he craved sleep. For a
moment he almost wished they would ask him something so he could tell them and be allowed to sleep.
But there was no one to ask him questions, just an ox
of a guard who seemed to enjoy keeping him awake.

A sudden noise came from the passageway outside.
The guard stood and checked the door, then came to
attention. The man who entered the room could only
be an interrogator, Murphy decided. The guard motioned Murphy to his feet, but he was too weak. Even
after repeated jabs in the ribs, all Murphy could do
was roll on the deck. Finally the interrogator pulled

him up by his soaked armpits, propping him against the bulkhead.

Murphy thought he was losing consciousness. The room swirled around him. The interrogator pulled over the swivel chair and sat Murphy down in it. Murphy looked up at the interrogator, whose Mao jacket showed no insignia or rank or ribbons. He was tall for a Chinese, Murphy thought idly. His face was cut from flat planes, his high cheekbones and thin lips making him appear severe. His build was not slight, not heavy, efficiently muscled like a decathlon athlete's body. His eyes were neither menacing nor friendly—just dark, glassy.

The interrogator pointed to Murphy's wrists. The guard unlocked the cuffs. For a moment Murphy was unable to move either arm. He tried to move the left first, finally pulling it up in front of him, the limb stiff and burning and tingling as circulation returned. He massaged the right arm with the left, the injured side of his body still numb and unmoving. The interrogator opened the stateroom door a crack and shouted, the Chinese dialect sounding oddly melodious and lilting, the sounds incongruous with the man's severe demeanor. Within seconds another guard brought a steaming mug. The interrogator handed it to Murphy. It was tea. Murphy tried to drink it; the tea burned his parched lips. He looked up at the interrogator, who dismissed the guard. The interrogator sat on the bunk so that his head was just below the level of Murphy's. He looked at Murphy and spoke, his English sounding vaguely British.

"My name is Tien. Leader Tien Tse-Min. I apologize if you have been treated badly. It took me some time to get here—all the confusion of this absurd revolution, you know, and the guards are stupid. Am I to understand you are the commanding officer of this vessel?"

Classic Good Cop technique, Murphy thought, hating himself for wanting to thank the bastard for easing up on him. For the last week the words from the Code had been running through his mind: *I will give no information or take part in any action which might be harmful to my comrades ... When questioned ... I am bound to give only name, rank, service number, and date of birth. I will evade answering further questions to the utmost of my ability ...*

The Code was like the Ten Commandments, an ideal ethical code, but who could live up to it? He thought back to a lecture at Annapolis by a Vietnam veteran, an aviator admiral named Ferguson, who had been shot down over Hanoi. He had been a plebe, and his roommate, Michael Pacino, had gotten up in front of the whole Brigade of Midshipmen to ask the admiral what he thought of the Code of Conduct. The upperclassmen and the Academy brass were ready to keelhaul him for asking such a wiseass question to so senior and venerated an officer about such a hallowed subject as the Code of Conduct. But Ferguson had taken the question. "What do I think of the Code?" he'd said. "I think it's a bunch of nice words written by old ladies who have never been in combat or taken prisoner. 'I am bound to give only name, rank, service number, and date of birth.' Let me tell you, guys, if Charlie wants to get some information out of you, by God you're eventually going to tell him. A man can take only so much pain before he breaks. That's any man. Folks, you saw my sketches of the torture gear, and with that stuff, I guarantee it, you're gonna talk. We tried to establish our own code. We'd resist for two beatings, two sessions. Then, halfway into the third beating we'd start giving the gooks a made-up story. They asked me who was in command of my aircraft carrier. After two torture sessions I told them it was Vice Admiral Mickey Mouse, and his Chief of Staff was Captain Donald Duck. That held them down for about a day, until they realized I'd made fools out of them. It only took them another two beatings to get the real information, but at least we made them work for every bit they got. The Code of Conduct assumes you're held by civilized folks serving tea and asking if there's any information you'd care to betray your country with. Bullshit, son. That answer your question?"

Pacino had nodded and taken his seat while the hall full of malevolent upperclassmen hissed him.

Murphy stared into the interrogator's eyes.

"My name is Murphy. Sean Murphy. Commander, United States Navy. I'd tell you my service number, but why the hell would you care?"

He expected a slap, a punch in the face, or perhaps a nudge in his bullet wound. At the very least, a shove back down to the hard deck. But Tien just smiled.

"Actually, Commander, we know all about you. The ship's office, you know. Has all the personnel files, complete with photos and backgrounds. We know who the officers are, who the weapons chief petty officer is, who the chief engineer is. I take it you forgot to burn those records with the other secret papers."

Murphy said nothing. Tien went on. "I only ask, Commander, because we intend to repair your ship so you can leave port and return home."

Murphy realized he was being manipulated. He tried to keep his face impassive, but apparently, in spite of himself, his expression had eased for a moment, giving Tien an opening.

"Yes, that's right. We just want to do what we can to repair your damage so you can drive out on your own power. After all, at a time such as this, we hardly need world public opinion against us, not when the thugs of the White Army are advancing on our People's government. How would you feel, sir, if Mexican troops had Washington surrounded? Before we complete your repairs, we have only one requirement of you. You know now how concerned we are with world opinion, and with our image with your own government. I do not know why your Navy sent you to spy on us, but I certainly hope it was not for the benefit of the White Army. I digress. I merely want you to record a statement. A statement to go on record that elements of your military ordered your ship here to spy on us, and that this shows the support of America for the Japanese-sponsored White Army. You will call for an end to this violation of international law and ask for help for my nation, telling how humanely we have treated you, and how we will be releasing your ship."

So, Murphy thought, here it was. And it now seemed obvious that the PLA and the Chinese government would try to make the most of the opportunity of catching the *Tampa* violating her territorial waters. He also had to at least consider the possibility of release, and how he was obligated to his men to do what he could to save their lives.

But the Code—*I will make no oral or written statements disloyal to my country and its allies or harmful to their cause.* How could he make a statement damning his command or his country?

"I've taken the liberty of having one of your officers make the same statement I want you to make," Tien said. "Of course, we could use his statement, but we both know it would be much more effective coming from you. In this situation, Captain, we need each other."

Tien stood then and opened the stateroom door. A guard wheeled in a television set and video tape player on a stand. The unit was plugged into an outlet and the tape was rolled. Murphy tried to keep the emotions out of his face, but when he saw Chuck Griffin's miserable face on the screen, he gave it up.

Griffin, of all people. Griffin, the most "conservative" member of the wardroom, an advocate of the use of military force in international crises. Griffin, in fact, had argued just a week ago that the United States should enter the war on the side of the White Army and use any means necessary to subdue Beijing. Now his face showed fear. His eyes were no longer young, they were eyes that had seen physical torture. He looked emaciated, as if he had lost at least fifty pounds. There were no discernible marks on his face, but it looked like he had been made-up. Pancake makeup could cover bruises and cuts. Griffin's face wore the look of a broken man as he read off the confession:

"... our heavily armed and battle-ready nuclear attack submarine was ordered into the territorial waters of the peaceful nation of the People's Republic of China. I deeply regret the naked act of aggression that the U.S. Navy has committed in this clear violation of international law in support of the Army of White Aggression ..."

Murphy knew Griffin would never be reading that statement unless he had been tortured beyond human endurance. Every man had his breaking point, himself included. The terrible question was, when ... ? Finally, after going on for twenty agonizing minutes, the tape ended, Griffin's voice sinking to a whisper as the picture dissolved into snow.

"I've had the text written for you on a TelePrompTer," Tien said. "Fighter Sai, bring in the camera."

Murphy watched as the guard set up the video camera and the TelePrompTer and the lights. A boom microphone was suspended over his head. The Tele-PrompTer flashed up with text, the large letters spelling MY NAME IS COMMANDER SEAN MURPHY. The lights came on, the video camera was trained on Murphy's face, and leader Tien Tse-Min smiled at him encouragingly. Murphy took a breath, looked into the camera, and began ... "I pledge allegiance to the flag of the United States of America and to the Republic for which it stands—"

He never felt Tien's fist crashing into his face, just the odd vision of the camera and lights and Tele-PrompTer slowly fading away from him, sinking into a thick blackness.

CHAPTER 15

SUNDAY, 12 MAY
1720 GREENWICH MEAN TIME

Bo Hai Bay
Point Hotel
USS *Seawolf*
0120 Beijing Time

Seawolf glided to a halt twenty-five yards east of Pier 3 in the deep supertanker channel, only two hundred yards south of Pier 1A, the PLA Navy berths—the location of the *Tampa*.

"Captain, ship's speed, zero point two knots and slowing," the battlestations OOD, Tim Turner, reported. "The ship is ready to hover."

"Off'sa'deck, commence hovering, depth band seven eight to seven nine feet."

"Hover, seven eight to seven nine feet, aye, sir." Turner turned toward the ballast-control panel and gave the orders to the Diving Officer and the Chief of the Watch.

Pacino looked like a modern-day pirate in his black coveralls, black crepe-soled boots and with a black eyepatch over his right eye designed to keep his periscope eye night-adapted. The darkened control room was rigged for red, only small red lamps lighting plot tables, and only the glow of the instruments and fire-control consoles illuminating the space.

The only sound in the control room was the low growl of the ventilation fans blowing cool air into the space and the high-pitched whine of the gyro forward of the ship control panel. The plot officers and attack-center officers waited, no new data coming in for them to plot, with the ship motionless and the targets tied up at the pier. The SEALs were in the upper level passageway waiting for Pacino's order to lockout. Pacino looked at his watch. Almost 0125. Time to scan the situation on the surface.

"Lookaround number-two scope," Pacino called out.

"Speed zero, depth seven nine feet," the Diving Officer announced.

"Up scope." Pacino rotated the hydraulic control ring in the overhead, the ring clunked into the UP position and the stainless-steel pole climbed out of the well, the large optic control module finally coming up and stopping. Pacino stepped up to the module, lifted off his eyepatch, snapped down the periscope grips and put his eye to the cold rubber of the eyepiece. Even in low power the adjacent pier looked dangerously close. The supertanker berth was empty, but the bollards and cleats for tying up ships seemed so close he could reach out and touch them. A lone sentry in the distance was walking toward him down the pier. Otherwise, the supertanker pier was dead.

Pacino scanned the sky to find the moon. The night seemed cloudy and overcast but the moon peeked out of openings in the heavy clouds to the south, opposite the direction of the PLA piers. Not good—moonlight could shimmer on the water, silhouetting the scope and giving him away. He turned the scope view to the PLA piers two hundred yards to the north. He could see the inboard Udaloy, the outboard Luda and the seaward-side Jianghu tied up at the pier—but no sign of the *Tampa.* He clicked the view to high power, magnifying the view by twenty-five times, and made out a black square-shape in the water against the flank of the inboard destroyer Udaloy. The shape could possibly be the *Tampa*'s rudder.

He pulled a trigger on the right periscope grip and magnification changed from 25× to 50×, bringing the Udaloy's hull so close that he could see two PLA

sailors leaning on the railing smoking. For a moment
he kept the two men in the view, the periscope reticle
filled with the forms of the midnight watch-standers.
They were looking down toward the water. Now one
of them tossed his butt into the water and walked on.
Then the second one followed. Pacino brought the
view down. There at the waterline was the black
shape. He could make out the draft markings on the
rudder, even the running light on top, the light off,
the glass of the bulb cracked. No doubt now that it
was the *Tampa*.

Pacino did a rapid low-power periscope search,
scanning the horizon for approaching contacts or aircraft, then checked the supertanker-pier one last time.
As he was about to lower the scope he stopped. There
had been something odd on the pier between the inboard destroyer and the end frigate. He returned the
periscope to the *Tampa*'s rudder, rotated it to the right
so that his view was between the destroyer and frigate,
then switched to high power and hit the doubler
trigger.

Buses. School buses. Two of them he could make
out, with the possibility of a third in between. Buses
suitable for removing the crew of a submarine, Pacino
thought. The vehicles were dark and unmoving. Perhaps they were there for taking the crew off later, or
had something to do with the surface warships. Whatever, it was not a good sign. Pacino shifted back to
low power, again checked the sentry on the
supertanker-piers and lowered the scope.

"Periscope exposure, eighty-four seconds, Cap'n,"
Turner reported. Not good, Pacino thought. Too long.
Periscope exposure begged for detection.

"Attention in the firecontrol team," Pacino said. "I
observed the two destroyers on either side of Friendly
One as well as the frigate aft on the seaward side of
the pier. I confirm the presence of Friendly One as a
submarine. In addition, there were buses on the pier,
not sure why. In the next twenty minutes the SEAL

team will lockout and commence the operation. Carry on."

He then phoned Morris. "You have permission to lockout and commence the operation." He was intentionally formal with Morris. "Be advised we've sighted several buses on the pier. The *Tampa* crew may or may not be in the process of being removed. Watch the pier for buses—if they start an offload, open fire on the pier guards—we can't allow a crew offload. I'll back you up with the Javelins."

"We'll play it by ear."

"Be careful."

"Don't you worry about us, Captain. Just you be there when we need you."

CHAPTER 16

SUNDAY 12, MAY
1728 GREENWICH MEAN TIME

Bo Hai Bay
Point Hotel, Xingang Harbor
USS *Seawolf*
0128 Beijing Time

The upper level passageway near the hatch to the escape trunk was crowded with men and equipment. Commander Kurt Lennox stood aft of the tall pile of clutter, heart pounding. He mistrusted his voice. When one of the SEAL operators asked if he was okay he nodded, trying to look it.

Lennox was fitted with full SEAL combat gear, not that he would use it, but rather he was functioning as a mule to carry spares for the commandos. Morris had insisted on it, saying contemptuously, "ain't nobody goes on a SEAL OP without carrying their weight." And weight he carried, perhaps a hundred pounds of it. He had on a black coverall with a heavy combat vest whose waterproof utility pocket contained a Beretta 9-mm model 92 automatic pistol with a loaded clip of hollow-point ammunition plus five spare clips. The right pocket, an oversized collarbone-to-waist container, held a MAC-10 submachine gun, official weapon of all self-respecting American drug dealers, complete with "hush puppy" silencer, with the additional burden of four 30-round magazines, each filled with jacketed hollow-point rounds. An upper central pocket stocked five flash-bang grenades and ten pounds of C-4 explosive. Below that pocket was a pouch containing the InterSat scrambled VHF walkie-talkie with its lip-mike headset. The vest, fully loaded, weighed over fifty pounds. On Lennox's thighs were pouches stuffed with Mark 114 satchel charges, each containing two charges, each charge a hefty twelve pounds with its wire reel for the parallel connection to the floating detonator receiver. On his back Lennox wore the combined buoyancy compensator vest and Mark 20 Draeger bubbleless scuba lung, the tanks feeling even heavier than the vest and the satchel charges.

With his mask on, Lennox felt like his head was in a goldfish bowl. He took it off and let it hang from his neck. He had always tried to hide a tendency to claustrophobia. Strange, it didn't bother him in the tight spaces of a submarine but surfaced when he found himself in large crowds. Of course, if the Navy shrinks ever got word of his problem his career would be over in a hurry. Ever since his Navy scuba training, he had stayed away from diving. Anxiety attacks could paralyze him. Now, in addition to having to overcome that fear, he would have to dodge bullets as they tried to take back the *Tampa*.

For a moment, as Lennox stood there in the passageway, he thought about his wife Tammy and the leave they had spent touring Japan. He had been shocked and happy that she had come. The WEST-PAC deployment of the *Tampa* had come at a particularly bad time for them, only a week after he had caught her in another man's car, in their own driveway, the car windows fogged, but not enough to hide his too vivid view. He had returned from the ship early at nine in the evening. He had told her he'd be aboard the ship for three nights straight attending to pre-underway emergencies, the staples of submariner's lives, but after one night on the boat he could no longer stand the loneliness, the mournful deep hum of the ventilating ducts, the moaning cry of the ESGN ball as it spun at thousands of RPM in its binnacle aft. In frustration he had left the ship and driven home, picking up a bottle of wine on the way. He had also found a florist who was still open that late on a weekday and bought Tammy's favorite red roses. He had craved one last romantic night before *Tampa* got underway. What he got was a black Mercedes in his driveway, the license plates spelling "RACY," the windows dewy, his wife inside. He had caught only a glimpse of her raising her head from below the steering wheel, her hair a mess, the car door opening, the sound of the wine bottle shattering on the asphalt, the roses now a bad joke.

He had thought about divorce, moving out right then. But in the early weeks of the deployment, all he could think about was how much he *still* wanted her, how he didn't want to lose her, and why in the hell he was in the middle of the Pacific welded into a steel pipe with one hundred and fifty other sweating men when his wife might be ... He tried to block it out of his mind.

Captain Murphy had insisted that Lennox go on leave, and when they made landfall in Yokosuka, Tammy was on the pier. Murphy had radioed Squadron to ask Tammy to come, even flying her out on a military hop. After a few days in Japan, Lennox's troubled marriage seemed to be healing, when the phone rang one evening at the hotel. A bureaucrat from NAVPERS had been on the phone, ordering him to report for duty aboard the *Seawolf*.

Goddamn Murphy, Lennox thought. Of all people, why did he have to get caught by the Chinese? Best skipper in the fleet, and now he was at gunpoint. A man who was more than Lennox's commanding officer—he was also Lennox's friend. At least the thought of being involved in an attempt to save Murphy made the claustrophobia recede for a moment.

The men from the first platoon opened the hatch to the huge escape trunk, the metal sphere with watertight hatches at the side and top. They began loading equipment into the hatch—heavy RPG grenade launchers and AK-47 machine guns. Bundles of Mark 114 satchel charges. Claymore mines. C-4 plastic explosives. An InterSat radio for talking to the COMM-SAT high above. When the gear was stowed, SEAL Commander Jack Morris climbed into the hatchway with his executive officer, a scrawny young lieutenant named Bartholomay, known to the SEALs as Black Bart, perhaps because of his jet-black hair.

Morris looked at the interior of the escape trunk, nodded he was satisfied, and called to Lennox to climb into the sphere. As the older commander climbed in, huffing from humping the heavy vest and scuba tanks, Morris shook his head at Black Bart. The toughest part of the operation would be getting this bubblehead submariner safely aboard the *Tampa*. Finally Lennox had climbed into the sphere and sat on the wood bench, precariously balancing the tanks on his back and the weapons in his combat vest, and began to put on his swimmer's fins, struggling to reach his feet over the bulk of the combat vest and buoyancy compensator.

"Ready, Lennie?" Morris asked Lennox.

"Let's go," Lennox managed to say, ignoring the derision in Morris's voice.

Morris raised a phone handset to his lips. "Upper level, escape trunk. Shutting lower hatch." He then unlatched the heavy spring-hinged steel hatch and shut it over the hole leading to the forward-compartment upper level. The light and warmth of the ship were suddenly replaced by the shadows of the interior of the escape trunk, lit only by a single pressure-resistant bulb. Morris rotated the wheel of the hatch, engaging the ring latch. "Lower hatch shut and dogged," he reported on the phone. "Flood and equalize the trunk."

A rush of loud noise filled the spherical airlock as cold sea water flooded in the bottom of the trunk from a four-inch line and began to lap over the men's feet. Lennox grabbed his Draeger mask and put it over his face, testing the regulator for air. He was getting air through the unit but was obviously anxious, the mask of the unit fogging up but not enough to hide his wide eyes.

Morris looked down at the water level rising and looked over at Black Bart in shared amusement at Lennox as the water climbed above the men's knees and rose to their waists. The air in the space was foggy from the pressurization. Black Bart yawned to clear his ears. Morris clamped his lips shut and blew, relieving his eardrums against the pressure, then yawned. By then the water was up to his chin, the air foggier and hotter from the compression. As the water filled the sphere to the upper hatch, Morris put on his Draeger mask and blew out the water with his nose, tasting the coppery air from the lung. He then keyed a button on his belt, inflating the buoyancy compensator until it overcame the weight of the vest, then deflated it slightly to avoid being overbuoyant—no sense popping to the surface and alerting the Chinese.

Morris peered through the dim light of the murky water to look at the faces of Bart and Lennox. Bart gave him an "okay" sign. Lennox, still wide-eyed, was under control and also returned an "okay" signal. Morris reached to the bulkhead of the sphere and rotated a switch-handle, cutting the light, and the sphere plunged into blackness. He felt up into the overhead for the wheel to the upper hatch, rotated it, and when the dogs clicked home he pushed upward, letting the spring hinge assist the heavy hatch to the vertical position. He pushed it until it latched and then swam out of the opening into the lukewarm water of the bay. Scarcely thirty feet overhead was the surface, their position less than a hundred feet from the supertanker-pier. He felt his way up and out of the chamber, holding onto the hatch and waiting for Black Bart to swim out behind him. The water of the bay was totally black, not so much from being dirty but from the absence of light. The moon would light their way close to the surface and on the boat, but this far down the moon was useless. The swimming would have to be done almost completely by feel.

Morris and Bart felt their way to the trailing edge of the sail, where a recessed lug was set into the sail's steel. Morris pulled out a line and attached it to the lug, then grabbed Bart and swam with him to a similar lug ten yards aft of the escape-trunk hatch and set flush into the deck. Once the tie-off line was in place Morris swam back into the escape trunk and pulled out Lennox, making sure his buoyancy compensator was filled to lift him up with the combat weights but not so light that he would have to struggle to remain deep. Satisfied, Morris pulled Lennox to the tie-off line and attached his lanyard to the line. No sense having the bubblehead float off into the bay.

Morris and Bart pulled the equipment out of the trunk and tied off the bundles to the tie line, then shut the hatch and tapped on the hull. Below, in *Seawolf*, the first platoon would be draining the trunk, loading their gear and locking out. With the dark water, it would take a half hour just to get everyone out of the ship. Morris frowned inside his Draeger mask—thirty minutes to lock out was not good enough. This operation should have been done with a swimmer-delivery submarine, one of the old missile subs that used the ballistic missile tubes as airlocks and could lock out thirty men in a few minutes. So much for progress.

While Morris waited for the second platoon he turned his mind to calculating how long it would take to lay the satchel charges, letting his thoughts drift to the days when he had been first trained in SpecWar techniques, to how they had practiced diving in enemy waters. He had been a platoon leader of Team One when his platoon had been ordered to lock out of the *Silverfish* in Severomorsk Harbor in the Soviet Union back in the eighties. He had been newly frocked to lieutenant then, still finding his style, and there he was diving in the sovereign waters of Russia, where he would have been shot or imprisoned if he were caught. The job had been to tap a submerged phone cable with an NSA device to record all the phone conversations. He should have been scared or at least anxious, but

instead had felt only a rush of pleasure. Maybe it was
sick, as some suggested, but it was what he lived for.

Six years after the Soviet bay dive he was in command of SEAL Team One out of Little Creek, Virginia, when the CIA asked them to insert into Libya
and destroy a chemical plant known to be making bio-
logical weapons. His SEALs had been inserted by un-
marked black helicopters, converging on the plant
from all points of the azimuth, and had watched until
the plant operator patrols had passed. Once the sentry
had retreated to the control building the SEALs wired
up two dozen explosive charges to the 120-foot-tall
distillation column, wired in their detonator charges
and retreated to watch the fireworks. When they were
a half-mile away in the sand, the column blew apart,
the white-hot fireball mushrooming into a brilliant,
poisonous cloud that rose over a thousand feet into
the air. The resulting secondary explosions and fires
took out the remainder of the site, killing every Lib-
yan within a thousand-yard radius of the column. His
team had escaped, using their Draegers for gas masks,
and vanished into the Mediterranean, where a second
set of helicopters picked them up and brought them
to the carrier *Nimitz*. The operation had earned him
a Bronze Star and the admiration of the SpecWar
community, and had finally led to his command at
Team Seven. It was also after Libya that he had been
given a free hand—unquestioned budgets, the finest
commandos in the fleet, and the choicest—most
dangerous—operations.

So much for his professional life. By contrast, things
at home were SNAFU. He had never married—
women only made life complicated—and had drifted
from bed to bed. In the last ten years he could recall
only a handful of women who had turned down his
many advances, including the married ones. He had
wondered why he lost interest in women after he bed-
ded them and had even talked to a unit psychologist,
who suggested it was a "self-esteem problem," and
had asked him how he felt about his mother. Morris

had nearly knocked out the man's front teeth. Still, for all his macho self-image, a woman he had picked up in a bar and gone to bed with over two months before and forgotten was calling him and telling him she was pregnant. "Sounds like you have a problem," he said, but the problem was now getting to be his, because he had, in spite of himself, started to think what it would be like to have a little boy. Of course, it would be a boy. He had almost called the woman and told her to have the child and he'd live with her. He had stopped himself from calling, but now here in this goddamned Chinese bay with an OP in front of him, he kept thinking about her. And the kid that maybe was his . . .

As he watched, the first and second platoons locked out and unloaded their equipment from the escape trunk. Finally the third platoon was locked out and the hatch was shut for the last time. Morris swam down the line and tapped the men on the shoulders— saddle-up time. It took a few moments for the men to tie the equipment onto their lanyards and adjust their buoyancy. The two hundred yards to the PLA piers might look like a short walk from the periscope, but hauling underwater enough ammo to blow a flotilla would be no piece of cake, never mind what he had told Pacino. He checked the men again, shining his hooded penlight into each face, getting an "okay" sign from each of them. He tied onto his own load, an RPG with six reloads, and tied his own lanyard to the tieline. When he tapped the man next to him, the signal was passed down the line to the men at the end, who untied the tieline from the submarine and looped the line onto their belts. Now all twenty-four men—the three platoons of seven plus Bart, Morris, and Lennox—were tied onto the line and could swim to the targets together without getting lost or separated. Also, should one of the lungs fail, the closeness to a swim-buddy would allow buddy-breathing off a spare regulator. And instead of having two dozen lighted compasses tempting detection, there was only Morris'.

He flipped the cover off his watch and held the face horizontal. When he clicked the light, the dial lit up, showing the depth and the compass bearing. Morris had memorized the chart, but the unknown was the *Seawolf*'s position when it locked them out. Still, he believed he could find the PLA pier.

He pushed off the hull of the submarine and swam over the cylindrical edge of the ship, diving down to the bottom of the deep channel, all the way to the one-hundred-and-twenty-foot level, his ears popping on the way down. Finally he felt the silt of the bottom and paused to let the others catch up. When they did he checked the compass again and swam northwest toward the piers. Almost immediately the silty bottom began to rise out of the supertanker channel to the shallower region of the piers, the sloping bottom there an average of thirty feet deep. Morris followed the up-slope, one hand in the silt, the other horizontal to see the compass, keeping them on course three four five. Now that they were shallow again, Morris looked up to try to find moonlight. There was a faint shimmer from overhead but no real light. The SEALs continued to follow the contour of the bottom until Morris hit concrete with his outstretched hand. Pier 1A. He waited for the team to catch up with him, then shined his light upward to see the surface. Instead of waves there was the black shape of a hull overhead—one of the ships tied up directly to the pier. Morris tapped the man on his right to confirm their position.

"Dogface" Richardson, a second-class petty officer, and "Buckethead" Williams, a chief, untied themselves from the tieline and swam up to the hull. When they returned after a few moments Buckethead shook his head—the hull above them was at the seaward end of the pier, making it the Jianghu frigate. The ships guarding the *Tampa* were further west. The team swam west along the pier until they reached the next hull, which would be the Udaloy guided-missile destroyer. Then the platoons split up.

First platoon took their gear and set it up near the

pier between the Chinese ships. Second platoon set up beneath the Udaloy, beginning work laying the keel-breaking satchel charges under the destroyer. Third platoon hauled their explosives beneath the hull of the *Tampa* further south to the outboard destroyer, the Luda, and began deployment of their charges.

Morris checked his watch. It was taking too god-damned long, he thought, wondering if he should have taken Pacino up on the offer to use the cruise missiles. But using Javelins here would be like a surgeon for-saking a scalpel for a chainsaw. He and Black Bart swam back and forth between the platoons, making sure the men were making progress, that the plan was proceeding.

Finally Morris signaled to Bart to come up to look at the pier, and the two divers ascended at the bow of the Udaloy. Morris disconnected from his lanyard and climbed a pier piling, the tar from it sticking to his hands. Near the top of the piling he climbed off onto a horizontal timber that was there to cushion the concrete pier from ship impacts. He cautiously lifted his head above the level of the pier, then ducked back down and silently reentered the water. The pier was crawling with guards, but the buses were not yet occu-pied and there was no evidence of a crew offload. He and Bart returned to the underside of the Udaloy.

Under the hull of the USS *Tampa*, on the bottom of the silty bay, huddled with the assault weapons, sat Commander Kurt Lennox, his mask fogged from his heavy breathing. Every few moments he turned his head to look at the submarine above him, seeing noth-ing but a black blur, thinking that in a very few mo-ments he would be back aboard her, and in a few moments after that he could be dead. Morris swam by and gave him a thumbs up.

Lennox appreciated it as he looked up again at the hull of the *Tampa* and told himself that just maybe Sean Murphy was going to get out of this in one piece.

CHAPTER 17

SUNDAY, 12 MAY
1730 GREENWICH MEAN TIME

Bo Hai Bay, Xingang Harbor
PLA Navy Pier 1A, USS *Tampa*
0130 Beijing Time

Sean Murphy had no idea how long he'd been unconscious. When he came to the butt of the AK-47 again in his ribs, his whole body was in pain. As he tried to focus on the interrogator's face, he realized that he now wanted to die. He tried to bring back Katrina, Sean junior and Emily, but the Chinese had taken the most prized thing he possessed—his memories of their faces. He could no longer remember the face of his wife of thirteen years, or the face of his firstborn. Death would be welcome.

"You are in pain," Tien said, his voice quiet. "Let's take you to the hospital where we can attend that wound and help you get rest. The base hospital has some of the softest beds in the world. Think of the cool crisp white sheets, the deep feather pillow in a cotton pillowcase. This is no way to live, my friend. All your resistance will do is make you sick—and delay the ship's departure. We have said we need your statement only for public opinion. If the words are not your own, your people will understand. After all, you are being detained, they will not hold any of this against you. I would guess the only matter your commanders will be annoyed with is allowing your ship's departure to be delayed by your insistence on *not* making the statement. Commander, if it were up to

178

me, I would let it go without the confounded statement, but I have senior officers overseeing my missions. Please see my side. We are not so different, you and I."

The words washed over Sean Murphy, he barely heard them.

"I have a present for you," Tien said, picking up a phone and speaking into it for a moment. After he put the phone down, he looked at the overhead as the Circuit One announcing speaker crackled with Lube Oil Vaughn's voice:

"THE REACTOR ... IS CRITICAL!"

Tien was as delighted as if he had just thrown Murphy a surprise party. "You see, I told you we would get your ship ready to go. We replaced whole sections of your steam-piping loop and reinsulated the lines. I am told that several of the steam valves needed to be replaced. Otherwise, your propulsion plant is, as you say, shipshape. Our nuclear-power experts have been over the plant inspecting it for the purpose of getting the ship ready to leave so you can return home. They say the ship is amazing."

The lights in the overhead flickered, and suddenly the ventilation ducts boomed into operation, blowing cool fresh air into the room. At least Tien had not been kidding about Vaughn starting the reactor and steam plants, even though they were probably only starting the plant to provide power. Without shore-power the battery would soon have run out of juice and they would have had to abandon the submarine. Probably they figured the statement could be gotten from him more easily aboard the ship than in a barracks ashore.

Again they brought in the camera and TelePrompTer, but before they turned it on, Tien popped a video in the VCR and turned on the television. He pressed the play button, and Sean Murphy's front yard flashed onto the screen, with Katrina and Sean and Emily looking into the picture.

"Sean, honey, we love you and we miss you. I don't

know when you'll get this," Katrina said into the camera, her auburn hair blowing in the breeze, "but maybe you can play it at sea and remember how much we love you."

His son said: "Hurry home, Daddy. Mommy says you're poking holes in the ocean but I know you can't make a hole in water. I told my class what you do at show-and-tell today. Everyone said it sounded neat. Come home soon, Daddy—"

Tien stopped the tape.

Murphy fought not to show his feelings as he became aware that the camera was focused on his face. The TelePrompTer stared at him: "MY NAME IS COMMANDER SEAN MURPHY" ... Murphy blinked hard and stared at the camera lens and began to speak, his voice a raspy croak.

"I am an American fighting man," he said, trying to recite the Code of Conduct. "I serve in the forces which guard my country and our way of life. I am prepared to give my life in their defense—"

"No," Tien broke in. "That is not what the script says." He waved to the guard. "Bring in Tarkowski," he said, resignation in his voice.

A shot of bile hit Murphy's stomach as he realized they were going to torture Tarkowski for his benefit.

USS *Seawolf*

The control room began to seem confining, Pacino thought, impatient with the need to act, to fire weapons, to do *something,* anything, to get Murphy out. Somehow the idea of trusting this rescue to swimmers who could only take out the hatch that they came in with seemed a bad idea. With the torpedo room full of weapons, with his number one and two tubes loaded with Javelin cruise missiles, both ready to fire, both tube outer doors open ... For the second time in a half hour he asked Tim Turner the status of the Javelins.

He reported the units had the destroyers targeted. "We can have both missiles in the sky within thirty seconds of your orders, sir."

Pacino decided to risk a quick look at the surface. There were no close contacts, no patrol boats or fishing vessels, or, God help them, a supertanker en route to the tanker pier. He did an air search, looking for the type of aircraft that Admiral Donchez hinted had detected Murphy. All he saw was the moon to the south, still going in and out of the clouds, and some dim stars to the north over the PLA piers.

Pacino turned the crosshairs onto Target Four, the Jianghu fast frigate, and rotated the grip of the scope to raise the magnification to high power. There was no activity. Further to the left was Target Three, the Udaloy destroyer, one of *Tampa*'s escorts. Not a soul in sight. A bit to the left was the rudder of the *Tampa*, the rest obscured by the stern of the Luda destroyer, the other escort for the *Tampa*. There was no evidence of the divers below the ships.

Pacino turned the view on the pier between the Jianghu and the Udaloy. The buses were still there but the pier looked dark. There were no guards in sight, no sign of them being used for a crew offload.

Pacino's earpiece crackled with the voice of Chief Dylan Jeb, the sonar supervisor. Chief Jeb was a tall, thin sonar expert from the hills of Tennessee. His drawl on the combat circuits was so thick as to be nearly another language. Pacino had taken an immediate liking to the lanky sonar chief, despite his impenetrable accent. Jeb ran the BQQ-5 as naturally and adeptly as his ancestors had run the family still.

"Conn, Sonar, we're getting new machinery noises off the hull and spherical arrays bearing north to the PLA piers. The bearing is ambiguous due to near-field effect. We're working up a narrow-band tonal profile but my guess is that *Tampa*'s engineroom is steaming ... wait ... we're getting a series of transients from the same bearing ... sounds like electrical breakers ..."

"Chief, what do you think they're doing?" Pacino

said, snapping up the periscope grips and lowering the scope.

"We're guessing, but it sounds like they're starting up the steam plant, maybe shifting the electric plant to a half-power or full-power lineup."

"Let me know when you've got the sound signature identified."

A startup of the *Tampa*'s engineroom . . . now what the hell could that be about? Would she be removed to another pier? And if so wouldn't she just do that under the power of the ships tied up to her?

"Conn, Sonar, sound signature identified. The noise is coming from a late-flight 688-class U.S. submarine."

"Any engineroom sounds or transients from Targets One through Four?"

"No."

All right, come on, Morris, Pacino thought, get this thing *going*.

USS *TAMPA*

Tarkowski's face was white, whether with fear or from starvation or beatings. Probably all three, Murphy thought. He had been brought in by the guard and deposited on the settee at the far end of Murphy's stateroom. He looked only once at Murphy. There seemed no recognition in his eyes, more the look of someone suffering so much pain he could not register the world around him. Whatever the *Tampa*'s navigator and acting exec had been through, there was no sign of it in his face, just the blank glaze on his eyes.

"Commander," Tien said. "I want the statement. I accept your indifference to your own welfare. But I know your men are important to you. You can save your executive officer now by making the statement. If you refuse, he will pay. Remember, Commander, I report to men less patient than I am. If it were not for my efforts, at considerable personal risk, I might add, they would have killed your crew long before now. I have also offended Beijing by insisting your ship be allowed to leave once we obtain your statement, but they have agreed. Look, here is the order."

Tien waved a piece of paper before Murphy, the Chinese symbols written on it meaningless. He waited, got no response from Murphy. "Commander, you force me to demonstrate my intent. Sai, give me Mr. Tarkowski's right thumb."

The guard pulled Tarkowski's hand from his lap, laid it flat on the table, produced a bayonet, and proceeded to saw Tarkowski's thumb from his right hand. Tarkowski howled in pain, the sound wailing high in pitch as if coming from an animal; his eyes were shut, his mouth open wide to let out the shriek of agony. The most frightening thing was that Tarkowski did not attempt to pull his hand away from the guard. What other unspeakable acts had he undergone? The guard wiped the bayonet on his thigh and held out the thumb to Murphy. When Murphy only stared at the guard, the guard dropped the flesh into his lap.

Tarkowski's hand was still on the table, blood spurting out with the rhythm of his pulse. Tien Tse-Min tossed a bath towel to Tarkowski, who finally moved his left hand from his lap to cover his mangled right hand.

"Commander," Tien began again, his voice calm, "you know a man may function without the use of his thumb, even without the use of his hand. Both hands. Both feet. But there is one thing that makes a man a man. Fighter Sai, put Mr. Tarkowski's penis on the table."

Like he was asking for a cup of tea. Sai pulled Tarkowski to his feet, unzipped his poopy suit, allowing the coverall to fall to the deck. He dropped Tarkowski's underwear to the deck, the coverall and underwear binding Tarkowski's feet together.

Murphy tried to find his voice, but his throat was dry. It was like one of those nightmares in which the dreamer tries to scream and can't.

"Ah . . . ah . . . I'll . . . I'll make the state . . . ment," he tried to say, but the words came out a choked whisper.

Sai had already raised his bayonet. Tarkowski continued to stand like a robot at the table. Sai brought the knife edge down to Tarkowski's penis. Tarkowski's mouth opened, again a shriek.

"Stop!" Murphy's voice finally came. "I'll make the damned statement, I'll make the statement ... I'll do it ... Just *stop, for God's sake stop!"*

Tien waved at Sai, who stopped the blade but did not release Tarkowski's penis.

Tien wheeled over the TelePrompTer and the camera. He rolled the camera. Just behind it Murphy could see the guard, the bayonet, the table, and Tarkowski's penis. Above the camera, Tarkowski's face had turned gray. Murphy tried to concentrate on the TelePrompTer. He began:

"My name is Commander Sean Murphy, United States Navy. I am the captain of the U.S. Navy nuclear-powered attack submarine *Tampa* ..."

The statement went on for minute after minute, into what seemed like hours to Murphy. Through it all he tried to read and ignore the meaning of the words, but even with Tien's flat face looking on, with Tarkowski still standing at the table, Murphy heard the words and wanted to throw up. He continued on, thinking that somehow Tien would pay, but also knowing the thought was a vain one. Finally the statement was finished.

Tien stopped the camera. "Commander, I thank you for being a reasonable man. Fighter Sai, release Mr. Tarkowski."

The guard released his hold on Tarkowski, underwear and coveralls still around his ankles.

"Let me help you, Tarkowski," Tien said, bending and gently lifting Tarkowski's underwear up and pulling his coveralls up over his shoulders. He zipped up the poopy suit and turned around to look at Murphy. The guard rolled out the camera and video equipment. For a moment Tien just looked at Murphy, then, his eyes still on Murphy's face, he picked up a phone and spoke some orders into it.

Immediately the fans wound down, the air conditioning stopped, the lights flickered. The Circuit One announcing system again broadcast Lube Oil Vaughn's voice to the ship, the voice empty of hope.

"REACTOR SCRAM," the voice said.

Tien turned to the guard: "Turn on the pier floodlights and prepare the buses. Get the prisoners offloaded immediately. I want these buses out of here in ten minutes."

Murphy began to protest.

Tien ignored him as he produced a pistol and put the barrel into Tarkowski's right nostril. After a moment's pause, he pulled the trigger, filling the small stateroom with a crashing report. Tarkowski's head blew apart, the back of his skull flying back against the far bulkhead. Slowly, he sank to the deck, his knees buckling.

Tien's pistol was still upraised at the place where Tarkowski's face had been a moment before. Finally he holstered the pistol and disappeared into the passageway, leaving Murphy alone in his room with the corpse of Greg Tarkowski.

CHAPTER 18

SUNDAY, 12 MAY
1835 GREENWICH MEAN TIME

Bo Hai Bay
Point Hotel, Xingang Harbor
USS *Seawolf*
0235 Beijing Time

"Conn, Sonar," Chief Jeb's Tennessee accent drawled, "Transients from Friendly One. The *Tampa* is shutting down her engineroom."

"What do you make of that, Captain?" Keebes asked from the deck near the attack center.

Pacino shrugged. "Lookaround number-two scope," he called as the periscope pole came out of the well, the optic control module clunking to a halt as it cleared the well sill. Pacino snapped the grips down, pushed up his eyepatch and put his eye to the scope trained to the bearing of the PLA piers.

He had expected to have to peer into the dim light, but the brilliance of the pier floodlights burned his retina. When his eyes adjusted he could see the floodlit pier and the dark shapes of the superstructures of the warships tied up pierside. Between Target Three and Four the buses were lit up inside. Both buses visible in the line of sight between the Udaloy and the Jianghu had drivers waiting inside them. Pier guards wandered on the narrow strip of concrete visible between the ships, rifles at the ready as if they were expecting something. The decks of the Udaloy, between *Tampa* and the pier, were lit up.

There could be only one thing going on with the

pier activity and the engineroom shutdown, Pacino decided. The Chinese were moving the *Tampa*'s crew to a POW camp.

The divers had been locked out for almost forty minutes. With fifteen minutes to get to the PLA pier, that had given them less than half an hour to set up the explosive charges on the surface ships. And Morris had predicted between a half-hour and an hour to lay the charges. He had also promised to keep an eye on the pier for any offload of the crew. Were his VHF walkie-talkies up and waiting for him to communicate?

"Radio, Captain," Pacino barked into his lip mike, "patch in the VHF freak to the SEAL team to the conn and line up the transmission on the Type-20."

"Conn, Radio, aye ... Captain, you're patched in. Type-20's ready to transmit." The periscope antenna was not usually a transmission device, but the radiomen had wired in the SEALs' walkie-talkie VHF frequencies into the antenna and rigged it for transmission, thereby avoiding Pacino having to raise the huge Bigmouth antenna for transmitting.

Pacino pulled a coiled-cord microphone from a console hanging on the aft stainless steel conn handrail, punched a toggle switch on the console, spoke into the mike:

"Whiskey, this is Bourbon, over." He listened while looking out the periscope at the pier. Any minute the prisoners would be moved, he thought. He had to *act* ... which meant launch the missiles. He fought for control as he called into the microphone a second time.

"Whiskey, Whiskey, this is Bourbon, over. I say again, Whiskey, this is Bourbon, come in, over."

Still nothing from the SEALs. There was the off-chance that they couldn't transmit, could only listen. Pacino decided to send his message and hope they received it. He didn't want to think what would happen if they didn't.

"Whiskey, this is Bourbon, break. I am executing

Plan Juliet. I say again, I am executing Plan Juliet, break. Bourbon, out.''

What else could he do? The satchel charges were not laid in time, the SEALs had not yet opened fire on the pier, and they didn't answer the radio call. Plan Juliet, "J" for Javelin, was the fallback.

Pacino snapped up the grips on the periscope and rotated the control ring, sending the pole back down into the well. He turned to stand at the railing and looked out at the assembled battlestations watchstanders. The time had come. The show was his now.

"Attention in the firecontrol team. We're executing Plan Juliet; the Chinese are getting ready to offload *Tampa*'s crew onto buses waiting at the pier. Firing-point procedures, Javelin missiles, tube one Target Three, tube two Target Two.''

"Ship ready,'' Tim Turner said.

"Weapons ready,'' Feyley reported from the weapon-control panel.

"Solutions ready,'' Keebes said in front of Pos Two.

"Tube one,'' Pacino ordered. "Shoot.''

"Fire,'' Feyley barked from the WCP, pulling the trigger. From the deck below the violent blast of the tube belching the missile into the sea popped the eardrums of the men in the control room.

"Tube two. Shoot.''

"Fire,'' Feyley said again. Again the tube ejection mechanism filled the ship with a roaring boom as the ultra-high-pressure air loaded a piston that pressurized a water tank surrounding the torpedo tube, the pressurized water pushing the Javelin's capsule out of the tube like a schoolboy's spitwad flying out of a straw.

"Tubes one and two fired electrically,'' Feyley reported.

"Conn, Sonar, own-ship's units, normal launches.''

Pacino wondered what the Chinese on the pier were thinking at that moment.

"Off'sa'deck,'' Pacino ordered Turner, "train the thruster to two seven zero and turn the ship around to the east. Let's get the hell away from the end of the pier."

"Aye, sir."

Somewhere above them two solid fuel rockets were igniting, sending two cruise missiles at two of the surface warships. It would not do for them to remain too long under the rocket plumes, two fingers pointing at their position.

"Conn, Sonar, we have rocket-motor ignition, units one and two."

Javelin Unit One was ejected from the starboard side of the *Seawolf* by the water pressure of the tube. Silently it glided from the tube, accelerating as it slipped past the skin of the ship and emerged fully over sixty feet below the murky surface of the Bo Hai Bay. As the stern of the encapsulated missile came out of the tube door, twin fins snapped down into place and acted as elevators, turning the missile toward the surface above. The missile was moving at thirty feet per second as it angled upward, reaching the surface three seconds after it left the tube. The nosecone of the capsule broached, sensing balmy May air on its surface, drying out two of the electronic sensors that proved it was no longer underwater. Next, the nosecone of the capsule blew off, exposing the nosecone of the Javelin missile inside.

For a moment the capsule bobbed in the water, the lid spinning in the night air twenty feet overhead. In the next instant the missile streaked out of the capsule, its rocket motor's white-hot flames sinking the capsule and hurling the missile clear of the water toward the overcast sky, the moonlight glinting off the flat black of its paint. The rocket's trail of flame extended vertically several thousand feet above the water, vanishing into a cloud.

Seconds later the Unit Two capsule of the second Javelin penetrated the surface, the second nosecone blowing toward the sky, a prelude to the second missile's liftoff sequence. Milliseconds later the second

unit roared out of its capsule and flashed toward the
sky, its flame trail illuminating the end of the supertanker pier and the water of the slip between the
tanker and PLA piers. The second unit flew up into
the night sky as if chasing the first unit, the twin missiles' exhausts blindingly bright, their noise deafening.

At four thousand feet the rocket motor of Unit One
cut out, the missile still rising skyward from the momentum of the initial thrust. At forty-five hundred feet
eight explosive bolts detonated at the ring joint between the missile and the solid rocket booster. At five
thousand feet the unit's upward velocity stopped and
for a moment the unit flew horizontally, until the missile nosed over and began a dive, popping out the
wings and the air-intake duct, the rudder turning, taking the weapon toward the north as it began to pull
out of its dive.

Moments later the second unit also discarded its
rocket motor, came to its peak altitude and nosed
down toward the ground, this unit turning south. As
both weapons picked up speed in their plunge toward
earth, the jet engine sustainers came on-line, propelling both units at speeds just under Mach 1, the better
to avoid a sonic boom that would give the missiles
away. Once their rocket trails vanished, the missiles
would likewise disappear, vaporizing into the radar
grass and ground clutter.

The first unit pulled out of its dive at an altitude of
forty feet, continuing to the north, flying over the PLA
Navy compound and continuing north and inland, flying over the dingy buildings of the village of Dagu.
The second unit pulled out and headed south, hugging
the coastline of the bay.

Both weapons had been "over-the-shoulder" shots.
The distance from the *Seawolf* to the targets had been
much too close for the units to perform their
climbouts, jet engine light-offs, pullouts and target approaches in a mere two hundred yards. The minimum
firing range was four thousand yards. The weapons
had to be ordered to reach their targets by first flying

away from them, then when stable at low altitudes to
turn and fly back.

Unit One continued north for a mile, then wiggled
the rudder and pulled three g's in a 180-degree turn.
Once settled on the southern course, back toward the
pier, the unit turned on its radar seeker, the superstructures of the enemy surface ships memorized. It
flew south at 570 knots, returning over the village of
Dagu, intent on finding its surface-ship target at the
PLA Navy piers. While Unit One flew in from the
north, Unit Two made its 180-degree turn, steadying
up on a course of due north, the ground of the bay's
coast streaking by beneath the fuselage.

Now at the pier, the two missiles flew in on straight
flight paths, one from the south, one from the north,
radar-seekers searching, warheads arming.

Fighter Sai climbed out of the hatchway and stretched
on the curving hull of the *Tampa*. He was hungry.
Leader Tien Tse-Min was obsessed, he thought, never
stopping an interrogation until he'd gotten the last
possible bit of information, and confession-reading.
The man was a pain in the ass. He put his outsized
hands in his pockets and slowly walked toward the
gangway leading to the *Kunming*, the destroyer tied
up between the American submarine and the pier. As
soon as the guards on the pier were ready and the
buses were started, he would begin offloading the prisoners for their all-night trek to the Shenyang Camp.
Sai wasn't told how long the men were to be kept
there, but if they were going to Shenyang the stay
would probably be permanent. Who cared? This was
all a welcome diversion in the war with the White
Army. As soon as the prisoners were moved he would
return with Tien to Beijing and join the PLA forces
guarding the city from the expected White Army of-
fensive. He felt better as he thought of killing Taiwan-
ese soldiers and turncoat mainland rebels.

Abruptly, the noise of a crashing explosion sounded
from behind him. He slammed into the deck of the

gangway, startled when the noise did not end but continued, an earsplitting shriek, from the direction of
the supertanker-pier. For a moment he thought that a
supertanker had exploded into flames. Slowly the
noise receded, and by the light of the fire behind him
he found the railing of the gangway and pulled himself
up.

In the sky to the south, two rockets were blasting
into the atmosphere, their tails spewing white smoke
that seemed to originate at the seaward tip of the
empty supertanker pier. He hurried back down the
gangway, turned toward the access hatch and lowered
himself down the ladder to the *Tampa*'s upper level.
It took several minutes to find Leader Tien Tse-Min,
and when Sai reported what he had seen, Tien's face
became flushed. It was the first time Sai could remember Tien showing any emotion.

Commander Jack Morris thought he had heard something, a thudding sound. Almost like one of his air
bottles had knocked against the other, but the bottles
were covered with rubber to deaden any such noise.
After a moment he heard the sound again, and then
nothing more. The trouble with interpreting sounds in
water was the sound velocity. With two ears, listening
in air, sound speeds were slow enough so that one ear
heard a noise before the other, giving the brain a clue
to the direction of the noise. Underwater, sound velocity was so quick that both ears heard a noise at the
same time, making it impossible to determine what
direction the sound had come from.

Morris decided to take another look at the pier. He
tugged on his buddy-line to Black Bart and the two
men slowly ascended to the surface between the bow
of the seaward frigate and the stern of the neighboring
destroyer. Morris was preparing to unbuckle the lanyard to Bart and climb up on the pier pilings when
he saw the white plume of a rocket exhaust overhead,
terminating at an orange point of light high in the sky
above.

Quickly Morris submerged, pulling on Bart's lanyard, pulling him deep. Morris hauled in the line, putting his mask up to Bart's. Morris directed him to the outboard destroyer while Morris headed for the inboard destroyer. Only an emergency would make Morris split from his swimming partner. This was definitely an emergency ... two cruise missiles were on the way in to hit the very ships on which his men were laying explosive keel charges. The demolition operation would have to be aborted; the men would have to be extracted and prepared for boarding the *Tampa*.

Morris gave hand signals to Bart in rapid Ameslan, the sign language for the deaf: "You and first platoon go to bow, attack ship immediately after missile impacts." As soon as the Javelins exploded, Bart's bow platoon would board and take the hatch forward of the sail. At the same time Morris's second and third platoons would board and take the aft section of the ship, third platoon going in the aft hatch to the engineroom, second platoon in the amidships access to the aft part of the forward compartment. "If no impact in fifteen minutes, missiles are dead and we go back to kill the destroyers." Bart nodded. "Lennox goes with me," Morris's hand signs added. Bart gave an okay sign. Morris slapped his head, a SEAL gesture for good luck.

As Morris swam the length of the destroyer's barnacle-encrusted hull, waving the men away from their demolition task, he had to consider why *Seawolf* had launched. What came to mind was that the *Tampa* crew were being moved and Pacino hadn't had time to tell him. Morris bit angrily into the rubber of his regulator—he hated a plan that stumbled. Now the element of surprise was gone, risking his men even more, unless he could get aboard the *Tampa* while the crews of the surface ships and the guards were still confused over the damage from the missiles.

He gathered with the second and third platoons under the *Tampa*'s huge spiral-bladed screw and checked his watch. Bart would be assembling the first platoon at *Tampa*'s bow. He pulled the platoon leaders close. One shone his hooded light on Morris while Morris gave the hand signals that relayed his orders for the platoon assignments, adding that he and Lennox would go into the forward compartment with the second platoon. He looked at Lennox, who seemed under control, but his eyes were just a fraction too wide, betraying his fear. Hell, Morris thought, if Lennox were to check my eyes he'd see the same thing. The only difference was that this was his job. And he was good at it.

Morris checked his watch again. 0249. He pointed to the surface and pumped his fins, taking his men shallow. The missiles should be impacting in the next few moments unless they veered off course or were shot down. He reached out, felt the steel of *Tampa*'s tapering aft-section under her screw and followed the curvature upward to the rudder, then continued forward to the top of the hull, still submerged. He put his fins on the top of the hull and swam the remaining few feet to the surface. The pier was lit with floodlights, as were the destroyer decks. The *Tampa*'s deck was lit only dimly by the wash of light from the neighboring ships. He caught sight of a guard hurrying into the forward escape-trunk hatch, a surprised look on his face.

Morris brought his watch up. 0250. He would have to wait another ten minutes before hitting the submarine's deck. That or the missiles would have to arrive. He ducked his head back below the surface and checked his men. All signaled okay.

For the next few moments Morris worked on a plan to hijack one of the smaller vessels, the seaward-parked frigate, and drive it out of the bay, or at least to a point that he could meet *Seawolf*. But that would be putting a few SEALs in an unfamiliar Chinese frigate against the whole PLA Navy. Well, at least he could try his hand at driving a ship. He checked his watch one last time. In four minutes they would be committed.

Morris rose the four feet to the surface to take another look. As the water cleared from his mask, he took in a scene beyond his imaginings.

Javelin cruise missile Unit Two approached the piers of Xingang from the south, the water of the Bo Hai Bay flashing by beneath the fuselage. The missile's navigation system updated from a star fix and confirmed the reading with a radar look at the coastline ahead. The unit adjusted the course for the final leg of the run before detonation. The warhead was armed, waiting only for the four-g's of deceleration required prior to receiving the signal to explode.

The radar-seeker scanned the pie-shaped wedge of earth in front of the missile, the high-frequency waves able to make out the difference between the structure of a crane and the mast of a ship. The unit flew on, nearing the supertanker-pier at the seaward end of the terminal. As the missile approached the pier, the point of its launch, its radar-seeker saw the ships of the People's Liberation Army at the pier. The seeker distinguished the frigates at either end and discarded the targets as too small. The middle radar-return was the correct size. The central processor compared the radar return with the programmed silhouette of the Luda-class and checked off the similarities—Double funnel. Check. Double mast, forward mast higher. Check. Topside missile batteries and surface gun. Check. Boxy superstructure forward, ahead of the mainmast. Check. Smaller structure aft of the second mast. Check. The ship was confirmed as the target. The missile lowered its nose just slightly so as to strike the hull of the ship just below the deckline.

At six hundred and fifty miles per hour the nose-cone of the missile smashed through the steel of the hull, destroying the radar seeker and the navigation equipment. The central processor survived, its detached thought-process recording the four-g deceleration as the steel of the hull slowed the weapon down. In the next ten milliseconds the weapon continued another eight feet into the ship, the tail of the missile disappearing into the small hole it had made in the hull above the waterline.

By that time the warhead received its signal to detonate and the fuse flashed into incandescence, lighting off an intermediate explosive set in the center of the main explosive, which erupted into a white-hot segment that detonated the high-explosive cylinder of the unit in the nosecone aft of the seeker and navigation modules forward of the central processor. The explosive burst into a sphere of energy, blowing the aft superstructure of the destroyer into the sky, vaporizing much of the aluminum framing and bulkheads above. The fireball also blew the aft stack apart, and with it the number-two boiler, which caused a steam explosion from the idling high-pressure steam drum.

The explosion of the Javelin blew downward, breaking the back of the ship, blowing the number-two boiler off its foundation, rupturing a fuel-oil tank. The force of the explosion carried away the main structure of the amidships-mounted HY-2 missile-launcher, blowing the remnants of the missiles into the forward superstructure. The units crashed through the gaping black wreckage of the superstructure, the remains of the officers' quarters and the ship's bridge. The missiles' explosives came to rest against an interior bulkhead in what was once a passageway and ladderway to the upper decks, bleeding jet fuel on the tile of the deck.

The fire caused by the missile engulfed the ship from the fireroom of the number-one boiler to the number-one turbine-room. Men ran out of their bunks in an attempt to bring the fire under control but the fire pumps were destroyed, as was much of the firewater piping. None of the battle-communication lines functioned as the ship rapidly filled with toxic smoke from the fire. Within ten minutes all of the crewmen who had not been able to jump overboard were killed by the smoke, the fire or the secondary explosion.

The missiles lying in the forward section of the superstructure were bathed in jet fuel, and when the flames leaped up the ladder from the number-one boiler's fireroom the jet fuel ignited in a rush of flames, the missiles' explosives detonating and blowing the remainder of the superstructure into the air and onto the foredeck. Now the ship began to take on a starboard list, leaning toward its captive submarine, the break in the keel causing it to settle into the water of the bay.

As the water level rose over the deck amidships, the ship began to buckle, the broken framework of the vessel rupturing its hull at the keel, the water pouring in unchecked. Some men did manage to swim away from the dying ship in the oil slick of the fuel tank. After another ten minutes of flooding and flames, the ship broke in half and settled into the water. All that remained visible forward was the bow-mounted gun and the scorched point of the bow. The aft portion was submerged except for an identical gun and the twisted black steel of the ship's mast, the flag of the northern fleet still flying from the masthead, the banner burned and charred but otherwise intact.

The fireball of what had been Javelin Unit Two was rising into an orange-and-black mushroom cloud spreading over the superstructure of the Luda when Javelin Unit One, coming in from the north, found the Udaloy destroyer and confirmed the target. The missile aimed for the main superstructure directly beneath the bridge, but instead of penetrating the hull, the missile impacted the stern section of the starboard SS-N-14 Silex quad missile-launcher. The nose of the Javelin passed through the canisters of SS-N-14s and continued on through the other side to the bulkhead of the superstructure. The missile's airframe barely made it into the hole in the bulkhead before the rocket fuel of the SS-N-14s detonated. Before the resulting explosion, the SS-N-14s had been rocket-launched torpedoes used in antisubmarine warfare. Now their rocket fuel's ignition made them as deadly to the ship as the Javelin launched by the *Seawolf*. The

rocket fuel exploded in a sloppy fireball, first blowing
outward before the force of the uneven explosion blew
the torpedoes into the forward gunmount. The explosion from the torpedo warheads was even more violent than the initial rocket-fuel ignition, blowing a hole
in the ship's deck in the former location of the
number-two 100-mm gun. At roughly the same time
as the detonation of the SS-N-14 torpedo warheads,
the warhead of the Javelin exploded, vaporizing most
of the interior of the forward superstructure and blowing the forward funnel into a crushed lump of metal.
Even if the missile had been a dud, it would have
succeeded because of the SS-N-14 detonations. The
blast of the Javelin warhead had the added effect of
blowing out the superstructure on the opposite side of
the ship, on the port side. The fireball engulfed the
port SS-N-14 missile canister and caused the unit to
detonate both the rocket fuel and the torpedoes' warheads at the same time. The explosion blew apart what
had been left of the superstructure, taking with it the
masts and antennae as the ship erupted into flames
amidships, the fire migrating aft to the fuel tanks,
where ruptured fuel lines spewed volatile fuel for the
gas turbines into the bilges.

   The Udaloy's main propulsion was by gas turbine,
a sophisticated power turbine turned by the gases of
the hot-gas generator, which was essentially a jet engine that ran on a light fuel of kerosene. Unlike the
viscous fuel oil of the neighboring Luda, which could
ignite only at very high temperatures, the kerosene
was so volatile that the vapor from the spill ignited
immediately, feeding the fire. The fuel tank, located
low and amidships, exploded into flames less than one
minute after the impact of the Javelin. The fire spread
throughout the ship. The crewmembers, those few
aboard, were not as fortunate as the men of the Luda.
No one could survive the white-hot fire in the Udaloy.
The ship's hull did stay intact, but the hole from the
port side SS-N-14 detonation began just above the waterline, and a slight list to port began the flow of water

over the lip of the hole into the ship's second deck. The flooding worsened the list until the ship began leaning hard aport into the hull of the black submarine alongside. The only sounds after the initial round of explosions were the intermittent explosions of ammunition rounds and the roaring of the fire from the deck.

Jack Morris could only stare at the scene. In one moment the *Luda* was intact and quiet. In the next her superstructure exploded into a ball of flame, the ball blowing up into a large sphere with a diameter half the length of the ship. Morris had the brief impression of the ship heeling over to her starboard side from the shock of the explosion, but at that moment two things happened. The shock wave of the explosion hit him, nearly blowing off his mask, and the Udaloy destroyer on the pier-side of the *Tampa* blew apart under another violent fireball, a secondary explosion shooting the fireball out over all three ships at the pier.

Pacino's missiles had been dead on.

As the fireballs from the destroyers shook the *Tampa* Jack Morris pulled off his mask and hit a quick-release button on his lung's harness. His buoyancy compensator, air bottles, mask and regulator fell off his back and sank into the bay, leaving him feeling light. Still underwater, he kicked off his fins. He found the hull with his sticky solid-rubber shoes and pushed himself along the sloping hull until his head and shoulders emerged from the water. He kept low, crouching down on the aft section of the hull. He cleared the barrel plug of the RPG launcher, loaded it with a mortar grenade and fired at his target on top of the sail.

As the grenade sailed in an arc toward the top of the conning tower, the light of the explosions from the destroyers revealed two men at the top of the sail trying to climb down from the tall fin, trying to escape the explosions, shrapnel and flames. The grenade hit the

lip of the sail and exploded, the fireball small compared to the spectacular detonations of the destroyers.
But it did its duty, dropping the guards at the top of
the sail to the deck, where they rolled off the cylinder
of the ship into the oil-coated water of the slip.

Morris glanced over his shoulder and watched as
the rest of his team jettisoned their Draeger lungs and
fins. Beneath the masks their faces had been painted
with black waterproof battle paint, a special makeup
that withstood sweat, the contact of rubber and sea
water. And blood. The other SEALs joined him on
deck, all falling into a crouch as they pulled equipment
from their vests.

Morris shouldered the RPG and scanned the deck
for any other guards. He could hear the popping of
the silenced MAC-10s of the first platoon targeting
guards who had manned the forward hatch. No guards
were visible on the aft deck after the RPG shot. Morris figured they dived down the access hatches at the
impact of the Javelins, or had gone overboard. In any
case, there was no one topside on the submarine.

Morris opened one of the waterproof pouches of
his combat vest and took out the MAC-10 machine
gun, checked the clip, slipped on the silencer. With
his right thumb he clicked the safety off, keeping the
weapon level in case he needed to put some rounds
forward while he got his other equipment ready. With
his left hand he reached into his combat vest and produced a black balaclava hood, a neoprene ski mask
that he pulled over his face, leaving only his eyes exposed. He plunged his hand back into the vest for the
Beretta and put it in an outside holster strap on the
left side of his belt, withdrew his InterSat VHF radio's
earpiece and lip mike and stuffed the earpiece under
the hood, which held the unit in place. Morris's deployment of his gear had taken less than ten seconds.
He could do it in complete darkness at that rate, and
so could his men.

Thirty seconds later sixteen of them were crouched
on the aft hull, all carrying machine guns, wearing

balaclava hoods and wired into their walkie-talkies. Morris spoke orders into his lip mike, signaling the start of the climb up the slope of the deck, the second and third platoons behind him, the men rushing forward.

As they ran up the deck, the destroyer on the starboard side, the Udaloy, erupted in a secondary explosion that knocked them to the deck and blasted their eardrums. Morris tasted blood in his mouth from a cut lip. He checked the men and saw that the blast from the destroyer had blown two of them overboard. Their forward progress was momentarily halted while the others hauled the men up the treacherous slope of the hull. Morris checked the destroyers. Both ships were burning violently but the secondary explosions seemed to have died down. The Luda was broken in half, its center settling into the bay, while the Udaloy was heeling toward the *Tampa*. Lennox's words in Pacino's stateroom came back to him, about the sinking destroyers sinking the *Tampa* by pulling her down by her own lines.

As the second man was pulled back from the oily water of the slip onto the deck Morris continued ahead, pointing his MAC-10 at the cleats and firing, the rapid burst of Hydra-shok bullets severing the thick manila lines. The aft lines were now cut but that still left six or eight more up forward. Morris discarded the clip and reloaded as he and his team ran on to the aft escape trunk.

The trip from the aft hull had taken less than a minute, but the aft escape trunk was still forty feet ahead. As the black circle of the hatchway neared, Morris thought he saw a dark shape illuminated by the fire raging in the misshapen hull of the neighboring Udaloy. It looked like the top of a head. A guard. Morris's muzzle lowered, his finger tensed, a burst of three shots blasted out toward the black shape, followed by scalp, brains and bone fragments spraying over the deck. A few more seconds and he was running past the aft escape trunk, the body of the

Chinese guard collapsing to the inside of the trunk below. Morris turned just long enough to wave third platoon down the hatch and watched as platoon leader Lieutenant Phil McDermitt ducked down the hatch, moving the body of the Chinese guard out of the way. Third platoon followed. Morris hurried on, leading the remaining men to the forward escape hatch. He watched the hatchway for another face but the opening was quiet. As he slowed to go down the hatch, sniper Chief Richard "Baron" von Brandt sailed past him, pulling Commander Lennox with him.

Morris half-stepped, half-fell down the forward escape trunk, his MAC-10's barrel pointing downward, heart pounding. It was the hottest target he had ever attacked.

As he had done in other SEAL operations, he let his bladder go, knowing that there was no time to "spring a leak" overboard yet there was no way he could let himself be distracted by a full bladder. As he went down the narrow ladder to the small sphere of *Tampa*'s escape hatch, and let go, he could almost hear Black Bart telling the others that Morris "got so scared he pissed his pants again." In a way, he wouldn't have been far off. Without fear Morris long ago would have been dead in the water.

CHAPTER 19

SUNDAY, 12 MAY
1855 GREENWICH MEAN TIME

Bo Hai Bay, Xingang Harbor
PLA Navy Pier 1A, USS *Tampa*
0255 Beijing Time

Chief von Brandt hauled the heavy sniper rifle in one arm and Commander Lennox in the other as he ran forward, dodging the piles of metal and shrapnel lying on the *Tampa*'s oily deck. Baron von Brandt was barely in his thirties, a short man with a deep tan and the round face of a mischievous schoolboy. Baron was also an electronics technician by training, but his value to the SEAL team, aside from his marksman's skills, was his ability to fly any aircraft, including helicopters, jets, ultralights, and even supersonic interceptors or multi-engined transports. He had been given the assignment of gaining the high ground and setting up a sniper station. On a submarine, of course, the only high point was the bridge at the top of the sail, nicely cleared out by Morris's first RPG shot. But there was no guarantee that the bridge had been permanently cleared of armed Chinese. The tunnel to the control room could admit any number of guards from the upper deck of the forward compartment to the bridge cockpit, which meant a guard might be waiting for them on the bridge. Lennox would have to cover him on this one, von Brandt thought. The sniper rifle was too long and bulky to be of much use in taking out a close-range guard, and von Brandt would need to keep the sub's deck clear until Lennox was safe in the bridge.

Von Brandt noted in his peripheral vision that the blown-off superstructure of the Udaloy would allow a firing position from the pier to the deck of the submarine. So they would have to reach the cover of the bridge in a hurry. As they got to the seaward side of the sail von Brandt pushed Lennox in front of him to the rungs of the steel footholds welded to the flank of the sail, the ladder from the cylindrical deck to the bridge above. Lennox began to climb the sheer side of the tall fin, clumsily holding his MAC-10 while climbing.

"Keep your finger in the trigger guard," Baron said into his lip mike, "and be ready to take out anyone in the cockpit!"

Lennox's choked voice acknowledged as he reached the top of the ladder and trained his muzzle right and left. His large body then vanished over the side of the cockpit.

"Anything?" Baron asked as he climbed the rungs of the ladder.

"It's clear," Lennox said, voice steadier.

Von Brandt jumped over the lip of the sail and ducked into the cockpit. At this height the heat from the destroyer's fires was intense. He peered into the shadows of the cockpit, looking for a hidden guard. None.

"Shut the hatch," von Brandt ordered, pointing to the hatch to the control room below. Lennox pulled up the grating under their feet and pushed the heavy hatch until it shut. "I can't dog it from above," he said. "The operator is only on the interior."

"Leave it. We'll know if we're getting company. You stay low and wait. The only time I want your head to come up over the edge of the sail is when we're ready to go."

Von Brandt peered out over the lip of the sail forward, then to either side. The deck of the ship was deserted. All three platoons had vanished down the hatches of the ship. Slowly Brandt climbed to the top of the sail from the aft bulkhead of the cockpit, keeping low to the top of the structure where he could see clearly yet not be picked off from the deck. He pulled the covers off both ends of the sniper scope, unplugged the muzzle, checked the magazine and sighted in on the mooring lines amidships.

It took two full magazines to cut the ship's mooring lines so that the ship was free, drifting in the oily slip.

"Hey, Commander," von Brandt said as he climbed back down into the cockpit, "we're underway. Shift colors and sound a long blast on the ship's whistle."

"Not funny. I need to look, need to see the current and the ship's position. If I'm gonna drive this thing out of here I need to visualize the slip."

"Okay, but make it quick. A snapshot."

Von Brandt wanted to raise third platoon. The escape plan called for a man to crouch in the aft escape trunk and maintain communications between the sail and the men in the engineroom. It wasn't likely the Chinese would anticipate commandos trying to control the ship from the aft end. More likely they would heavily defend the control room, figuring it to be the key to the ship. But if the nukes aft could get propulsion they could take control of the rudder, and with Lennox in the sail and communications with the walkie-talkies, Lennox and the nukes alone could drive the ship away from the pier. It was all up to third platoon now, von Brandt thought as he tried the radio, knowing that the VHF signal could not penetrate the steel of the hull but would be heard by the SEAL in the escape trunk.

"Stinky, this is Baron. You up?"

No answer. Von Brandt crawled back on the top of the sail to get a look at the aft deck. Still no guards on deck, but there was also no sign of Petty Officer David "Stinky" Welsh. Probably too early for the engineroom to be taken, von Brandt thought. He climbed back into the cockpit and looked out over the forward deck. Still nothing on deck.

So far, at least from what could be seen from the sail, the operation had gone off as planned—until the armored column of PLA troops raced up the pier and screeched to a halt on the other side of the burned-out hulk of the Udaloy. Four armored personnel carriers, three tanks and five units of self-propelled artillery began training their weapons on the sail while heavily armed PLA troops deployed from the APCs. Typical, von Brandt thought. He spoke into his lip mike:

"Stinky, if you're up, we've got company, man. Hurry the hell up with the nuclear power."

Lennox popped his head up for a moment then dropped back down, his voice coming over von Brandt's headset. "Shit."

"Deep," von Brandt added, setting up to shoot at the PLA troops. "Those troops will be opening fire any second."

"What troops?"

"You didn't see them on the pier? What'd you say 'shit' for?"

"The frigate astern," Lennox said. "Didn't you see it? It's getting underway ..."

"Tanks on the pier, a sub-killing frigate started up and pulling into the bay. A perfect end to a shitty day."

"Could be worse," Lennox said.

"How?"

"We could have helicopters inbound," Lennox said.

Van Brandt was about to agree when the sound of helicopter rotors sounded from the distance, the chopping sound beating out a death knell for the operation.

Lieutenant Phillip McDermitt was a red-haired, freckle-faced Irishman, slightly heavy for his height but the strongest in his platoon, leading his men in every physical activity the SEALs trained in. An Academy grad, McDermitt was single and known as a womanizer or a romantic, depending on the observer's point-of-view. His radio handle was "He-She," from an incident in Naples, Italy, when the gorgeous "lady" he had picked up for the evening had turned out to be a transvestite. Still hungover, he had told the story the next day, forgetting that SEALs have long memories. The nickname had stuck ever since, in spite of his move from the west coast to the east. Before his arrival at SEAL Team Seven a phone call had been received at Black Bart's desk informing them that Lieutenant Phillip McDermitt was to be addressed properly. When he first reported to Morris's office, in dress blues, at rigid attention, Morris had smiled and said, "Welcome aboard, He-She." McDermitt had cursed but taken it like a man. He had no choice.

McDermitt was the first SEAL down the hatch of the aft escape trunk after Morris shot the Chinese guard who had been lying in ambush inside. McDermitt dropped the five feet to the bottom of the spherical escape trunk without using the ladder, his feet coming to rest on the body of the Chinese guard. For a moment he considered dropping the body inside the ship to see if it drew fire but decided against that, pushing the body aside with his foot, making sure the hatch to the deck below was clear. His chief, Lyle "Padre" Gerald, landed next to him as McDermitt tossed the grenade down to the deck and immediately began to climb down the ladder. A second later the grenade exploded.

Lube Oil Vaughn had noticed the guards' alarm when the first explosion had rocked the ship. For the first time in days, Vaughn felt a sliver of hope—a rescue mission had to be underway. He had kept a careful eye on the anxious guard, who seemed distracted enough to be overcome. Vaughn made eye contact with his reactor operator and electrical operator. Both men were obviously thinking the same thing, nodding at Vaughn knowingly. When the second explosion came, the guard was momentarily knocked against the jamb of the door to maneuvering, and without thinking, Vaughn launched himself toward the armed guard, wondering where the guard's AK-47 bullet would hit him. The reactor operator and electrical operator were just behind him. The RO went low, grabbing the muz-

zle of the AK-47 while the EO came at the guard
from his other shoulder. In a crazy instant that extended into what seemed an hour Vaughn saw the
guard's throat coming closer, his fingers wrapping
around it, the guard's head slowly turning to look at
Vaughn, his eyes registering what was happening to
him.

Time seemed to speed back up as the force of
Vaughn's body impacted the guard. The guard's head
hit the wall with a cracking noise, Vaughn plowed into
the guard's chest, the man's weight dragged him
toward the deck. By then the RO had a grip on the
AK-47 and the EO was pulling the guard's feet up,
dumping him to the deck. Vaughn saw the AK-47 barrel rising, then turning back down toward the deck—
the RO had the rifle and was aiming at the guard. For
the third time in a minute an explosion filled the
room, the rifle-muzzle blast inches from Vaughn's face
as the RO fired into the guard's chest. Vaughn's ears
rang as he pulled himself upright. He grabbed the
AK-47 from the RO, ready to shoot the next Chinese
he saw, when the grenade exploded below the after-
escape hatch. Not five seconds after they had over-
powered the one guard, the other guard on the upper
level had lobbed a grenade.

McDermitt shut his eyes for an instant after tossing a
grenade to the deck of the aft compartment. It exploded directly below him, but it was a simple flash-
bang unit producing an incredibly loud explosion, a
blinding flash and a roomful of smoke, but no other
damage. Under the cover of the grenade's smoke
McDermitt came down the ladder two steps at a time,
the other SEALs behind him. By the time the smoke
cleared the seven SEALs of third platoon were in-hull
and running from the impact point of the grenade.

Four of them bolted for the ladder to the lower
levels, where a two-man team would clear the middle
level and a second team would secure the lower level
of the aft compartment. McDermitt and Chief Gerald

hurried for the walled-in room aft of the escape trunk—the maneuvering room that was the control for the entire propulsion plant and would be a key space to secure in order to get the *Tampa* out on its own power.

As McDermitt approached the side-entrance door to the maneuvering room he saw the barrel of the Chinese AK-47 rifle coming down and forward, aimed right at him. McDermitt pointed his MAC-10, his finger tensed on the trigger guard as he ran toward the door and saw the edge of a head in the clearing smoke, and aimed for it ...

When the heavyset broad-shouldered man in black pajamas, black ski mask, black vest and black submachine gun materialized out of the smoke of the grenade blast Vaughn nearly got off a round—when he realized that Chinese guards did not wear ski masks, did not stand over six feet tall and did not have eyes as blue as the ones staring at him.

"Hold your damn fire," the man's voice boomed in a Mississippi accent, "we're a SEAL team. We're here to get this ship the hell out."

Vaughn felt like hugging the commando, who seemed to be sizing him up.

"You the engineer?"

"Yes."

"How fast can you start up the reactor and get ready to crank out power?"

"By the book, an hour, for you, the main engines at full RPMs in a couple minutes."

The SEAL handed Vaughn a walkie-talkie and a Beretta pistol. "I'll be back," he said, and disappeared.

"Have the scram breakers reset and latch all rods and pull," Vaughn ordered.

The rods were already coming out of the core as the muffled sound of automatic rifle fire sounded from the lower levels of the aft compartment. The reactor power meter's needle came off zero and rose to forty percent. The steam in the headers filled the space with roaring heat and the sound of the turbines whining at thirty-six hundred RPM aft of maneuvering was the sweetest sound Vaughn could remember hearing.

CHAPTER 20

SUNDAY, 12 MAY
1858 GREENWICH MEAN TIME

Bo Hai Bay, Xingang Harbor
PLA Navy Pier 1A, USS *Tampa*
0258 Beijing Time

Ensign Ted "Buffalo" Sauer, the leader of the first platoon, was worried as he glanced at the forward deck of the *Tampa*. The first problem was the slick sonar dome of the ship at the bow—its surface was incredibly slippery, the combination of smooth plastic, slimy buildup from the ship's days in port and the oily scum from the Chinese bay on top of the slime. The dome would be tough to climb, the only available path right up the centerline. But that would cause their insertion aboard the *Tampa* to be a single-file climb, leaving them naked. That led to the second problem, the guards on the deck. One guard had been smoking a cigarette, leaning on the forward leading-edge of the sail. At least one other guard, perhaps two, was visible on top of the sail in the bridge cockpit, and they had an excellent firing position for killing off the first platoon. Buffalo could only hope Morris would come through, and that the Javelins would fly straight and not forget to explode.

Buffalo pulled his MAC-10 out of his vest while still floating in the bay and unplugged the muzzle, motioning to Chief Buckethead Williams to do likewise. The sudden roar of the Javelin explosion on the destroyer to their right slammed their eardrums, the mushroom cloud lighting up the sky. The platoon ducked underwater, waiting for the second impact. Soon the second Javelin hit, the crippled destroyers filling the sky with pulsating fireballs. The second detonation, stronger than the first, blew flames and shrapnel onto the deck of the *Tampa,* even knocking one of the guards by the sail overboard. Buffalo and Buckethead opened fire on the guards, shooting in three-round bursts, and Buffalo dropped the two remaining guards on the deck.

It was then that the RPG exploded on the port lip of the cockpit. Buffalo could see one guard drop to the deck. He didn't wait for the second. He motioned the platoon on, and as he kept his machine gun aimed at the deck, four of his shooters made their way slowly up the slick slope of the bow, gaining ground at the more level hull near the hatch. They crouched under the cover of the sail, rapidly pulling gear out of their combat vests. The SEALs were vulnerable but it had to be done. When the four shooters from his platoon had their weapons deployed, he and Buckethead tucked their guns in their vests and climbed the slope of the sonar dome. Once on deck, Buffalo pulled out his ski mask, radio and MAC-10, replacing the clip with fresh ammunition. He tested his radio, then ordered the platoon to go below.

As usual on a SEAL OP the commander of a unit went first—SEALs did not believe in leading from the rear. Buffalo took the ladder rungs two at a time and dropped silently to the deck, leveling his machine gun at the approaches to the ladder. The space seemed deserted. He was in a narrow passageway running fore-and-aft.

At six feet five inches tall and two hundred and fifty pounds, "Buffalo" (short for "Water Buffalo") Sauer was the proverbial gentle giant, except on an OP. His moniker and radio handle came from his inordinate need for water—drinking, not swimming, although some thought the latter was linked in some mysterious fashion to the former, and hence his joining up with the SEALs. Unlike Morris, Buffalo Sauer seemed quiet to passive on the outside, but Morris and those around Sauer knew that that had nothing to do with the toughness inside, all of which Sauer needed now.

He ordered the assembled platoon to go, and covered the ladderway to the hatch above while the men proceeded up the stairs to the middle level. As he joined them he thought he heard something in the captain's stateroom, some sort of struggle, but his orders were to stick to the plan. The upper level of the forward compartment was Commander Morris' assignment. To stay here would put the team in danger of being in the path of Morris' bullets. Buffalo continued down the steep staircase to the middle level, emerging into a narrow passageway that ran the length of the compartment.

He sent a two-man team into a door leading to the petty officers' quarters, a second team to the port crew berthing rooms, while he and the remaining men continued aft along the passageway to its termination at the crew's mess. For a space that should be holding the entire ship's crew, the level so far had been lifeless, as had the upper level. It wasn't possible that all the guards had been killed when he and the platoon had come aboard . . . or could the Chinese have evacuated the ship before the SEALs got there?

Buffalo and Buckethead slowly approached the mess, one of the largest spaces aboard, roughly the size of a small restaurant. The last time Buffalo had raided a 688-class ship the men in the mess had been watching a movie. Taking it had been easy. But now the room could be a holding pen for several dozen prisoners, guarded by ten or more armed Chinese. Buffalo looked into Buckethead Williams's eyes. No question, the man was pumped, his forehead broken out in sweat, his pupils dilated.

For a moment Buffalo wished he could just lob a stun grenade into the mess. He had considered it when he and Morris had drawn up the assault plan but Morris had vetoed it. The prisoners would be suffering from lack of food, respiratory infections and weakness. A stun grenade that would paralyze a Chinese guard for a half hour might well kill a man suffering from pneumonia and starvation.

As Buffalo neared the end of the passageway, he could see men in the crew's mess. He waved Buckethead in behind him as he accelerated into a sprint and ran into the room.

The next seconds seemed hours, the effect of the shot of adrenaline as he crashed into the room, a world of slow motion. Every bench was full of seated men, all wearing blue coveralls, most with their heads on the table tops. The floor space between tables was crammed with bodies, also wearing the blue submariner's coveralls. Their faces were paper white, thin, emaciated. A memory was keyed in his mind; the faces reminded him of the pictures he'd seen depicting the prisoners in Nazi death camps. The next impression that hit him was the awful stench. The men had been in a sweatbox for days, sitting in their own filth. It was like a stockyard.

Buffalo looked up to the aft bulkhead. Along the wall a row of Chinese guards stood at semi-attention, all wearing Mao jackets and liberty caps with the red star in the center. The guards' faces were starting to move in reaction to the entry of the SEALs. The next sound Buffalo heard was automatic rifle fire, the cough of a close MAC-10. The sound was coming from his own gun, his body reflexively aiming and firing. The chests of the guards spotted red as the bullets smashed into them. Surprise had neutralized them—for a moment.

He heard a rapid series of shots from over his right shoulder, gunshots that were not the rapid *blips* of the silenced MAC-10s but the deep-throated barking of an AK-47. He pivoted, bringing up his weapon, and saw a guard standing against the forward bulkhead in the blind corner along the port side. The guard was emptying his clip, shooting every round he had, not at the SEALs but at the helpless, prostrate men on the deck and at the tables. Buffalo, in a rage, leveled his MAC-10 at the guard, and fired ten rounds into the man's chest, knowing he should have budgeted only three but the fury of the moment had taken over. He had a brief impression of the other SEALs targeting the guard, the man's chest exploding, yet he continued to fire into the prisoners, as he sank to the deck. At least a dozen men had been hit or killed.

Buffalo started to call Doc Sheffield to attend them while he and Buckethead took the remainder of the middle level deck. The call was interrupted by the sound of rifle fire coming from the starboard side of the middle level. Officers' country. He reloaded, checked Buckethead and ran forward to the passageway and toward the door to the wardroom. He took a deep breath, allowing himself just a moment to try to clear his mind of the awful scene he'd just left and prepare himself for what was coming.

Jack Morris shielded his eyes as "Cowpie" Clites' acetylene torch burned through the side of the forward escape trunk. They were forced to cut through it rather than exit by the lower hatch, which led down to the crew's mess. With the hostages being held there, an entering team would be shot by the guards. Finally, Clites and "Pig" Wilson pulled in the circle of steel cut by the torch. Morris stepped into the navigation room, blinking as his eyes adjusted to the comparative brightness of the compartment's fluorescent lights. He felt the strange sensation of his mind fissioning into two separate but parallel parts, one side focused on the action of the present, a second on recording and analyzing. The forward compartment, as Morris knew from his raids on other 688-class submarines, took up roughly the forward forty percent of the submarine. It was separated from the reactor compartment by a thick-shielded steel bulkhead with only one door in the middle level. So even though he came from the forward escape trunk, he was now in the furthest aft portion of this part of the sub. The port end of the room led to the fan room, the starboard to the radio room. A forward door led to control. A ladderway dropped to the lower decks.

Morris stepped away from the trunk to allow the other men of the second platoon to follow him, while he crouched down, his weapon seeking guards who could come from the radio room door, the fan room, or forward. For a moment he thought back to Norfolk Naval Air Station, where Admiral Donchez had given him the full picture of the Bo Hai Bay operation and assured him that he and his men could liberate the *Tampa*.

Now he wasn't so sure. *Something* inevitably went wrong with every operation—nothing was ever all right. What was it this time? The screwup with the cruise missiles? Something else waiting to mess them up? Now that his men's footsteps were coming from the escape trunk the time for worrying was over.

As the last man entered, Morris gave the order to go. The second platoon assignments paired platoon leader Lieutenant "Pig" Wilson with platoon chief "Python" Harris. They would act as a two-man team and head for the torpedo room on the forward end of the lower level. A misdirected bullet or ricochet could detonate a torpedo's self-oxidizing fuel or explode a warhead, and if that was to be the flaw in the operation it would be a fatal one for everybody aboard. "Cowpie" Clites and "Droopy" Garnes were also to go to the lower level and take the aft end including the auxiliary machinery room, then cover Pig and Python. "Mad Dog" Martin and "Red Meat" Reynolds would take the critical middle level, critical because the bulk of the guards were expected there, as were the hostages, since the middle level contained the crew spaces. That left Morris paired with "Bony" Robbins to take the upper level, including the radio room, navigation space, the control room, sonar and the captain's and XO's staterooms. The assault would have to be surgical, to avoid damaging equipment. Only a few physical systems could take a bullet and survive. A bullet hole in a sonar equipment cabinet would mean they would be deaf on the way out. A bullet hole in a periscope optics module would make them blind.

After checking the radio room and the fan room, Jack Morris and Bony Robbins advanced to the door to the control room. Morris peered in through a small round red-glassed window, and seeing no one, kicked the door open.

At that moment the Chinese guards in the control room opened up, all ten AK-47s bursting into violent life at once, the blast of the Chinese bullets shattering the door and cutting it to ribbons.

Chief Baron von Brandt raised his head after the helicopter rotor noises subsided. The flyover had been a reconnaissance, at least on the first pass. As the choppers flew back to the east a half-mile away, von Brandt sighted his sniper scope on the man who seemed to be in command of the PLA troops on the pier. No head shots, Baron thought, only hearts. He put the commander's upper left chest in the crosshairs, exhaled slowly and steadily and slowly squeezed the trigger, hoping to make the shot a surprise even to himself, to keep him from jerking the rifle. The unit barely recoiled as it sent the heavy grain Hydra-Shok bullet toward the commander at thirty-eight hundred feet per second.

The bullet spun out of the barrel, dropping slightly as gravity dragged it down toward the pier and the water of the slip. After a total flight time of twenty-eight milliseconds, the bullet penetrated the fabric of the man's tunic two inches from the central seam. The fabric vaporized as the round contacted it, its kinetic energy at the tip the equivalent of an acetylene torch. The skin below the fabric yielded next, then the thin layer of fatty tissue before the muscle that lined the chest. The bullet entered a cavity between two ribs and proceeded on through the lung, blowing apart several airways, then on to the outer layer of the man's heart, where it severed two coronary arteries before entering and destroying the right ventricle.

The damage from the bullet by this time would have been enough to kill the PLA commander, but the Hydra-Shok round was specially designed to resonate within the cavity of the man's abdomen, setting up a shock wave in his chest area, the pulsations causing what ballistics scientists called hydraulic shock. The effect of the shock wave was the immediate traumatization of the entire abdominal cavity, shutting down every organ, shorting out every nerve, cracking several ribs and vertebrae, bursting veins and arteries. The effect of the nerve-shorting trauma was an instantaneous overload of the brain stem receiving the electrical impulses from the spinal cord.

As life was being extinguished, the bullet, now wobbling and misshapen, passed out of the body, flew out over the north end of the pier and splashed into the water of the slip. As it sank, steam boiled from it for just an instant, its surface temperature elevated from the friction of the flight. On the pier the PLA commander's face froze as he collapsed onto the oily concrete. He never knew what had hit him.

By the time the PLA commander's knees had begun to buckle, von Brandt had drawn a bead on the vice-commander and fired, then targeted the lieutenants on the pier. As their officers died, the troops hit the concrete. The only problem now, von Brandt thought, was that there was no antidote to the tanks. They hadn't planned on using LAW rockets on this OP—who could expect tanks on a warship raid? Now it looked like they were going to pay for that mistake. On the pier, two of the tanks rotated their turrets, their guns aiming at the *Tampa*'s sail. Von Brandt ducked back into the cockpit, not sure how to break the news to Lennox that they had only seconds until the tank fired.

The sound of the helicopter rotors rose into a crescendo as the two Dauphin choppers returned, swooping in from the northeast, their flanks bristling with large-bore guns. The bullets from their guns blasted across the top of the sail, sparks flying from the impact of the heavy bullets against the high-tensile steel.

Once the helicopters flew by, one of the tanks on the pier opened up, the sound from its gun echoing across the calm water of the slip, a *whoosh* marking the flight of its projectile as the round flew overhead and dropped down into the water, the first explosion rocking the submarine.

Von Brandt shouted into his lip mike: "Stinky? If you're up talk to me. We've got trouble up here—"

"BARON, THIS IS STINKY. WE'VE GOT PRO-PULSION—GIVE US AN ENGINE ORDER."

"Go," von Brandt yelled at Lennox. "Get us the hell out of here!"

Lennox lifted his head up over the starboard aft lip of the sail, looking for the position of the Jianghu fast frigate, which was nowhere in sight. Only the gentle waves in the slip testified to its rapid departure. Off in the smoke-filled distance to the south, toward the supertanker pier, Lennox thought he saw the super-structure of the frigate. It would be going after the *Seawolf,* he thought.

As Lennox began to speak the second round was fired from a tank on the pier, this shot grazing the forward lip of the sail, its explosive force dissipating over the grave of the neighboring Luda but the force still enough to smash Lennox and von Brandt into the deck.

"All back full," Lennox shouted.

"ROGER, ALL BACK FULL," his earpiece replied.

Lennox waited, hoping the ship would move, the agonizing seconds ticking off as the first tank adjusted the aim of its gun at the sail, the third shot guaranteed not to miss. Lennox thought he could hear helicopter rotors again, but the sound no longer bothered him— the ship was *moving,* it was really moving. The pier and the burned-out hulls of the destroyers were fading forward of them, the open water of the bay ap-proaching from aft. For a moment he couldn't tell whether the shout of exultation he heard was his or Baron von Brandt's.

The tank on the pier, now almost a shiplength away,

fired and missed, its aim now off, the *Tampa*'s motion
confusing the turret operator. Lennox popped his head
up to watch the end of the pier sail by, the wake of
the ship's motion white and glowing from phosphorescence in the water of the slip, the warm salty breeze
over the sail dissipating the smells of the gunfire.

The sail neared the end of the pier, the tanks and
troops now far away.

"Right full rudder. I say again, right full rudder."

The helicopters zoomed in low for another pass,
their bullets strafing the sail. Lennox ducked as the
bullets whizzed by, amazed that again he'd survived a
strafing run. For the first time in years he felt totally
alive. Coming this close to death enhanced the sense
of life. There was something about the approach to
death, especially the evasion of it, that was unique.
Lennox waved his fist in the air at the troops on the
pier and at the receding silhouettes of the choppers.

He even shouted: "You missed me, now you can kiss
me." He looked over at von Brandt, to share the moment, when he noticed that Baron wasn't moving, and
that a dark stain was spreading over his face. Lennox's
balloon was instantly deflated.

CHAPTER 21

SUNDAY, 12 MAY
1905 GREENWICH MEAN TIME

Bo Hai Bay, Xingang Harbor
USS *Tampa*
0305 Beijing Time

Jack Morris looked over at Bony Robbins, both men's faces pressed down on the cool tile of the deck aft of the control room. Gunfire from the control room had suddenly stopped. Every weapon had exhausted its clip of ammunition at the same time. Stupid, Morris thought, to shoot at shadows and use a whole clip at once. He gave Robbins a shrug as he reached for a stun grenade, pulled the arming pin with his index finger and rolled it into the control room. The stun grenade sounded, and soon after, the panicked coughing of a room full of Chinese guards.

Morris grabbed a second grenade and tossed it in after the first one. As it went off he heard the sound of weapons clattering to the deck. He reached into his vest's side pocket and pulled out swimming goggles and a spongy filter mask similar to a surgeon's except that it had no straps and was moist—a wet filter. He slipped the mask under his balaclava hood and strapped on the goggles over his eyes. A glance at Bony confirmed that his teammate was similarly equipped. Morris gave the order to go in.

He rose up slightly and ran into the room, cutting to the right. The place was completely filled with the smoke of the stun grenade, traces of it leaking through the gaskets of Morris's goggles and making his eyes water. Actually the grenade was a simple smoke bomb surrounded by the stun solution, which was nothing but the juices of pepper, including jalapenos; the pepper juices had the effect of causing mucous membranes to water and swell. An exploding stun grenade within twenty feet of a man's face would literally shut his eyes with a painful watering, cause his nose to run and nearly close off his throat. The gunmen would be on the deck, grabbing their throats, gasping for breath, blinded. The grenade was far more effective than tear gas, though within some thirty minutes a victim would be normal. The major problem was keeping the mucous membranes of the attackers from suffering the same effects as the targets.

Morris heard the spasms of men coughing as he ran forward along the attack center row of consoles. He could make out the shapes of the enemy on the deck, still suffering from the stun grenades. Morris aimed his machine gun, careful that his bullets would not hit equipment or ricochet into consoles. A scene like this would never play well in Hollywood, he thought—too cold-blooded. The movies would show the commandos roping the Chinese together as prisoners. Bullshit, he thought as he fired. This was real time, real life. A killing job. Them or us.

The ten guards were dead. Morris ejected his clip and replaced it. He looked up at Robbins, who nodded back at him. They moved to the door on the forward bulkhead, on the centerline, which led to the captain's and XO's staterooms, the sonar display room and forward to the weapons-shipping hatch and the sonar equipment space. The two crouched on either side of the door. As Morris was about to kick the door open, a rumbling sound began, followed by a deep growl. The room's smoke vanished in a blast of cool, clean air. The nukes back aft must have gotten the reactor restarted, he decided. He kicked the forward door open, and saw that down the passageway the captain's stateroom door was opening. He aimed his weapon at the doorjamb, and as the Chinese officer came out of the door he prepared to fire—when he saw something that stopped him.

"Hold it," he whispered into his lip mike to Bony.

The PLA officer was holding a hostage, one of the ship's officers, and had an automatic pistol up against his hostage's head. By the look on the hostage's face he was in bad shape, perhaps unconscious.

"I'm holding the ship's captain," the PLA officer said in an odd accent, the lilting sound of it partly Chinese, partly aristocratic British. "Withdraw or I will be forced to kill him."

"Go for it," Morris said. "You realize you'll never make it to—"

And interrupted himself by opening fire.

He had been through hundreds of training scenarios like this one, and had connected with the terrorist ninety-eight percent of the time. He would have been dead-on with this shot too, if the ship had not unexpectedly lurched just as he was firing. The good news was that the *Tampa* was obviously underway, accelerating backward away from the PLA pier, the mission to free the ship now into its second phase.

The bad news was that Jack Morris, inadvertently, had just hit the hostage.

USS *Seawolf*

The sound of a faint rumbling noise could be heard through the hull of the control room. Pacino looked up at the sonar monitor selected to the hull array and noted the noise streaks on the screen.

"Sonar, Captain," he said into his boom microphone, "what'ya got?"

"Conn, Sonar," Chief Jeb drawled, "explosions bearing three four eight, bearing to PLA piers. Sounds like secondary detonations after the two main explosions. Tough to tell."

Pacino raised his voice to the watchstanders in the room: "Lookaround number-two scope." The Diving

Officer reported their depth at seventy-nine feet, speed zero knots.

The periscope seemed to take a full minute to climb out of the well. Impatiently Pacino crouched, snapping the grips down as soon as the optic module came up at the deck level, putting his eye on the eyepiece before the unit rose to knee level.

The view was black, the scope lens only breaking the oily water of the bay as the optic module thumped into the stops at the overhead. Pacino had moved the ship two thousand yards down the channel to the southeast of the supertanker-piers, then turning so his bow faced the action at Xingang, hoping to be positioned to get a better view of the PLA piers than he had had of the tanker-pier point. But when the lens cleared Pacino saw nothing but orange-and-white flames, the massive balls of fire sent up by the impact of the Javelin explosions. As he watched, a secondary explosion flared from the PLA piers, this fireball's diameter a shiplength wide, the glow from it making the scene seem lit by the sun at midday. Pacino could only hear one thought in his head: *I sure hope that's not your ship I see burning, Sean.*

"Down scope," Pacino called reluctantly.

Now that his window to the outside world was again shut, Pacino paced the periscope platform, frustrated. For the moment the operation was out of his hands. He had to trust that the SEALs could pull this off. But what about the Javelins? Had the SEALs realized what was happening in time? Or had the explosions fried them as they had the ships at the pier? And what if the missiles had ripped into the *Tampa*? What if the detonations had killed the SEALs in the water, or set off their contact charges while they were still diving beneath the hulls of the destroyers? *And* what if the Chinese were now sending warships to kill the *Seawolf,* now that her position was compromised from the Javelin launches? There was no way of knowing, short of more periscope exposure, which would imperil the crew of *Seawolf.*

He itched to get the *Seawolf* into action, a chance to do something to save his friend, something other than pace the conn in suspension—suddenly, his headset crackled.

"Conn, Sonar, we have a diesel engine startup bearing three five two. Bearing correlates to the pier position of Target Four, Jianghu Type II fast frigate. Captain, we now have twin screw noises at high RPM. I'd guess Target Four is getting underway to come see us."

Pacino didn't acknowledge Chief Jeb. At his last words Pacino had already called out "lookaround number-two scope" and raised the periscope. As the lens broke the surface he saw the Jianghu frigate backing into the bay from the pier, the wake at her stern foaming up as she reversed her screws. The bow of the vessel turned toward him, the bow wave building up as the ship accelerated, the tall central mast waving flags lit by a spotlight, the wash of the light illuminating the exhaust smoke pouring out of her stack. Pacino called out to the control room watchstanders without removing his eye from the scope.

"I've got Target Four, Jianghu-class frigate, underway and making high-speed turns directly toward us. Standby for observation ... Bearing mark. Range mark, two divisions in low power, angle-on-the-bow zero. Down scope."

"We have a firing solution, Captain," Firecontrol coordinator Keebes reported from the firecontrol consoles of the attack center. "Recommend shooting."

"Very well. Attention in the firecontrol team. We're going to shoot two torpedoes down the bearing to Target Four, give him something for breakfast. Weps, set Mark 50 torpedoes in tubes three and four to surface homing mode, shallow transit, medium-to-low active snake search, wake homing mode on reacquisition, anti-self homing disabled, anti-circular run disabled. Report status."

"Sir, tubes three and four are lined up, Mark 50s," Feyley reported from the weapons console, repeating back Pacino's mode selections, his voice sounding doubtful at Pacino's orders to disable the safety interlocks on the weapons. Pacino looked at Keebes, waiting for Keebes to object to risking the ship with torpedoes that could turn around and impact *Seawolf*. None came.

"Firing-point procedures, tubes three and four, Target Four," Pacino ordered, raising the periscope. "Final bearing and shoot."

"Ship ready," Officer of the Deck Turner reported.

"Weapons ready," Feyley called.

"Solution pending," Keebes said.

Pacino's eye hit the eyepiece at waist level as the optic module rose from the well.

"Observation, Target Four . . ."

"Ready," Keebes said.

"Bearing . . . mark!" The frigate's bow was plowing directly toward them, her slender bow slicing the calm waters of the bay, her guns trained on their position, a crew of men standing at the antisubmarine mortar launcher in the fo'c'sle. The crosshairs of the periscope reticle framed the graceful form of the ship, and the odd thought came to Pacino that the frigate was truly beautiful, an elegant efficient design. He smirked in self-mockery: a beautiful ship, bent on killing him. "Range mark! Four divisions in low power, angle-on-the-bow zero. Down scope."

The screws of the ship could be heard with the naked ear through the steel of the hull, the throbbing thrashing sound of their angry cavitation a clear indication of the frigate's hostile intention.

"Solution ready," Keebes said.

"Set." Feyley.

Pacino was about to call *shoot* when sonar called over his headset:

"Conn, Sonar, we've got steam turbine transients and screw noises from bearing three four five, correlates to Friendly One. The *Tampa*'s underway!"

"Check fire!" Pacino half-shouted, realizing that the two torpedoes, if they missed the frigate on the first attempt, would surely detect the hull of the *Tampa* and put her on the bottom. The screws of the frigate got louder, the sound of the violent pumping noise now blaring through the space, forcing Pacino to shout to be heard.

"Diving Officer, flood depth control at full-open and keep flooding till we bottom out," Pacino ordered. If the frigate didn't turn it would run right on top of them, easily shear off the sail or rip open the pressure hull. The deck sank under Pacino's feet, his stomach rising as if he were on an elevator in a skyscraper, the ship plunging to the bottom of the deep channel.

The screw of the frigate passed overhead, its loud *floosh* rising to a crescendo from directly overhead, then fading away again astern. The deck below thumped as the ship's keel hit the bottom of the channel.

"Ship's on the bottom, Captain," the diving officer reported.

"That bitch ran right on top of us, Skipper," Keebes said, looking down at the Pos Two display. "Let's hope he's not going to drop depth charges this way."

"Conn, Sonar, Target Four is turning around and heading back for the PLA piers at max speed."

"Probably heading back for the *Tampa*," Keebes said.

The screw of the frigate passed overhead again, just as loud and insistent as the first time.

"Dive, blow depth control and get us back up, fast, depth seven nine," Pacino commanded. *"Observation number-two scope, target four."*

The scope was up before the Diving Officer was able to get the ship back to periscope depth. Pacino waited, his lens trained upward, watching the lights from the pier fires reflecting off the gentle waves above, cursing the ship's inertia. But now, though he felt the same impatience, he felt the steely sensation of control. He was back in command, once again able to influence the outcome of this fight. And the *Tampa* was underway.

His exhilaration plunged when chief sonarman Jeb

reported over the headset the sound of helicopters
hovering at the bearing to the *Tampa*.

USS *TAMPA*

Buffalo Sauer crouched outside the door to the wardroom in the forward compartment middle level, straining to hear the radio report from Buckethead
Williams, who had slipped through a passageway to
the second door to the wardroom. As Sauer set up
with Williams, he was nearly thrown to the deck by
the lurch of the ship as it accelerated backward. Buffalo glanced at his watch—Baron and the ship's XO
had gotten the vessel underway right on time, he
thought.

When Buckethead reported that he was ready, Buffalo called out the order to storm the room and then
kicked in the locked door. Actually the door did not
open fully but stopped halfway. And even as Buffalo
saw the reason for the door stopping he realized that
he was in for another scene like he'd just survived
from the crew's mess. The body of a man on the floor
had kept the door from opening all the way. The man
leaned against a sideboard, legs thrown out in front
of him, eyes sunk deep in his sockets, face terribly
pale.

Buffalo launched himself into the room, trying to
avoid stepping on the man's legs. Once he was inside
the stench hit him, as bad as it had been in the crew's
mess. He had a brief impression of the room around
him, the central feature being a large table used for
the officers' meals and meetings. On top of the table
were two bodies, the skin of their faces green with
decay, the foreheads open and raw from bullet
wounds. Both men looked vaguely young, although
the bloating of the corpses hid their ages, as did the
facial wounds. They were both wearing the silver dual-
bar insignia of lieutenants. The thought occurred to
Buffalo that the men in the room were meant to see

the butchered, decaying corpses of their fellow officers, perhaps as a reminder not to do what they had done. Perhaps the dead lieutenants had tried to escape or defy the guards.

Seated around the table were the ship's officers, eight of them. The scene was eerily grotesque, as if the Chinese captors had insisted that the officers sit about the table with the dead bodies lying out on it like some sort of nightmare meal. Each man's chair was drawn up to the table, and the men on the far side of the room all had their heads on the table. The others, the ones with their backs to the doors, were sitting straight up, as if at attention. Whether that was by order of the guards or because of revulsion at the dead bodies, Buffalo had no clue. For a moment Buffalo was reminded of plebe year at the Academy, the harassed plebes sitting around their tables at attention, forbidden to look at their plates, their eyes locked into the distance by order of the first-class midshipmen. The men at the table had eyes staring blankly like that, except haunted by madness rather than mere fear.

Buffalo looked toward the wall of the room opposite his door and saw Buckethead sailing into the room. For a moment he wondered what had taken Williams so long, but then as he saw the way Buckethead's body seemed to float slowly into the room he realized that he was experiencing the dilation of time peculiar to intense injections of adrenaline, and that he himself had only been inside the room for less than a second. Williams saw the scene in the corner of the room at the same time Buffalo did.

A Chinese guard had a pistol to the head of one of the officers seated at the table. As he watched, the guard pulled the trigger. Before Buffalo or Buckethead could react, the guard turned his pistol to the next man at the table and fired. The man slouched in his chair, his head hitting the table. It was only then that Buffalo realized that the men against the far wall had their heads on the table because each of them had already been executed.

For a moment Buffalo was thrown off-balance as the guard continued to execute the men at the table rather than defend himself by shooting at the invading SEALs, and by the awful reality of watching men being executed at a table without resistance. What had these men seen that paralyzed them so, even in the face of certain death?

One answer came as Buffalo aimed his MAC-10 at the guard and squeezed the trigger, the Hydra-Shok bullets exploding the interior of the guard's abdomen, his pistol dropping to the ground as his body slammed against the aft bulkhead and slipped toward the deck. The answer in Buffalo's mind kept his trigger finger tensed, continuing to shoot into the guard's body. These men had seen things so horrible that they no longer wanted to live. For them, death was a deliverance.

Buffalo was suddenly thrown into the sideboard by the force of the ship turning, the deck tilting as the ship came around. He found himself staring into the glassy eyes of the man lying on the deck, the one who had been lucky enough not to have had to sit and stare at the rotting corpses. The man wore the single silver bar of a junior-grade lieutenant on the collar of his coveralls. Above his left pocket was a set of gold submariner's dolphins. His eyes were dead, as if he had been lobotomized. Buffalo waved his hand in front of the man's eyes. At first the man blinked, then shut his eyes. Buffalo shook him, heard mumbling. He put his ears next to the man's lips, straining to make out a voice distorted by thirst and hunger and sickness and fear. Finally came the words.

"What took you so long? God, what took you so damned long? . . ."

The man lost consciousness, collapsing in Buffalo's arms. Buffalo glanced at Buckethead Williams, whose jaw had tightened.

Buffalo reloaded his MAC-10 while speaking into

his lip mike, trying to raise the men he'd sent to the chief's quarters, "Peach" Pirelli and "Roadrunner" Kaplan.

"Peach, Roadrunner, you up?"

"Roger, One."

"What's the status?"

"CPO quarters are a meatgrinder, Mr. Buffalo. They'd executed five of the chiefs before we could nail the guards. Just like the crew's mess. Almost as if they were carrying out orders in case of a raid. Like they were expecting us."

"How are the survivors?"

"Pretty bad, One. Must have been tortured. They seem like they're in deep shock."

"Roger. Keep Roadrunner there and meet me in the passageway to make sure the level is clear."

Any remaining guards hiding in cubbyholes or staterooms would need to be dealt with before the middle level was considered secure. When it was, they'd help the other teams on the other levels. Until then, it would be best to stay out of the line of fire.

As Buffalo made his way down the narrow passageway, he almost hoped to see another Chinese guard. The more he saw of the prisoners, the greater the itch in his trigger finger.

CHAPTER 22

SUNDAY, 12 MAY
1907 GREENWICH MEAN TIME

Bo Hai Bay, Xingang Harbor
USS *Tampa*
0307 Beijing Time

Leader Tien Tse-Min felt the rush of air as the bullet flew by his ear, felt a sticky wetness on his neck from the blood that came from Captain Murphy, who twitched in his arms. The commando had shot at him and instead hit the captain. He dropped the hostage and the pistol and bolted for the ladder behind him, thrusting himself out of the cavern of the submarine, wondering if he would feel the rounds of the American's machine gun crashing into him. What he heard were the sounds of the commando's footsteps as the man ran toward him, but fear propelled Tien out of the hatch and onto the deck before the man got to him. Tien wondered momentarily if the commando had been running to catch him or to attend to the captain. It no longer mattered. He felt more than heard the two additional bullets from the direction of the American, but the shots missed and by then Tien had reached the top of the ladder.

He emerged from the forward hatch to a fiery landscape, the destroyer hulks burning, the fuel in the water of the slip burning, gunfire coming in from the pier, the helicopters overhead spraying bullets onto the ship. He had a brief impression of motion, of the destroyers and the pier moving away from him as the submarine, incredibly, moved backward, the water of the slip flowing swiftly over the bow as the ship backed up. It was true—the Americans had somehow found a way to recapture the submarine and were driving away with it in spite of the platoon of heavily armed guards Tien had stationed in the ship's control room. How could his troops have been overcome in seconds since the explosions sounded from the pier?

Impossible or not, it was happening right before his eyes. He continued out of the hatch, his body's momentum propelling him forward along the sloping bow of the submarine. He took a deep breath and dived into the water of the slip, closing his eyes against the scummy oil floating on the surface, came up for air, spitting out brackish bay water, and watched as the submarine backed clear of the slip, two heads visible at the top of the ship's conning tower, one of them driving the submarine.

Tien swam to the berth that had been occupied by the frigate *Nantong* astern of the sub. He could only hope that it would be chasing the American submarine. He found a maintenance ladder leading up to the pier, and climbed out of the oily bay water. In front of him were the troops of an armored unit of the PLA, the troops firing their weapons without effect at the retreating submarine.

Tien watched as the ship pulled out, the wake boiling around its bow as it reversed its way into the channel water of the bay.

He found the man who seemed to be in command and took his radio, calling for the Hangu airfield, where he knew there was a fleet of Hind assault helicopters. On the third try he reached the base and convinced the duty officer to scramble the helicopter gunships.

"How long for the Hinds to get here?" Tien shouted.

"Five minutes."

Tien waited, hoping that five minutes would be soon enough.

*　　*　　*

Lieutenant Pig Wilson lay on the deck forward of the port rack of torpedoes in the forward compartment's lower level torpedo room, waiting for the last Chinese sniper to make a mistake. When he and Chief Python Harris had first inserted into the room there had been at least a dozen guards. The initial volley of shots had dropped four, sending the others for cover. Unfortunately, there were too many places to hide in the room, including inside the tubes themselves.

In the rush of taking the room Pig had heard a torpedo tube door slam shut. No doubt one of the guards had dived into an empty tube, hoping to pop back out unexpectedly and shoot the SEALs from behind. But Pig knew how to lock a tube from the central console in the room. He peeked up at the torpedo room central console. The top of the console was burned out and full of holes, but the controller section for the port tube bank looked as if it had been hastily repaired and rewired, the plastic function keys ripped out with crude toggle switches installed in their place. Hoping the repaired switches worked, he had thrown a switch and watched as the thick steel ring rotated over the dogs of the inner tube door. He could hear the faint sound of a man shouting, the sound muffled and resonant, as if the noise came from inside a metal can, which in a way it did. Pig threw a second switch to vent the tube to the torpedo room, opening a valve in a pipe on top of the tube, the pipe intended to make sure no trapped air remained in the tube when it was filled with water. The third switch was the best; the marking above it said FLOOD. Pig hit the switch, opening up the tube to the water in the tube tanks, filling the tube with seawater all the way to the vent valve, which automatically shut when the tube was full of water. There followed a rushing noise, louder shouts from the tube. By the time the vent valve shut, the tube was full of water, and all human sound was extinguished.

But they couldn't all be that easy, Wilson knew. The room was the most vulnerable of all the spaces they would be raiding, full of weapons and their high-explosive warheads as well as the volatile fuel. A single bullet would be enough to cause a fire that could kill the whole ship ... the self-oxidizing torpedo fuel, once lit, could not be extinguished by anything—it burned under water, it burned when blasted by a CO_2 or PKP or foam-extinguisher, it just burned until the fuel was gone. That kind of violent fire would blow every warhead in the room, creating a chain reaction that would breach the hull, perhaps even cutting the ship to pieces. One goddamned bullet.

When the stun grenade exploded in the space, Pig held his breath, but heard only the clatter of guns dropping to the deck and the screams of the guards as the stun juice hit them. After a moment of quiet, Pig and Python began to search the space.

Fighter Sai, the last Chinese PLA guard remaining alive aboard the *Tampa*, managed to escape Pig and Python and bolted for the stairs leading from the torpedo room to the middle level, his AK-47 clattering against the rails of the stairs as he ran. He ran aft along the passageway between the crew quarters and officers' country, heading toward the crew's mess to the tunnel and the aft compartment. He knew a hiding place where he hoped they wouldn't look for him. When the Americans thought they were safe in their recaptured boat, he would emerge and take over the ship, killing the complacent, overconfident Americans with some of their own weapons. Or at least he could sabotage the vessel, sufficient to sink the ship somewhere in the bay.

Sai reached the corner of the galley and turned into a short passageway leading starboard. He thought he heard an American shouting something and worried he'd been seen. At the end of the passageway was the massive hatch to the aft compartment that lay open on its latch. Without stopping to shut the hatch Sai climbed through and ran along the tight tunnel leading to the aft compartment, and felt the deck tilt as the ship turned at high speed.

Midway along the tunnel Sai stopped at the door to the room he privately called the forgotten compartment. Forgotten because it seemed to be between the forward and aft compartments, but other than the one tunnel going through it there was no access to the space. The one door to the space was set into the wall of the tunnel and it had a window with a mirror that rotated with a handwheel, providing a view into each corner of the room. Inside the space there were large pieces of equipment, mostly tanks or storage containers. Sai knew that no one ever ventured into the room because the oval door to the space was locked with a thick chain and padlock. No one went in, no one ever came out. There were a hundred places where no one would see him from the tunnel. He was feeling better.

As Sai shot the chain of the lock and turned the wheel of the door's latch, he ignored the yellow-and-magenta-colored sign set above the door as well as the panel next to it flashing red letters. He pulled the thick door open, marveling at its thickness and heaviness. Once inside the room, on a grating platform on the other side of the door, a suffocating steamy heat assaulted him. What was the compartment's original purpose? Part of the engineroom? But if so why would it be locked? Why was it so hot? Sai pushed the thoughts from his mind and shut the door, then climbed down the two ladders to the grating at the lower level and found a place to sit next to a large steel tank, keeping the tank between himself and the window of the door high above.

The sign Sai had been unable to read was printed in block letters in English: CONTROLLED ACCESS—NO ADMITTANCE—HIGH RADIATION AREA. The panel flashing the red letters read: WARNING—REACTOR CRITICAL. The tank that Sai sat next to, his hiding place, was the pressure vessel of the *Tampa*'s nuclear reactor, which was then at fifty percent power.

Sai could not feel the radiation as it went through his body. The gamma radiation ionized the molecules of his cells as the waves penetrated, the radiation some ten million times the strength of an X-ray, the equivalent of standing next to a nuclear explosion. The neutrons from the uranium atoms' fissioning slammed into his tissues, the flux of the radiation vaporizing the structure of his cells.

The first indication Sai had that something was wrong was his hair standing on end as if he had grabbed a hot wire. The second sign came within ten seconds, when Sai's eye lenses changed from being clear to being black and opaque, leaving him blind. His abdomen began to swell with fluid buildup as his tissues tried to compensate for the massive damage. When his stomach ballooned he could no longer see it from the blindness.

Unfortunately, in a sense, for Fighter Sai, his brain was the last organ to be affected by the radiation, protected as it was by the bones of his skull, which acted as a partial shield, leaving a capacity to feel the effects of the radiation inflating his body to several times its normal size. He was still alive when his abdomen exploded. An observer standing at the window of the door to the compartment would have seen only a dark stain in the bilges.

Fighter Sai's death marked the end of the occupation of the submarine *Tampa* by the Chinese PLA. Inside, the ship again belonged to the U.S. Navy.

The same could not be said for the outside.

HANGU PLA NAVAL AIR FORCE STATION

Aircraft Commander Yen Chitzu jogged out of the ready-building off the taxiway at Hangu, pulling on his flight helmet and blinking the sleep out of his eyes. He only half-cursed the late hour. A year before he would have been mumbling obscenities about the senior officers and whether they had any idea what time it was. Now, with the White Army closing on Beijing, the landscape of reality had changed. Now when the alarm to scramble to an aircraft blared in the ready-building Yen rushed to his aircraft without a complaint.

He climbed up the step over the 23-mm forward gun into the upper cockpit of the Mil Hind-G helicopter, pulled his feet up and over the sill of the door and landed in the thinly padded seat, then shut the cockpit door after him, already starting in on his pre-flight checklist while his weapons systems officer, Leader Ni Chihfu, checked the weapons pods and, apparently satisfied, climbed into the lower forward cockpit. The Hind was the largest assault-helicopter gunship in the Chinese PLA Navy, the ship licensed for construction from the Russians, the new variant named the G, although it was essentially identical to the F variant of the old Red Army. This particular helicopter was fairly new, its interior still smelling of the vinyl and plastic and paint.

Below in the forward cockpit Ni ran through his checklist, tested the intercom, announced he was ready. Yen waved at the fighter out on the pad, who backed away, and put on ear protectors, then snapped the toggle for the electrical starting motor for number-two turbine on the port-engine control-console and watched the engine tachometer as the turbine spun up to speed, the whining noise coming from over his left shoulder. At ten thousand RPM he snapped up the second toggle marked FUEL INJ, beginning the fuel injection to the combustors, then toggled in the IGNITION switch, lighting off the combustion cans. The tachometer needle lifted as the engine became self-sustaining. He pushed up the throttle-tab to stabilize the turbine above the idle point, then repeated his actions for the starboard number-one turbine, the sound of it spooling up adding to the earsplitting noise-level in the cockpit. When both turbines were up, he engaged the clutch, connecting the power turbines' output shafts into the main reduction gearbox. The gears began to moan as the main rotor overhead began to spin slowly, taking some five seconds to complete its first revolution of the seventeen-meter-diameter four-bladed rotor.

It took almost a minute for the main rotor to accelerate to full idling speed, and while Yen waited he plugged in his radio headset and adjusted the UHF to the frequency designated for this mission. Immediately he heard a man speaking his callsign on the radio. Yen listened for a moment and acknowledged, transmitting that he was now taking off.

He lifted the collective lever on his left side, checking the tachometer to ensure that the automatic throttle was compensating for the drag of the increased rotor pitch. As the aircraft lifted off the pad he pushed on his right anti-torque pedal. The heavy assault helicopter lifted slowly off the asphalt of the pad, lights marking the boundary of the pad rotating to the left as the chopper slowly turned to the right. For a moment Yen paused, waiting for the second Hind helicopter to start its main rotor and lift off. When the nose of Yen's Hind pointed south, he stopped the rotation with his left anti-torque pedal while easing the collective. The helicopter hovered above the pad at two meters, and Yen frowned, aware he was burning fuel while waiting for the second Hind. Finally the other chopper was ready. Yen raised the collective and pushed forward on the cyclic stick between his knees. The helicopter took off from the pad and accelerated forward, suddenly getting a burst of lift as it passed through transition velocity, the rotors now in air undisturbed by the rotor-wash blasting off the ground.

The Hind accelerated to one hundred and fifty clicks, the Hangu base fading away, the terrain of the land coming in rapidly from ahead. Within a few minutes the water of the bay flashed below the fuselage, and a few moments after that, the piers of the PLA complex at Xingang came into view.

Yen smiled as his target became visible.

The ship began to respond to the rudder, the bay beginning to turn beneath Lennox. His mind momen-

tarily fogged by Baron's death, it took him a moment
to realize that the ship was in fact turning in the wrong
direction, the stern headed south toward the supertanker-
pier instead of north. Lennox had intended to have
the stern come around to the north, where he would
have put the rudder amidships and gone ahead flank,
just like pulling a car out of a driveway and heading
off to work. But goddamn if the screw wasn't walking
the stern in the opposite direction as the rudder and
so pulling his tail in the wrong direction. No wonder
they always used tugs to get out of the slip.

Lennox realized hundreds of lives depended on his
next decision. The stern was now pointing almost
southeast, too late to reverse the direction of the turn.
He would either have to continue in a semicircle going
backward until his bow was pointed east or go forward
with the bow pointing north and do a one-hundred-
eighty-degree turn to the south. The first option could
cause the stern to ram into the supertanker-pier. The
second would cost him extra time.

Whatever, he couldn't continue to be at the mercy
of the goddamned rudder and screw. He had to get
the ship to be predictable again. As he watched the
bay turn around him in the wrong direction, he felt a
pain in his chest and wondered if he was having a
heart attack. No ... it had to be the anxiety from the
screwed-up maneuver. Good thing Murphy was below,
Lennox thought. At least the captain couldn't see this
amateurish shiphandling.

"All ahead full," Lennox barked.

"ROGER, ALL AHEAD FULL."

The screw aft of the rudder, a moment before
pumping water forward, slowed, stopped and began
rotating in the opposite direction, now pumping water
aft, thrusting the ship forward. The water above the
scimitar blades of the spiral screw boiled and churned
in angry phosphorescence. Lennox felt the deck tremble, the hull not accustomed to the force-reversal. The
ship slowed to a stop and then began to accelerate as
it surged forward. Around them the water was a bub-

bling foam from the power of the main engines, the PLA pier drifting by amidships. The only problem was that they were now going north, not south.

Lennox raised his head above the scarred steel of the top of the sail to look aft, making sure the rudder was turned to the right instead of left. A wrong rudder direction could send them crashing into the PLA piers, which would be the end of the rescue attempt.

The deck's vibrations steadied out somewhat, but the power of the main engines at fifty percent reactor power and the full-rudder order still caused perceptible vibrations. As the ship came around to the south Lennox heard the sound of the Dauphin helicopters coming closer, preparing for another strafing run. He ducked down and reached for a clamshell on the port side of the cockpit—the clamshells were hinged panels that covered the top of the cockpit when rigged for dive, smoothing it out with the contour of the top of the sail. Without the clamshells the cockpit hole would cause a flow-induced resonance, like a breath of air over the mouth of a soda bottle. The clamshell was heavy, made of inch-thick HY-80 steel for breaking through polar ice. While Lennox struggled to raise the panel into the horizontal position he silently thanked the design engineers who had replaced the old fiberglass clamshells with hardened steel. Once the port shell was up, he raised the center forward-and-aft shells, which left him only a small cubbyhole to look out of on the starboard side.

As the choppers approached for their strafing run Lennox ducked into the clamshells on the port side. The bullets impacted directly over his head, zinging off the heavy steel. Lennox poked his head out the starboard clamshell, ducked quickly back in as he saw the second chopper in its approach. This time he hugged the deck of the cockpit, the loud clanging of the bullets seeming closer, harder. When the noise died down he put his head out again and saw that the ship was now almost completely turned around, head-

ing south into the deep channel. They should be out
of there in no time . . .

He was about to order the rudder amidships, thinking ahead to his next order to increase speed to flank,
when he saw the buoys just ahead of him. Sure as hell
he was no expert on Chinese coastal buoys, but it
struck him that the only plausible reason he could
think of to put a line of buoys this close to a deep
channel was that there was a submerged obstruction
or, God forbid, a sandbar.

"Right hard rudder!" he shouted into the VHF
radio. Too late.

The *Tampa* hit the submerged sandbar at over
twenty knots, slowing down to a complete stop in less
than two seconds, plowing her bow deep into the sand.
Lennox was thrown into the forward bulkhead of the
cockpit, smashing his cheek, breaking his nose. The
deck was tilted absurdly to the port side, a twenty- or
twenty-five-degree list. Lennox looked aft and saw
that the foam was no longer boiling up around the
screw. The deck no longer vibrated with the power of
the main engines—they must have lost propulsion
when they hit the sandbar, which meant he couldn't
use the engines to back the sub off the sand.

Lennox tried his radio, wondering if it broke when
he hit the cockpit lip. He heard a new sound, the
sound of the rotors of a big assault chopper approaching from the north. He looked up in time to
see the flying bulk of the Hind helicopter circling
around to approach the crippled submarine from the
bow. As it drew up, it went into a hover, its rockets
and guns hanging on struts protruding from the gunship's flanks. Then a second Hind pulled into a hover
behind it.

For a moment Lennox forgot the radio. The painful
truth was that the operation was almost surely blown,
and it was his fault.

Aircraft Commander Yen Chitzu looked through the
plastic bubble of the Hind's upper cockpit at the scene

below. The reason for the Hind's call-up from Hangu was immediately apparent. Pulling out of the PLA slip was a large black submarine, the one that had been captured spying on the Chinese coastline. The destroyers that had been its guards were smoldering and sinking into the water of the pier's slip, the water around them in flames as the kerosene and diesel oil burned. An armored PLA force on the pier was firing tank guns and artillery into the water, the rounds missing the sub as it entered the bay channel still going backward. Two kilometers to the southeast a Jianghu-class frigate was reversing course to turn and come back to attack the escaping submarine. To the south, two poorly armed Dauphin helicopters were coming in on a futile strafing run. Yen activated his radio and ordered the Dauphins out of his airspace, then called the second Hind in his formation to follow him in. Next he radioed the captain of the Jianghu frigate and told him to hold his fire while the Hinds lined up. He brought the aircraft around a wide circle, crossing over the deck of the frigate and approaching the submarine, slowing to a hover.

Now he spoke into his intercom to the weapons officer, Leader Ni Chihfu, ordering him to arm the Spiral missiles and the UB-32 rockets and to commence firing, then sat back to watch the fireworks.

On the *Tampa*'s bridge the VHF radio sputtered:

"REACTOR SCRAM! WHAT THE HELL HAPPENED UP THERE?"

Lennox spat into the radio. "We ran aground." We, hell, he thought, *I* ran us aground. "What happened to the reactor?"

"WAIT ONE, THEY'RE CHECKING."

The Hind helicopters hovered barely a half-shiplength in front of the sail at twenty feet. Lennox, still standing with his head exposed out the starboard clamshell opening, stared at the missiles slung on missile rails on booms extending from the flanks of the choppers. He could even see the laser sights on the

helmets of the chopper pilots in the nosecone cockpits
as they aimed the missiles. Further ahead in the channel, south of the supertanker-pier, he could see the
Jianghu frigate driving up closer, its 100-mm gun up
forward moving, the barrel lining up on his position.

Lennox's VHF radio squawked:

"CAUSE OF THE SCRAM WAS SHOCK OPEN-
ING THE SCRAM BREAKERS. WE'LL HAVE
POWER IN ABOUT TWO MINUTES. THE ENGI-
NEER WANTS TO KNOW HOW BAD THE
GROUNDING IS. CAN YOU GET US OUT OF
THIS?"

The frigate had come to a stop a shiplength in front
of them. The helicopters hovered, at most one hundred feet away. Lennox continued to stare at the choppers' and frigate's guns and missiles, the world tilted
in a twenty-five-degree slope. Forget answering the
radio, he thought. He ducked down into the cockpit
and waited for the missiles and gun projectiles to hit,
wondering how it would feel to die.

CHAPTER 23

SUNDAY, 12 MAY
1910 GREENWICH MEAN TIME

Bo Hai Bay, Xingang Harbor
USS *Seawolf*
0310 Beijing Time

The periscope lens finally broke the surface and
cleared, revealing the scene Pacino had most worried
about. The Jianghu frigate was dead in the water just
a few hundred yards in front of the bow of the *Tampa*.
Two huge helicopters hovered just in front of the sail
of the motionless submarine. But the worst of it wasn't
the frigate or the choppers, it was the appearance of
the *Tampa*. The sail was canted over in a twenty- or
twenty-five-degree angle, leaning hard to port, and
there was no bow-wave, no disturbance of the water
at all from her stern—she must have hit an underwater
obstacle. She must have run aground on the way out
and was now a cripple in the channel while the PLA
Navy was getting ready to deliver the coup de grace.

"Conn, Sonar, no propulsion noises from Friendly
One. Looks like—"

Pacino interrupted and shouted over the noise of
his headset:

"Belay the report, Sonar. Off'sa'deck, arm the
SLAAM 80 missiles. Weps, report status of tube-
loaded Javelins."

"SLAAM 80 missiles armed, Captain," Tim Turner
said from the Mark 80 Submarine-Launched Antiair
Missile console, the control unit mounted on the port
railing of the conn, the console no bigger than a lunch
pail. "All missile doors indicate open."

Pacino lifted the protective cover over a red button on his left periscope grip.

"SLAAM 80, SLAAM 80," he said as he hit the key. He punched it two more times, chanting the launch notice twice more. There was no telltale sound of the missiles leaving the ship—for a moment Pacino wondered if the missiles had actually been launched, then . . .

"Four Mark 80s away, sir," Turner reported from the SLAAM control box.

"Javelins tube-loaded in tubes five and six, Captain," Feyley said. "Both are spun up and ready in all respects."

"Open outer doors, tubes five and six," Pacino commanded. "Firing point procedures, Javelin units five and six, Target Four, over-the-shoulder shots, five to go west, six to go east."

"Ship ready," Turner said.

"Weapons ready." Feyley.

"Solution ready," Keebes reported.

"Shoot five, shoot six," Pacino ordered, hoping the Jianghu frigate would show up better on the cruise-missile-seeker radars than the *Tampa*. Tubes five and six barked, slamming Pacino's eardrums, sending two Javelin cruise missiles up to the surface to kill the frigate.

Pacino waited, hoping the Javelins would be able to tell a frigate from a submarine.

USS *TAMPA*

Commander Jack Morris ran the ten steps to the prone bleeding body of Captain Sean Murphy, glancing up once to see the Chinese officer's feet leaving the hatchway above, the feet lit by the glow of the pier. Gently Morris pulled Murphy up into a sitting position and looked at him, trying to see if he was still alive.

Blood was coming out of Murphy's neck but at least

the flow was not from an artery. It oozed out, dark and dull. With a good field dressing and some antibiotics Murphy should make it. *If* he had been healthy before getting the wound, which did not look to be the case. Murphy had lost consciousness, his breathing unsteady, face pale, skin clammy.

The ship's roll to starboard threatened to knock Morris into a bulkhead. He steadied himself on a rung of the ladder, felt drops of water splashing down on him from above. The hatch shouldn't be open, he thought, laying Murphy back down on the deck while he stepped to the top of the ladder and looked out the forward hatch.

One look was enough. The pier was fading away in front of them, the tanks on the pier were getting ready to shoot. Morris reached up and shut the lower hatch, spinning its wheel to engage the dogs. No sense letting in Chinese commandos or shipping water into the boat once Lennox started going forward. Next he came back down the ladder and looked at Murphy. As soon as Tien had bolted up the ladder Morris had sent Bony Robbins aft to see to the security of the upper level. Morris knew he should have been joining Robbins in the control room, but Murphy's helplessness ... He picked up Murphy and carried him to the captain's stateroom. When he saw a dead body, on its back, knees bent, blocking the doorway, he carried the wounded captain to the next stateroom, almost stumbling as the deck rolled hard to port—Lennox had to be turning the ship to leave the harbor. He ducked into the executive officer's stateroom, which was empty, put Murphy on the bed, wrapped a towel around his neck wound and covered him with a wool blanket. For a moment he looked down at the man who had commanded the submarine but who now was perhaps only moments from death. Well, Morris thought, there was nothing else he could do for the man.

He left and moved into the control room, nodded at Bony and joined in a search of the space. The smell of the stun juice was still pungent in the room, mixed with the smell of gunfire, the meaty smell of blood, and of the guards' bodies as they died. He had begun checking the cubbyhole between the ship control panel and the ballast-control panel when the room seemed to turn upside down, tossing him into the console, smashing him in the head and dumping him onto the deck.

Somehow he got himself up, nearly overcome by dizziness, and soon realized it wasn't dizziness that had tilted the world but something they had hit. The deck was quiet, no longer vibrating with the power of the reactor aft. Morris went for the hatch to the bridge tunnel, Bony Robbins right behind him. He rebelled against the thought that filled his mind but there was no sense denying it. Lennox had run the ship aground. They were now sitting ducks.

At the top of *Seawolf*'s sail four small doors opened. Below the doors were circular seals that kept the Mark 80 SLAAM missiles from being damaged by seawater. Below each seal a Mark 80 missile waited for the launch signal. The four signals arrived at the base terminal box one after another at half-second intervals. The first missile to receive the electronic signal to fire experienced a warm sensation at its base as the gas generator lit off—the gas generator was a small casing around a solid rocket motor, the nozzle of the rocket pointing downward into a reservoir of water. The rocket motor ignited and sent a stream of superheated gases toward the reservoir. The water in the reservoir immediately boiled, forming a high-pressure bubble of steam. When the steam at the base of the Mark 80 missile reached a pressure higher than the external sea pressure, the seal above the missile ruptured and the missile was expelled from the sail by the high-pressure steam bubble. It rose to the surface, never even getting wet from the seawater, the steam bubble that followed it surrounding it all the way to the surface.

As the missile rose out of the sail a tiny relay designed to measure acceleration registered two g's, twice normal gravity. The missile then armed its rocket motor ignition circuits as it prepared to light off its own solid rocket fuel. The bubble of steam rose steadily toward the surface, taking less than two hundred milliseconds to go from the top of the sail to the waves above. When the missile reached the surface the momentum of its upward journey threw it clear of the water until all its eight feet were completely out of the water and rising. At ten feet the missile froze as its upward velocity gave in to the downward acceleration of gravity. At that point the zero-g relay closed, completing the rocket-motor ignition circuit. Before the missile had fallen backward an inch the thrust from the rocket motor had climbed to ten g's, taking the missile from being motionless to Mach 1.2 in seconds, its path straight up. The heat-seeker in the missile's nosecone activated as it sought a target, any target, as long as the target emitted heat and was at least ten feet above the ground level. Immediately the seeker identified two targets, each coming from the hot exhaust of the turbines of the jet-powered helicopters. The missile switched the seeker from omni-mode to target-vector mode, the onboard microprocessor moving the control surfaces at the missile's tail to turn the unit toward the stronger of the two signals. The flight time to the target was approximately a second, the target-vector seeker keeping the helicopter's exhaust pipe in sight, and at the end of the missile's supersonic journey everything happened at once.

The missile flew into the hot tailpipe of the target, making the seeker blind, as if it had looked into the sun. The seeker going blind was the signal the microprocessor had waited for. It sent a faint twenty milliamp signal to the high explosive in the missile's forward section just aft of the seeker in the nosecone. By the time the signal reached the detonator the nose of the missile had actually flown some six inches into the helicopter's tailpipe. When the missile had traveled another two inches the explosive detonated, no longer a solid mass, but exploding in a furious fireball of a chemical reaction that blew the helicopter to pieces, its remains raining down on the water of the bay below.

Aircraft Commander Yen Chitzu adjusted the collective, keeping the Hind helicopter in a stable hover, waiting for Ni Chihfu to fire the Spiral missiles at the sail of the listing submarine. Out his plastic windshield he could see down into Ni's cockpit and make out the green light on Ni's status panel that indicated the missile was ready for launch.

Yen was not aware of the launch of the Mark 80 SLAAM missile behind him, and since it approached his aircraft at supersonic speed, there was no sound as the missile's nosecone entered his port turbine's exhaust pipe. There was, however, a loud noise as the missile exploded, blowing the Hind apart and igniting its fuel. Yen felt the cockpit of the helicopter disintegrate around him. He had been looking downward toward Ni's cockpit, but now down at his legs, and by the light of the aircraft's fireball he saw his body being torn apart, his torso leaving his legs behind in what had been the seat of the helicopter. He had the briefest impression of being thrown away from the exploding aircraft, of a rotor blade whipping by him, its rotating velocity throwing it away from the fireball, and then a view of the blood erupting from his severed midsection. Gradually the light of the fireball faded as Yen began to pass out from loss of blood pressure and from the nerve overload of trauma. By the time Yen's upper half hit the water of the Bo Hai Bay, he had been dead for almost five milliseconds.

At the top of Pacino's periscope view four small heat-seeking missiles flew toward the horizon, as if they were in formation. One hit the Hind helicopter on the right, blowing it into a hundred-yard-diameter fireball. The other three impacted the Hind on the left at about the same time, likewise blowing that aircraft into several large pieces. As the fragments of the helicopter splashed into the water they exploded into flames, probably, Pacino thought, the result of a delayed secondary explosion of an onboard rocket.

Pacino rotated the periscope to look at the trajectories of the Javelins, trying to determine if they had flown true. Off to the left a bright trail of fire marked the first missile's takeoff. Pacino turned the scope to the right, where another smoke trail showed the liftoff of the second unit. The missiles should be turning around about now, Pacino figured, to return and find the frigate, which had decided to leave the *Tampa* alone and come for him. That made sense, since *Tampa* wasn't going anywhere, and an intruder submarine had just launched two more cruise missiles.

As the frigate turned toward him, Pacino could see that the ship's two 37-mm gunmounts were turning, one to starboard, one to port. For a moment he wondered if a Javelin cruise missile could be shot down by anti-aircraft fire if the target was alerted. As if in answer, both 37-mm guns began firing at either side of the frigate, the bright orange flashes reaching out from the muzzles even though to Pacino's eyes there was nothing to shoot at.

PLA NAVY VESSEL *NANTONG*

Aboard the frigate *Nantong* Commander Chin Chi-wei raised his binoculars to his eyes, searching the dark horizon for any traces of an incoming cruise missile, but could see nothing but the sea lit by the reflections of the moonlight from the waves. Ahead, two smoking missile-exhaust plumes pointed to a spot in the ocean where the launching submarine had been only minutes before. First, thought Chin, he would down the cruise missiles and after that the firing submarine would be history.

The intercom from the combat-control center blared as his weapons officer reported:

"COMMANDER CHIN, INCOMING MISSILES BEARING ZERO NINE FIVE AND TWO SEVEN THREE, BOTH SUBSONIC, BOTH AT LOW ALTITUDE. FIRECONTROL RADARS ARE LOCKED ON AND THE 37S ARE ENABLED IN AUTOMATIC."

Chin acknowledged, calmly waiting for the missiles to fly into view. He trained his binoculars to the bearings called out by combat and found them as dark as before. Then in a sudden burst of sound the 37-mm gun immediately below the bridge began to fire, the reports from the gun barrel rattling the plate glass of the bridge's windows, the 180-rounds-per-minute firing rate making the sound a sustained roar. Chin watched down the bearing line, telling himself that any second the cruise missiles would be arriving, and that even if he couldn't yet see them the firecontrol radars did ...

Javelin Unit Six sped in toward the Jianghu class frigate at six hundred knots, altitude thirty-five feet. The waves flashed in under the fuselage, the target still invisible up ahead. The missile's radar-seeker felt out ahead of the unit, searching over the surface of the water for the shape of the frigate's hull. After a few moments the seeker saw the shape forming up ahead, the boxy bridge, the pointed bow, the tall central mast and the funnel aft, with the box of the hangar for the Dauphin helicopter and the flat helo-deck aft. The target was confirmed. The Javelin armed the warhead and aimed at the vessel's hull just below the bridge.

The first 37-mm bullets hit the nosecone of the missile like a spray of a shotgun's buckshot, stinging and ripping open the skin of the nose section, knocking out the seeker-radar, then paralyzing the arming mechanism. This particular buckshot consisted of rapidly fired bullets, each weighing over a half-pound, three of them coming in per second. The missile drove on toward the target, blinded by the rain of bullets,

until it took a round in its air intake duct that shot
through the compressor, which lost four blades and
disintegrated, rupturing the airframe and spilling jet
fuel out the hole. Another bullet lodged in the navigation unit, another in the targeting computer, several
in the warhead. As the missile lost thrust, its engine
seized, it fell down toward the water, its fuel beginning
to ignite.

Two hundred yards from the target the missile hit
the water and exploded, its fuel and high-explosive
warhead detonating in an impotent flash, to be swallowed and forgotten by the sea.

USS SEAWOLF

It happened so fast Pacino could hardly believe his
eyes. The Javelin missile flying in at the frigate from
the east exploded, crashed into the water, the splash
from the detonation rising high in the moonlit sky. A
moment later the second cruise missile detonated, its
fireball bigger and brighter and perhaps closer to the
frigate, but no more harmful to the PLA vessel. As
he watched, a wave began at the frigate's bow while
it accelerated and turned toward him. He also caught
sight of a helicopter being rolled out onto the helo-
deck aft as he pulled his eye away from the eyepiece,
snapped down his eyepatch and lowered the periscope.

He now calculated the angle between the frigate
and the *Tampa*, wondering if he dared risk it. No matter how he positioned the ship in the next few seconds
the angle was too slim. But he had to take the risk,
now that his Javelins had failed.

"Snapshot tube seven," he called to the firecontrol
team, ordering a quick-reaction torpedo shot. "Direct
contact mode, active low-speed snake, shallow surface
transit, run-to-enable zero, ASH and ACR disabled.
Get the outer door open, now!"

Feyley worked the panel. "Sir, tube seven set at

shallow direct-contact, active snake at low speed, enabled at zero yards, ASH and ACR disabled."

"Bearing and bearing-rate matched," Keebes said. "Range eleven hundred yards and closing."

"Door's open, sir," Feyley said.

"Shoot," Pacino ordered.

"Fire." Feyley pulled the trigger on the horizontal panel of the console.

The tube fired, barking as it ejected the torpedo, the air in the ship compressing in a shock wave from the high-pressure air ram venting inboard.

"Tube seven fired electrically, sir, and we're active."

The pinging of the torpedo could be heard outside the skin of the ship, the sound fading as the torpedo drove away to the northwest down the bearing line of the frigate.

"Lookaround number-two scope," Pacino called, raising the periscope and lifting his eyepatch. The scope was trained to the bearing of the frigate as it came out of the well.

He put the crosshairs of the scope on the frigate, now approaching at flank speed directly toward him, the hull of the *Tampa* a mile behind it but on almost the same bearing line. He realized that if he missed, not only would *Tampa* take the torpedo hit, but *Seawolf* would be rammed and sunk by the frigate.

As the frigate plowed toward him, its knife-sharp bow looming bigger each second, he wondered what Admiral Donchez would say if he heard that both submarines had been lost.

"COMMANDER, STILL NO SONAR CONTACT, BUT THE WOK WON RADAR IS GETTING A DETECT OFF THE SUBMARINE'S PERISCOPE, BEARING ONE TWO FOUR."

"Steer one two four, Fighter Tse," Commander Chin ordered the helmsman. Up ahead he thought he could see the reflection of the moon off something in the water, perhaps from a periscope lens. "What's the status of the helicopter?" he asked the Deck Officer.

"He's on deck now, sir, and should be starting his engines any minute."

"Tell him to *hurry*." Chin clicked the intercom button. "Are the Whitehead torpedoes armed?"

"ARMED AND READY, COMMANDER, STILL NO SONAR CONTACT."

"Standby."

Chin raised his binoculars to look at the bearing to the periscope, and when at first he didn't see it he dropped the glasses and searched with his naked eyes until he saw the periscope silhouetted in the moon's reflection on the bay's waves.

"Got him now," he mumbled to himself. An instant later the fo'c'sle of his frigate disintegrated in a blooming fireball while the deck jumped up two meters, the explosion throwing him against the aft bulkhead of the wheelhouse and cracking open his skull.

The ship's forward momentum, without her bow section, drove her into the water of the bay, the water soon flooding the bridge after the bow of the ship exploded. As the *Nantong* sank, Commander Chin Chi-wei sputtered, coughing and inhaling water as the wheelhouse filled with water. For a few moments he swam in circles, his lungs filled with water, then lost consciousness in the blackness of the bay.

Moments later the hull of his ship hit the bottom of the bay and rolled over, burying the bridge in the silt.

The crosshairs of the periscope were centered on the bridge of the frigate, and when Pacino switched to high power he could see the face of a man staring at him with binoculars in the redlit windows of the bridge. He switched back to low power, the hull of the frigate almost filling the periscope view.

The bow of the ship vanished for a moment, obscured by a column of water and an orange cloud of fire, black chunks of shrapnel flying away from the bright flash. Almost as quickly as it came, the fireball and water-column receded as the ship plowed into the water, taking a down angle. The sea swallowed the gunmount forward of the bridge, then the bridge went under, the central mast following. The funnel vanished in the foamy water, then the helicopter hangar and finally the helodeck, until there was nothing left but the Dauphin helicopter, which for a moment bobbed in the waves caused by the frigate's sinking, then gave up and sank itself, either from being flooded or being sucked down by the vortex from the frigate.

The bay was empty except for the *Tampa*, which still leaned helplessly against the sandbar.

CHAPTER 24

SUNDAY, 12 MAY
1917 GREENWICH MEAN TIME

Bo Hai Bay, Xingang Harbor
USS *Tampa*
0317 Beijing Time

As Jack Morris climbed the ladder in the dark bridge-access trunk he felt the explosions from outside the submarine. He had no idea what was going on topside but figured it wasn't good.

At the top of the tilted bridge trunk he stopped before the closed hatch, pushed up on it with all the strength he had, thinking that since it was almost two-inch-thick steel it would be heavy. He hadn't counted on its spring-loaded hatch, the spring designed to balance the weight of the steel pancake so that a child could open the hatch from below. With Morris' mighty heave on the hatch, the spring coiled and pulled the hatch upward, launching Morris out of the trunk and smashing the hatch against Kurt Lennox's thigh. Morris lost his balance and fell to the deck grating of the bridge cockpit, then stood abruptly and hit his head against the closed canopy of the steel clamshell.

"Son of a *bitch*." He found the square of light coming from the one opening on the starboard side and crawled toward it. Lennox's large frame was standing in the opening, his head exposed above.

Morris shouldered him aside and pushed his own head up above the lip of the sail, craned his neck to see around Lennox and observed the flames on the water from what looked like crashed aircraft or perhaps the remains of patrol boats. Ahead a Chinese frigate was sinking, vanishing into the water of the bay, a smoky column of fire rising from its dying hulk. Within moments the frigate vanished into the foam of the bay water, leaving only a small airframe of a helicopter behind, and then it too sank. The bay was quiet, the moon lighting the bay water with a bright white glow.

"What the hell happened?" Morris barked. "Where's Baron?"

Lennox said nothing. Morris saw von Brandt's corpse on the deck. He looked up at Lennox, his face dark with anger.

"You ran us aground, didn't you?"

Lennox nodded.

"Well, get us out of here. Use the engines, do *something*."

Lennox stared into the distance, still saying nothing.

Morris reached inside his vest to his radio and switched frequencies so that he was on the channel that Stinky was using back in the aft escape trunk.

"Stinky, it's Boss. Get the Engineer up there and put him on the VHF."

"HE'S RIGHT HERE." There was a brief silence on the line. "BRIDGE, ENGINEER HERE."

"Eng, we're hard aground on a sandbar or obstruction. You got power?"

"REACTOR'S CRITICAL. IT'LL BE ANOTHER MINUTE TILL WE'RE IN THE POWER RANGE, A FEW MORE TO SPIN THE TURBINES UP."

"Leave someone with brains in charge and get your ass up to the bridge—you're driving this bucket of bolts out of here."

"ON THE WAY, ENG OUT."

Morris pulled Lennox around so the man was facing him, then slapped his face a few times, enough to focus his eyes.

"Get below, Lennie," Morris said quietly. "Find some men who can take over the control room below and get them ready to dive the ship. In the meantime the Engineer'll drive us out, if he can get us off the sandbar."

Lennox handed Morris a chart and a red flashlight and his headset, and as if sleepwalking, left the bridge and lowered himself down the access trunk ladder. As the hatch shut after him, a tall man with a dirty face and disheveled hair appeared from the port side of the sail. He had just climbed the ladder rungs set on the outside.

"Permission to come up," he said.

"Get the hell up here," Morris told him.

The man climbed over the panels of the clamshells, reached under and retracted them, expanding the bridge to its former size.

"I'm Vaughn," he said. "Ship's engineer. Who're you?"

"Morris, Jack Morris, SEAL Team Seven CO. Here's the radio headset. Here's Lennox's chart and here's a flashlight. Now do us all a big goddamned favor and *get us the hell out of here*."

Vaughn looked over the port and starboard lips of the sail, took the headset, chart and flashlight. As he studied the chart in the glow of the light he gave Morris orders as though the SEAL were a green ensign just reporting aboard.

"Get below and go to the ballast control panel. It's on the forward port corner of the control room. Above the console you'll see two big stainless-steel levers. When I give you the word pull the plungers on the levers down and rotate the levers to the up position. The levers will initiate an emergency ballast-tank blow. Got all that?"

"I just killed thirty, forty Chinese guards to save your butt. I think I can flip a couple of levers."

"Good man. Get going."

Morris scrambled down the ladder, annoyed but glad to have someone on the bridge who seemed ready to take charge. As he entered the control room he saw Lennox sitting at the shipcontrol panel.

"Lennie," Morris said, "where are the emergency blow levers?"

Lennox pointed to the BCP. Morris went to the levers and waited for Vaughn's orders.

On the bridge above, Vaughn's radio crackled.

"BRIDGE, WE HAVE PROPULSION!"

"Bridge aye," Vaughn replied. "Shift the coolant recirc pumps to fast speed and prepare for a flank bell."

Vaughn looked up from the chart and checked the water below one final time. He was gambling that the ballast tanks had leaked air out over the last five days in captivity, letting in water from the vents below. Usually that happened in port, and when at the pier the daily routine called for the duty officer to blow the ballast tanks full of air. Otherwise, after a week or two, the ship would lose a foot of draft. Left unattended and with no ballast tank blow a submarine would probably sink after a month at pierside.

The way the vents had jammed in the struggle with the Chinese, and with the port list, there was a good chance the tanks had a considerable amount of water in them, which meant they were low in the water. If he could blow the tanks and refill them with air it might give him some added buoyancy to get off the sandbar. But he couldn't use the blower—that would take a half hour to fill the tanks and time was what they did not have. He would have to use the emergency blow system—the EMBT blow system would force the water out so violently on the surface that the air flowing out of the tank gratings at the ship's keel might blow the sand away from them. The blow would empty the high-pressure air bottles, making it impossible for them to emergency-surface once they were submerged, but that was a problem that might never come.

So, the emergency blow and a max speed order might get them off the sandbar ... then again, it might just dig them deeper into the sand. And if that happened the only alternative would be to get the rescue sub to surface, throw them a line and get towed off the bar. Odds were that the two operations would take so long that the Chinese would recapture them... They could, he supposed, abandon ship and get aboard the rescue sub, but that would take even longer than being towed off the bar. Which meant that either the emergency blow worked or it was back to Xingang for everyone aboard *Tampa*. Vaughn took a deep breath and spoke into his lip mike.

"Emergency blow! Hit the levers!" Almost immediately a violent foam of bubbles boiled up around the bow and stern, the air from the ballast tanks blowing out as the emergency blow system engaged.

"All ahead flank!" Vaughn ordered into the radio.

The deck of the ship began to tremble as the water aft of the rudder erupted into foam and the screw began to spin at maximum RPM. The ship eased up off the sandbar, just slightly, in reaction to the emergency blow in the ballast tanks. Then in a sudden surge the port list came off the ship and the submarine accelerated forward, the waves protesting and boiling up at the bow as the ship plowed into the channel.

The ship drove ahead, the bow wave building up over the sonar dome, the piers of the PLA fading behind. Vaughn ordered the rudder left and right, following the course of the channel until the ship was five miles away from Xingang and into deeper water.

Vaughn looked at the water of the bay around him, allowing himself a moment of satisfaction. They might not be home free yet, but at least, it seemed, they were on the way home.

Bo Hai Bay, Xingang Harbor
PLA Navy Pier 1A

Leader Tien Tse-Min fumed at the commander of the Huchuan-class fast-attack torpedo boat. The twenty-two-meter-long patrol craft was a hydrofoil boat capa-

ble of going sixty clicks armed with two type-53 torpedoes and two twin 14.5-mm guns. Its commander was
a short, slight southerner, probably from Shanghai or
one of the cities in rebellion, Tien thought.

"Start your engines and get out on the water now.
We have to get that American sub. Can't you see it?
Two torpedoes and we'll blow it apart. We must keep
it from escaping."

"I'm sorry, sir," Commander Soo Chi Meng said,
realizing what he was about to say might well determine whether he lived through the night. "The diesels
are not in good shape. Two were being worked on at
the time of the missile attack on the destroyers. The
third was bounced around by the shock. My engineering technician says it has wiped its bearings."

Tien glared at the commander. "Show me. I will
start the diesels myself." Tien, of course, was bluffing.
He had no idea how to start a diesel engine.

"I'm sorry, sir, but I'm afraid I can't let you do that.
It could be dangerous, it could explode and wound
you."

"Commander, I am ordering you to start the motors
on this boat and go after that submarine. Do I need
to get you on the radio to Chairman Yang?"

"Sir, you must believe me—the engines are not
working." Soo felt sweat drip down his forehead. If
the senior officer actually boarded his ship and
checked the engines he would find the engineroom
spotless. As for starting a diesel engine, there was not
much to it. The officer would only need to find the
red button on the control panel marked START and
push it. Ten seconds after one of the diesels roared
to idling speed, the officer would shoot him. But he
felt it was worth the risk, after seeing what the invisible submarine had done to the frigate that had chased
it, the entire bow of the supposedly invincible frigate
blowing up, sending the sub-killing ship to the bottom
in less than a minute, not to mention how it had managed to down two massive Hind helicopters and sink
the pierside destroyers too. Somewhere out there that

rescue submarine lurked, waiting to sink any ship that threatened the captive submarine.

For a moment Tien simply stared into Commander Soo's eyes, trying to look into the man's mind and see if he were telling the truth. Off in the distance of the bay water the formerly captive submarine kicked up a spray of water from its tail and surged ahead, obviously free of the sandbar it had been stuck on, and began sailing off into the distance. Tien felt like grabbing the patrol boat commander's face and smashing it, but he realized it was too late. The patrol boat would probably be sunk just like the *Nantong*. As he watched, the submarine's hull shrank into the distance until, even in bright moonlight, he could no longer see it. Commander Soo continued to stand in front of him. Finally Tien turned away, walking down the pier to a PLA command vehicle he had commandeered from the armored force, got in, stared at Soo one more time, and drove off.

Soo's sense of relief was what any condemned man might feel at the news of an unexpected reprieve.

An hour later at Hangu navy base Tien was linked into a UHF secure voice circuit to Fleet Commander Chu Hsueh-Fan at Lushun. Chu had been asleep and was annoyed to be awakened. Tien's report on what had happened made him wish he were still asleep and this was only a nightmare.

Tien waited for the jet that Chu had sent for him, a vertical takeoff jet that would take him to the aircraft carrier *Shaoguan*, Fleet Commander Chu's ship. He might have lost the American submarine out of Xingang, but there was no way that sub would get out of the Bo Hai Bay alive, not through the tight channel at the Lushun/Penglai Gap. The northern fleet at Lushun was a formidable force, enough to kill the submarines, not the PLA Navy skeleton force that had been tied up at Xingang.

There would be two destroyed subs by the time he

returned to Beijing, Tien told himself. If not, he might as well never go back to Beijing at all.

USS *TAMPA*

A half hour after leaving the harbor of Xingang, Vaughn had managed to get the control room operational—at least, the equipment was operational. The crew were still in shock from their captivity. Vaughn scanned the horizon with his binoculars. The night sky had grown overcast with the approach of a storm. That could only help, lowering visibility for the forces that would inevitably begin searching for them. Vaughn called into his VHF radio down to the control room:

"Control Bridge. Morris, where are you?"

"I'VE GOT YOU, OVER." Morris' voice was calm.

"What's going on there? We need to submerge ASAP."

"I KNOW. LENNOX IS READY TO TAKE THE CONN. I'VE GOT SEALS ON THE HELM AND PLANES AND I'LL BE ON THE BALLAST PANEL."

SEALs driving the submarine out? Vaughn had to find out what had happened to the men held up forward—he'd heard they were all like zombies. It would be a hell of a transit without a competent crew. But before he could take on that, he had to get the submarine *down*. He pulled all the clamshells up except the one on the starboard side of the bridge. He had rigged the bridge for dive, with the exception of latching up the final clamshell and shutting the upper hatch to the bridge-access tunnel. Baron von Brandt's body had been lowered down the tunnel and was in the frozen stores room. Vaughn called Lennox to the radio and passed on his course and speed and approximate position, then handed over the conn. After a last look at the surface he closed the clamshell, ducked into the bridge-access trunk and shut the hatch above him.

He came down the ladder two rungs at a time and dropped to the deck of the upper level passageway, shutting the lower hatch and spinning the operating wheel to engage the dogs. He stepped into the control room.

"Last man down, hatch secured, Chief of the Watch ... uh, Commander Morris," he said once he'd dropped to the deck of the control room.

He looked at Executive Officer Lennox. The man's eyes were sunk into his skull, dark bags below them; his mouth was slack, his posture a slouch. Still, there was some intelligence in his eyes, which was more than could be said for some of the men who had been held forward, if Morris's report was to be believed.

"XO, you want to take her down or do you want me to?" Vaughn asked.

"You do it, Eng," Lennox said dully.

"Aye, sir." Vaughn looked around at the control room for a moment, the operating stations manned with SEALs who didn't have the slightest idea what they were doing. In spite of his audience he announced formally, solemnly, "This is Lieutenant Commander Vaughn. I have the deck and the conn." He waited a moment, then spoke to the SEAL at the helmsman's station. "You at the helm. Say, 'helm aye.' "

"Helm aye," Buffalo Sauer said, trying not to smile.

"XO, raise the number-two periscope. Commander Morris, open all main ballast tank vents. Oh hell, move over a second."

Vaughn stepped to Morris's console and snapped to the up position six toggle switches—the solenoid valves to the main ballast tank vents. He then reached into the overhead and rotated a handle on a communication box and the ship's klaxon horn blared throughout the ship its *OOH-GAH OOH-GAH*. Vaughn raised a microphone to his lips and ordered, "DIVE, DIVE" on the Circuit One, expecting to hear a cheer from the crew in the middle level, but there was no sound except the growling of the ventilation system.

Vaughn watched the ballast control-panel vertical-console, waiting for the indication that the ballast tank vents had opened. But in the next seconds, no red telltale circles appeared; the old green bars remained lit. Vaughn stepped up to the conn, took hold of the grips of the periscope, trained it forward and aft. No sign of any venting from the tanks.

Vaughn told Lennox: "Damned vents are stuck shut. Still frozen from the depth charging."

"What now?" Morris asked.

Vaughn reached into a toolbox built into a bench-box against the starboard curvature of the hull, back behind the attack consoles. Inside was a sledgehammer. He handed it to Morris, who looked at him in disbelief.

"What now? Why, we hammer them, of course. XO, grab all the lanyards from the first lieutenant's locker and a harness."

Lennox walked forward and came back with a pile of tangled canvas straps. Vaughn had undogged the lower hatch to the bridge-access trunk, opened it and latched it in the up position. He looked over at Morris.

"I need a volunteer, someone with some balls who's not scared of a little water."

Morris looked at Vaughn. "Let's go."

"I figured." Vaughn walked to the pile of straps and untangled a harness. "Put that on. The XO will show you how."

"I know how to put on a harness."

"XO, link the lanyards together. We'll need about twenty of them."

Vaughn took the periscope, searching the water around them. There were no other ships visible, and no aircraft in the impenetrable clouds above. He looked for another periscope but saw nothing but the faint line of demarcation between bay and sky.

"Ready, OOD," Lennox called, handing Morris a coil of canvas, the twenty lanyards linked end to end. Morris, suspecting what was coming, latched one end of the long tether to his harness and tossed the coiled lanyard over a shoulder, stuffing the sledgehammer into one of the straps of the harness.

"Good," Vaughn said. "XO, take the radio and make sure my speed and bowplane orders are followed."

Lennox nodded. Vaughn and Morris walked to the hatch of the bridge.

At the top of the sail Vaughn opened the clamshells and looked out again into the blackness of the sky. Only two hours till dawn, he thought. He looked at the sky, hoping there were no airborne patrol craft on the way. All he could hear was the noise of the bow wave below. Vaughn spoke into his lip mike.

"All ahead one third!"

The radio crackled its acknowledgement and the bow wave died down, its roar quieting to a whisper as it lapped against the sonar dome forward. Vaughn took one end of Morris's lanyard and tied it to one of the steel rungs set into the side of the sail and looked at Morris.

"Okay, Commander, here's the drill. You climb down the ladder and go aft to the ballast-tank vents, the shiny metal plates in pairs along the centerline. See them? Get the ones furthest aft, then work your way forward."

"What do you mean 'get them'?"

"Smash them with the hammer. Hard. Hard as you can. Get your face away from the vent once it opens," Vaughn said, "or else it'll be like staring into Old Faithful just as it's erupting. And hurry it up because once those vents start venting the ship is going down."

Morris climbed over the lip of the sail and lowered himself down to the cylindrical deck of the ship, then walked back aft. Vaughn watched Morris work his way aft, letting out his tether as he went, until he was at the far aft-point of the hull where it sloped down into the water. Morris then hit the first vent-valve with an overhead smash.

Nothing happened. Morris raised the sledgehammer

again, high over his head, and brought it down in a rapid arc, his muscles straining.

The hammer hit the vent-valve plate with a solid thunk, and a tremendous spray of water roared out of the opening, knocking Morris down to the deck and nearly washing him overboard. The water sprayed out like a firehose, rising over forty feet above the deck. Morris got to his feet on the wet deck and moved forward to find another set of vents further forward. He repeated the action, smacking the valve as hard as he could. Another spray of water blasted out of the vent. He continued forward to the last set aft, opening it, then headed forward.

As he reached the sail the ship was already submerging, the deck sinking into the sea. Morris hurried toward the forward deck, the water beginning to rise on the cylindrical hull until only a few feet of width remained. He glanced aft long enough to see that the after-deck had vanished into the water, which left only the forward deck exposed. He found the first of three forward vents and smashed the first, running from the spray, then hitting the second, the spray from it knocking him to the deck. He somehow regained his footing, smashed the third and let go of the hammer.

Morris now began the walk aft along the sail to climb back up, but by this time the ship had settled into the water so that only the sail remained above the waves. The water flow over the hull was only five knots but as the hull sank into the flow the water washed Morris off the deck.

He shouted up at Vaughn as the sail went by. "Slow *down*. I've got to hand-over-hand the lanyard to get back to the sail."

"I can't! If I slow down we'll sink. Our speed over the bowplanes is all that's keeping us up!"

Morris didn't care what the reasons were. He pulled in on the lanyard, seeing the sail slip away from him, continuing to grow smaller as the ship drove on, still sinking.

The lanyard began to pay out. Morris spun in the

water as the lanyard untangled itself from his shoulder, where he had coiled it as he had walked forward. He decided to wait until the lanyard unwound so he could pull himself up on it. Even though it would be a two-hundred-foot trip to the sail, at five knots the hand-over-hand was not much ... he had done this hooked onto a ship plowing through the water at twenty knots with a five-hundred-foot line testing a counter-terrorist insertion method.

But when Morris saw the rudder approaching, only the top of the vertical surface showing, his confidence vanished. Being this close to the rudder meant that the screw was just a few feet astern of it, and the screw vortex from a scimitar-bladed submarine screw would suck him in immediately and grind him into shark bait. He grabbed his lanyard and pulled with all his strength, trying to avoid the screw. Hand-over-hand he climbed, taking in the lanyard, thinking he was still going to make it—when the lanyard behind him caught in the screw and began pulling him toward it.

Morris saw the rudder coming up on him, the tail of the ship fast approaching as the screw pulled his lanyard in like a fishing reel. He knew he couldn't fight against the horsepower of the screw. When the rudder went by he was dragged underwater. Now only a few feet from the screw, he frantically tried to detach his lanyard, searching his harness for the release hook. He couldn't find the lanyard release, he was about to go into the screw ...

CHAPTER 25

SUNDAY, 12 MAY
1945 GREENWICH MEAN TIME

HANGU PLA NAVAL AIR FORCE STATION
0345 BEIJING TIME

Leader Tien Tse-Min spoke into a microphone as he looked out the tower window at the Nimrod antisubmarine patrol plane idling on the runway.

"You have orders to release weapons and sink the submarines. Any submarine contact you find will be a hostile target. Sink it. There are two subs, one crippled, possibly on the surface, the second submerged."

The patrol craft's engines roared from the end of the runway as the oddly shaped plane prepared to takeoff, its bulbous bow and stinger-tail making it appear ungainly.

"Understood, Leader Tien. We'll search until we run out of fuel or weapons or both."

The Nimrod released its brakes and accelerated, finally lifting off the runway and turning to the south, to search and destroy the enemy submarines.

USS *TAMPA*

"STOP THE SHAFT! STOP AND LOCK THE SHAFT!" the walkie-talkie blared in the maneuvering room. The throttleman at the steam-plant control-panel slammed the ahead turbine throttle shut, spinning the wheel two turns until the poppet valves of the throttles seated on the casings of the huge main

270

engines. He looked up at the panel and saw the steam box pressure falling to vacuum, then whipped open the smaller chrome wheel set inside the larger wheel. The small wheel was the throttle valve for the astern turbines. By applying steam to the astern turbines there was a chance that they could counteract the momentum of the heavy drive train and bring the shaft to a stop. But the problem was control—the astern turbines had a tendency to be either shut tight or wide open. Not enough steam and the shaft would continue rotating—too much steam and the screw would begin to spin rapidly in the astern direction. The other problem with sticky throttle valves was that when they slammed open they could pull so much steam from the boilers that the reactor could overpower and shut down the entire system on a power-to-flow scram. Then the shaft would certainly continue spinning in the ahead direction with no brake to stop it.

The throttleman sweated as he watched the steam-pressure gages on the astern turbine steam boxes, heard the Engineroom Supervisor shouting out "more steam" and "less steam" trying to stop the tons of steel spinning a hundred feet aft. As the attempt to stop the shaft entered its second half-minute the throttleman wondered *why* he was stopping the shaft. There could only be two reasons: either there had been a complete loss of the main lube oil system ... or there was a man overboard. The MLO system was fine, which meant that if he failed to stop the shaft, he could be grinding somebody to a bloody pulp ...

"More steam!" the ERS called. The throttleman puffed the astern turbines one last time.

"Shaft is stopped, lock the shaft," the ERS shouted. After a moment, the throttleman heard the report: "Shaft is locked."

He shut the throttle wheel and sat heavily in his seat, the sweat pouring over his face, wondering if he had been in time.

*   *   *

Jack Morris shut his eyes as the screw approached, its vortex roaring in his ears as the blades spun in the dark water. When the screw hit him, the blades were frozen in the water. The ship was still moving from its own momentum, but the screw had stopped. He was pinned against three curved, polished brass scimitar blades.

It was only after being trapped against the screw by the water flow for another minute that Morris realized he had been underwater for maybe three full minutes. He had survived only because his lungs were so used to diving. Although he was too disciplined an underwater swimmer to thrash for air and gulp water, he well knew that in another ninety seconds or so he would be faint from lack of oxygen, and thirty seconds after that he would pass out. He reached down to his waist to feel for the lanyard hook but couldn't find it. He reached around to the small of his back, remembering that the lanyard's shock absorber was hooked onto a metal loop in his back—rigged that way so that if it pulled him hard his momentum would bend him rather than break his back as it surely would if he had worn it in front. As he searched for the lanyard, he felt his ears pop. A moment later they popped again.

This meant the submarine was sinking, submerging with him wired to the screw by his goddamned lanyard. He gave up trying to reach the back hook, pinned as he was to the screw, and began to try to undo the straps of the safety harness. If he could escape the harness it wouldn't matter what the lanyard was doing.

As he pulled on the straps of the harness his ears popped again. His body longed for air, even to the point of tempting him to breathe water. He struggled against the harness, loosening one leg strap but realizing he had one more leg strap, a chest strap and two arm straps to go.

Never make it, he thought as he struggled against the straps. He began to suffocate, his body beginning to react to his brain stem alone, ignoring the higher levels of his mind. He was thrashing hard, left and right, the convulsions beyond his control, like a fish pulled from the water on a hook. He had one clear thought ... remembering that when he instructed recruits in Survival Swimming School he used to call the near-drowning panic "seeing God."

And Jack Morris was about to see God.

The ship settled into the water faster than Lube Oil Vaughn would have thought. The main ballast tanks were flooded, thanks to the SEAL commander, and the shaft of the screw was stopped and locked. But now that the ship was heavy, with no speed, it had begun to sink. The only thing keeping her sail above water had been the bowplanes and sternplanes, the water flowing over them giving the control surfaces enough lift to be able to "fly" the ship up over the surface. With the screw stopped, she was losing the lift, like an airplane trying to take off with failing engines. Vaughn couldn't even emergency blow back to raise the ship back to the surface—the vents were jammed open and the EMBT blow system had no more high-pressure air left.

The water came up to the lip of the sail and began to flow over it, running down to the deck of the bridge and down the access trunk. Vaughn could hear the shouting from the control room below, the men wondering if he was still on the bridge. He could sense their instinct to shut the lower bridge-access tunnel hatch to save the ship. That was the code of the Silent Service—save the ship, save the plant, *then* save the men.

And yet, even though the ship was flooding, and he might be washed overboard, he couldn't just dive down the hatch and leave Morris out there. Without Morris the crew would still be in Chinese hell, dying of starvation or beatings by now. But he also couldn't order the engines to add speed, because turning the screw might well mean carving up Morris's body if he were caught on the blades.

But Vaughn wouldn't be much use dead, to Morris or the ship. Reluctantly he finally left the bridge, fought the water flooding the access trunk, jumped down the hatch and shut it after him. He hung onto the ladder in a blacked-out tunnel, dogging the hatch above. He climbed down the ladder in the unlit tunnel and banged on the lower hatch. He could hear the latch being spun open, then saw the crescent of light from the passageway below as the hatch was opened.

He stepped down onto the stepoff pad and into the control room, soaked, and found the men in the room looking at him. He could see the questions in their faces. Where was Commander Morris . . . ?

He told them without being asked . . . "He's overboard," Vaughn said, his voice dead. "His lanyard got caught in the screw."

"I know," Commander Lennox said, lowering the periscope. "I saw it all in the type 20. Vaughn, there was nothing you could do."

Vaughn looked at Lennox in surprise for a moment, wondering if the XO had gotten over his dazed confusion when the ship went aground. He seemed to be functional now, if still somewhat haunted. Perhaps thinking he was losing Vaughn had startled him back to reality, for if Vaughn had gone overboard with Morris, Lennox would have been the only man capable of driving *Tampa* to freedom.

"Is the screw still stopped?"

"Yes," Lennox said. "I took the conn when it looked like you were having trouble, but we're still at all stop."

"Order up ahead standard and plane up to the surface," Vaughn said. "Do an Anderson turn and come around to the point we lost him. I'll try to see if I can spot him. You keep looking on the scope. Get a boathook from the first lieutenant's locker and pass it up."

"Helm, all ahead standard," Lennox ordered.

Buffalo Sauer turned the needle on the engine indicator to STANDARD. An answering needle matched the ordered needle.

"Maneuvering answers ahead standard," Buffalo called out.

Vaughn waited at the ladder to the bridge, his face grim.

Through the haze of panic that had taken over Jack Morris's mind, there was, amazingly, still a kernel of rational thought, though it was fast disappearing. It was that one point of dim light left in his mind that allowed him to feel the screw begin to rotate again, slowly at first, then speeding up, spinning Morris like a pinwheel. As the massive brass screw moved it sliced through the canvas of his lanyard. The screw turned even faster until the blood rushed to Morris's head, the force of the motion nearly snuffing out what little life was left in him.

At sixty-four RPM of the fifteen-foot-diameter screw, Morris's remaining harness strap broke, and the motion of the spinning propeller sent him twisting off into the sea. His body rose up toward the surface some twenty feet above with such force that he was tossed out of the water and up into an arc. Finally he crashed back down into the black bay water, submerging again for just an instant, then bobbing back to the surface. Instinctively his body coughed up a lungful of water and sucked in the air.

He was not aware of breathing or coughing or floating. He had lost consciousness, partly from the lack of oxygen, partly from the rush of blood to his head while spinning on *Tampa*'s propeller. He floated in the water of the bay, his face raised to the cloudy sky, wheezing as he breathed in the sea air. Off to the south, lightning flashed. Moments later the thunder rolled over the water and the rain began.

"I see him," Vaughn shouted into the radio. "All stop. Right full rudder . . . rudder amidships! All back one third. All stop!"

Vaughn had pulled the ship up so that Morris was just a few feet forward of the sail, against the hull, but the hull was thirty-three feet in diameter, which put Morris sixteen feet away from the deck. At least where the deck used to be—as soon as Vaughn stopped the ship it began to sink. It was trimmed too heavy, and in spite of pumping out the depth-control tanks and the bilges, the ship was too heavy to stay up on the surface at low speed with the ballast tanks full. As Vaughn watched, calling out to Morris, the sail was going down until the water lapped at the lip of the sail. Once again Vaughn dived down the hatch and emerged below, the boathook in his hands.

"You want to try again?" Lennox asked.

"I couldn't pull that close to him in ten years of trying," Vaughn said. "Without being stable on the surface I can't reach him. And I can't maneuver because I'll suck him into the screw."

"He might already be dead—"

"*No.* He was breathing."

"You could tell that in the dark, in the rain?"

Vaughn was silent.

"Lube Oil, we have to leave him. It'll be light in a few hours and with the rain we may never see him again. Save the ship, Eng."

"Wait." Vaughn moved to a console set into the overhead immediately aft of the periscope stand. He screwed in two fuses that were taped to the front of the console and flipped up a toggle, pulled a microphone off a hook, stopped and looked at Lennox.

"We got a callsign?"

Lennox nodded. "We're Black Sheep. The *Seawolf* is Sheepdog."

"*Seawolf* came for us? I'm surprised they risked her." Vaughn spoke into the microphone, his voice bouncing back at him as if coming from the bottom of the sea. "Sheepdog, this is Black Sheep. Sheepdog, this is Black Sheep, over." Stupid goddamn callsigns, he thought.

The console's speaker sputtered. It was the UWT,

the underwater telephone, an amplifier tied into the sonar system's active transducers, that transmitted human voices in the ocean rather than pulses or beeps.

"BLACK SHEEP, THIS IS SHEEPDOG. GLAD YOU MADE IT, OVER."

"Skip that," Vaughn said, trying to speak slowly and distinctly. "We have a man overboard at our position. Vents and blow system broken. Need you to rescue. Do you copy, over?"

"ROGER, BLACK SHEEP. WE HAVE YOUR POSITION CHARTED AND WILL ATTEMPT RE-COVER. PROCEED TO POINT GOLF-SUB-ONE. SHEEPDOG OUT."

"Pacino will handle it if anyone can," Lennox said. "Meantime we need to get out of here. Take us deep and head for golf-sub-one."

"Pacino? Name rings a bell. Who's he?"

"*Seawolf*'s captain, new guy, just took command."

"Okay. Point golf-sub-one, here we go." Vaughn looked down at the chart table at the chart of the Bo Hai Bay. The bay seemed terribly big. At standard speed it would be another twelve, thirteen hours before they reached the Lushun/Penglai Gap, the exit of the bay. "Helm, all ahead one third, turns for two knots."

Buffalo acknowledged. Vaughn continued to look at the chart, taking in hand some dividers and a calculator. After a few minutes Vaughn spoke again, still examining the chart.

"Helm, all ahead standard, steer course one zero two. Maintain depth eight zero."

"Aye, sir, standard at one zero two, depth eight zero, maneuvering answers ahead standard."

"Not bad, Buffalo," Vaughn said, trying to sound positive, but not succeeding.

Jack Morris began to wake up from the rain pounding in his face. He blinked the water out of his eyes, realizing he was being pulled by a rope. He tried to think back to what had happened but all he remembered was being sucked underwater by his lanyard. His head hurt, his whole body ached, but he seemed whole.

He saw a bright light in his eyes as the rope pulled him in, a long hook grabbing his coverall collar and hauling him up onto a deck. He remembered he was in Chinese waters and saw that he was being recaptured. He tried to struggle, but his strength drained. He felt himself collapse, and several men carried him, bumping him into the sides of the ship's superstructure. As the light went out in front of him he went blind, the world swimming in front of him in odd colors. He felt himself swaying from side to side as he was taken down a ladder.

It wasn't until the men carrying him stood him up, still holding him by his arms, that he realized he wasn't in a PLA ship but in the control room of the submarine *Seawolf*, staring into the face of Captain Michael Pacino.

"Morris, what would you do if I weren't here to save your sad ass? Take him to the doc and get him fixed up."

Morris, back from the dead, smiled and closed his eyes as the needle of a syringe punctured the skin of his arm.

USS *SEAWOLF*

"Conn, Sonar, we have aircraft engines bearing three three zero. Probable antisubmarine warfare aircraft ... confirmed, we have sonobuoy splashes from the north."

"Depth seven five feet," Pacino commanded.

"Probably detected us when we surfaced to get Morris," Tim Turner said, his voice tight.

The periscope came out of the well. Pacino could see the aircraft on the horizon when he selected the infra-red, which normally he would not do because it could be detected, but at least the IR would find an aircraft quickly, eliminating the need for a long air search. In the view of the IR, hot objects were colored light, cold objects dark. In the distance he could see the aircraft, or rather, in effect, an X-ray of it. At high power he could see through the wings to the engines, the turbines and compressors standing out in relief. He could even see consoles inside the plane's fuselage, and men at the consoles. The plane approached, flying overhead and circling back around.

"Mark on top," Pacino called. "Aircraft is a Nimrod ASW aircraft. Looks like he's in a final approach pattern for a torpedo launch. Arm the Mark 80s, OOD."

"SLAAM missiles armed, sir," Turner replied.

"SLAAM 80, SLAAM 80," Pacino called, hitting the missile key on the periscope grip. "Two launches," he said, watching the white splotches of the missile exhausts on the IR. He switched the scope to visual, de-energizing the IR view. A missile explosion would white-out the IR. As soon as he switched to normal visual, the first missile hit the Nimrod and blew off the right wing. The second hit the fuselage aft of the jet exhaust, cutting the aircraft in half. It came down into the water in flaming fragments.

"Aircraft is neutralized. Lowering number-two scope," Pacino said. "Right fifteen degrees rudder, steady course one one zero. Off'sa'deck, you have the conn. Secure battlestations and the rig for ultraquiet. Have the galley crank out a hot meal for the crew. Keep us on course for point golf-sub-one and make sure you track range and bearing to Friendly One at all times. Call me if you have problems. Any at all. Got it?"

"Yessir," Turner said, showing a weary smile, "Good night, sir."

Pacino yawned. "Later." He walked up the ladder to the upper level and forward to the corpsman's office to look in on Morris.

"How is he?" Pacino asked the corpsman chief.

"Mostly bruises, some water in his lungs, a bad headache and exhaustion. Tough man. Lucky man."

CHAPTER 26

SUNDAY, 12 MAY
2230 GREENWICH MEAN TIME

Bo Hai Bay
USS *Tampa*
0630 Beijing Time

Doc Sheffield, the SEAL corpsman, walked into the control room. It looked strange to see the muscle-bound SEAL wearing submarine coveralls. Vaughn stood alone on the conn, the ship control console and ballast control panel manned by SEALs, the firecontrol screens dead and unmanned. Vaughn had to tell the SEALs every switch to throw, every control to move. He had taken the watch as OOD until Lennox woke up to relieve him at 0800. Vaughn was beat.

"How are the crew?" Vaughn asked Doc Sheffield.

"The eighteen shot in the crew's mess are dead. Even the ones that took hits in their limbs, wounds that originally weren't that bad, are gone. It's more than just torture and starvation—after a while their will to live died. It happens, I guess. The Chinese executed five officers and six chiefs. The rest of the men are still spaced out from the torture. We need to get them off this ship. I'm not a shrink, but I think the confines of the sub are making them worse—it's not their ship any longer, it's their former prison. Once we're out I'm recommending a medevac."

"Doc, what the hell happened to them? What made them so zoned out?"

"I'm not sure you want to hear, Eng," Sheffield said. "It's taken me half the night to work this information out of the two or three half-sane men left aboard. They were held in close quarters, not allowed to get up or move for *any* reason, including to defecate or urinate. They were made to sit in their own stink for five days. They were not even allowed to stretch. They were starved, no food, no water. Several were shot and laid out on tables in front of the survivors. Not sure yet, but it looks like most of the ones shot were the NSA cryptologists, although at least five weren't. This gets worse. The Chinese made it clear that the crew had a choice—die of starvation and de-hydration, or eat the flesh of the dead men. From what I've gathered, for two days no one touched the bodies, they just sat there, staring at the decaying men who used to be their shipmates. Then a few began eating—they were reduced to desperate animals. The ones who held out had to watch the ones who didn't, and the ones who ate had to live with what they were doing.

"It only took a few hours to drive both groups to near madness. They were left like that for three more days. No wonder they just sit there and stare into space. Most of them now won't eat or drink. If we give them food they start screaming. They'll all die in a couple of days if we don't get them out of here."

"Jesus," Vaughn said. "Why would the Chinese do that? What did they have to gain?"

"It was a sort of blackmail to make the captain agree to record a statement condemning the President and the Pentagon. Maybe they thought a tape like that would turn the West away from supporting the White Army, I don't know. But I know they didn't have to use the crew—the captain broke and recorded the tape *before* they showed him what they'd done to the crew."

"How is the captain?"

"He's unconscious. Bad bullet wound in his shoulder that traveled deep into his upper chest, it's badly infected. Another bullet wound in his neck. Without surgery, I'd give him only hours. His blood pressure is down, pulse weak. He's barely alive."

"You mentioned surgery."

"To take the bullet out of his shoulder and clean the wound. It's deep in there, and pulling it out could cut a pulmonary artery. You'll need a damn good surgeon."

"Well, looks like you're it. I'll get Lennox out here to take the conn and I'll help you set up in the wardroom. We have surgical supplies—anesthesia, scalpels, suction. I'll try to assist you. Go get whatever you'll need." Vaughn picked up a phone and buzzed Lennox's stateroom.

"*Wait* a minute, sir. I'm a med-school dropout, not a doctor, much less a surgeon, and I just told you you'd need a great surgeon."

Vaughn spoke quietly into the phone and replaced it in its cradle.

"I heard you," Vaughn said quietly. "I heard you say the captain has only hours to live if he isn't operated on. We're *twelve* hours from international waters, and there's a fleet of Chinese warships between us and freedom. Number one—we could use the captain to help us out of this. Number two—he's not only the captain, he's my friend. I'm not going to let him die without trying every option, even if the option kills him. What are you worried about, a malpractice suit? *Now get going.*"

A voice came from the back of the room, the young SEAL lieutenant, Bartholomay, Morris' XO.

"You heard him, Doc. Let's go. Scrub up and get your stuff to the wardroom."

Doc Sheffield looked at the two officers for a moment, shook his head and left the control room.

"Any word?" Kurt Lennox asked Black Bart Bartholomay, who had brought a pot of coffee to the control room.

"They're still in there. It's tough to say if Doc is making any progress."

"Well, at least Murphy's still alive or they would have quit."

"I guess ..."

"How about the crew?"

"They'll probably be sleeping until we get to the Korea Bay. I wouldn't be surprised if they're still sleeping when the medevac choppers land on the hospital ship. I've seen hostages have a post-traumatic shock before, but never like this."

"What did you guys find in the torpedo room?"

"A goddamned mess. Blood everywhere from gathering the Chinese bodies and loading them into the torpedo tube. I don't think we're going to be shooting anything."

"Is there an intact torpedo?"

"Five or six, but they're all locked in by broken units. From what I've been able to see of the hydraulic loading system, the only way to get a torpedo into a tube would be to push it in by hand."

"What about the air rams?" Lennox asked, referring to the pistons that pressurized the torpedo-tube water-tanks.

"They look okay but I'm not familiar with the system."

"And the tubes?"

"One and three are leaking bad. But the port tubes seem okay. The firing panel switches were rewired for them. The one on the port side is where we stuffed all the Chinese bodies. But as far as the tubes being able to fire, who am I to say?"

"Until I get a crew back, you're it. So here's the deal—we do this the old-fashioned way, with muscle power. Get your guys below and break some grease out of the auxiliary machinery room. We'll fire a water slug out tube two to get rid of the bodies, then grease the racks and the weapons and shove two of the good ones into tubes two and four."

"What about that?" Bart asked, pointing to the dead firecontrol panel. "How are you going to shoot the fish if the computer's broken?"

"We'll set them manually from the torpedo room console."

"How will you know where to shoot?"

"Manual plots. I'll show you how."

Lieutenant Commander Vaughn walked into the room from the forward door. His coveralls were soaked with sweat, his hair plastered to his bearded face. Dark circles rimmed his eyes. He slouched against the doorway. Bart and Lennox froze, waiting for the word.

"Well," Vaughn said, "we're finished. The captain's stable, but Doc's not sure if he'll last more than another twenty-four hours. We need to get him to a hospital."

"We'll have to break radio silence to tell the fleet about what medical help we'll need," Lennox thought aloud. "I want choppers standing by to get the boys off."

"Risky," Vaughn said. "The bad guys could vector in on our position with direction finders."

"We'll send it in a buoy with a three-hour time-delay. They could still get a lock on our track, but it's no secret we're headed for the bay entrance at Lushun/Penglai Gap at maximum speed. My guess is the Chinese will be waiting in force at the Gap no matter what we do with the radio."

"I'll draft the message," Vaughn said, walking aft to the radio room.

Vaughn loaded the UHF satellite message buoy, roughly the size of a baseball bat, into the aft signal ejector, a small mechanism much like a torpedo tube set into the upper level of the aft compartment. When the buoy clicked home in the ejector he armed the switch that would activate the unit, then shut the ejector door. On the way back to the control room he ducked his head into the maneuvering room.

"You guys okay?" he asked the reactor operator.

"Real beat, Eng," the RO answered. The watch-standers aft were the same who had been on watch aft for the five days of captivity. Other than Lennox, Vaughn and the SEALs, the single engineering crew seemed the only men aboard who were sane.

"Hang in. A few more hours and we'll be out of the bay and off this boat—"

"Off the boat?"

"There's no way we can get this ship into Yokosuka with this crew—the guys on watch now are all we have, and by the time we reach Japan we'll be asleep on our feet. I'm calling for a replacement crew as soon as we reach international waters."

The electrical operator asked about the crew. Vaughn told him the truth, his stomach turning as he finished the story.

"Do us all a favor, men," Vaughn said. "Stay awake and keep this plant up, no matter what. If we get a shock that opens the scram breakers, do a fast recovery startup. Don't wait for orders."

"Aye, sir. Good luck, Eng."

Vaughn walked into the tunnel leading through the hatch to the forward compartment, up the ladder and down the passageway into control.

"Ready to launch, XO," he said.

"Launch the signal ejector," Lennox ordered.

Vaughn keyed a button on a small panel by the conn.

A hundred feet aft, the outer door of the signal ejector opened, and twenty seconds later a solenoid valve in a branch pipe from the auxiliary seawater system popped open, sending high-pressure seawater into the bottom of the signal ejector tube that pushed out the radio buoy. The buoy climbed the fifty-five feet to the surface and began to float, barely visible in the brown water of the bay. A timer inside the unit began a three-hour countdown ...

At the end of the countdown a whip antenna extended from the buoy and the UHF radio activated, transmitting the message from the *Tampa* to the western Pacific COMMSAT high overhead in a geosynchronous orbit. Within thirty seconds the message transmission was complete, the buoy flooded and sank to the silty bottom of the bay.

By the time the Harbin Z-9A sub-chasing helicopter flew over the square mile of water from which the buoy had transmitted, the submarine *Tampa* was over fifty miles further east, approaching the entrance to the Lushun/Penglai Gap.

KOREA BAY, 130 MILES EAST OF LUSHUN
SURFACE ACTION GROUP 57
AIRCRAFT CARRIER USS *RONALD REAGAN*
0947 BEIJING TIME

Admiral Richard Donchez stood in Flag Plot in the carrier's island with a wall of windows overlooking the flight deck below. The central chart table was taken up with a chart of the Lushun/Penglai area, the Bohai Haixia Strait in the center. Donchez, in working khakis, leaned over the table. After a moment his aide, Fred Rummel, brought in a satellite photo of the PLA Navy fleet piers at Lushun. Donchez studied it for a moment, then straightened up and looked at Rummel's fleshy face.

"The Northern Fleet's getting underway."

"Yes, sir. Every ship they have."

"Including the *Shaoguan*," Donchez said, pointing to the largest ship in the outbound fleet, the aircraft carrier that looked like a battleship with half the deck lopped off for the installation of a flight deck. "Which means they'll be flying ASW aircraft and helos. We'll need the air wing. Call the SAG and the Air Boss to flag plot and get me a NESTOR circuit to the White House and the SecDef."

Rummel grabbed a phone and gave a series of orders, then replaced the handset and looked out the windows at the sea, at the formation of the surface ships surrounding the carrier.

"What do you have in mind, Admiral?"

"We'll launch a squadron of F-14s and a squadron of F/A-18s to blow out their helos and their jet torpedo-carriers. I'm counting on *Seawolf* to take care of the surface ships, but she'll be damned low on Mark 80 SLAAM missiles by the time she and *Tampa* get to the strait."

"Washington will never go for it, Admiral. That's a direct attack on PRC naval assets. It would look like we're starting a war with China."

"I don't care *what* it looks like, I care about getting our subs out."

"I'LL try, sir, but I wouldn't count on it."

"Admiral," an ensign said, knocking on the door. "Immediate message for you, sir."

Donchez took the steel clipboard.

"Is the SAG on the way?" He meant the admiral in command of the surface action group comprised of the *Reagan,* two nuclear cruisers, two Aegis cruisers, five destroyers, four fast frigates, two fleet oilers, a supply ship and a hospital ship. Rear Admiral Patterson Wilkes-Charles III, the SAG, was a capable surface officer, but, in the opinion of both Donchez and Rummel, unaggressive and more concerned with his career than with the mission at hand.

"He'll be here in another five minutes, sir," the ensign said.

"So, Fred, you think the SAG will launch aircraft on my authorization without getting permission from Washington?"

"Patty? Patty the shrinking violet? Never, sir."

Donchez looked down at the message, read it, shut the metal clipboard cover and shoved it at Rummel.

"Look at paragraph four."

Rummel glanced at the message, a status report from the *Tampa.* The first three paragraphs consisted of a report of ship's material condition, ship's position and the miserable weapon situation. Rummel skimmed down to the fourth section of the message:

4. CREW SITUATION POOR. TWENTY-NINE (29) MEN AND OFFICERS KILLED BY CHINESE GUARDS DURING REPOSSESSION OF SHIP. COMMANDING OFFICER CDR. S. MURPHY IN GRAVE CONDITION AFTER EMERGENCY SURGERY. SURVIVING MEMBERS OF CREW IN SEVERE SHOCK AND UNABLE TO PERFORM DUTIES. SHIP OPERATIONS BEING CONDUCTED BY SHIP'S EXECUTIVE OFFICER, ENGINEER, SINGLE SECTION WATCH AFT WHO WERE GIVEN SPECIAL TREATMENT DURING CAPTIVITY, AND SEALS. CREW SHOCK CAUSED BY TORTURE—CREW GIVEN CHOICE OF STARVATION OR EATING CORPSES OF MEN EXECUTED DURING CAPTIVITY. ALL ATTEMPTS TO FEED CREW CAUSE VIOLENT HYSTERICAL REACTIONS. DUE TO STARVATION AND DEHYDRATION AND PSYCHOSIS, CREW WILL NEED MEDEVAC TO HOSPITAL FACILITIES IMMEDIATELY UPON REACHING INTERNATIONAL WATERS.

"Jesus," Rummel said.

A whooping noise rang out. Rummel answered a sound-powered phone making the noise. He listened for a moment, hung up.

"NESTOR circuit open, Admiral. SecDef is standing by."

Donchez reached for the red handset of the UHF satellite secure-voice NESTOR radio and began to speak. And as he did, a thundercloud passed over his face.

TWENTY KILOMETERS SOUTH OF LUSHUN, PRC

The fuselage of the two-seat YAK-36-A Forger trembled as the pilot throttled down the main cruise engine and started the lift engines. Up ahead, barely visible in the rain-swept fogged plastic of the aft canopy, the dark gray shape of the carrier *Shaoguan* materialized out of the clouds, the deck of the ship seeming impossibly small in the vast waters below. The lift engines were apparently working because the vibrations of the main jet were quieting. The VTOL jet coasted to a halt about thirty meters over the deck of the carrier, the lift engines now roaring in the tiny cockpit. After a moment suspended motionless, the jet came straight down in what seemed a barely controlled crash, slamming into the steel deckplates and bouncing twice, its weight finally settling down on the wet non-skid paint of the flight deck. The whine of the lift jets died to a low howl, then cut off, leaving the cockpit eerily quiet. The comparative stillness was interrupted only by the rain on the windshield, the sound of the wind and the ringing of sore ears.

A crowd of men came running toward the jet, each wearing oversized helmets, each performing a different function, one attaching a kind of tractor to the nose wheel, a second connecting a cable to a connection in the nose, two more tying the wings to the deck while another rolled a ladder to the cockpit. The canopy of the jet slowly opened, admitting a salty wet sea breeze. The man on the ladder pulled, and after a moment the man in the rear seat of the plane stood, his muscles aching from the ride. He allowed the technician on the ladder to help him down the rungs, and in a moment his boots rested on the solid deck of the Northern Fleet vessel *Shaoguan*.

An officer in a rainsuit ran up and saluted, pointing to the superstructure on the starboard side. The door in the island opened and the officer and the man from the newly arrived jet ducked inside. The noise of the wind and the rain died down when the officer shut the door.

"Welcome to the *Shaoguan*, Leader Tien Tse-Min. I have been authorized to escort you to your quarters—"

"No time. I need to speak to the Fleet Commander."

The officer walked quickly to a ladder on the starboard side. Five flights up and down a passageway guarded by an armed PLA soldier, Tien was led to a heavy steel door. Inside the fleet commander's suite, Tien pulled off his sweat- and rain-soaked helmet and tossed it on a couch, then went to the chart table on the port side of the room. Behind the massive table stood Fleet Commander Chu Hsueh-Fan. Chu stared out at Tien from under bushy gray eyebrows, his black eyes rimmed by a network of wrinkles, his mouth set into a tight line, the muscles of his jaw clenched. Tien did not need any further signs to understand that the fleet commander did not want him there. Too bad. He was to be in charge of the search-and-destroy operation, and the sooner Chu realized that the better.

"Beijing came up on the tactical net." Chu bit off the words. "I have orders to assist you to find the American submarines."

"Fleet Commander, excuse me, your orders are not to *assist* me. Your orders are to deploy the fleet as I request and find those submarines."

Chu glared over the chart at Tien Tse-Min, hating the idea of deferring in a military matter to a political crony of the Chairman. But now that he was here there was nothing Chu could do except perhaps stand back and let the political commissar ruin the operation. Chu reminded himself that if the operation failed, it was to Tien's account, not his own. And yet, finding the two submarines coming out of the gap was the core of Chu's job, it was a mission he had trained decades for, it was his profession, his life's work. But then, if he interfered with Tien, all that would be over. And even if Tien thought he was in command, perhaps he could guide the political officer's actions and still get the American subs. Even if Tien got the credit, it would be a small price to pay.

Besides, three decks below, in the ready room of the Fourth Antisubmarine Forger Squadron, Chu's son, Aircraft Commander Chu Hua-Feng, waited to board his aircraft and seek out and kill the submarines. No matter what happened, he would try not to let a mistake by Tien endanger his son. His son was a warrior and a pilot, but he wasn't invulnerable.

His thoughts collected, Chu spoke, his voice level.

"Leader Tien, I—and my fleet—are at your disposal."

Tien nodded. "Very well, then. I will be cleaning up. After a hot meal I will return to review the deployment of the fleet."

Tien turned and left the Fleet Commander's quarters. As the door slammed, Chu shook his head and went back to his chart.

CHAPTER 27

MONDAY, 13 MAY
0505 GREENWICH MEAN TIME

Bo Hai Bay
Sixty-seven Miles West
   of the Lushun/Penglai Gap
USS *Seawolf*
1305 Beijing Time

Pacino stood up from his stateroom's conference table as the knock sounded at the door. He was still staring at the chart taped to the tabletop when Jack Morris, Greg Keebes, Bill Feyley and Ray Linden walked in. All were noticeably tense as they gathered around the table. On the aft wall Pacino had taped a large chart of the Bo Hai and Korea bays, the Lushun area in the center. The channel leading through the Lushun/Penglai Gap's forty-mile length was about twenty inches long on the wall chart. The conference table's blown up photocopy was larger, the forty-mile-long channel taking up too much of the large table's surface. The chart was covered with a sheet of clear mylar. Colored grease pencils lay scattered on the table.

Pacino went up to the wall chart and took a pen from his coverall pocket to use as a pointer. The eastern mouth of the bay ended at Lushun to the north, Penglai to the south. The Lushun peninsula was a finger of land pointing southwest, the PLA Northern Fleet main base on the furthest south point of a bulbous tip at the end of the peninsula. Sixty miles south of Lushun Point was the northern hump of the broad

Shantung Peninsula, the blunt point of land that separated the Bo Hai from the Korea Bay at Penglai, and extended further east to separate the Korea Bay from the Yellow Sea to the south. In the center of the restricted waters between Lushun and Penglai were the islands of Miaodao. The passage for shallow draft ships was fairly broad north of the islands, and there was also plenty of water for transit south, closer to Penglai. On the chart Pacino had drawn a red mark along the twenty-fathom curve, the minimum depth they would need to transit submerged through the gap. For the twenty-fathom depth, there were two channels open to passage east. The larger of the two was the Bohai Haixia Strait, a tube of water forty nautical miles long and six miles wide at its narrow throat. The smaller channel lay to the south, the Miaodao Strait, south of the islands in the middle of the gap. Although the Miaodao Strait was wider at the mouth and the exit, it narrowed to a mere thousand yards in width north of Penglai.

Pacino said: "In less than three hours we'll be at the mouth of the gap. In the next half hour I want to come up with our final exit plan. Our only constraint is our previous arrangement with the *Tampa*. The four of you consider yourselves the Chinese. Your force strength is listed in front of you. Leading the fleet is the aircraft carrier *Shaoguan*. It has four squadrons of Yak antisubmarine vertical takeoff jets, each jet equipped with MAD detectors." He looked at Morris. "Jack, that's a magnetic probe that senses a disturbance in the earth's magnetic field caused by large deposits of iron, like submarine hulls. Only works when the ship is shallow and when the jet is directly overhead, but it will confirm a sub's position when sonar probes sniff it out. The carrier also has two squadrons of Harbin Z-9A choppers, also MAD-equipped, each designed to kill subs with torpedoes and depth charges.

"The fleet has five subs, three Han-class nukes, two Ming-class silent diesel-electric boats. Destroyers—

seven Ludas, four Udaloys, three Luhus. Frigates—thirteen Jianghus, three Jiangweis and one Jiangnan. Thirty-four fast attack torpedo patrol boats. And two dozen land-based Hind helicopters modified for anti-ship service. Now, I'm going to the conn to get to periscope depth and grab our traffic off the satellite and get a final navigation fix. I'm hoping for some last minute intelligence on the deployment of the fleet. I'll be back in, say, twenty minutes. When I get back the four of you will outline your plan to keep the two American subs from escaping your bay. You got all that?"

The officers nodded. Pacino left them, knowing that if they sweated over the plan as much as he had they would be more likely to understand his reactions over the next few hours.

In their shallow transit it took only moments to slow and come up to periscope depth. Pacino hadn't seen the outside world since the evening before, when he had been shooting at the Chinese aircraft and the frigate. When he raised the periscope, he was surprised by the grayness of the sky and the ugly brown of the bay water. Raindrops clouded the scope lens as a fierce wind blew on the surface. Visibility was still good, unfortunately, but the wind was blowing the wave tops to a height of two to three feet, a high sea for an enclosed bay like the Bo Hai. Radio reported the satellite transmission had been received in the computer buffer. The global positioning system had swallowed their navigation fix from the GPS NAV-SAT, pinpointing their location with an accuracy of a few inches. Pacino lowered the periscope and ordered the ship back down, then walked to the wardroom to grab a cup of coffee. He nodded at the officers gathered around the table, most of them unable to sleep knowing that the evening watch would be a combat watch. Pacino splashed the coffee into a *Seawolf* cup, the steam of the dark brew rising to the overhead. He downed a sip, burning his tongue, and saw Sonar Officer Tim Turner and Communications Officer Jeff Joseph looking at him.

"What's the word, Captain?" Turner asked.

"We breaking outta jail tonight, Skipper?" Joseph put in.

"We'll do our damndest," Pacino said quietly.

"Are you gonna brief us on how?" Turner asked.

"Nothing to brief. We line up our torpedoes and our Javelins and our Mark 80s and we come out shooting. At the end of the day we'll see who's left."

"That's it?"

Pacino looked at them. What more was there to say? Finally Pacino spoke: "Trust me. We'll be back in Yokosuka before you know it, and then you'll get Captain Duckett back."

The two junior officers shared a look. Joseph spoke. "Sir, we were hoping that you'd be staying on as captain."

Pacino looked up from his cup.

"Thanks, but after this is over I'll be run out of town on a rail. Admiral's orders."

"Then is it true, sir? The rumors that you're here ... because you're not afraid to shoot?"

"I don't think so, Jeff. True, I have no career to protect, no ass to cover, but the reason I'm here is that I've done this before. Two years ago, under the polar icecap."

"What happened?" Joseph pressed.

"My ship went down. Lost the crew to the sea and radiation." Pacino said, amazed at his voice staying level.

"What about the other guy?"

"We took care of him."

The lieutenants smiled. Pacino headed for the door. Turner called after him: "Sir?"

"Yes, Mr. Turner." Pacino looked into the younger man's eyes.

"Good luck, sir. Kick their butts."

Pacino nodded solemnly, realizing the young officers

had just told him they trusted him in spite of the news
about his last mission.

Pacino walked back down to his stateroom, taking
the radio message board from the radioman. He
paused outside his door, reading the message from the
Tampa to Donchez stating the wounded ship's status.
The line about Murphy being operated on was news—
Morris had told him about the rest, and it had sick-
ened him, making him look forward to the moment
when he could release his weapons. He fought hard
to keep his mind from flooding with images of the old
days with Sean Murphy, the friend who had shared
his whole adult life, the friend who had risked his own
Navy career to go AWOL to attend Pacino's father's
memorial service, the friend who had sat up night after
night next to Pacino's hospital bed when death was
close, the friend whose wife and children formed a
second family. A friend who now lay dying from two
bullet wounds and the torture of men who now would
try to sink them. Pacino stuffed the message into his
pocket. Beneath it was the intelligence message he
had hoped for, Donchez's relay and interpretation of
the deployment of the Chinese fleet. But something
seemed wrong.

Either the Chinese were screwing up, or the intelligence was flawed.

Lushun/Penglai Gap, Bohai Haixia Strait
Eight Kilometers From International Waters
PLA Navy Aircraft Carrier *Shaoguan*
1312 Beijing Time

The strategy room's huge tabletop was covered with a
large-scale chart of the Lushun/Penglai Gap. Northern
Fleet Commander Chu Hsueh-Fan held a long pole in
his hand, the end of the instrument shaped like a hoe,
used for moving small ship models on the table. He
had arranged a fleet of destroyers and frigates to the

west of the gap, the ships organized in a forward-deployed mobile force, a hunter-killer group. In the northern Bohai Haixia Strait, at the channel entrance, a large force of attack vessels was stationed. The zone in between the forward force and the channel entrance force was filled with the symbols of helicopters and Yak-36A VTOL planes.

Leader Tien Tse-Min stared at the chart from its west end.

"Give me the pointer," he said, reaching for Chu's implement.

"Sir, this is the way the fleet should be deployed," Chu protested, but handed over the hoe anyway.

Tien pulled all the ships and aircraft to a corner of the table, and began setting them up his way. When he had finished, Chu nearly felt sick. Instead of having a forward-deployed force searching in the east corner of the bay at the approaches to the gap, Tien had arranged most of the destroyers and frigates at the entrance and exit of the smaller channel to the south, the Strait of Miaodao. The surface forces had been relegated to the positions of sentries, gate guards. He had put a token surface force at the throat of the wider Bohai Haixia Strait, at the exit of which the *Shaoguan* was positioned.

"The submarines," Tien went on, "will transit through the southern strait, here at Miaodao. They may execute a feint to the north but they will be headed through the southern channel. I have arranged a gate-keeper force here at the entrance, another here at the exit. The center throat of the channel will be mined with acoustic and contact mines. Fast patrol boats will be stationed on either side of the mined area. And to ensure that the Americans are not tempted to change their plans and go through the northern passage at Haixia I have stationed an impressive though small force at the mid-point of the channel, with the *Shaoguan* at the exit of the channel."

Chu almost laughed. It was obvious to him that Tien was placing himself out of the combat zone by ordering the aircraft carrier to the farthest point from the anticipated action in the southern passage.

"Sir, the Americans will transit through the north channel, not the south. The Strait of Miaodao is much too tight, only a kilometer wide at the throat. They will have no room to maneuver there."

"Yes. That is why they will go to the southern passage. Since it is tight they will assume we will neglect it. But I am not assuming, Chu. My intelligence people assure me they will go to the southern passage."

"Please, tell me how they know that, sir. We have not even been able to track the subs after they left Tianjin. One aircraft was blown up trying to follow up a possible detection. An enemy radio transmission turned out to be a false alarm. So how do you know where the Americans will go?"

"I know the mind of the American commander like my own."

"Because you interrogated him?" He didn't say "tortured." "And, sir, we know nothing of the mind of the commander of the rescue sub."

"Or commanders, Chu. There are more than one, which is another reason we will use a gate-keeper force instead of a mobile force."

"Sir, grouping a task force together like this in restricted waters is like lining them up in a shooting gallery."

"No. If the Americans shoot they give away their location. When and if that happens we launch the helicopters and Yaks from the *Shaoguan* and together with the missiles and depth charges and torpedoes of the main and auxiliary forces we will prevail."

Chu reluctantly nodded, seeing that even though the plan was flawed, it just might barely suffice.

"Can we at least strengthen the northern task force, just in case?" Chu calculated, betting that Tien was a coward. "That would better protect this vessel in case of an ambitious, suicidal American escape plan."

"Yes, yes, I believe you are right about that. Perhaps a few more destroyers and frigates."

"And this zone to the west of the northern task force—it should be patrolled by helicopters continuously. Similarly for the sea to the east, between the task force and us."

"No," Tien said quickly. "The area to the west is a free-fire zone for Silex rocket-launched depth bombs. If there are friendly aircraft there the Udaloy destroyers cannot launch the rocket units. And we will need to keep our aircraft in a state of readiness onboard *Shaoguan,* so that they will have sufficient fuel when the Americans disclose their position, which will be when they fire on the southwest gate-guard task force."

Chu sighed, realizing Tien was using the aircraft to protect the carrier, and thereby his own hide. But then, Chu thought, what benefit would come from exposing his own son to the murderous weapons of the rescue submarine, the one that could reach up into the sky and shoot down helicopters? Again he remembered a promise to the boy's mother that he would never allow his own son to come to needless harm.

"Very well, Leader Tien. I will deploy the fleet as you have ordered."

"No need, Fleet Commander. I have already given the orders, the fleet is already deployed."

Chu stared at Tien, who only smiled pleasantly.

USS *SEAWOLF*

"Well, men, what's it look like?" Pacino asked the four senior officers bent over the stateroom's conference table.

Keebes stood up and pointed to the chart. Instead of being covered with grease-pencil marks it was crowded with pieces from a Monopoly game. Rows of red houses and green hotels were arranged in lines, and the tin battleship and dog and iron board pieces were put in places deemed significant.

"Sir, I took the liberty of raiding Captain Duckett's game cabinet. He used to like Monopoly. Anyway, the dog game piece is us, you know, dog for *Seawolf*. The battleship is the Chinese aircraft carrier, the iron is the *Tampa*, since it has no weapons it's dead iron. The hotels are major combatants, the Udaloys, the Luhus. The houses are the other destroyers and frigates. Thumbtacks are choppers, paper clips are VTOL jets, and the Han and Ming subs are dice. We ran out of stuff, so where we wanted to indicate mines we just spit on the table."

Pacino smiled. "Go on, XO."

"Well, sir, we put a force of destroyers and frigates out here, in the approaches to the bay, sort of a mobile search-and-destroy outfit. Then we put a bunch of choppers out there to search in open water, some over the channels. We're assuming the northern passage is the exit point, and we put sentry task forces at the entrance and exit, including the carrier at the exit. Just a token force here in the southern passage at Miaodao, couple PT boats, a few choppers. Jets patrolling here, rotating back to the carrier in sections to get refueled. It's leakproof, sir. You'll never get out of this."

Keebes must have listened to his last sentence, because his light tone vanished.

Pacino examined the chart for a long time, nodding.

"That's pretty much how I saw it," he said.

"So how do we get out, Skipper? And what did we tell *Tampa*?"

"You guys won't believe this," Pacino said, glancing at the intelligence message on the clipboard. He began pulling off hotels, game pieces, thumbtacks and paper clips. "The main entrance to the northern passage at Bohai Haixia is wide open. Nothing there for twenty-five miles. Then a small surface force patrolling at the throat of the channel. Two Udaloys, four Ludas, a few fast frigates. Then nothing all the way to the carrier, which is here, only five miles from international waters. All the emphasis is on the southern channel at

Miaodao. Two main surface task forces, including submarines, at the entrance and exit. The channel's being mined here in the middle. PT boats orbiting on either side of the minefield."

"What the hell?" Keebes said, looking at Pacino's positions of the game pieces. "Why would they guard the tiny channel to the south and leave the north damn near wide open?"

"Maybe they're trying to sucker us north," Morris said. "Defense in depth. Lure us in deep, then flank around the west task force from the entrance to the southern channel here, closing in on us from the west, squeezing us from either side."

"Goddamn," Keebes said. "Those guys are sneaky. That beats hell out of the Chinese plan we had."

"I don't think that's it," Pacino said. "The task force to the south is too far away to come in and act like a cork in the bottle of the northern passage. Those guys are two hours away from the entrance to the northern channel. They may be filling the holes in the north coverage with aircraft but I don't think so."

"So what do you think they *are* doing?"

"I think they're convinced we're going to the southern channel, and are setting up to catch us there. The forces to the north are tokens, just to keep us from thinking we've got a clean shot going through the northern channel."

"Why in hell would they think we'd try to escort *Tampa* out through that little channel on the south end?" Linden asked. "That channel is so tight we'd all get hard-ons going through it."

"They think we'll go through the south channel because they know we know it's too tight," Pacino said.

"I can't handle it," Keebes said. "So what do you want to do, then, sir?"

"We start here at the entrance to the northern channel. We launch the Javelin cruise missiles. Each one will have the time delay set for a future launch, when we're far into the channel. Then we launch half of the decoys, the Mark 38s designed to imitate the sounds

of a 688-class sub. Most go east in the Bohai Haixia
Strait, but we send a few south to the Miaodao Strait.
Meanwhile, *Tampa* begins the transit through the
strait in front of us, her passage screened by the decoys. It'll sound like half a dozen subs coming down
the channel. But before the Chinese hear them we
launch torpedoes down the channel, and a few down
to the south to confuse the task forces."

"Sir, torpedoes will hit the *Tampa*," Keebes put in.

"No. They'll be in transit mode, on the run-to-
enable. They won't enable and go active till they're
right on the central task force in the mid-point of the
Haixia channel. Then all hell breaks loose. The decoys
are spotted by the Chinese, then the torpedoes go
active and hit some, maybe all, of the ships in the task
force. The Javelins liftoff, and two minutes later we
have ten Javelin cruise missiles and eleven Mark 50
torpedoes hitting the thirteen ships of the task force.
Meanwhile, the decoys and the *Tampa* and *Seawolf*
go under the trouble zone."

Feyley asked: "Then what? They know you're there,
and the southern task forces come north to get you
while the carrier launches all its ASW aircraft to put
you on the bottom."

"We increase speed to twenty knots and get the hell
out. We'll launch the remaining Mark 80s at the aircraft and we launch the standoff weapon, the Ow-sow,
at the aircraft carrier."

"Captain," Keebes said, "it'll take us an hour to get
from the point where we dive under the sinking task
force to where we get to international waters. That's
an hour since you launched a bunch of Mark 80s and
an Ow-sow, an hour since the surface group got
pounded by a bunch of torpedoes and cruise missiles.
In that hour the decoys will have shut down. The Chinese will scramble their aircraft and their surface ships
from the south and they'll pound us. The surface
forces don't need to get close to be lethal—they have
the SS-N-14 rocket-launched depth charges and the

fourteen-variant rocket-launched torpedoes. We'll be dead meat five minutes after our Javelins impact."

There was silence in the room while Keebes's analysis sank in. Finally Pacino spoke:

"If we were alone we would be in big trouble. But we're not."

"Who else is here?" Keebes said. "Did I miss someone?"

Pacino went to the desk and took up a paperweight, a chunk of heavy steel left over from the ship's construction, with an etched inscription dedicated to Captain Duckett. Pacino slammed the steel chunk on the table, at the far corner to the east of the gap.

"The cavalry is here. Surface Action Group 57, with Admiral Donchez in charge aboard the USS *Ronald Reagan,* the biggest, hairiest aircraft carrier in the goddamned world. About the time our missiles start flying, Donchez will cover the bay with an umbrella of aircraft. It'll be a 'no-fly' zone for the Chinese."

"You know for a fact he'll cover our ass here?" Morris said. "He told you this?"

"Nope. But I know Dick Donchez. When he sees the flames coming from the bay, and a bunch of angry bees buzzing over our position in the channel, he'll know what to do."

"You better hope you're right, Captain," Morris said, "or it'll be your last mistake."

Pacino nodded. Morris, of course, was right.

KOREA BAY, 130 MILES EAST OF LUSHUN
SURFACE ACTION GROUP 57
AIRCRAFT CARRIER USS *RONALD REAGAN*

Admiral Richard Donchez shouted into the red handset of the UHF satellite secure-voice connection.

"What the hell do you mean, no air cover? Did anyone mention to the President that without air cover these subs will be sunk? They're fish in a goddamned barrel! What the hell have we done all this for to come here and have no air cover?"

The speaker in the overhead blasted out the distorted voice of the Secretary of Defense, Napoleon Ferguson.

"DICK, THIS HAS ALL BEEN EXPLAINED TO PRESIDENT DAWSON. HE IS EMPHATIC ON THIS POINT. THERE WILL BE NO PENETRATION OF BO HAI AIRSPACE BY YOUR JETS. IT'S TOO THREATENING, THE WORLD WILL THINK WE'RE STARTING A WAR WITH THE CHINESE. THE U.N. IS VOTING TONIGHT ON IMPOSING SANCTIONS ON THE UNITED STATES. WE'LL VETO IT, OF COURSE, BUT WE'LL GET A BLACK EYE. AND IT'S BECAUSE OF YOUR OPERATION THERE IN THE BAY. DAWSON DOESN'T WANT TO RISK IT. I'M STILL TALKING TO HIM."

"No, Napoleon, you've done enough talking. Donchez out."

The Admiral slammed the handset into its cradle and looked at Fred Rummel. "Well, Fred, you still think the SAG won't launch aircraft on my orders without authorization from Washington?"

Rummel shook his head: "Sir, we're grounded."

Donchez looked out the bulkhead windows, toward the west, out at the rain falling on the water of the bay.

Mikey Pacino was on his own. Donchez threw his cigar butt to the deck and mashed it in disgust.

CHAPTER 28

MONDAY, 13 MAY
0920 GREENWICH MEAN TIME

Bo Hai Bay, Lushun/Penglai Gap
Entrance to the Bohai Haixia Strait
USS Seawolf
1720 Beijing Time

Pacino hunched over the chart table in the control room, checking the plotting of the Chinese task forces and Seawolf's position at the entrance to the northern passage at the Bohai Haixia Strait. The Tampa had already entered the channel and was on the way east, the dot on the chart marked with the time of her position. Pacino stood and looked at Lieutenant Tim Turner.

"Tim, you ready?"

"Yessir."

"Off'sa'deck, man silent battlestations."

"Man silent battlestations, aye, sir. Chief of the Watch! Man silent battlestations!"

The COW acknowledged and spoke into his headset: "All spaces, Control, man battlestations."

The control room filled with men, each taking his watchstation and putting on cordless headsets with boom microphones. Usually manning silent battlestations took ten minutes before the space's phonetalkers could get everyone out of bed with the verbal announcement that the ship was manning battlestations, then it would take the men two minutes to dress and get to their watchstations, another two minutes to relieve the watch, a minute for a relieved watchstander

305

to go to his own battlestation and relieve that watch-stander. By the time the daisy chain of watch reliefs ended it could be fifteen minutes later. But when Turner reported battlestations manned it was less than sixty seconds later—the on-edge crew had been waiting for the order.

Pacino leaned over Bill Feyley's weapon-control console, checking the tube-loading status indication on the CRT display. "Weps, I want tube eight to be loaded at all times with a Mark 50 torpedo for a quick-reaction firing—our insurance. Tube eight is mine—one through seven are yours."

"Aye, sir."

"I want a thirty-second firing interval, no more. When I shoot a tube I expect the crew to be reloading immediately, and I want that operation to be *quiet*. You pass the word to your people below. What have you got in one through seven?"

"Tube-loaded Block III Javelin encapsulated cruise missiles with time-delay systems. All weapons powered up and self-checks nominal."

"Very well." Pacino checked the time. He was ahead of schedule. He moved up on the elevated periscope stand and looked out over the faces in the crowded control room, one of them belonging to Commander Jack Morris, who covered his nerves with a war face. "Attention in the firecontrol team." The room became instantly quiet, the only sound the whine of the spinning ESGN ball and the booming of the ventilation system. "Operation Jailbreak is now into its second minute. Here's the deal.

"In a few minutes we'll be launching Javelins set for delayed launch. When they're all gone we'll be putting out a salvo of Mark 38 decoys down the channel and a few to the south. Then a salvo of Mark 50 torpedoes, most down the channel. Then another round of decoys. The *Tampa* will be beginning her run down the strait any minute now. At approximately 1900, everything happens at once. The surface force will detect the initial wave of decoys, the torpedoes will go active and seek out targets, the Javelins launched between 1730 and 1830 will liftoff, the torpedoes will acquire and detonate, the Javelins will impact, and *Seawolf* and *Tampa* will transit beneath the distracted surface force.

"The only thing between us and freedom will be the Chinese aircraft carrier guarding the exit of the channel. I expect an aircraft attack, which we'll answer with our remaining Mark 80 SLAAMs. When we get close to the carrier we'll launch the Ow-sow, and with luck the ship will be damaged enough or too distracted to attack us on the way out. I hope you're all ready for a tough watch tonight. It's now 1732 Beijing time. Our ETA at the channel exit in international waters is 2115. We've got some shooting to do between now and then."

Morris went up to the conn and looked out at the activity in the room. Pacino nudged him, noticing he had his holstered Beretta pistol with him. What the hell, Pacino thought, it was probably his security blanket.

"Ready, Jack?"

"Just get us the hell out of here, Cap'n."

"Helm, right fifteen degrees rudder, steady course south, all ahead two thirds. Weps, pressurize all tubes and open all outer doors. Confirm targeting vectors to all Javelins and report status."

"Aye, sir," Feyley said. "All tubes pressurized and equalized to sea pressure. All outer doors coming open now. Target vectors tubes one through seven confirmed, targets bearing one zero five to one one three, range fifty-two thousand yards. All time delays set for liftoff at time 1900 local, an hour-and-a-half from now. All outer doors now open. Ready to fire, Captain."

"Very well," Pacino said, glancing at the chronometer. When it clicked over to 1735:00, he gave the next order: "Weps, shoot tube one."

"Fire," Feyley called. Down below the tube barked,

the noise loud in the room. "Tube one fired electrically, Captain."

"Shoot tube two."

The firing sequence continued. When Feyley launched a tube, the torpedo room crew shut the outer door, drained the tube, opened the inner door and rammed another Javelin in, connected the power and signal leads and shut the door so that when the tube's turn came up three or four minutes later the weapon was spun up and warm and ready to fire. By 1750 the room's Javelin missiles were gone, all of them floating silently in their watertight capsules below the surface of the bay, waiting for their timers to reach zero hour, 1900, when they would broach, open their nosecones, and unleash the rocket-powered cruise missiles. By that time, *Seawolf* would be far down the channel, within a few hundred yards of the northern channel's task force. Pacino ordered the ship to enter the channel and proceed east at twenty-five knots while the crew began to load Mark 38 decoys, the torpedo-sized noisemakers programmed to radiate the same noises as a Los Angeles-class submarine, able to be programmed to maneuver in set patterns or follow a channel. By 1812 the initial volley of Mark 38s had been fired and the torpedo room was set up to launch Mark 50 Hullcrusher torpedoes. When they were all gone, except the one earmarked for tube eight, the final volley of Mark 38 decoys was launched.

By 1830, less than an hour after he had started, Pacino's torpedo room was empty, all weapons gone except tube eight's Mark 50 and the ASW Standoff Weapon. Pacino took a deep breath and leaned against a railing of the periscope stand, his ears aching from the forty-three tube launches. He checked the chart. *Seawolf* was twelve miles into the channel, the boundaries of the restricted water narrowing on either side. The throat of the channel was another thirteen miles ahead. Somewhere further down the channel, eleven Mark 50 torpedoes, twelve Mark 38 decoys and the *Tampa* were making their way east. To the south, there were eight decoys and two torpedoes heading for the entrance to the southern passage at Miaodao, designed to confuse the southwest surface task force.

Pacino couldn't help wondering what was going on inside the *Tampa*. At least he had, more or less, control of his destiny. Those guys were passengers, along for the ride. Pacino looked at Jeff Joseph's Pos Two display at the circle marking Friendly One, now ahead of them by six miles to the east. Pacino plotted a dot on the chart, the position of the *Tampa*, then stared at the dot, as if by looking at a mark of pencil on the paper on the chart table he could project his mind into the hull of Murphy's submarine.

At 1851 the first decoy's acoustic emissions alerted the surface force at the channel mid-point that the intruder submarine was inbound. From that moment on, Pacino had no more time to think about the *Tampa* or even about Sean Murphy.

BOHAI HAIXIA STRAIT
USS *TAMPA*

Lieutenant Bartholomay looked up from the chart table in the control room, hoping to see in Lieutenant Commander Vaughn's face that what showed on the chart was not real.

"Eng, what are you doing here?" Bart asked, his finger pointing to the chart.

"I'm driving down the channel," Vaughn said, leaning on the periscope pole.

"But you're driving straight for the surface ships. Can't they detect you? Won't they depth-charge us or something?"

"Come and look at this."

Bart joined Vaughn in front of the Pos One console. Set into the overhead was the sonar display console, the broadband waterfall display selected off the sonar spherical array in the nosecone.

"See the waterfall? Those vertical streaks falling down the screen are noises, each noise a contact, and their horizontal positions on the display are their true bearings from us. The vertical position is time, the new at the top, the old at the bottom, the new replacing the old. The old falls off the screen, giving it the name waterfall. How many vertical streaks do you see?"

Bart counted: "Twelve. No, thirteen with this dark trace at one hundred degrees."

"The one zero zero trace is the surface force directly ahead. The other twelve traces are twelve *Tampa*s."

"Say what?"

"Every one of those noises is a 688-class submarine. At least so it will appear to the Chinese. Those are Mark 38 decoys. They are torpedo-sized, with large fuel tanks and a computer brain that steers them on a programmed course. In the nosecone of the unit is a sonar transducer that emits noises sounding exactly like this submarine. To the surface ships, it will look like there are thirteen subs coming."

"So?" Bart said. "So they shoot a dozen more depth-charge things than normal, and kill us a few seconds later. Is this the great plan you and Lennox have been hatching?"

"Only part of it."

Vaughn pressed a sequence of touch keys on the lower face of the monitor panel, dividing the waterfall display into two waterfalls. "The upper screen shows the last thirty minutes of history instead of just the last thirty seconds. The dark traces are the Mark 38 decoys. Look here at these lighter traces, the ones that sloped flat about fifteen minutes ago." Eleven new traces were visible, each vertical at the bottom, sloping flat in the middle and vertical again at the top of the display. "Those are torpedoes. They came out of our baffles and passed us here, where the traces are horizontal, then drove on ahead of us. They are now catching up to the decoys. In another twenty minutes or so the first wave of decoys will swim into the task force zone. The Chinese will detect them—I *hope*—and get confused, since there are apparently several submarines. Then the volley of torpedoes will reach them, and after that, we and those closer decoys will reach the task force. By that time the Chinese should be sinking."

"Won't you be shooting at the surface ships?"

"Can't. None of the torpedoes are working. We thought we had some healthy units but they all failed their self-checks. Two tubes work, but without an intact torpedo there's no chance. We've got vertical launch tubes for cruise missiles, but without the fire-control computer they're just useless scrap metal."

"So what happens after the *Seawolf* runs out of torpedoes? Will we be out of hot water?"

Vaughn pushed the function keys on the sonar monitor, returning the original waterfall display, and turned to Bartholomay.

"Who the hell knows? Look, Bart, either we get out of the bay or we don't."

"I just don't like being along for the ride. On an OP at least I have a finger on the trigger. Here, all I can do is wait inside this sewer pipe for you to drive us out."

Lube Oil Vaughn looked at the SEAL, his face a mask of confidence, his stomach a nest of butterflies, his hands in his pockets to prevent anyone seeing them shake. He was one of only two officers who could get the ship out, and if he didn't look steady it would be that much harder to keep the men's trust. But the truth was, Vaughn was just as much a passenger as Black Bart.

At 1845 Kurt Lennox came into the control room, his black-rimmed, bloodshot eyes giving away the fact that he had been unable to sleep for days. Each minute stretched into hours, each hour a month. Lennox, Vaughn and Bartholomay stood over the chart table as if gathered around a campfire on a cold night.

"How much longer to international waters?" Lennox asked.

Vaughn walked his dividers across the chart, measured the distance, then grabbed a time-motion slide rule and spun the inner circle twice.

"About ninety minutes," he said, "assuming we speed up to full when we hit the task force at the channel mid-point."

"Goddamned long time," Bart said.

"It's a big *goddamned* channel," Vaughn said, looking at the chronometer, wishing they had just one lousy torpedo.

PLA Navy Destroyer *Jinan*

Weapons Department Leader Chen Yun held up the binoculars and looked out the bridge windows at the water to the west. The wind blew the rain against the windshield, the sound like a sandblast rig from the shipyard. Outside the windows, the bay water was black, the sky turning dark brown as the light faded. The water of the bay was choppy, the whitecaps phosphorescent in the dim light. The ship was on course north, two kilometers astern of a Jianghu frigate, which was two kilometers astern of another frigate.

Chen walked to the surface search radar display and put his face down to the hooded display, the rubber of the hood cold on his forehead. The circular scope was green, the rotating beam lighting up the land around them. The point of Lushun was sharp and clear to the north. The hump of Penglai was more distant, its shoreline fuzzy in the rain. Close to the center of the circle, a group of islands lit up and slowly faded with each rotation of the radar beam. Chen adjusted a range-display knob, setting the radius of the display circle to eight kilometers. The points of land vanished, the scope taken up with twelve dots arranged in an oblong rectangle, the center of the display on the east elongated edge of the rectangle. The dots were the twelve other ships of the task force, all steaming one behind another along an eleven-kilometer by two-

kilometer racetrack, pacing back and forth over the
deep channel through the Bohai Haixia.

Chen didn't like it. A Udaloy-class destroyer was
not meant to march back and forth in formation as if
on a parade ground; it was built to prowl the open
seas in search of submarines, and when they were detected, to kill them. The ship should have been steaming independently, in a forward deployment, searching
over open water for the submarines. To bottle them
up here at a choke-point was stupid. Certainly that
was fine for the frigates, but to put a sub-hunting Udaloy here made no sense. Even if they detected the
subs now, the Udaloy would have a tough time getting
to them in the restricted waters of the channel.

The water to the west, from the direction of enemy
approach, was a free-fire zone for their SS-N-14 Silex
missiles. That at least had been done right. The most
lethal weapon in the task force was the SS-N-14, a
rocket-launched depth charge. Usually one per cus-
tomer would be enough to kill any sub. But if they
needed to launch torpedoes down a west bearing line,
they could not do it from the eastern branch of the
pace pattern because they could acquire on the ships
of their task force to the west, the ones pacing south.
And they were prohibited from shooting in the east
direction because the aircraft carrier *Shaoguan* was
patrolling the end of the channel to the east, and it
would not do to hit the carrier with a volley of Type
53 torpedoes.

It made no sense, confining a deadly Udaloy to this
battle tactic, but then, who was he to say? Chen was
still in his late twenties, barely out of the Second Surface Vessel Academy at Canton. He could not hope
to match the tactical minds of the fleet commanders
and task force commanders or of Ship Commander
Yang Pei Ping, the *Jinan*'s captain. They must have
agreed to this force deployment. Still, the tactics
course at the academy had always insisted that fast
ASW destroyers like the Udaloy operate in open
water, leaving choke-point entrapments to lesser ships

like the Jianghu frigates. And what about the fleet
deployments to the south? The fleet commander had
stationed most of the fleet at the entrance and exit of
the southern passage, the Miaodao Strait, expecting
the subs to try to leave through the narrow channel.
Chen didn't see it. If he were a submarine commander
trying to make his way out he'd keep to the wider
channel. But perhaps the fleet commander had satellite surveillance or some reason to believe that the
subs would come out via Miaodao.

Chen swallowed his frustration. His life since ado-
lescence had led up to this moment, and not only was
his ship put in the secondary task force, a halfhearted
contingency force, but they were doing the job of a
PT boat. He walked to the port bridge wing and
searched the bay to the west with his binoculars.

"BRIDGE, COMBAT CONTROL," a speaker
blared out from the overhead, its rasping volume star-
tling Chen, who put his binoculars down and concentrated on the announcement. "WE HAVE
BROADBAND SONAR CONTACT ON MULTI-
PLE SUBMERGED HOSTILE TARGETS TO THE
WEST."

Chen felt the rush of excitement spinning him to
an accelerated speed. With one hand he grabbed the
microphone of the ship's announcing system: "GEN-
ERAL QUARTERS, CAPTAIN TO THE BRIDGE."

With his other hand he grabbed the handset of the
tactical net radio and clicked the button for transmitting, tried to make his voice slow and distinct.

"Task force flag, this is destroyer *Jinan* reporting
initial detection of multiple submerged hostile contacts, bearing west, supplemental report to follow,
over."

"*JINAN,* THIS IS TASK FORCE FLAG, AC-
KNOWLEDGING INITIAL DETECTION, OUT,"
the tactical net's speaker crackled.

Commander Yang Pei Ping hurried into the bridge,
his face set in a mask of concentration.

"I've been in combat control, Chen," he said. "They are tracking twelve contacts. A dozen submarines!"

"No. That's impossible," Chen said. "Is it a trick?"

"Perhaps the Americans sent a fleet of submarines to rescue their ship. From the destruction at Xingang it is beginning to make sense. Are general quarters manned?"

"Yessir."

"Good. Arm the SS-N-14 Silexes and the Type 53s. Prepare for a Silex launch of the entire battery to the west."

"Yes, Commander, but the range to the targets is unknown. We can't throw away missiles without a fire-control range. Perhaps the Commander would consider using the active sonar to locate the mean range."

"No," Yang said, dismissing the younger man. "Passive sonar only. Orders of the fleet commander. He does not want to fill the channels with active echo ranging signals that might impede our longer range detection of threats. The more we transmit, the more noise in the water and the less we'll hear."

"Sir, I don't mean to doubt the fleet commander, but an active sonar transmission will determine beyond a doubt if any of these hostile contacts are ... decoys."

"There are no such things as *decoys*, Chen. These are submarines."

"We'd get a range to the ships much quicker going active, sir. The subs could be driving up close any moment. We need to release weapons, at least fire torpedoes to the west."

"Chen, the tactics are being evaluated in combat control. Your function is to help me drive the ship, *not* comment on strategy. We'll continue our target motion analysis by turning around when we have the first leg bearing rates. The task force will maneuver in a moment." Yang took up the intercom mike. "Combat control, do you have a steady bearing rate?"

"BRIDGE, COMBAT, YES."

"Task force flag, this is destroyer *Jinan* reporting

first leg complete and ready for maneuver, over," Yang reported on the tactical net, which replied immediately:

"TASK FORCE NORTH, THIS IS TASK FORCE FLAG, STANDBY FOR IMMEDIATE EXECUTE, BREAK, TURN STARBOARD ONE EIGHT ZERO RELATIVE, BREAK ... STANDBY ... *EXECUTE*."

"Right full rudder, both engines ahead full speed," Yang ordered.

The ship responded, the deck vibrating and tilting as the rudder and gas-turbine engines brought her one hundred and eighty degrees around to the south. At the same time every ship in the task force turned a half-circle, reversing course, the ships now driving their racetrack clockwise instead of counterclockwise, the better to get a parallax range to the incoming submarines. Two minutes later it was apparent that the contacts were extremely close. Much too close. Inside the minimum range of the Silex missiles, Chen thought bitterly, resenting the mindless rigidity of his senior officers. If they had gone active, the Silex missiles would have blown up the submarines three minutes ago.

The task force had lost their opportunity. It was now, he felt, too late to shoot. Once the submarines came between the surface ships and the aircraft carrier they would have to use the fleet's helicopters to kill the subs—the firing of torpedoes going east toward the aircraft carrier and the fleet commander had been prohibited.

PLA Navy Aircraft Carrier *Shaoguan*

Fleet Commander Chu Hsueh-Fan put the handset of the tactical net back in its cradle and looked at Tien Tse-Min, who was leaning over the chart table and scratching his chin.

"Leader Tien, we have detected twelve submerged

contacts in the Bohai Haixia Strait. They are heading east and approaching the north task force. The task force will be releasing weapons in the next few moments." Chu bit back a smile now that the notion that the submarines would depart via the south passage was obviously disproved. There would be no more interference from Tien—they could get on with the business of destroying the submarines.

"No. Your north task force shall not release weapons. The submarines will be coming through the south channel at any moment."

Chu could not believe what he was hearing.

Tien grabbed the tactical net handset and called the southwest task force commander. "Southwest task force flag, this is Tien. Is there any sign of a detection, over?"

"LEADER TIEN, THIS IS SOUTHWEST TASK FORCE FLAG, STANDBY, OVER."

"Leader Tien, I do not understand."

"Chu, if you were a commander of a sub you would understand. The Americans are launching decoys at us to confuse us. They will wait until all our weapons are depleted and then they will sail through the bay making fools of us."

"Sir, decoys or not, no one has decoys that can make a sound like a submarine. There are units that can make noise, even generate a screen of bubbles to fool torpedoes, but *these* contacts are a flotilla of submarines. Can you expect me to let these contacts go without shooting them?"

"Commander Chu," Tien said, "any noise, any weapons, any active sonar, any activity of our forces in the northern passage will make the Americans believe that they have confused us. I am telling you, they are coming out through the Miaodao Strait."

"LEADER TIEN, THIS IS SOUTHWEST TASK FORCE FLAG, OVER."

"Go ahead, Flag."

"WE HAVE DETECTED TWO SUBMERGED CONTACTS CLOSING THE ENTRANCE TO THE

MIAODAO CHANNEL AT APPROXIMATELY TWENTY-FIVE CLICKS. CONFIDENCE IS HIGH THAT THESE ARE THE AMERICANS. REQUEST IMMEDIATE WEAPONS RELEASE, OVER."

Tien smiled. "I told you the Bohai Haixia detections were a feint. A smokescreen to draw our attention to the north."

"Sir, if you won't allow a weapon release for the north task force, we at least need to verify these contacts in the Bohai Haixia with our helicopters, the units with magnetic anomaly detection."

"Mag detection won't work in a shallow channel," Tien said.

Chu raged beneath his forced calm. Leader Tien Tse-Min knew just enough about naval matters to be dangerous, but certainly not enough to sink a PT boat, much less a flotilla of motivated and lethal American submarines. The first crack formed in Chu's professional front.

"Leader Tien, listen with your ears and launch the helicopters."

For a moment Tien just stared at Chu. After a moment he raised his eyebrows and smiled indulgently.

"Very well, Fleet Commander. I suppose it would not hurt to do some overflights."

Chu gave an order into the phone. Down the flight deck below, the jet turbines of twelve Harbin Z-9A helicopters began to spool up, reaching full power a few moments later, the main rotors of the big machines beginning to spin, beating the rainy air of the storm-darkened dusk.

PLA Navy Destroyer *Jinan*

At 1854, the first of the contacts drove under the task force, the submarines inside minimum weapons range. The other submarines likewise were too close to shoot, and one by one they transited under the channel where the task force sailed. *Jinan,* like the other vessels, allowed the ships to go, knowing that once the subs were outside one kilometer they could shoot SS-N-14 Silex missiles at the ships, as long as the *Shaoguan* gave permission.

At 1900 ten cruise missiles lifted off from a point at the far west entrance to the channel, their orange flames lighting up the bay as the ten missiles climbed into the clouds and vanished. Immediately Commander Yang ordered the port SS-N-14 quad launcher trained on the position, the range set for forty kilometers, and the battery launched. The first and second Silex missiles were lifting off when the 30-mm six-barrel anti-missile guns began to train over to the west. The speaker of the intercom boomed through the bridge.

"BRIDGE, COMBAT, INCOMING CRUISE MISSILES, SEVERAL CONTACTS, INBOUND AT SUBSONIC VELOCITY. FIRECONTROL RADAR LOCKED ON AND 30-MM GUNS IN AUTOMATIC."

Commander Yang acknowledged while the third Silex missile lifted off and climbed to the west, en route to the vessels that had launched the missiles. Yang's binoculars were on the position forty kilometers to the west, where the American submarines, the ones that had launched the hostile cruise missiles, were about to be blown apart.

"Combat control, bridge," Yang called on the intercom. "Report status of the second leg to the submerged contacts—do we have a firing range set into the computer?"

At 1906 the sonar operator in the combat control center clicked his microphone to respond, then stopped and listened hard into his headset. He heard a strange screeching noise, then two noises, then five, then seven. His screen filled with angry bright traces, all of them loud and fast. Too late he realized what was on the screen.

PLA Navy Aircraft Carrier *Shaoguan*

Chu watched as the Harbin helicopters of squadrons one and two lifted off and flew to the west, soon vanishing into the dark and the rain until only their flashing beacons could be seen, then those too were swallowed up by the darkness. As he watched he thought he saw flashes of fire far to the west, beyond the horizon, the cause of the fire not clear in his binoculars. He hurried over to his tactical net radiotelephone when the task force commander of the north beat him to it, the radio speaker loud and insistent as the commander's voice rang out in the room:

"FLEET FLAG, THIS IS NORTHERN TASK FORCE FLAG, WE HAVE MULTIPLE LAUNCHES OF ROCKETS FROM THE ENTRANCE TO THE CHANNEL FORTY KILOMETERS WEST OUR POSITION. MISSILES ARE BEING TRACKED NOW. WILL RELEASE WEAPONS INTO THE FREE-FIRE ZONE."

"Northern Task Force Flag, this is Fleet Flag. Release weapons to the west and report incoming missile status."

"FLEET FLAG, THIS IS NORTHERN TASK FORCE FLAG, INCOMING MISSILES ARE SEA-LAUNCHED CRUISE MISSILES. WE CAN KNOCK THEM DOWN."

"Roger, Fleet Flag out."

Before Chu could press Tien to commit to vectoring the southern task forces to the Bohai Haixia Strait, a radio transmission came into the room, the southeast force commander's voice rushed and urgent:

"FLAG, THIS IS SOUTHWEST, WE ARE UNDER TORPEDO ATTACK. THE *DONGCHUAN* AND THE *WUZI* ARE SINKING. REQUEST IMMEDIATE AIRCRAFT SUPPORT."

Tien replied to the task force commander, then looked at Chu. "We must divert the helicopter squadrons to the southwest task force. Radio the instructions."

"If you send our helicopters to the south, can I at least launch the VTOL jets down the Bohai Haixia?"

"Keep the jets on deck until we have pinpointed the exact locations of the submarines. Then the jets can deliver the killing blows."

It was madness, Chu thought, that whatever facts presented themselves, Tien Tse-Min would see them through the filter of his preordained conclusions about the submarine escape through the south passage. Chu realized there was nothing more he could do but wait for the subs to reach the *Shaoguan* after the weapons in the south were proved to be a diversion. Then it would be up to the jets, helicopters and ASW weapons of the *Shaoguan* to neutralize them, even if he had to chase them into the Korea Bay.

PLA NAVY DESTROYER *JINAN*

At 1907 the first torpedo smashed into *Jinan*'s hull at the forward funnel, a geyser of water exploding two hundred meters into the sky, blowing a hole in the ship so big that it looked like a bite had been taken out of the ship's port side with jaws a half-shiplength wide. The engines stopped, the gas turbines dying from the destroyed fuel delivery and computer control systems.

At 1908 a Javelin cruise missile slammed into the superstructure under the starboard bridge wing, entered the interior of the ship and detonated. The resulting explosion and fire set off one of the SS-N-14 canisters on the starboard side, which swallowed the remainder of the superstructure in a fireball that grew into a billowing mushroom cloud, turning from orange to black over the hull of the ship, rising up into the wet clouds.

Chen and Yang were both smashed into the starboard bulkhead of the bridge when the first torpedo exploded. The Javelin explosion blew a hole in the floor of the bridge, the glass windows still remaining after the torpedo hit. Yang and Chen were alive, even after the cruise missile hit, but the explosion of the Silex battery vaporized the bridge wing where they had collapsed. Their bodies would never be found. After the SS-N-14 explosion there was nothing left of them bigger than what could be poured into a thimble.

At 1911 the second Mark 50 torpedo swam under the keel of the crippled *Jinan,* the hull proximity sensor firing the detonator train, the ton of high explosive blowing the water under the keel into a sphere of expanding gases. With the water suddenly gone beneath the keel, the ship's weight supported only by the bow and stern, the ship collapsed, breaking like a bridge carrying too great a load. The hull snapped, the bow section rolling starboard and sinking immediately, the stern half rolling to port and vanishing by the screw, the grotesque twisted and burned metal of the ripped hull sticking straight up into the rainy air, then slowly settling.

At 1913 the only sign that a mighty Udaloy destroyer had been there was the oily slick from her fuel tanks and the foam and debris from her sinking.

At 1914 the USS *Tampa* transited east, passing within four hundred yards of the corpse of the *Jinan.* At 1917 *Seawolf* followed. By 1920 Beijing time the thirteen ships of the northern task force were destroyed and on the bottom of Bohai Bay.

Sixteen kilometers to the east, the aircraft carrier *Shaoguan* turned to the north, across the line of sight to the fiery explosions of what had been the northern task force, its sensors straining to detect the submarines that had caused the destruction. In the strategy room, the fleet commander stared at the radar screen, which was now empty except for the ships in the Miaodao Channel.

CHAPTER 29

MONDAY, 13 MAY
1130 GREENWICH MEAN TIME

Bo Hai Bay, Bohai Haixia Strait
USS SEAWOLF 1930 Beijing Time

"What's your range to the carrier?" Pacino asked Lieutenant Jeff Joseph on Pos Two.

"Sir, showing seventeen thousand yards, but the solution is sloppy."

"Close enough. Weps, spin up the Ow-sow in tube one."

Feyley acknowledged. Keebes looked up at Pacino.

"Captain, once we launch that thing, we'd better have some air cover or that's the end," Keebes said, and turned back to the firecontrol computer.

"We won't launch until the last moment," Pacino told him.

Morris looked over at Pacino from the chart table.

"This had better work, Pacino."

Pacino just held his gaze. No way he could promise it would.

PLA Navy Aircraft Carrier SHAOGUAN
1938 Beijing Time

Fleet Commander Chu Hsueh-Fan ignored Leader Tien Tse-Min as he looked at the radar repeater's hooded screen while holding the handset of the radio-telephone to his ear. Other than the contours of the land to the north and south, the screen was empty in the Bohai Haixia Channel. The northern task force no longer existed. Chu left the radar hood and stared out the port bulkhead windows at the channel to the west, the flames slowly dying out on the horizon as the last of the ships of the northern task force sank. When he put his binoculars down, the look on his face was murderous rage.

"The northern fleet is *gone*. Sunk by torpedoes and cruise missiles from the submarines in the Bohai Haixia. While you sent our forces south and refused air cover to the north, we lost every ship and every man, men who trusted me and our Navy."

"I disagree. Those torpedoes and missiles could have been launched from the mouth of the Bohai Haixia *before* the submarines went into the south passage. If not for the blunders of your southwest task force we would have caught the subs by now—"

Chu grabbed Tien's tunic above the pocket, the button on the pocket flap falling to the deck. "You damn fool, I've had enough. I relieve you of tactical command. Maybe the Chairman will let me live if I can recapture or kill at least one submarine today. But we are both sure to die with you in command."

Tien, not so much a fool as to challenge Chu now, said nothing. If they survived, he would take credit. And Chu, it seemed, had been right . . .

Chu found the microphone to the bridge and turned his back to Tien. "Bridge, Strategy, move the ship to a position two kilometers west of the line marking international waters, max speed. Alert the Yak squadron to man their planes. As soon as we reach our new position launch the Yaks and sweep to the west for submarines."

"FLEET COMMANDER, THE SHIP IS SPEEDING UP TO FORTY-FIVE CLICKS, HEADING NINETY-FIVE DEGREES. YAK SQUADRONS ARE MANNING PLANES."

"Very well. Alert the Ship Commander to begin an active sonar search with all hull arrays, short range first, then medium as we come around back to the west."

The ship's deck began to vibrate, then to tilt as the bridge put the rudder over and the ship went into a tight turn to the east. Chu steadied himself on a sideboard while he reached for the tactical net.

"All helicopter aircraft, this is fleet flag. Turn immediately and proceed at maximum speed to the western mouth of the Bohai Haixia and begin an active sonar sweep of the channel to the east. Use leapfrog tactics. Weapons release is authorized upon any submerged contacts."

Chen then ordered the southwest task force flag to proceed north to the western mouth of the Haixia and sweep to the east following the helicopter forces. He next directed the southeast task force flag to detach two of his fastest and closest destroyer or frigate assets and vector them to the east mouth of the Haixia at absolute maximum velocity. The ships were to standby with the *Shaoguan* and form a search-and-destroy task force.

The reply came: "FLEET FLAG, SOUTHEAST FLAG, DETACHING UDALOY-CLASS DE-STROYER *ZUNYI* AND LUDA-CLASS DE-STROYER *KAIFING,* REMAINDER TASK FORCE EN ROUTE EAST HAIXIA AND PRE-PARING TO COMMENCE SONAR SWEEP FROM EAST TO WEST, SOUTHEAST FLAG, OUT."

Chu looked at Tien.

"The submarines will be captured or dead within the hour. No doubt the Chairman will be very pleased with you."

"You have not even left a token force guarding the south."

"The channel is mined, PT boats are patrolling both sides of the minefield. No one would make it alive out of the south."

The intercom blared out the bridge officer's voice: "FLEET COMMANDER, BRIDGE, THE SHIP

IS NOW POSITIONED AS YOU ORDERED, TWO
KILOMETERS FROM INTERNATIONAL WA-
TERS, TURNING NOW TO THE WEST. YAK
SQUADRONS WILL BE LAUNCHING AIR-
CRAFT IMMEDIATELY."

Chu walked to the port bulkhead overlooking the
floodlamp-lit flight deck, hoping to see his son's VTOL
jet taking off.

Aircraft Commander Chu Hua-Feng jogged through
the rain to his waiting Yak-36A, strapping on his flight
helmet just before he reached the ladder to the cockpit. As the technician enabled his ejection seat, his
weapons officer strapped himself into the small aft
cockpit. The attack model of the Yak was a single
seater, but the ASW version had a rear seat for the
weapons officer, who spent more of his time detecting
submarines than releasing weapons.

Chu's weapons officer, Lo Yun, was a young, aggressive officer straight out of the Quingdao Aviation
School. Lo shared many of Chu's opinions on the rebellion, on flying, on the navy as a career. He did not
seem to mind that Chu's father was the fleet commander, as so many of the other officers in the squadron did, always being careful of what they said when
Chu was present. Lo was not afraid to be irreverent
about their leadership, and more often than not Chu
agreed with him. Chu was beginning to think of Lo
as a friend, a very good friend. As he pulled the stick
toward his crotch and the plane flew away from the
deck, Chu suspected in the next hours a friend like
Lo might well be as important as the weapons they
carried.

USS SEAWOLF

Pacino stood next to Keebes overlooking the firecontrol console. The Pos One display showed the geographic presentation of the channel sea. At the

opening of the Haixia, the Chinese aircraft carrier was stationed as if guarding the exit. To the southwest and southeast, the ships of the task forces were heading north to the Bohai Haixia Strait, as if abandoning the southern passage and coming to help the carrier scour the Haixia. For a moment Pacino wondered if *Seawolf* or *Tampa* had been detected. Yet there were no aircraft overhead, so how could they have been detected?

"Sonar, Conn," Pacino called, "any aircraft contacts? Close or distant?"

"Conn, Sonar, no, but we have two surface contacts coming out of the southeast task force bearing one five nine, bearing drift left. Both contacts approaching at high speed between thirty and thirty-two knots. The rest of the task force is only doing twenty-four or twenty-five."

"XO, designate the two contacts Targets Fourteen and Fifteen. Let's get a solution on them and let me know their ETA to the channel mouth."

"We'll need to maneuver to the south to get a passive leg," Keebes replied.

"Mr. Turner" Pacino called, "take the conn and drive the ship for a TMA solution on the incoming contacts."

"Aye, sir. Skipper, if we start doing target motion analysis here in the passage we'll lag behind the *Tampa*. She'll be out there by herself."

"Don't worry," Pacino said. "We're going to be enough of a distraction that *Tampa* won't be noticed."

"Conn, Sonar," Chief Jeb's voice announced on Pacino's headset, "the Mark 38 decoys are shutting down. Seven so far. The others will be down in a few minutes. The two inbound warships from the southeast are classified destroyers, one Luda-class, the other a Udaloy . . . Conn, *all* decoys have now shut down."

"Conn, aye," Pacino replied, feeling Keebes's eyes on him. Pacino concentrated on the firecontrol display and on the chart, watching as the solutions developed to the two inbound warships, noting that the Chinese carrier, Target Thirteen, was maneuvering toward the east, toward the "finish line" denoting the boundary between international and Chinese territorial waters.

"Conn, Sonar, we're getting helicopter engines."

"Where are they?"

"The bearings are scattered, but it looks like most of them are concentrating in the west at bearing two eight five."

"What do you figure they're doing, Captain?" Keebes asked.

"Probably overflying the Javelin launch zone at the west mouth of the channel. Maybe they think we were there when we launched and they're searching a zone around the liftoff."

"From liftoff point to the east down the channel," Keebes added, "which means they're on the way."

"Sonar, Captain, are the choppers converging on one bearing?"

"Yes, all choppers are now bearing two eight zero to two nine zero."

"Coming or going?"

"Doppler's not applicable here, sir."

"What do your *ears* tell you?"

"Coming, sir. Definitely inbound."

Pacino looked at Keebes. "They're sweeping eastward, squeezing us between the choppers on the west and the carrier on the east. And the only noises they'll hear in this channel are us and the *Tampa*."

"And *Tampa* is a lot louder than we are."

"I know. Mr. Turner, can you arm and launch the Mark 80 SLAAMs without the periscope being up?"

"Yessir."

"Arm all of them."

"What are you going to do?" Keebes cut in.

"Score a few choppers."

"We've only got nine missiles."

"That's nine choppers," Pacino said.

"Conn, Sonar, we are now getting jet engines out of the east. Looks like the carrier is launching the Yaks at us. Jets are inbound at high speed."

"Sir," Turner reported, "ETA of the destroyers at

our position is eighteen minutes. But they should be in SS-N-14 range within nine."

"Helicopters are getting closer, Captain," Sonar Chief Jeb reported. "Bearings to the aircraft are spreading."

Pacino waited, ears straining, waiting for the first ping of a dipping sonar indicating the helicopters had found the *Seawolf.*

"Conn, Sonar, we're getting distant dipping sonar pings, some east, some west. The closer ones are west."

"So, Captain," Jack Morris said, his arms crossed over his chest. "Did you think it would be this bad?"

"You call this bad, Morris? So far no one's launched a single weapon at us. Wait till the ordnance starts going off before you get in a sweat."

But what Pacino was thinking as he stared at the firecontrol display was: Where the *hell* was Donchez's air support?

KOREA BAY
SURFACE ACTION GROUP 57
AIRCRAFT CARRIER USS *RONALD REAGAN*

The Nimitz-class carrier USS *Ronald Reagan* steamed through the rain and the mist and the dark, plowing through the Korea Bay's whitecaps, her search radar rotating once every ten seconds, the American flag flapping from the highest yardarm of the tall central mast, the masthead lights illuminating the spray of the rain and the number 76 painted on the island, her air wing's aircraft secured in the hangar decks in the bowels of the 105,000-ton ship. A ring of dim red lights in the island marked the bridge, where the officer of the deck drove the ship, the ships of Surface Action Group 57 in formation around the carrier, each in her assigned position and monitored by the bridge crew.

One level below, the flight-operations center was

quiet, the room stuffed full of consoles for the radars and communications gear that would provide tactical control of the air wing once it was airborne. A level below flight ops was the tactical flag command center, also known as the flag plot room, where Admiral Richard Donchez stared out over the darkened flight deck of the *Reagan* and held the red handset of the NESTOR satellite secure-voice radiotelephone to his ear, a deep frown on his face.

"Mr. Secretary, I have a lot of American lives at stake here. I can't get the submarines out without air cover. I need an hour of flight operations and I can neutralize the Chinese fleet—yessir, I know that ... I understand that, but do you realize they will bomb these ships to the bottom of the bay? We've monitored every weapon launch by the *Seawolf,* and by our calculations she is out of weapons. That's right, sir ... I know, but if you count sunken ships, that's at least one torpedo per sinking. The Chinese have several squadrons of ASW helos and jets up, scouring the bay. The subs only have a few miles to go, and they're out of there ..."

Donchez paused for a long moment, listening, rubbing his forehead. Finally he nodded and spoke, saying only "Roger, Donchez out." He replaced the red handset, then looked up at Rummel.

"Sir, what did the SecDef say?"

"He's worried that our international partners will think we're beating up on the *poor Chinese.* That we still don't want it known that we were in the bay spying. That this is an embarrassment to the Administration. That this is more firepower than we asked for in the first place. That torpedoes shot from subs are one thing, that carrier-launched aircraft are another. That this whole thing is turning into the President's personal flap. He said he was convening a meeting with the President and the national security staff and that he'd make our case. He said he'd contact us in an hour."

"That could be too late—"

"I *know*. Get the SAG up here."

Rummel called the bridge and told them to send the SAG to Flag Plot. It only took a few minutes, during which Donchez hunched over the oversized Bo Hai Bay chart.

The door opened and shut behind Rear Admiral Patterson Wilkes-Charles III, the commander of the surface action group, including the carrier, the fleet and the air wing. Wilkes-Charles, a tall, thin blond man, was in working khakis, his only insignia his admiral's stars and his surface warfare pin over his left pocket. It was unusual for a SAG to be a surface officer, even though the task force was primarily surface ships—usually SAGs were ex-carrier commanders. Carrier captains were inevitably fighter pilots first, surface ship commanders second. But Wilkes-Charles had commanded a frigate, a destroyer, a nuclear cruiser and Aegis cruiser, as well as a helicopter carrier, just before his promotion to rear admiral. He was the hero of the surface warfare community, living proof that a black-shoe officer could command a carrier group without flying an F-14 fighter first. Wilkes-Charles had been marked as a golden boy when he was a midshipman at Annapolis, groomed for command, always the first promoted in his class of officers. Still, Donchez couldn't help but wonder why. Wilkes-Charles had never been close to combat, had been in Korea during the Gulf War, and had never done anything special during his command tours to justify the Pentagon's apparent love of him. But then, neither had he run aground, had any serious accidents, gotten divorced, gotten drunk in front of the brass, or any of the other things that could ruin a Navy career. He was competent, personable, friendly, but hardly original or aggressive. Still, he was the SAG, which meant he controlled the operational deployment of the surface and air forces, which in turn meant Donchez would need to go through him to get this operation going.

"Admiral Donchez, good to see you. Should I have some sandwiches brought up, sir? Would you like coffee?" Wilkes-Charles smiled, his even teeth shining even in the red fluorescent lights.

"No thanks, Pat," Donchez said. He decided to give it to the SAG straight. "Listen, Pat, we still don't have authorization from the President to go."

"We're at a point of no return, Admiral."

Donchez looked at him, wondering if he were hoping to avoid a fight over the bay, something that could definitely go wrong, stopping his career-flight to the top.

"Exactly, a point of no return. Which is why we're going to launch aircraft now. I want you to get your F-14s and F-18s airborne immediately, as well as your EA-6s and a couple Hawkeyes. And don't forget the Viking ASW jets and all the LAMPS choppers we're carrying."

"But, sir, I can't do that. You just said Washington hasn't given us permission—"

"Washington won't let us shoot. No one said we can't fly. Get those aircraft up and keep them fueled with tankers. The minute the President says 'go' I want every fighter and attack aircraft crossing the line and mixing it up. Until then our boys will fly to an orbit point this side of the line of demarcation."

"We'll launch, sir. But I can't keep everyone fueled indefinitely. We'll have to come back sooner or later."

"I know that. Get going."

Wilkes-Charles left. Donchez listened to the announcements on the Circuit One ordering flight ops, watched the deck fill with planes as the elevators lifted the jets onto the deck, watched as pilots manned the planes and taxied over to the catapults. The ship turned into the wind at full speed, the steam from the catapults wafting over the ship, half-obscuring the men working on the aircraft. And quickly, the first F-14 Tomcat supersonic fighter was positioned on the number-one catapult. Ready for liftoff.

USS SEAWOLF

"Conn, Sonar, the helicopters have all flown over. All chopper contacts now bear east. I don't think we were detected."

"That anechoic coating does a good job against active sonar," Pacino said, but Keebes's face remained grim.

"Conn, Sonar, we now have multiple high-frequency transmissions from a helicopter HS-12 dipping sonar, bearing zero nine eight. We think they've locked onto Friendly One."

"They've got the *Tampa,* Skipper," Keebes said.

"Range to the *Tampa*?"

"Ten thousand yards."

"Mr. Turner," Pacino said, "take her up to seven nine feet. Lookaround number-two scope."

Officer of the Deck Turner brought the ship shallow to a keel depth of seventy-nine feet, then reported the depth to Pacino. Pacino rotated the hydraulic control ring for the periscope and waited for it to come out of the well. When it arrived he snapped down the grips and pressed his eye to the cool rubber of the eyepiece. Outside, the sky was dark, the sea choppy, the rain beating against the lens. The remaining light was steadily vanishing.

"Chief of the Watch, rig control for black," Pacino ordered. The lights were turned out, which made clearer the view out the scope.

To the east he could make out the dark shape of the Chinese carrier in the distance, much of its hull obscured by the curvature of the earth, only its superstructure visible. He turned the scope to the southeast, looking for incoming destroyers, saw nothing. He did a quick surface search and found nothing close, then tried an air search, nearly impossible in the rainy dark. But at the bearing to Friendly One, the *Tampa,* he thought he could see the flashing beacons of helicopters.

"Mark 80 status?" Pacino asked.

"Armed and ready, sir."

"Launching now, one, two, three, four—" Pacino counted to nine, waited, still looking out the periscope toward the position of the *Tampa,* not concerned about being detected since he had just informed the entire Chinese fleet of his presence with the missiles, and besides, detection fit his tactical plan. The missiles in the sail silently floated out of the water and flew into the sky, heading for the helicopters gathered around the position of the *Tampa.*

Several missile trails appeared at the top of Pacino's periscope view, the nine Mark 80 SLAAMs en route to the helicopters flying over the *Tampa.* One, then two, then a half-dozen fireballs bloomed in the dark at the bearing to Friendly One. Pacino lowered the periscope and fished in his coverall pocket for his eyepatch. As he strapped it on, he called for the Chief of the Watch to rig the room for red. The fluorescent red lights in the overhead flashed on.

"Attention in the firecontrol team," Pacino announced. "The Chinese now know we're here and I'm expecting company any minute. Once the choppers and jets pin us down we won't have an opportunity to launch the Ow-sow, so even though the carrier is still eight miles to the east and the *Tampa* is still four miles from international waters I'm going to put up the Ow-sow now. With luck the carrier will be distracted enough so *Tampa* can slip through and make it over the finish line. That is it, guys. Weps, status of the Ow-sow?"

"Dry loaded in tube one, sir. Power is up, gyro is up, self-checks are go, solution is input to Target thirteen, and readback is sat." Feyley turned to look at Pacino. "We're ready to launch, Captain."

"Flood, equalize, and open the outer door, Weps. Firing point procedures, tube one, ASW standoff weapon, Target Thirteen, the carrier."

"Ship ready," Turner said.

"Solution ready." Keebes.

"Tube is flooding now, sir." Feyley.

Pacino waited, cursing the time. The helicopters would be up on him any minute.

"Conn, Sonar, we have incoming helicopters, from the bearing to Friendly One."

"Sonar, how many?"

"Hell, Captain, ten, fifteen—so many onscreen it's hard to say."

"Tube one ready, Captain," Feyley said.

"Shoot," Pacino ordered.

"Fire!"

The tube fired, the noise violent and loud in the room.

CHAPTER 30

MONDAY, 13 MAY
1143 GREENWICH MEAN TIME

BOHAI HAIXIA STRAIT
USS *TAMPA*
1943 BEIJING TIME

The noise of the explosions was loud, even through two inches of HY-80 high-yield steel hull plating. Vaughn counted, finally coming up with eight explosions. He looked over at Lennox.

"Those choppers, they're gone. Maybe we've got our air support from outside the bay."

Lennox shook his head.

"That was just a few SLAAMs from the *Seawolf*, the sub-to-air missiles, like they used against the choppers when we were aground on the sandbar."

"How do you know?"

"Look at the traces on the screen. The choppers still up are all headed west to a single bearing. It has to be the launch position of the *Seawolf*."

"So now *Seawolf*'s in trouble."

"Looks like it, but her skipper's a good one."

"Who is her skipper?" a weak voice asked from the forward control room.

Vaughn stared. There in the doorway to the forward passageway was Captain Sean Murphy, bandaged and in a sling, his throat wrapped in a bloody gauze bandage, his shoulder in so many bandages he looked like a mummy. His eyes appeared to drift, as if he were about to fall asleep on his feet. In fact, as Vaughn hurried over to him, he began to sink to the floor, and passed out. Vaughn was able to keep the captain from hitting the deck, but Murphy was clearly out cold.

"I should take him back to his stateroom," Vaughn said.

"No, leave him here or he'll just try to get up and get in here when he comes to. Bartholomay, grab the captain's mattress and pillow and set him up on the deck by the door to sonar."

Black Bart hurried forward, returning with the mattress. He and Vaughn lifted Murphy onto the makeshift bed and covered him with a blanket. He was shivering, his skin pale. As Vaughn looked down at him, Murphy lifted his eyelids, squinting through the slits.

"Who?"

"What Skipper? You should try to rest, sir—"

"Who is . . . *Seawolf*'s . . . captain?"

"Pacino, sir," Lennox said. "Michael Pacino. He said he knows you."

Murphy half-smiled, some color returning to his face, just before he lost consciousness again, this time his breathing slow and steady.

Vaughn stood. "At least he's alive."

"Not for long. As soon as they're done with *Seawolf* they'll be coming after us."

"Look," Vaughn said, pointing to the waterfall sonar display. "What the hell is that?"

A broad, incredibly loud sound blanked out the waterfall display for a few seconds, the noise narrowing to a streak that moved rapidly through the bearings, ending up on the bearing to the Chinese aircraft carrier.

"I don't know, but I'm going to see."

Lennox didn't need to raise the scope to see what happened next. The sound of the explosion from the carrier was enough.

BOHAI HAIXIA STRAIT

When the ASW standoff missile floated to the surface, its central processor waited for the feel of air on the unit's skin. The momentum of the tube launch quickly brought it to the choppy surface, and its accelerometer told it that its upward progress had momentarily stopped as it lost the buoyant force of the water. A broach sensor dried out and sent its signal to the central processor, the signal the unit waited for.

The rocket motor's solid fuel lit with the energy of a barely controlled explosion, thrusting the missile from the sea into the air. Unlike a Javelin cruise missile, whose rockets merely did a popup to give the jet sustainer engine a chance to spin up, the ASW standoff weapon was altogether rocket powered. Although its range was significantly less than a Javelin, it did not carry a jet engine or a large fuel tank or a set of control winglets or an elaborate navigation system, all of which took up volume and weight. Instead, it had a lightweight processor, a simple tailfin positioner, a small radar transponder for final target confirmation, a relatively small rocket motor and a large charge of explosives. Its warhead was three times the size of the Javelin's, the explosive power more than three times the punch because of its state-of-the-art shaped-charge. The Ow-sow's nosecone was pointed, designed for supersonic flight, allowing it to cover enormous stretches of ocean in mere seconds, and making it more difficult to shoot down in mid-flight than a subsonic Javelin.

The missile now climbed to its apogee, a mere thousand feet, then began a dive to its target. By the time its transponder found the large target some two thousand yards ahead the missile was traveling at Mach 2.4 and still accelerating. It approached the target, having been airborne less than thirty-five seconds, and hit the aircraft carrier amidships on the port side, crashing into the number-two turbine room before detonating.

The explosion from the warhead blew a sixty-foot-wide hole in the flight deck, knocked four turbines off their foundations, killed one hundred and seventy-five men and put a fifteen-foot gash in the ship's hull.

At an altitude of twelve hundred meters, the limit of visibility, pilot Chu Hua-Feng was traveling east, intent on closing the submarine contact that had been pinpointed by the helicopters of first and second squadrons, when the white-flame trail burst out of the sea west of the submarine contact. As he watched, stunned, the rocket traveled in a graceful flat arc. He barely realized that he had jerked the aircraft's stick in a violent motion, trying to keep the rocket in view as it descended back toward the sea, never having risen more than a few hundred meters. He had the odd momentary thought that the rocket was beautiful, that its perfectly shaped arc was sculpted by the wonders of Newtonian physics. But in another compartment of his mind he began to realize that the missile was headed east, toward its target, and that the target could only be the *Shaoguan,* his father's flagship.

And as the missile descended and hit the carrier and exploded into a hundred-meter-wide mushroom cloud of flame and smoke and shrapnel, Chu Hua-Feng felt an explosion in his mind, an explosion of anger, as well as a trembling so intense that the jet was picking up the vibrations in his stick hand and converting it to aileron and elevator motion. His aircraft began to shake so violently that Lo Yun asked over the intercom if they had been hit. Only then could Chu focus his energy on flying and away from the sight of his father's burning ship.

He brought the aircraft around and headed for the foamy sea that marked where the missile had been launched from below. The enemy submarine was there, he thought, but it would not be there long.

"Extend the MAD probe, Lo," Chu ordered. "And arm the depth charge."

Two minutes later Chu's Yak was over the sea from where the missile had come and he flew a tight circle around the spot, the magnetic anomaly detector picking out the position of the submarine contact.

"Depth charge armed and ready," Lo reported. "We have contact on a submerged vessel on MAD. Contact is definite and shallow."

Chu cut in the lift and idled the cruise engines. The aircraft hovered over the exact position of the submarine. In a few seconds the people who had dared launch the destructive rocket at the *Shaoguan* would be dead. Only then could he fly back to what was left of his father's ship.

USS *TAMPA*

"All ahead flank!" Lennox ordered as the sounds of a hull breaking up came through. The sonar screen showed the bright angry trace at bearing zero six seven, now northeast instead of due east as the ship made progress and got closer to the "finish line." Now that the carrier was hit by whatever it was the *Seawolf* had fired, Lennox wanted to get beyond her and to international waters as soon as he could. He was no longer concerned with leaving a wake on the surface that would pinpoint their position. It was clear that the aircraft and surface ships were intent on attacking *Seawolf.* And since *Tampa* was useless in a fight, the only thing he could do was get the ship and her crew out of the bay and into the safety of international waters.

Still, even as the ship's deck vibrated with power, he couldn't help feeling guilty and frustrated at not being able to help. For a moment he wondered how he could live with himself if *Tampa* survived and *Seawolf* went to the bottom. *Seawolf* had seemed so invincible that he had always assumed it would be *Tampa* that would never make it. Abruptly he heard Murphy's voice:

"XO," Murphy's voice rattled, "we can't leave *Seawolf.* We've got to help."

Lennox and Vaughn looked over at Murphy, who had been lifted from his mattress and was now sitting in front of Pos Two.

"Sir," Vaughn said, "three of our tubes leak, not one of the torpedoes is whole and the firecontrol computer is blown to pieces. The torpedo room console is shattered. There's nothing we can do to help—"

"The Javelins, we have to launch the Javelins."

"Sir," Vaughn said, looking at Lennox, "the computer is gone and we can't target them manually. The Javelins are inert."

"No," Murphy said. "Get one of the firecontrol techs. Get a signal simulator and"—Murphy coughed, a rattling hacking sputter—"open up the signal cable, input a signal to open the door and launch the weapon."

"But there will be no target," Lennox told him.

"Just launch them. The liftoffs will ... confuse the Chinese."

"Sir," Lennox said, "we don't have a missile tech, they're all in shock, unconscious or dead. And we don't have a signal simulator. And who knows where the cable connectors are? I'm very sorry, Captain, somewhere in Korea Bay there's a carrier air group that's *supposed* to take over now ... *Seawolf,* with whatever help she can get from the air group, will have to get out of this without us. Our cards have been played."

Murphy stared up at Lennox, then lowered his head, and for a moment Lennox thought he'd lost consciousness again. He hadn't. He was trembling slightly, from anger and frustration, Lennox guessed.

"Eng, mark our ETA at the finish line," Lennox ordered, the bite in his voice showing some of his own frustration.

Vaughn went to the chart table, glanced at the sonar display one last time, took out his dividers, checked the ESGN position a second time, then said to Lennox:

"The ETA is negative, XO. We're here. We crossed

the finish line two minutes ago. We're now 1.1 nautical miles into international water. We made it!"

Lennox looked at the sonar display, his face still grim. The *Tampa* had indeed made it out of the bay.

But now there was no way *Seawolf* would.

KOREA BAY
USS *RONALD REAGAN*

Commander Jim Collins taxied the F-14 to the number-one catapult while latching his oxygen mask to his flight helmet, the word MUGSY printed in block letters above the visor of the helmet. Collins commanded VF-69, the *Reagan*'s F-14 squadron. He was on his last sea tour as a pilot, and hated the idea of leaving the flying fleet for nuclear power school, where he was assigned to learn how to command a nuclear aircraft carrier. The thought of spending a year with a bunch of green submarine-bound ensigns at nuke school was an unhappy one, as was the notion of spending two years as XO of a carrier before he could spend four years in command. He wasn't a fool and realized he should take some satisfaction in having been chosen for higher command, but he would still find it hard to give up flying supersonic fighters. It was what he *did*. Watching the action from the bridge of the carrier didn't exactly compare to seeing it from the cockpit. The thought of this operation being the last for him made the adrenaline flow. The cockpit was an extension of his body, the sky waited for him, as did the Chinese fleet. He would not need to wait much longer. His body ached from the hours in the ready room preparing for the mission, the hours without sleep, waiting for the go order.

Finally, his F-14 was lined up on catapult one, the deck sailors attaching the catapult to the nosegear. Collins checked his instruments, the twin turbines purring aft, waiting to be kicked into full thrust. Collins tested his ailerons, rudder, and elevators, the last item on the checklist. He spoke into his intercom to his radar intercept officer, Lieutenant Commander John Forbes.

"Ready, Bugsy?"

"Ready, Mugsy." The radio handles had developed separately years before, but now somehow it seemed fitting that the squadron commander and his RIO would go by gangsters' names. To some deck-bound types they were considered loose cannons.

Collins nodded to the deck officer below. Aft of the aircraft a large thrust-deflector shield rotated upward to protect the deck crew from the F-14's jet exhaust. The deck officer signaled with his wands, and Collins's gloved left hand reached the throttle levers and pushed them forward to their stops, the jet turbines aft shrieking as they spooled up. Collins watched the instruments, then pulled the levers right past the detents and forward again into the AFTERBURN position. Far aft, the turbines' nozzles opened and injected fuel into the jet exhaust, the hot gases igniting for the second time, adding even more thrust to the jet's push.

Collins looked out his canopy to the Deck Officer and saluted. The Deck Officer, now crouched low on the deck, his forward leg bent, his aft leg ruler straight, quickly waved his wand forward in a big arc, the wand finally touching the deck, then coming up to point straight ahead down the deck into the wind. The catapult operator activated the cat, and Collins's F-14 rocketed down the carrier's deck under the three-g acceleration of the steam-driven catapult and the F-14's own jets on full afterburners.

Collins's skin stretched aft, his body thrown into the seat as the big jet accelerated. The deck and the dark sea flew toward him as if he were falling through a blurred tunnel. At the end of the cat the jet was doing one hundred and fifty knots, enough to stay airborne, but barely. Collins felt the jolt as the catapult disconnected, freeing his nosewheel of the deck, and the ship faded astern as he retracted the landing gear, the jet

surging forward as the gear pulled up out of the slipstream. The jet continued accelerating as Collins
pulled the stick back, and the sea and the carrier
shrank behind as the fighter clawed its way skyward,
the airspeed and altimeter needles winding up on the
panel. Collins smiled at the sheer joy of flight, pulling
the jet over into a tight turn, entering the pattern to
wait while the other pilots in his squadron took off
and joined him. As soon as they were aloft he would
lead the way to their hold-point two nautical miles
east of the line from Lushun to Penglai, the line of
Chinese international waters.

With luck, once they were there, they would get the
word to fly in and kick ass.

PLA Navy Aircraft Carrier *Shaoguan*

The ship had taken on a fifteen-degree list to port and
had begun to settle noticeably into the water. Fleet
Commander Chu Hsueh-Fan continued to stare out
the port bulkhead glass windows toward the west, hoping to catch sight of the fleet sinking the American
submarine. The ship seemed quiet now, the engines
long since dead, the fires continuing to rage but the
firefighting given up by order of Ship Commander Sun
Yang. The flooding was uncontrollable, the damage
extending through four major compartments to port
and amidships. The abandon-ship routine was almost
complete. All the lifeboats and rafts were over, all the
survivors floating in the boats watching the crippled
vessel.

Somewhere far below an explosion rumbled through
the bowels of the dead ship, the detonation sharp at
first, then settling into a sustained roar. Chu shivered
at the sound, the carrier's death-rattle. The ship's heel
increased suddenly to twenty-five degrees, the deck
becoming a steep ramp. Ship Commander Sun Yang
broke into the room, the door slamming against the

bulkhead, the tilt of the ship keeping the door from latching open, as Yang stared at Chu.

"Fleet Commander, our helicopter is waiting. It can't hold onto this deck much longer. The ship is about to capsize."

Chu turned around, his face lit only by the dim battery-powered battle lantern. His face was deeply lined.

"You go. Transfer the flag. Get that submarine. I will stay here—"

"Sir, you can't do this. Tien is already waiting in the helicopter. This is Tien's fault. If you go down with this ship his story will be the one they believe."

"You tell the story. I let Tien botch this operation . . . I will join my men who suffered for it. Now go."

Sun Yang was about to speak when the deck began to roll further to port, now a dangerous thirty-degree angle. He shook his head, turned and made his way up the steep deck to the door.

"At least try to swim out of here, sir. My helicopter will circle the water to find you . . ."

Sun ran down the steps to the flight-deck level, the passageways barely illuminated by the battle lanterns, emerged from the superstructure and paused while his eyes adjusted to the dark. He made out the gaping hole in the deck, a brief hellish impression, the torn steel girders, the ripped piping, the dangling cables, mangled deckplates, the jet-fuel fires and reflections of fires from the lower decks, and the sight of some two dozen torn bodies. Another distant rumbling explosion shook the deck, the energy of it more a feeling than a sound, the bass of the shock vibrating Sun's chest, the treble barely registered in ears already abused by the earlier explosion when the missile hit the ship.

He became aware of the sound of beating helicopter rotors and ran toward the sound, skirting the deep gash in the ship, and found the Hind helicopter hovering over the ship, no longer able to idle on top of the deck because of the steep angle. Sun threw himself toward the door, and men grabbed him as the helicopter lifted off the ship.

Just as the Hind cleared the deck the huge carrier, now inert scrap metal, began to capsize, its huge form rolling to port, the splash a phosphorescent burst of foam as the superstructure hit the water on the port side. Soon the entire superstructure vanished into the sea and the deck became vertical, exposing the flank of the ship's hull. For a moment the hole in the hull revealed itself as the ship continued to roll, then stopped, the ship completely upside down, the bow deeper than the stern. After another minute, all that was left of the ship was her four huge brass screws, the blades waving mournfully toward the sky. Finally the stern went down, and the PLA Navy aircraft carrier *Shaoguan* vanished into the rain-swept water of the Bo Hai Bay.

The pilot of the helicopter flew around the bubbling turbulence of water where the ship had once been, but finding no survivors outside the lifeboats and rafts, flew on to the west.

Tien Tse-Min looked out the window at the foam marking the spot where the aircraft carrier had been.

"Stupid fool. He should have listened to me. I tried to tell him the submarines would be coming out of the north passage, not the south . . ."

In the darkness Tien could not see Sun Yang's eyes glaring at him.

Forty meters under the dark water of the Bo Hai Bay, the strategy room of the *Shaoguan* was now upside-down and flooded with water. Fleet Commander Chu Hsueh-Fan was still conscious, still aware of the water around him. He had been a strong swimmer all his life, and even now he instinctively had held his breath. The room had toppled quickly, and he remembered taking his last deep breath as the windows shattered and admitted the flood of bay water, the water cold as it smashed him against the starboard bulkhead. The room had rolled completely over, leaving the battle lantern on the floor instead of the ceiling, its weak light insistently illuminating Chu's too real nightmare. The ship had gone down so fast that the pressure rise had ruptured Chu's eardrums. He held onto the hood of what had once been the radar repeater, which now hung from the ceiling. It was almost a welcome event when the crushing grip of sea pressure smashed his ribcage and he gave up his last air to the sea. The battle lantern failed, leaving darkness. Chu lost consciousness, and four minutes later was brain-dead. The corpse of the *Shaoguan* came to rest on the bottom of the deep passage of the Bohai Haixia Strait. One last explosion sounded from one of the boiler rooms, and then she remained quiet.

USS *SEAWOLF*

Michael Pacino shut his eyes in concentration as Jeb's announcement came over his headset.

"Conn, Sonar, multiple aircraft overhead circling our position. If you put up the scope I think you'll see about five of them. Most of the contacts are helicopters but I've got a definite jet in the mix. And that's not all. The two destroyers are close now and slowing. I'm guessing they're inside of their weapons range."

"Jeb called it, Skipper," Keebes said. "Firecontrol range to Target Fourteen is twenty-six thousand yards. He's within SS-N-14 range."

"What now, Captain?" Morris asked, an edge in his voice.

Pacino ignored him.

"Conn, Sonar, the aircraft overhead are backing off."

"Say again?"

"The aircraft are flying away, they're bugging out."

"That's good," Morris said.

"No," from Keebes, his face grim. "It means the Udaloy destroyer, Target Fourteen, has decided he's the senior man and wants to fire the killing weapon. An SS-N-14 will be on the way any minute."

Morris stepped close to Pacino, who was staring into space in deep thought. Morris tapped his shoulder.

"Pacino, what are you gonna do?"

Michael Pacino blinked and looked at Jack Morris for a long moment, his face blank and hard. When he spoke his tone was that of someone stating the obvious.

"We surrender."

CHAPTER 31

MONDAY, 13 MAY
1153 GREENWICH MEAN TIME

BOHAI HAIXIA STRAIT
1953 BEIJING TIME

Aircraft Commander Hua-Feng's radio headset crackled with the voice of the squadron commander:

"ALL UNITS, SQUADRON ONE LEADER, THIS IS TO ADVISE YOU THAT THE CARRIER HAS BEEN SUNK BY THE AMERICAN MISSILE. WATCH YOUR FUEL AND BE READY TO DIVERT TO LUSHUN, OUT."

Chu Hua-Feng's jaw muscles tightened as he listened to the flat tone of the squadron leader marking the sinking of the flagship, and very possibly the death of his father.

"What's the status of the Type-12, Lo?"

"Armed and ready. We have a good estimated depth of the submarine."

"Prepare to drop," Chu said, jockeying the jet directly over the position of the submarine.

"ALL AIRCRAFT UNITS BOHAI HAIXIA STRAIT, THIS IS UDALOY DESTROYER *ZUNYI* APPROACHING ESTIMATED POSITION OF ENEMY SUBMARINE SUSPECTED OF FIRING MISSILE ON FLEET FLAGSHIP. WITHDRAW TO A SAFE POSITION NO CLOSER THAN THREE KILOMETERS FROM SUBMARINE POSITION. I SAY AGAIN, WITHDRAW TO A SAFE POSITION NO CLOSER THAN THREE CLICKS FROM THE SUBMARINE. WE HAVE IMMEDI-

ATE SILEX MISSILE LAUNCH PENDING IN THREE ZERO SECONDS, COMMANDER DESTROYER *ZUNYI,* OUT."

"You ready, Lo? Drop on my mark."

"Chu, we've just been ordered out of here, you need to clear the area—"

"*No.* We're dropping the Type-12."

"Chu, the commander of the *Zunyi* obviously wants a piece of this action. Let him have it. After he fires his damned Silex we'll come back and let this submarine have a real treat. Come on or we can be taken out by that Silex—"

"This guy down there may have killed my father. I don't care about Silexes—"

"You'd better, he just launched the damned thing and it's incoming—Chu, don't be an idiot, get us *out* of here."

Chu, hating it, knew Lo was right. He throttled up the cruise engine and flew the Yak away from the position of the submarine. As the jet flew outside the one-kilometer radius from the sub, the bright flame trail from the Silex missile illuminated the cockpit.

USS *Seawolf*

"Conn, Sonar, incoming missile—"

"All ahead flank!" Pacino shouted.

The helmsman rang up the flank order. The deck began to tremble with the power of *Seawolf*'s main engines as the turbines spun at maximum revolutions, accelerating the ship away from the missile launch position. The crew held onto consoles and handholds, waiting for the detonation, except for Pacino, who looked from the firecontrol display to the chart to the sonar repeater. The wait for missile impact seemed to stretch on and on. Pacino looked over at Jack Morris. Sweat had broken out on the SEAL's forehead. This wasn't his game, waiting instead of acting. The ship continued accelerating to 44.8 knots as the reactor plant reached one hundred percent power. Pacino looked back toward the firecontrol geographic display, calculating ... With a missile average flight speed of Mach 1, firing range of thirteen nautical miles, the missile flight time would be a little over one minute. With *Seawolf*'s average speed since he accelerated thirty knots, in the one minute of flight time he would have the ship a thousand yards from her position at launch. If sonar had only given him half the flight time's warning, and if the commander of the Udaloy had fired at his future position instead of his actual position, the ship would perhaps only be two hundred or three hundred yards from the missile impact point, maybe less. In a worst case, only a hundred yards, three hundred feet.

Now, Pacino thought, would three hundred feet away from a rocket-launched depth charge be enough to save the ship?

BOHAI HAIXIA STRAIT

The Silex missile lifted out of the quad launcher of the destroyer *Zunyi* and accelerated away from the sleek warship, its tailfins moving slightly in response to the onboard processor's commands. The missile reached apogee and arced back down toward the dark sea, the inertial navigation system aiming the missile for the position of the submarine, not its position at launch but the position it was calculated to be at time of impact. After forty seconds of rocket-powered flight, the rocket motor cut out, exhausted, the explosive bolts in the ring separating the motor from the depth charge below, jettisoning the inert rocket-motor canister. The warhead flew on, the surface ahead approaching at Mach 0.95.

The impact of the water jarred the missile's warhead. The accelerometer tied into the arming circuit felt the negative four g's of deceleration and completed the circuit to the depth-charge arming-circuit.

The depth indicator felt the pressure increase of the water as the unit sank, the pressure rising as it fell to ten meters, twenty, thirty ... At a depth of forty-five meters the depth-indicator output matched the limits set by the processor's setpoint, and the detonation circuit software logic interlock was satisfied. The detonator went off, exploding the depth-charge warhead in an underwater fireball. The shock wave of the explosion traveled outward, seeking the hull of a submarine.

Which it did not take long to find.

WASHINGTON, D.C.
WHITE HOUSE

The White House basement's situation room was walled with painted cinder block, full of Formica-topped tables and cheap carpet. An entire wall on the west side was lined with communication and crypto gear. The east wall was filled with television screens, some of them selected to cable feeds from Langley, CIA Headquarters; Ford Meade, home of NSA; or the Pentagon. But two were selected to CNN, since the open media often got stories as quickly as CIA, DIA or NSA. The north wall of the room was reserved for charts and maps, in this case the Bo Hai Bay. The south wall had a table filled with stale sandwiches and donuts and another one with a large coffee urn on it. Coffee cups filled the waste cans and cigarette butts were piled high in the ash trays. A door in the east wall led to the situation room's conference area, lined with curtains, where the President would meet with the National Security Council. The press or the White House photographer often captured the NSC in situation-room meetings, the conference table neat, the curtains pressed and clean. But this morning, the table was strewn with top-secret briefing papers and the curtains were drawn.

Secretary of Defense Napoleon Ferguson stood in

the conference area, chewing on a tasteless donut and washing it down with cold coffee, waiting for President Dawson and Secretary of State/National Security Advisor Eve Trachea to arrive. He had been in the situation room all night. He had hoped he could catch Dawson's ear when Trachea wasn't around, but that seemed more and more difficult in recent months. Trachea was apparently becoming Dawson's favored advisor, and Ferguson had begun to wonder why the hell he continued in the job. He had begun to feel Trachea's guiding philosophy was to disagree with anything he wanted, which tempted him to argue for what he did *not* want and count on Eve to disagree. But now Dawson relied so heavily on Eve Trachea's guidance that often Department of Defense personnel weren't invited to meetings. NSC meetings had grown less frequent, as had Cabinet meetings.

When Dawson and Trachea arrived, Ferguson checked his watch, then sat down. He only took a few moments updating them on the situation in the Bo Hai Bay, ending with his request to allow the *Reagan*'s air wing to overfly the bay and escort the subs out. Dawson seemed inclined to go along, but then Trachea spoke up:

"Mr. President, this course of action would be an all-out attack against the Chinese fleet. Our agreement with your admiral was to use the *Seawolf* to get out the spy sub. Now there's pressure to escalate. Why does that sound so familiar, Secretary Ferguson? 'Just give us a few troops now,' you say, and later it's 'we need to support the troops we already have.' We cannot commit to a killing air war ..."

Ferguson looked from Trachea to Dawson, who clearly was unhappy with his choice.

"She's right, Napoleon. I only authorized the use of force for the *Seawolf*. The country can't go to war over this ..."

Ferguson pulled a crumpled sheet of paper from his pocket, spread it on the desk and smoothed it out before handing it to Dawson. Dawson began to read, with Trachea, who sat next to him, reading along with him. The paper was the message transmitted from the *Tampa* describing the torture the men had undergone when the Chinese had taken the ship. Dawson's face went pale at first, then changed to the flush of anger.

"These are the people we're dealing with," Ferguson said.

"Is it possible this is exaggerated, Napoleon?" Dawson asked, the certainty on his face from a moment before seeming to evaporate.

Ferguson tried to control himself. Somehow he needed to find something to shock this well-meaning but misguided president into unleashing the aircraft. But *what* . . .

USS SEAWOLF

"Chief of the Watch, prepare to emergency blow all main ballast tanks," Pacino ordered, his eye on the chronometer.

"What are you doing?" Morris asked.

"Sonar, Captain, report the splash of the SS-N-14 as soon as you have it."

"Captain, Sonar, aye."

"We're going to surface," Pacino finally told Morris.

Morris began to protest when the overhead speaker blared out the report from sonar:

"SPLASH FROM THE MISSILE DIRECTLY ASTERN!"

"*Emergency blow fore and aft!*" Pacino shouted. "*Take her up, ten degree up bubble! All stop!*"

The emergency blow system levers were thrown upward to the BLOW position, forcing ultra-high-pressure bottled air into the ballast tanks of the *Seawolf*, blowing them dry of sea water. At her already shallow depth, it took only a moment to blow the tanks dry, and the sudden increase in buoyancy forced the ship toward the surface, her nose rocketing upward.

A split second before *Seawolf*'s sonar dome

broached the sea, the depth charge from the Silex missile exploded directly astern of the ship.

BOHAI HAIXIA STRAIT

Aircraft Commander Chu Hua-Feng watched as the Silex missile impacted the water, the splash still phosphorescent in the bay. He flew around in a circular pattern, waiting for orders to finish off the submarine, waiting for the Silex missile's depth charge to explode.

He watched the spot of foam for signs that the depth charge had succeeded. In a way he hoped it would fail and give him the chance to put the submarine on the bottom. He glanced at his fuel gages, saw how little fuel he had left. As he looked back down to the bay he saw a black shape coming out of the dark water. For a moment he could not believe his eyes. Half a kilometer east of the depth-charge detonation, the American submarine had surfaced, either surrendering or damaged beyond the ability to stay submerged, he decided. As the water of the depth-charge explosion rained back down into the bay and its spot of foam calmed, Chu flew his Yak toward the submarine, which now bobbed in the water, no longer underway, as if it had lost its engines.

USS SEAWOLF

The deck jumped with the explosion. The bank of fluorescent lights in the overhead flickered and went out. The firecontrol displays and sonar repeater monitor winked out, then the lights came back on, illuminating the room in a red glow.

"Weps, get your firecontrol back and hurry," Pacino said.

"Conn, Sonar, loss of sonar. We're reinitializing."

"Get it back up, Chief," Pacino ordered. Two firecontrol technicians scrambled to the outboard side of the attack center consoles and began typing into a console hidden from the conn platform. The screens of the firecontrol system came back for a moment, then winked out.

"We're doing a cold start, Captain," Feyley reported, frowning over the technicians.

"Chief of the Watch, any damage aft?"

"No, Captain, all nominal. We're checking aux machinery now." He held up a finger. "Sir, some leakage in the auxiliary seawater piping to the diesel. Otherwise, we seem okay."

The deck rocked gently in the waves of the bay. The depth indicator showed the ship on the surface. The speed indicator read zero.

"Turner, get to the bridge and open the clamshells," Pacino ordered. "We'll send up a white sheet for you to wave and a walkie-talkie to transmit that we surrender—"

"Sir, are you really going to do this?"

Morris stepped close to Pacino as he raised the number-two periscope and looked out toward the east, centering the periscope on the approaching Udaloy and Luda destroyers.

"Pacino, submerge this ship and get us out of here," Morris said, removing his Beretta from its holster. "If you actually surrender I swear I'll put a bullet in your head."

Pacino pulled his face from the periscope and looked at Turner.

"Get the hell up to the bridge and follow my orders," he barked, and Turner went to the upper level carrying the white sheet and walkie-talkie the phone-talker had handed him.

Pacino then looked over at Morris, put his face as close to Morris' as he could with his hand still on the grips of the periscope.

"Morris, I still have one torpedo and two main engines. Are you reading me?"

Jack Morris stared at Pacino for a moment, then holstered the pistol.

"Attention in the firecontrol team," Pacino called from the periscope. "We have the Udaloy destroyer, Target fourteen, and the Luda destroyer, Target fifteen, closing in on our position. I'm betting these guys are going to try to take us alive. Status of firecontrol."

Feyley turned to Pacino. "Firecontrol is a cold start complete. I'm configuring the positions now and I'll be ready in a minute."

"Sonar, Captain, status of sonar?"

"Still working on it, sir."

"Hurry up. XO, looks like we'll be launching by periscope observation. You ready? Observation Target fourteen. Bearing mark, range mark, four divisions in high power. Observation Target fifteen, bearing mark, range mark, three-and-a-half divisions in high power."

Pacino lowered the scope, waited for a minute, then raised the periscope again. This time the destroyers were very close. He called out another observation, then lowered the scope.

"Sir, we have a firing solution to both targets," Keebes said.

"Stand by for torpedo attack, Target fourteen, tube eight," Pacino said. "Set the Mark 50 torpedo for shallow, low speed, direct-contact mode, active snake. Disable ACR and ASH interlocks. We will fire the unit as Target fourteen approaches, then submerge and head out of the bay."

"Sir," Keebes said slowly, "we only have one torpedo and there are two destroyers."

"I know," Pacino said. "Standby. And Chief of the Watch, get a man up to the bridge and tell Turner that as soon as we accelerate to shut the hatch and get below, fast. We'll be submerging immediately. Prepare to dive."

On the bridge Lieutenant Tim Turner stood beside the open hatch of the bridge trunk, being careful not to fall the twenty-five feet down to the deck. The clamshells were open, allowing him to stand up and look out. Turner looked around at the moonlit bay, sniffing the salty air that smelled oddly bad after being submerged with their canned stink for so long. The evening was pleasant, the sea and the moon beautiful. But Turner had no thoughts of beauty, no ability to sense anything other than the urgency of the coming battle.

He looked to the east at the approaching destroyers and began to wave the white flag, even though he knew the ships were still too far away to see him.

"Approaching Chinese destroyers, this is U.S. Navy submarine *Seawolf*. I say again, approaching Chinese destroyers, this is U.S. Navy submarine *Seawolf*. We surrender. We are standing by for you to come alongside. I say again, we are standing by for you to come alongside, over."

The ships were headed directly for them, picking up speed. Turner waved the white sheet and made the surrender call again, continuing to transmit and wave the flag for the next ten minutes, all the while expecting to see more missiles or torpedoes or aircraft with depth charges. But all he saw were the surface ships approaching the ship, the destroyers purposeful and steady. Finally his VHF ship-to-ship radio crackled with a Chinese accent:

"AMERICAN SUB *SEAWOLF* STANDBY FOR US TO COME ALONGSIDE AND BOARD YOUR VESSEL."

Turner had no idea what Captain Pacino was planning. It was time for blind faith.

WASHINGTON, D.C.
WHITE HOUSE

Secretary of Defense Ferguson leaned over the table, his face intense and flushed.

"Mr. President, I want an order to launch aircraft to rescue the *Tampa* and I want that order now. I'm sorry to be blunt but—"

A Marine colonel came in at that moment.

"Sorry to interrupt, sir, but we just got a message from CINCPAC aboard the *Reagan*. The *Seawolf* has surfaced in the Bohai Haixia Strait, and she's transmitting a message to the Chinese fleet that she's surrendering ..."

Ferguson reacted first. "What's the Chinese fleet doing?"

"CINCPAC says they're approaching to take her alive. They're coming alongside."

Ferguson looked to President Dawson. "Sir, that's it. Now we'll lose the *Seawolf*, the most advanced submarine in the world. And her crew can enjoy Chinese hospitality, until they're dead—"

"Ferguson, *enough*," Dawson snapped. "Launch the damned aircraft. You have twelve hours and unlimited weapons release authorized. You get that submarine back, understand?"

"Yes*sir*," Ferguson said, hurrying to the radio console, where he hoisted the handset to his ear, waiting for Donchez's voice to come through the connection.

BOHAI HAIXIA STRAIT

Chu felt like spitting into his oxygen mask.

"I don't believe it," he said to Lo. The commander of the Udaloy destroyer *Zunyi* had ordered all aircraft to stay outside of a one-kilometer radius of the American submarine, declaring that the sub had surrendered and that they were going to take it captive.

"Don't they see it's a trick?"

"Maybe it isn't."

"Just keep us armed and your eyes on that submarine."

USS *SEAWOLF*

Pacino looked out the periscope at the approaching destroyers. The closest was the Udaloy, now at six hundred yards bearing zero nine five. The Luda was at bearing one zero five, only eight hundred yards away. That was about as close as he intended them to get.

"Chief, tell Turner to get ready to come down, but tell him to keep waving that white flag until the torpedo detonates."

"Yessir."

"Firing point procedures, tube eight, Target fourteen," Pacino called, his periscope crosshairs on the approaching Udaloy.

"Ship ready, solution ready," Keebes said.

"Weapon ready," Feyley said.

"Shoot!"

"Fire!" Feyley said, pulling the trigger.

The tube fired, the pressure slamming Pacino's ears. He watched the Udaloy, waiting.

Finally a brilliant orange-and-white-and-black fireball bloomed from the port side of the destroyer's superstructure. Pacino turned the crosshairs to the Luda, seeing its bearing, now one zero six degrees, then lowering the scope.

"All ahead flank, steer course one zero six!"

Only then did the sound of the explosion reverberate through the hull, the violent sound of a warship dying.

"Ahead flank aye, one zero six, maneuvering answers all ahead flank, steering course one zero six, sir," the helmsman replied.

"Sir, you're headed straight for the Luda—"

"Chief of the Watch, tell Turner to get below! Diving Officer, submerge the ship to nine zero feet!"

The Chief of the Watch shouted into his headset and reached to the ballast-control panel to open the main ballast tank vents at the same time. The diving officer ordered the bowplanes to twenty degrees dive, the sternplanes to five degrees. The deck began to take on an angle. The Chief of the Watch, still following the rig for ultraquiet, called "Dive, Dive!" into his headset rather than on the Circuit One P.A. system.

The deck began to incline as the ship drove deep, then flattened as the Diving Officer pulled out.

On the bridge Tim Turner felt the deck beneath his feet tremble as the ship began to move. He dropped the white sheet and bent to snap up the heavy clamshell on the port side. When he stood to fold up the central clamshell he saw the Luda destroyer directly ahead. The bow wave was gone, the hull already under. His eyes were level with the shoes of the men running on the main deck of the destroyer, men running away from him ... Turner stood half-frozen as the hull of the destroyer grew closer. The captain was going to ram it, he thought dimly, the thought breaking his inertia. He dropped the walkie-talkie down the bridge hatch and jumped down after it. He had reached up for the hatch when the ship hit the destroyer, the force of the collision throwing him down the tunnel.

The sail of the *Seawolf* hit the hull of the Luda destroyer *Kaifing* at a speed of twenty-eight knots, forty-seven-feet-per-second. The sail's top five feet still protruded above the water as it hit the hull of the *Kaifing,* but the destroyer had a draft of about fifteen feet, reaching deep enough that only a few feet separated the top of *Seawolf*'s cylindrical hull from the bottom of *Kaifing*'s keel. The leading edge of the sail crumpled, the hardened steel yielding but not rupturing, the sail designed to impact submerged icebergs under the polar icecap without giving, the designers knowing that a six-foot-thick chunk of polar ice was equivalent to a half-inch plate of steel, at least when approached at two-feet-per-second. But now *Seawolf* had hit the *Kaifing*'s hull at twenty times that velocity, and the target's hull was not just a single plate of steel but a matrix of steel plates stretched over structural-shaped frames. As the sail slammed into the port-side hull, the steel dented, then gave way, finally tearing open into a gash large enough to allow the sail to pass through. The sail continued inward, slicing through a fuel tank, through a berthing compartment and shower room, through a passageway into a row of engineering maintenance offices and through the plate steel of the starboard side.

By the time the *Seawolf*'s sail emerged from the far side of the *Kaifing,* the submarine had slowed to two knots, her kinetic energy almost expended in ripping open the hull of the *Kaifing*. The *Seawolf*'s screw continued to turn, eventually accelerating her back to flank speed, but *Kaifing*'s screw would never turn again. The destroyer settled in the water, her lower compartments flooding as she sank to the silty bottom of the strait.

BOHAI HAIXIA STRAIT

"I told you it was a damned trick," Chu said into Lo's intercom.

Below them the Udaloy destroyer was in flames and dead in the water, starting to sink by the bow while listing to port, crippled and near death. A half-kilometer to the southeast the Luda destroyer was closing the position of the submarine, but the sub was developing a bow wave and sinking into the water. Chu had to believe his eyes. The American submarine was not hurt at all but speeding eastward, not toward open water but directly toward the Luda-class destroyer. As he watched, the submarine's hull vanished, leaving only its conning tower behind. The Luda's stern boiled in foam as the ship tried to accelerate out of the way—too late.

The conning tower of the American submarine hit the Luda destroyer's hull amidships, slicing into it. Smoke rose from the collision, and Chu brought his jet closer to observe. The conning tower of the sub had vanished, not emerging from the other side. The Luda destroyer began to slow down, coasting to a halt, the hole in her hull now invisible as the ship settled into the water and began to list starboard, now completely stopped. Chu no longer wanted to wait to see what would happen to the second destroyer. A glance over his shoulder revealed that the Udaloy was gone, sunk, nothing left but a foamy oil slick, a few boats, and men floating in the water.

"It's up to us, now," he told Lo. "I'm flying over the continuation of the submarine's course. Do you have a detection?"

"Yes, four hundred meters ahead. Depth shallow but getting deeper."

"Drop the Type-12 on my mark."

Chu cut in the lift-jets and throttled back on the cruise engine, finally matching the submerged submarine's speed.

"Call it," Chu said.

"Directly overhead now."

"Drop!"

"Type-12 away, clear the area."

Chu throttled up the cruise engine and sped away, waiting for the results of the depth charge.

CHAPTER 32

~~DAY~~, 13 MAY
~~GR~~EENWICH MEAN TIME

Bohai Haixia Strait
USS *Seawolf*
2004 Beijing Time

Lieutenant Tim Turner was able to grab a rung of the ladder on the way down, preventing himself from falling the distance down to the deck below, but breaking his fall sprained an ankle and dislocated his shoulder. The pain shot through his body and he winced, certain he had broken something. He reached for the next rung up in the tunnel ladder, and as he looked up he could see water beginning to trickle down the hatchway. Below him the hatch to the upper level of the forward compartment shut as the petty officer sent to warn him to come down shut the lower hatch.

Which left Turner alone in the sealed-off trunk with an open hatch overhead, the water ready to drown him. With all his remaining strength he moved up the ladder to the hatch and reached for the hatch ring, feeling the gusher of water in his face as he tried to reach to the hatch and pull it down.

He was only able to pull it a few inches, the roar of water down the hatch threatening to wash him down the tunnel, but the water flow beat against the closing hatch and slammed it into the hatch seat. The flooding stopped, but left Turner hanging over a fifteen-foot-deep hole by one hand. He reached up with his right hand, engaged the hatch dogs, and felt for the ladder rung with his foot, then lowered himself down the tunnel to the deck and found himself in water up to his waist.

He banged on the hull with his flashlight, and after a moment the water began to drain slowly out of the tunnel as the man below opened a drain valve. After another few minutes the hatch opened and Turner could climb down the ladder to the deck. He dogged the lower hatch over his head, and had turned to the petty officer who had abandoned him, ready to say something, when he was thrown to the deck by a violent force, barely conscious as he slid over the wet deck to the door of the galley. The deck tilted, and looking aft, it seemed the hundred-foot-long passageway was a stairwell, a ramp, inclined toward him, the lights no longer illuminating it, just some automatically activated battle lanterns. Turner wondered if it was his head injury that caused the illusion, but then a flashlight loosened from its cradle fell to the deck and rolled down to his position at the galley door. No illusion, he realized, the ship was diving. And with no lights.

The detonation of the depth charge made the deck jump more than Pacino would ever have expected for a ship of nine thousand tons, and he was thrown into the periscope pole, banging his forehead. The lights went out, the room lit only by battle lanterns. The firecontrol console displays went blank for a second time. The sonar repeater stayed blank, never having come back up from its initial injury.

A dim voice came over the emergency communications network:

"Flooding in auxiliary machinery, flooding in—"

Pacino shouted over the announcement: "Chief, make the phone announcement and send the casualty-assistance team to the torpedo room."

Before the chief could do it a speaker in the overhead crackled:

"REACTOR SCRAM, REACTOR SCRAM," Engineer Linden reported.

Pacino turned to the ship control console and the Diving Officer. "Flood depth-control tanks and put her on the bottom." He reached for a phone to the aft compartment. "Maneuvering, Captain, report cause of scram."

"Sir," Engineer Linden's voice said over the connection, "I think it was just shock to the scram breakers, or a rod jump that caused a flux spike that tripped the protection systems. We're setting up for recovery—"

"Don't," Pacino ordered. "Shut down the engineroom. Shut the main steam bulkhead valves and shut down all your pumps. Shift the reactor to natural circulation and keep that compartment *quiet*. Have your guys take off their shoes if you have to."

"Aye, sir."

"Chief of the Watch, have you got a report from the torpedo room?"

"Nothing, sir."

"XO, go to the torpedo room and take over. Get that flooding stopped and do it quietly."

Keebes took off his headset and dumped it on the Pos Two console, then quickly headed for the aft stairway.

"Attention in the firecontrol team," Pacino called. "We're out of weapons, we're surrounded by aircraft, we've shut down the engineering spaces and we're sitting on the bottom. Within minutes I expect that the aircraft will be turning around and coming for us with more depth charges, and the surface forces will soon be here with their own weapons. Meanwhile, we're not going anywhere until the flooding in the lower level is stopped, particularly since the flooding is too close to our only power source, the battery. In any case I'm hoping that with the reactor shut down we won't be detected by passive sonar. And that since we're on the bottom, active sonar won't be much good either. The only thing we have to worry about is magnetic detectors, and there's nothing we can do about that. Carry on."

"That's it?" Morris said. "You're just going to play dead and hope they don't shoot?"

Pacino nodded.

"Conn, Sonar," his headset intoned, "sonar is back."

Pacino stared at the screen, the digital images of the broadband sonar suite now forming on the chart, the screen taking a few moments to generate history as the sounds fell down the waterfall display.

"What have you got out there, Chief?"

"Bad news. Helicopters every point of the compass. One real close, must have a magnetic anomaly detector. Closer now, sir. Definite helicopter hovering directly overhead, and he isn't moving."

"Talk about worst case scenario," Pacino muttered.

"Conn, Sonar, the other aircraft are closing."

Pacino shook his head. Morris watched him, seemed to be studying him.

"Conn, Sonar, we have approximately thirty helicopters and one jet aircraft on our screens, not counting anyone in the baffles, and they're all hovering within a thousand yards ... Sir, I've just gotten two splashes directly overhead. We're getting depth-charged."

The depth charge detonated, and Pacino's only impression was that Jack Morris's face vanished, to be replaced by the deck, and when the darkness came he couldn't tell whether it was because the lights went out or that he was no longer alive.

BOHAI HAIXIA STRAIT

The explosion from the depth charge lifted ten thousand liters of water skyward in an angry fan of phosphorescent foam. Chu pulled his stick to his thigh, circling the Yak in a tight circle to port, trying to find evidence of the submarine's presence. To the east and west several dozen helicopters were inbound. The other Yaks of his squadron had already gone back to

Lushun, their fuel low. Chu's tanks were going dry but he didn't care. He would orbit the position of the submarine until his turbines sucked fumes if he could just see the American ship sink. It would be worth ditching the jet in the bay as long as he could have a piece of the damned Americans.

Chu climbed for a better view as the helicopters of the task forces, the squadrons from the *Shaoguan* and the land-based Hinds jockeyed for position along the channel as they searched for the sub, preparing to drop their ordnance. Chu half-expected the air commander to order indiscriminate depth-charging if for no other reason than to relieve their frustration over the submarine so far evading them. Finally he did order that, the helicopters with depth charges forming up into a line of aircraft, each to drop a depth charge in the channel midpoint with horizontal longitudinal separation of a hundred meters. The air commander then ordered that once the depth charges were gone, all torpedoes would be shot, going from west to east. No submerged vessel should last long with that kind of weapon saturation.

For the first time in his flight Chu smiled in satisfaction as the helicopters moved into their depth-charging positions. Even if his Yak only had another ten minutes of fuel, he would still be airborne when the submarine sank, and he would have a grandstand seat.

"Razor Blade, this is Shaving Cream, over."

Commander Jim Collins heard his squadron's callsign on the UHF tactical control frequency and lined up his radio to transmit. This was probably the order to abort the mission, he thought. The F-14s of VF-69 were only a minute from their hold points, and he had expected only one radio exchange, either go or no-go.

"Shaving Cream, this is Razor Blade, read you five-by, over."

"Roger, Razor Blade, break, you are authorized to proceed to the store and purchase all groceries on the list, I say again, you are authorized to proceed to the store and purchase all groceries on the list, break, over."

"Roger, Shaving Cream, Razor Blade out." Collins cut out the transmitting circuit-breaker on the radio console, annoyed that he had been asked to transmit. But what the hell, he thought, the Chinese would soon know they were there. "You hear that, Bugsy?"

"Yeah, Mugsy. We're going in."

"Arm everything and track everything."

Collins put the stick down and dived for the deck, pulling up at an altitude of only twenty-five feet, the waves of the Korea Bay coming at the plane at Mach 2, the shock wave astern sending up twin rooster tails in the sea. A few minutes later the firecontrol radar was locked on to multiple airborne targets, all of them orbiting a single point in the sea.

"Mugsy, we're in range, I'm tracking thirty-seven helicopters and a fixed wing aircraft all within a couple miles of each other. No surface contacts, all airborne. The Mockingbird missiles are all armed, all locked on, I'm calling Juliet."

"Roger, releasing now."

Collins hit his stick button a dozen times, launching the supersonic air-to-air Mockingbird missiles, the sky lighting up with each launch, the plane's inventory quickly gone.

"Missiles away."

To the north and south other flashes of light shone briefly as the other planes of the squadron of F-14s also fired their missiles, the squadron still on approach at supersonic speed.

Aircraft Commander Chu Hua-Feng had looked away from the scene of the helicopters dropping their depth charges just long enough to check his fuel gages and note with dismay that both read empty. He wondered whether he would be airborne long enough to confirm the kill of the submarine. As he looked up from the panel he felt a small jolt, looked out the canopy to starboard and saw his right wing disintegrate and explode into flames—for no apparent reason. It seemed to take a long time for the plane to start falling to the sea below, but after a moment frozen in mid-air, it began to spin toward earth.

Chu's hands were already grabbing his crotch, where the ejection seat's D-ring was located, the position of the D-ring designed to keep his arms tight to his body in case of ejection, high-speed ejections tending to cause amputations from the high-speed airstream. He pulled the D-ring nearly up to his waist, felt the ring pulling the pin that would blow off the canopy and ignite the ejection seat's rocket motors. He waited . . . nothing happened. He was about to let go of the ring and pull the canopy off manually when he noticed the view out the window had frozen—a helicopter was engulfed in a ball of fire but the ball was static, unmoving, and the chopper was not falling. Moreover, Chu's own jet was no longer tumbling out of control but lazily floating toward the water. As he watched, another piece of the wing detached and flew off into the slipstream, but it looked more like a feather floating in a breeze than shrapnel whipping into a six-hundred-click airflow.

Chu vaguely realized he had gotten such a huge dose of adrenaline that his time-sense had crazily accelerated, nearly stopping time. Now, as he watched, the canopy overhead blew off, leisurely flying upward and away, tumbling gracefully off out of view. Beneath him the ejection seat rockets cut in, and the cockpit of the airplane began to move, the instrument panel slowly moving downward and away as the rockets flew him out of the plane—except to Chu it seemed he was only going at walking speed as his seat left the aircraft. As soon as his legs cleared the cockpit the airstream hit him and the aircraft faded away in front of him, shrinking slowly as it moved off. Chu stared at his crippled tumbling plane, still spinning gracefully and slowly when it exploded in a violent blooming fireball.

The explosion seemed to kick Chu into normal time, the seat jostling, the sound of the air a roar in his ears, his parachute deploying overhead, the seat falling away, the sea coming up from below while his chute canopy blossomed overhead. He floated toward the water, dimly aware of the fireballs surrounding him as the helicopters of the northern fleet exploded in flames just as his Yak had. It occurred to him that he and Lo might be the only survivors of the attack, since only they had ejection seats. He looked briefly for Lo but saw no other parachute or ejection seat. He was calling his friend's name as the water came up and smashed into his back. He sank in the lukewarm water, but managed to detach his parachute and swim away from it.

He finally got his head above the water and saw a huge Hind helicopter flying overhead, flying low and fast toward the north as if trying to escape. He pulled a cord, inflating his life vest, took off his flight helmet, and let it sink into the bay. He kept watching as the Hind flew over, and a supersonic missile flew by in hot pursuit.

Leader Tien Tse-Min looked out the windows of the Hind helicopter at the formation of choppers about to drop their loads of depth charges. He looked south-southwest to see if the ships of the surface task forces were nearby; none was visible in the dim moonlight. He looked back to the sea below and watched as the first helicopter dropped its two depth charges, then flew off. He waited for the explosion from the water, but before it came the helicopter that had dropped the charges vanished in a violent white-and-red ball of flame, the rotor spinning off into the sky, the mis-shapen airframe spinning down to the water. Its remains hit the water at the same time the depth charges exploded, throwing spray and foam and water into the air, the fan of water from the explosion swallowing the burning helicopter. When the water calmed, there was no trace of the chopper. As Tien watched, stupe-fied, the other helicopters exploded and crashed to the sea. The lone VTOL jet remaining, the Yak-36A, blew apart, its canopy opening and belching an ejection seat that popped a parachute, the airplane blowing apart and raining shrapnel on the water below. Tien felt the jolt as the pilot of the Hind turned and headed north away from the battle zone.

Only when the Hind settled on its northern course did Tien begin to realize what had happened ... The Americans had launched some kind of air-to-air missile attack on the helicopters. He blamed Fleet Commander Chu for losing the carrier that would have made impossible Americans flying over Chinese territory and launching their missiles.

Tien's thought was disrupted as the Mockingbird heat-seeking missile flew into the Hind's port engine exhaust duct and exploded. Tien's body was blown apart, the blood from his dismembered body boiling into vapor as the fireball grew. And within seconds there was no trace left of the Hind except pieces of fuselage floating in the bay water below.

"We're out of air targets," Bugsy Forbes called on the intercom as the last of the fireballs flamed out into the bay.

"What about surface ships?" Mugsy Collins responded.

"Whole lot of folks to the south, another task force to the southwest."

"I'll call up the F-18s to take on the southwest force. Our guys will go see the south fleet," Collins said, clicking his radio to call the other F-14s. Moments later Collins put the stick over and turned the jet to the south while Forbes armed the Mohawk air-to-surface missiles ...

Twenty minutes later the two dozen F-14s of VF-69 streaked in formation over the burning, sinking ships of the southeast task force of the Chinese Northern Fleet, the sonic booms of the jets a farewell as they climbed and turned back to the northeast and vanished over the horizon.

KOREA BAY
SURFACE ACTION GROUP 57
USS *RONALD REAGAN*

Admiral Richard Donchez lit his cigar as the F-14s of
VF-69 landed on the deck of the *Reagan*. As the carrier recovered the F-14s, she launched the squadron
of S-3 Vikings, the twin-jet ASW aircraft detailed to
search the bay for the *Seawolf*.

"Any sign of *Seawolf*?" Donchez asked, unable to
wait any longer.

Captain Fred Rummel shook his head. "The jets
took out all the helicopters but the *Seawolf* never surfaced. The Vikings will be able to see if she's still
there, but so far, nothing."

"What about the LAMPS helos?"

"They're already on the way, sir. We'll have active
and passive sonar and MAD detectors scouring the
strait in another few minutes."

"I want to know the instant we know anything."

"Yessir," Rummel said, wondering how long it
would be before it became obvious that *Seawolf* was
lost.

2315 BEIJING TIME

"Any word?" Donchez asked.

"Maybe you'd better come up to flight ops," Rummel told him.

They climbed the steps and walked into the stuffy
air of the flight-operations center, where the air operations boss, the ship's captain and the SAG hovered
over the radar screens listening to the distorted voices
of the pilots on the UHF tactical frequency.

Donchez stood in the back, listening as the pilots
reported that there was no submarine contact at the
location that the helicopters had been hovering. It
took time for the news to sink in, but finally Donchez
began to feel the heavy weight of the inevitable.

Seawolf was gone, and with her, Captain Michael Pacino.

"I'm going to the bridge," Donchez told Rummel.

"I'll hang around here, sir. I'll let you know if . . ."

Donchez was already gone and entering the blacked-out bridge, with its expanse of windows overlooking the flight deck and the sea. Off to port the Officer of the Deck was scanning the horizon with his binoculars.

Donchez immediately demanded: "What's the word on the *Tampa*?"

"She'll be intercepting the group in another five minutes, sir. We're standing by with a helicopter and a diver when she comes up. Her ballast tanks vents are jammed open so she can only stay on the surface when she's steaming ahead. Our chopper will be dropping a diver to her deck. He's going to be bolting some gasketed covers over the vents. Once that's done she can blow the ballast tanks and stay on the surface. She'll be pulling up alongside the *Port Royal*, one of our Aegis cruisers. We're going to offload her crew and replace them with a transit crew. Once the transit team is aboard they'll be sailing to Yokosuka for refit, and the original crew will be airlifted to the hospital ship *Mercy*."

"Off'sa'deck, combat reports a surfacing submarine bearing two nine one, range five thousand yards," the junior officer of the deck reported.

"Very well. Status of the chopper?"

"Lifting off now."

"We'll have her alongside the *Port Royal* within the hour, Admiral."

Donchez nodded, then returned to Flag Plot. Rummel was waiting for him. Donchez could tell by his face that the news was bad.

"Nothing on the *Seawolf*, sir. The search continues, we've got till dawn before the President's authorization expires, but the ASW guys aren't hopeful . . ."

"I'm going down to get some rack," Donchez said, knowing he wouldn't sleep but wanting to be alone.

"Yessir. And, Admiral, there's this . . ."

"What's that, Fred?"

"At least we got the *Tampa* back."

Donchez nodded, but his thoughts were that the price was too damned high.

USS *TAMPA*
ALONGSIDE CRUISER USS *PORT ROYAL*
2345 BEIJING TIME

Lieutenant Commander Jackson Lube Oil Vaughn stood on the deck of the *Tampa* watching the corpsman lifting out Captain Sean Murphy. As soon as he was out of the hatch he said something to the two men carrying him and they brought him to where Vaughn stood. Beside Vaughn was Lieutenant Black Bart Bartholomay, the SEAL XO.

"Captain," Vaughn said, "don't fight these guys, let them take care of you, okay? I'll be up to visit you soon as I get the crew turnover done."

"Lube Oil," Murphy said, his voice weak, "I just wanted to thank you and Lennox for all the fancy shiphandling you did to get us out of there. I was ... damned proud of you guys. I'm sorry I couldn't help ..."

"You did fine, Skipper."

"And, Black Bart, when I get healed I want to pin a medal on every one of your SEAL team. Without you guys we'd all be dead meat by now."

Bartholomay thanked him, and added, "I wish Jack Morris could hear you say that."

Vaughn looked at Murphy. Either Morris had drowned at sea when he went overboard, or he was picked up by *Seawolf*. And God alone knew where *Seawolf* was. If she was anywhere ...

The corpsmen took Murphy up the gangway to the weather deck of the *Port Royal,* the massive cruiser towering over the submarine, then put Murphy in the waiting helicopter on the cruiser's fantail. The chopper's blades spun into a blur and it lifted off into the darkness, disappearing except for its blinking beacons.

"Well, I'd better get my guys and their gear off-loaded," Bart said.

Vaughn stretched out his hand. Black Bart shook it, turned and walked toward the hatch.

Vaughn turned away, looking out toward the west to an empty stretch of seawater.

CHAPTER 33

TUESDAY, 14 MAY
0004 GREENWICH MEAN TIME

BOHAI HAIXIA STRAIT
0804 BEIJING TIME

The ASW officer, Lieutenant Victor Samuels, sat in the rear starboard seat of the S-3 Viking twin-jet submarine-hunting aircraft, staring at the magnetic anomaly detector display.

"Anything cooking on MAD?" his sonar technician asked.

"Maybe," Samuels said. "I'm getting four detects in the area but the whole channel has been like this."

"All four are weak on the sonobuoys," the technician replied. "Same detects we've been hunting all night."

"Hey, guys, Momma's calling. Playtime's over," the aircraft's pilot said on the intercom.

"Give me one last active dipper," Samuels replied. "These four detects are still bugging me."

Down below, a LAMPS III Seahawk helicopter hovered over the spot marked by the Viking, dropped its dipping sonar and sent out a series of active sonar pings. Twenty-five hundred yards to the west a second Seahawk dropped a dipper, and the two choppers pinged over the area, hoping to come up with something solid over the four MAD detects.

Samuels listened on his radio to the LAMPS choppers for a moment, then nodded somberly and called the pilot on the intercom.

"The LAMPS guys say the detects are the hulls of

the destroyers and some helicopter debris. Nothing strong enough to be a nine-thousand-ton submarine. Let's bug out."

"Roger, concur."

Samuels pulled off his sweaty headset and looked down one last time at the bay water south of the Lushun peninsula. Somewhere down there were the bodies of over a hundred Navy submariners. Out the window the sun had risen high over the bay, the water reflecting a deep blue. The western Korea Bay was a shimmering landscape—it would have made a beautiful painting. Samuels leaned his head against the window and shut his eyes. It had been a long night.

Below them, in the area that had been searched by the Seahawk helicopters, four hulls lay on the bay bottom, two hundred and forty-five feet deep at that point. One was the broken and burned-out remains of the Udaloy destroyer *Zunyi*, the second and third the forward and aft halves of the Luda destroyer *Kaifing*, sliced cleanly in half by the sail of the *Seawolf*. The fourth hull was the *Seawolf*, lying inert, her misshapen sail tipped over in a twenty-five-degree roll, her anechoic tiles blown off her hull, the steel of the cylindrical hull almost completely buried in the silt of the bottom from the explosions of the depth charges.

The S-3 Viking flew in on final approach to the aircraft carrier *Reagan*, Samuels on the radio to flight ops that all detects of the night had proved to be either outcroppings of rocks or the hulls of other ships known to be sunk in the previous day's battle.

Inside the hull of the half-buried *Seawolf* all the lights were off. Only the dim beams of battle lanterns fought the darkness. The atmosphere was close, stuffy, damp. The decks were tilted into a twenty-five-degree roll to starboard. Men lay scattered on the tilted tiles of the decks, some half-conscious, most out cold. Of those unconscious, several were out because of injuries, others because of the diminishing levels of oxygen.

In the control room Pacino tried to open an eye but

couldn't. Had he gone blind? He reached up and put a hand to his face and felt that his right eye was swollen shut. His left seemed normal. While he tried to open his good eye, he tasted copper, as though he were sucking on a penny. He stuck his tongue out in distaste, but his tongue seemed to dissolve into a ball of sparks, the feeling from his mouth turning into an odd combination of partial numbness and coppery taste. He felt something with a part of his tongue that wasn't numb. A tooth. He spit it out, tried to raise his head but vertigo hit him so hard that he had to drop his head again.

After a moment he heard a pinging noise, a sonar ping. Only then did he fully realize where he was. He grimaced as he tried to stand, pulling himself up to a seat at the attack center's Pos Two console. He looked around the room, his good eye blurry, and saw only dim lights. He took a headset and called into it for someone, anyone. He tried to move to the aft end of the room but immediately felt tired and dizzy. He found a cubbyhole locker and pulled out a gas mask, wrapped it on his sore face and plugged it into an air manifold in the overhead.

He took a slow breath, wondering if the air system might be contaminated, it seemed dry and stale. He took another deep breath, feeling his head clear. It had to be the levels of oxygen in the ship. For a moment he considered going to the lower level to the oxygen bottles and opening up the bleed valve, then dismissed the idea. Oxygen was not enough—they needed to clear the air of carbon dioxide. Hell, they *needed* to get the hell out of the bay.

Pacino began to make his way aft to the shielded tunnel, unplugging and replugging his mask every forty feet until he was in maneuvering. He pulled a mask out of the overhead and strapped it onto the engineer's face. Ray Linden opened his eyes, shook his head to clear it.

"We need to restart the scrubbers and burners," Pacino told him.

"We need to restart the reactor," Linden managed to get out. "The battery's down, must have shorted out and opened the battery breaker . . ."

"We're in big trouble with no battery," Pacino said.

"Don't need it to restart," Linden said, getting fresher. "The reactor protection circuitry has backup batteries and we don't need coolant pumps. You say the word and we'll start this thing out of here."

Another reverberating sonar ping through the hull.

"Not yet, they're still looking for us. Get everyone into a mask. I'll call you."

Pacino headed forward to the control room and began strapping masks on the men. When two, then three regained consciousness Pacino told them to help get the rest of the crew in masks and went into the sonar room and found Chief Jeb in a mask staring at him, his face badly swollen.

"Hear the pinging?" Pacino asked. Jeb nodded.

Pacino figured as long as they could hear the pinging through the hull they wouldn't need sonar and could stay on the bottom.

After a few moments the pings died down.

Pacino went back into control, trying to find out how many men were hurt seriously. So far the worst had been some broken bones. The men had fairly well recovered with the breathing air, but the supply was limited. One way or another they had to get the hell out of the bay. He checked his watch. It had been a half hour since the last sonar ping he could remember.

He called Linden aft.

"Start up the reactor and get the atmospheric equipment up, full power lineup, but no main engines yet."

In twenty minutes the fans were working, blowing cool air into the stuffy room. The ESGN navigation system came on with a moan, its ball spinning up to several thousand RPM. The firecontrol and sonar screens lit up as the ship's computer came back to life. The control panel's displays flashed up. *Seawolf* was back.

Pacino pulled on his headset over the straps of his air mask.

"Chief Jeb, can you hear me?"

"Yessir."

"Is sonar up? I'm getting a waterfall screen."

"I'm initializing, sir, but we'll be up in no time."

"Listen for surface and aircraft contacts. I want to know if they're still waiting for us. There hasn't been an active ping in a while."

"Yessir."

Pacino hoisted a phone to his ear.

"Eng, how's the plant?"

"Normal full power lineup, turbines working in spite of the heel. But I'd like to get us horizontal. The condensers don't drain very well like this."

"I'll get back to you. How's the air?"

"Analyzer says we have high CO and CO_2, very low oxygen. We should all be dead."

"Clean it up as fast as you can."

"Conn, Sonar," Jeb's voice announced, a ring of pride coming through. "Sonar's up, no surface contacts, no air contacts. We're cleared for takeoff, Captain."

Pacino liked the sound of that.

"Eng, start the main engines and prepare to answer all bells."

Pacino leaned over the chart, wondering where the ship was. The navigation systems were out of line after the depth charging.

"Conn, Maneuvering. Propulsion is on the main engines, ready to answer all bells," Linden said.

"Diving Officer, blow depth control number two empty and don't let us broach if that's too much buoyancy. Helm, all ahead two thirds!"

First water, then air blew out of the *Seawolf*'s underside as the depth control tank went dry. The propulsor aft spun, still submerged in silt. As the ship grew buoyant she lifted out of the mud, righted her roll and surged ahead, the stern lifting out of the silt.

The deck leveled and the speed indicator rolled the numerals up on the ship control display.

"Helm, all ahead full. Steer course east. Depth one five zero."

When they had gone down, Pacino remembered having less than ten miles to go. At full speed he could be out of the Bo Hai Bay before the Chinese realized he wasn't dead. He watched the chart and when he was sure they'd gone at least twenty miles he stood up on the conn, grabbed the microphone to the Circuit One P.A. system and put the mike to his gas mask exhalation filter.

"Attention, this is the captain." His voice rang out through the decks and the compartments of the submarine. "We are now in international waters in the bay of Korea. Because our atmosphere is still contaminated I intend to surface, which will give us a chance to check out the sail and see how bad the damage is. That's all, carry on."

He took a last look at the sonar display console. The surface was clean.

"Diving Officer, surface the ship."

"Surface the ship, aye. Chief of the Watch, prepare to start the low-pressure blower on all main ballast tanks. Bowplanes to full rise, five degree up angle on the ship. Depth eight zero, seven five, six zero, sir. Depth three eight, three seven. Open inboard induction, drain the header, okay. Open the outboard induction valve, and, Chief, start the blow."

"PLACING THE LOW PRESSURE BLOWER ON ALL MAIN BALLAST TANKS."

With a howl from the fan room aft, the huge displacement blower began blowing the ballast tanks dry. Ten minutes later the Chief of the Watch stopped blowing air into the tanks and began to ventilate the ship with the same blower.

"Captain," the Diving Officer announced, "the ship is on the surface, atmosphere is in spec. Recommend securing air masks."

"Very well," Pacino said. "Mr. Keebes, announce

to the crew to remove air masks and let's get a navigation fix, then get Mr. Turner up here to check out the sail. If it will work let's get the radar mast up and find out where the surface action group is. Once you've got their position, recommend a course to intercept the task force."

"Yessir," Keebes said, already working on the navigation system.

Pacino sat back down on the Pos Two control seat and put his feet up on the console. The best feeling on the run was taking off the gas mask and breathing pure, clean outside air.

USS REAGAN

Admiral Richard Donchez stood on the starboard bridge wing looking out to sea, chewing on a cigar that had gone out a half hour before. Next to him Captain Fred Rummel waited for Donchez to speak.

"I'm sorry, Fred, what did you say?"

"We'll have to notify the Pentagon, sir, that *Seawolf* is lost."

Donchez stared at the blue waves running down the starboard side of the massive aircraft carrier, not seeing the waves but the face of a man he considered his own son.

"Admiral, sir, the Officer of the Deck wants you," an enlisted man announced from the bridge.

Donchez walked into the bridge.

"Sir," the commander said, "we have radar contact on an unidentified submarine that just surfaced about two minutes ago, about twenty miles east of the line marking international waters."

Donchez dropped his cigar.

"What are you doing about it?"

"Trying to raise it on UHF. So far no reply. But she's giving off radar that's classified as a BPS-14."

"What radar did the *Seawolf* have?"

"BPS-14, sir."

The VHF radio monitor blared out into the room the unmistakable voice of Michael Pacino.

"USS *REAGAN,* USS *REAGAN,* THIS IS U.S. NAVY SUBMARINE *SEAWOLF,* I SAY AGAIN, THIS IS U.S. NAVY SUBMARINE *SEAWOLF,* OVER."

Donchez grabbed the VHF microphone, not quite believing it.

"God*damnit,* Mikey, where the hell you been?"

"WE WERE LOST, BUT NOW WE'RE FOUND."

Donchez smiled and handed the microphone back to the OOD. He walked out to the bridge wing and stared back out to sea, the wind howling in his face. Down below, a school of dolphins began to jump in the waves of the ship, as the carrier plowed through the bay, heading south toward the waters of the Yellow Sea, and from there to the Pacific.

EPILOGUE

MONDAY, 20 MAY

"I'm glad you could make it, Sean, but you sure you're okay to sit through all this?" Pacino asked, holding onto Murphy's arm as he walked slowly to the seat in the front row.

"I'm fine, Patch, better than I've ever been, thanks to you and your crew ... and those SEALs."

"Well, take it easy, and if you don't feel good get out of here."

"I wouldn't miss this for anything, old buddy."

"Hey, I'm just giving the ship back to Captain Duckett. That's not such a big deal." Especially since privately he hated separating himself from the *Seawolf*. But that was the deal from the first.

Pacino moved back down the aisle of chairs to the south wall of the pier and looked out over the spread. On the north wall of the pier the *Seawolf* was tied up, her sail ruined, smashed almost in two on the front edge. The jagged metal at the top of the sail begged for a shipyard crew to come and torch it off. Almost all the anechoic tiles were blown off her deck, revealing bare metal beneath—not even the paint remained

385

after she had been depth-charged. She looked like hell, but she was his beauty. Or had been ...

Big white letters had been hung on the ruined sail that read SSN-21 SEAWOLF. Along the pier and draped over the ship were red, white and blue banners. American flags whipped in the wind of the sunny day. All over the pier sailors and officers stood in their dress whites.

Pacino's own whites were starched so hard they felt like cardboard, the high choker collar coming almost to his chin. Over his left pocket the gold of his submarine pin gleamed in the sunshine. Around his neck he wore the Navy Cross—Donchez insisted he wear it. On his left hip he wore a ceremonial officer's sword and on his head he wore a new white senior officer's cap, the gold scrambled eggs shining on the brim. His captain's shoulder boards were brand new, the four broad stripes laying perpendicular to the line of his shoulders.

On the sub's deck a carpenter's crew had made a platform and handrails, and on the platform was a podium with a microphone and the emblem of the *Seawolf,* its head facing out at the crowd.

Admiral Donchez came up to him.

"How do you feel, Mikey?"

Pacino let out a breath. How did he feel to be returning command of the *Seawolf* to Captain Duckett? Over the last ten days he had become a part of the submarine, and it of him.

"I'm gonna miss this girl, Admiral. I admit it. Well, I guess I'd better get up there, we're already late."

Donchez reached into his pocket and handed Pacino an envelope.

"Here are your orders, Mikey. Now get up there and carry on."

As Pacino moved down the aisle and up the gangway to *Seawolf*'s deck he heard the Circuit One P.A. system blast out one last time: *"SEAWOLF ... AR-RIVING!"* He proceeded up to the platform that extended most of the length of the hull aft of the sail, the seats near the sail for senior officers like Donchez and for him and Duckett. Pacino nodded at Captain Henry Duckett, the permanent commander of the submarine. Donchez went to the podium, spoke a few words, led the crowd through the national anthem and a prayer. Pacino then stood, pulled his orders out of his pocket, and walked up to the podium.

The sun was in his eyes as he looked out over the crowd but he could identify the men from *Tampa* who had been well enough to leave their beds for the ceremony. There in the front row were Sean Murphy, Kurt Lennox and their engineer, Vaughn. To their right, filling the rest of the front row and nearly all of the second, were the contingent of SEAL Team Seven, Jack Morris actually smiling up at him. For a moment Pacino stared as he saw his wife in the second row and next to her their son, Tony. The crowd quieted down as Pacino opened the envelope and laid the orders out on the podium, telling himself to get on with it, give Duckett back his ship and get on with his life. But he held back, folded the orders for a moment and stepped up to the microphone.

"Ladies and gentlemen, before I turn over this lady to Captain Duckett, I'd like to say a few words. Less than two weeks ago ... it seems like a lot longer ... I took temporary command of this submarine for a particular operation that went pretty well, thanks to the SEALs of Team Seven and to the men of the USS *Tampa* and the *Seawolf*'s crew. To all of you, I want to say thank you. *Thank you*."

The crowd was silent as Pacino unfolded his orders and squinted through the sun at them as he read:

"From NAVPERS, Washington, D.C., to Captain Michael A. Pacino, U.S. Navy. You are hereby ordered to take permanent command of the USS *Seawolf* and—"

Pacino stopped, stared into the crowd that burst into applause. It went on so long it was embarrassing. He felt his good eye blurring with water as if it were as sore as his injured eye.

Pacino was relieved when Donchez, next to him on the podium, pushed up next to the microphone.

"That's right, people. This isn't a change-of-command ceremony, it's a take-permanent-command ceremony. A reward for a job well done, Captain Pacino. Besides," Donchez grinned, "Captain Duckett says the boat is too much of a wreck to take back, so Captain Pacino, it's now your job to get this boat put back together."

Donchez saluted him, he returned the salute, and then the crew broke ranks and crowded around him, half-carrying him down to the pier.

The speaker system rang out "*SEAWOLF* ... DEPARTING!" and all Pacino could remember of the ceremony from that point on was that he was hugging his wife and son, shaking hands with the crew, and especially with Sean Murphy.

After the crowd had left, only his family remained on the pier as the sun began to set. Then they too left for their hotel and Pacino sat in a chair in the front row and stared at *his* submarine, still not quite believing it was really his.

There was no one else except the deck sentry as he got up and walked to the gangway, intending to go below to his stateroom and change out of his dress whites, when the Circuit One system blared out over the pier the two words that were the most beautiful Pacino had ever heard:

"*SEAWOLF* ... ARRIVING!"

GLOSSARY

ACR (Anti-Circular Run)—A torpedo interlock that prevents the weapon from acquiring on the firing ship. When the torpedo turns more than 160 degrees from the approach course to the target, the onboard gyro sends a signal to the central processor to shut down the unit. It then sinks.

Active Sonar—The determination of a contact's bearing and range by pinging a sound pulse into the ocean and listening for the reflection of the ping from the target. The time interval between transmission and reception gives target range using the speed of sound in water. The direction of the return pulse indicates the target bearing. Generally not used by submarines since it gives away the ship's position.

Anechoic Coating—A thick foam coating attached to the outside of the hulls of some submarines. It absorbs incoming active sonar pulses without reflecting them back, while damping out internal noises before they can get outside the ship. Analogous to stealth radar absorptive material on a stealth aircraft.

Angle On The Bow—The angle between an observer's line-of-sight to a target ship and the target's heading. A ship coming dead on has an angle on the bow of zero degrees. If the contact is going on a course at a right angle to his bearing from the observer, the angle on the bow is port (or starboard) 90 degrees.

ASH (Anti-Self Homing)—A torpedo interlock that measures the distance from the firing ship. If the torpedo comes back toward the firing ship, at 80% of the return trip, the ASH interlock will shut down the unit, and it floods and sinks.

ASW—(1) Antisubmarine warfare. (2) Auxiliary seawater system.

ASWSOW—Antisubmarine warfare standoff weapon. A supersonic solid rocket fueled missile launched from a submarine at either a surfaced or submerged target. Also called "Ow-sow."

Baffles—A "cone of silence" astern of most submarines where sonar reception is hindered by engines, turbines, screws, and other mechanical equipment located in the aft end of a submarine.

Ballast Tank—Tank that is used solely to hold seawater ballast, weight that allows a ship to sink, or, when blown, allows a ship to be light enough to surface.

Battleshort—A condition in which the nuclear reactor's safety interlocks are removed. Used only in a severe emergency or in battle, when an accidental reactor shutdown is more dangerous to the ship due to loss of propulsion than the potential risk of a reactor meltdown. Only the captain can order Battleshort.

Bearing—Direction to a contact, expressed in degrees. A contact to the north is at a bearing of 000. A contact to the east is at 090, etc.

Bigmouth Antenna—Slang name for the AN/BRA-34 multifrequency antenna. A radio antenna suitable for transmission or reception of several frequencies including HF, VHF, and UHF. Shaped like a telephone pole, it protrudes from the sail about 25 feet.

Bridge—Small space at the top of a submarine's sail used for the Officer of the Deck to control the movement of the ship when on the surface. The height allows a better view of the surroundings of the ship.

Bridge Access Trunk—Tunnel from the interior of the submarine to the bridge.

Broadband—Noise containing all frequencies; white noise, such as heard in radio static, rainfall, or a waterfall. Broadband detection range is high for surface ships, which are noisy. Broadband detection range is low for submarines, usually less than five miles, due to quiet submarine designs.

Bubblehead—Derogatory slang for submariner, used by aviators (Airdales) and surface sailors (skimmers).

Check Fire—Order to abort a pending weapon launch.

CINCPAC—Commander-in-Chief Pacific. Admiral in command, U.S. Pacific Forces.

Clamshells—The steel or fiberglass hinged plates that cover the top of the bridge cockpit when rigged for dive and are opened when rigged for surface. When shut, the top of the sail is completely smooth.

Clear Datum—Tactical euphemism meaning run away.

C.O. (Commanding Officer)—Official title of the captain of a ship.

COMMSAT—Communications satellite in a geosynchronous orbit that sends and relays Navy radio traffic.

Contact—Another ship, detected by visual means, sonar, or radar. A contact can be hostile or friendly.

Course—The direction a ship is going measured in true compass degrees. North is 000. East is 090. South is 180, etc.

Critical—The point that a nuclear reactor's fission rate is constant without an external source of neutrons. The chain reaction keeps fissions continuing using neutrons from fissions.

Deck—(1) Floor of the submarine. Each compartment is either two or three decks high. (2) Responsibility for the physical operation of the ship. The officer who has the Deck makes decisions about equipment lineups, how to run and operate ship systems, etc., while the conning officer concerns himself with ship navigation, course, speed, and relationship to the target. Usually the OOD has both the Deck and the Conn.

Depth Control—Ability to control a ship's depth within a narrow control band. Done either manually, with a computer, or with the hovering system (when stopped). Particularly vital at periscope depth because failure to maintain depth control can cause the sail to become exposed (broach), giving away the ship's position.

Dogs—Banana-shaped pieces of metal that act as clasps to keep a hatch shut.

Dolphins—Pin worn above left pocket of submariner's uniform, indicating the person is qualified in submarines. Qualification typically takes one gruelling year. Enlisted men wear silver dolphins; officers wear gold. Dolphins, when not worn on the pocket, are a general symbol of the Submarine Force.

Doppler Effect—Effect responsible for train whistles sounding shrill when the train approaches and low pitched when the train is past. When a moving platform emits sound waves, the waves are compressed ahead and rarefacted (spread apart) behind the source. The compression of the waves raises their frequency, making a higher note.

EMBT Blow—Emergency main ballast tank blow.

Emergency Blow—Blowing the water out of the main ballast tanks using ultra-high-pressure air. Empties ballast tanks in seconds, lightening the ship, allowing the ship to get to the surface in an emergency such as flooding.

Emergency Propulsion Motor (EPM)—A large DC motor aft in the engineroom, capable of turning the shaft to achieve 3 knots using battery power alone. An electricity hog.

EO (Electrical Operator)—Enlisted nuclear-qualified watchstander who mans the Electric Plant Control Panel and reports to the EOOW.

EOOW (Engineering Officer of the Watch)—Nuclear-qualified officer who runs the nuclear power plant. Responsible to the OOD for propulsion and propulsion plant damage control.

Escape Trunk—A spherical airlock used on American nuclear submarines. The device can be used to make emergency exits from a sub sunk in shallow water. Principally used for divers to lock in or lock out.

ESGN—Ship's inertial navigation system using a small metal ball that spins at about 10,000 RPM to gyroscopically maintain a constant reference (north).

ESM (Electronics Surveillance Measures)—The gathering of intelligence through the analysis of enemy signals, including radars and radio transmitters.

EWS (Engineering Watch Supervisor)—A Chief who is a roving supervisory watchstander in the engineering spaces. Reports to the EOOW.

Fathom—Unit of depth equal to six feet.

Fathometer—Bottom sounding sonar that directs an active sonar pulse down to the ocean bottom and measures the time for the pulse to reflect back and hence the distance to the bottom. New units transmit a secure pulse, using a short duration random high frequency pulse.

Final Bearing and Shoot—Order of the captain to shoot a torpedo after he takes one last periscope observation of a surface target.

Firecontrol Solution—A contact's range, course, and speed. A great mystery when using passive sonar. Determining the solution requires maneuvering one's own ship and doing calculations on the target's bearing rate. Can be obtained manually or with the firecontrol computer.

Firecontrol System—A computer system that accepts input from the periscope, sonar, and radar (when on the surface) to determine the firecontrol solution. The system also programs, fires, steers, and monitors torpedoes. If a ship is cruise missile equipped, the system will program and fire the missile.

Firecontrol Team—A collection of people whose task is to put a weapon on a target. Includes the sonar operators, OOD, JOOD, Captain, XO, firecontrol operators on Pos One, Pos Two, Pos Three, the firing panel, and the manual plotters (geographic, time-bearing, time-range, and time-frequency).

Firing Panel—A console section between Pos Two and Pos Three. The vertical section is a tube/weapon status panel. The horizontal section has the trigger, a lever used to fire a torpedo or cruise missile.

Firing Point Procedures—An order by the captain to the firecontrol team to tell them to prepare to fire the weapon, done during a deliberate approach when the solution is refined, as opposed to a Snapshot. The solution is locked into the weapon and the ship is put into a firing attitude.

Fix—A ship's position. Determined by visual triangulation or radar when close to land on the surface, or by NAVSAT or BC sonar when at sea.

Flag Plot—A chart room used by flag officers (admirals) to plot strategy or determine the distribution of forces.

Flank Speed—Maximum speed of a U.S. submarine. Requires fast speed reactor main coolant pumps and running at 100% reactor power.

FLASH—The highest priority of a radio message. Receipt required within minutes or seconds.

Forced Circulation—Forced flow of water coolant through a reactor using pumps, as opposed to natural circulation.

G—A measure of acceleration. The acceleration due to gravity is one g. Two g's is twice, etc.

Geographic Plot—(1) A manual plot saved from World War II submarine days using the plot table to deduce a firecontrol solution. Works well on unsuspecting targets. Target zigs cause confusion on this plot. Useless in a melee situation. (2) A mode of display of the Mark I firecontrol system showing a God's eye view of the sea with own ship at the center and the other contacts and their solutions surrounding it.

GMT (Greenwich Mean Time)—A worldwide time standard using the time at longitude zero at Greenwich, England. Also called Zulu time.

GPS (Global Positioning System)—A series of satellites and shipborne receivers enabling extremely precise navigation fixes. Also called the NAVSAT.

Gyro/Gyroscope—Electrical compass using a rapidly spinning gyroscope.

Head—Seagoing term for bathroom.

Helm—The wheel that turns the ship's rudder. Also short for helmsman.

Hovering System—A depth control system managed by a computer that keeps the ship in one point underwater. Used by boomers when launching missiles. Used by fast attack submarines to establish a desired vertical speed (depth rate) to vertical surface through polar ice.

Hull Array—One of the sonar hydrophone element assemblies (arrays) of the BATEARS sonar suite, consisting of multiple hydrophones placed against the skin of the hull over about one-third of the ship's length. Used mostly as a backup to the spherical array because the hull array's sensitivity is reduced by own ship noise inside the hull.

HUMINT—Human intelligence, that gained from foreign agents or American intelligence officers.

IR—Infrared.

JOOD—Junior Officer of the Deck; Assistant to the OOD. When in transit, the JOOD is usually an unqualified officer in a training position, given the Conn and supervised by the OOD.

KH-17—Newest generation of Bigbird spy satellites. The KH stands for Keyhole—appropriate for a spy platform.

LAMPS—Light airborne multipurpose system. Cute acronym for a Seahawk ASW helicopter carried aboard a U.S. Navy surface ship.

Leg—The straight line travel of a submarine doing passive sonar Target Motion Analysis (TMA) between maneuvers. During a leg the crew attempts to establish a steady bearing rate to the target and establish speed across the line-of-sight to the target. Two legs determine a firecontrol solution. Three legs confirm the solution. Four legs indicate the captain is afraid to shoot. A large sign at Prospective Commanding Officer School in Groton, Connecticut, reads "YOU DON'T NEED ANOTHER GODDAMNED LEG!"

List—Tilt of a ship to the side.

Locking In/Locking Out—Entering or leaving a submerged submarine through the escape trunk (airlock).

Lookaround—(1) A periscope observation. (2) A warning by the OOD or captain to the ship control team that the periscope is about to be raised. The Diving Officer and helmsman report ship's speed and depth as a reminder, since high speeds can rip the periscope off and flood the ship through the periscope hole.

MAD (Magnetic Anomaly Detector)—A detector flown on an aircraft that measures changes in the earth's magnetic field that could be caused by the iron hull of a submarine.

Main Ballast Tank—Tank that is used solely to hold seawater ballast, weight that allows a ship to sink, or, when blown, allows a ship to be light enough to surface.

Main Engines (Propulsion Turbines)—The large turbines that extract energy from steam and convert it to power to turn the screw.

Main Steam Valves One and Two (MS-1, MS-2)— Large gate valves on the port and starboard main steam headers, at the forward bulkhead of the aft compartment. These can isolate the main steam system in the event of a major steam leak.

Maneuvering—The nuclear control room, located in the aft compartment upper level. Smaller than most closets.

Maneuvering Watch—The watch stations manned when a ship gets underway in restricted waters.

Mark 36 or 38—A torpedo-sized decoy vehicle that transmits the sounds of a submarine and can be programmed to maneuver through the ocean like a submarine; used to evade a trailing hostile ship or torpedo.

Mark 50—Latest breed of torpedo. Also called the "Hullcrusher."

Mark 80 SLAAM—Submarine-launched anti-air missile.

Mark On Top—Term used to note that a hostile aircraft is flying directly over the submarine. Generally means the submarine has been detected by the aircraft and will be under attack almost immediately. Usually followed by an expletive, i.e., "P-3 mark on top, dammit."

Natural Circulation—Water flow through a reactor caused only by the heat of the core—hot water rises and cold sinks. Eliminates use of noisy main coolant pumps, allowing quieter operation.

NESTOR Secure Voice—A UHF radiotelephone communication system that encrypts a voice signal prior to transmission and decrypts it after reception. Can be transmitted to the satellite and beamed worldwide. Fast, secure means of communication.

New Kuomintang (NKMT)—A Chinese revolutionary group modeled after the unsuccessful faction of the 1940s. The NKMT, with Japanese support, is dedicated to the overthrow of the Chinese Communists.

NMCC (National Military Command Center)—A nerve center in the Pentagon where, in theory, orders would originate for fighting a nuclear war. Seasoned officers scoff at the idea that NMCC would survive the first ten minutes of a surprise decapitation assault.

Nukes—(1) Nuclear weapons. (2) Nuclear-trained officers and enlisted men.

OOD (Officer of the Deck)—Officer in tactical command of the ship, a sort of acting captain. Directs the motion of the ship, giving rudder, speed, and depth orders. Responsible for ship's navigation, operation of the ship's equipment, and employment of the ship's weapons. Usually has the Deck and the Conn. Needs captain's permission to do certain operations, such as go to periscope depth, start up the reactor, transmit active sonar or transmit radio, or launch a weapon. Done best while smoking a cigar and telling sea stories.

OP—Operation or mission.

OPAREA—A specific ocean area devoted to a particular exercise or operation. Some OPAREA's are permanent, some are established only for one exercise.

OPREP 3 PINNACLE—Name of a message that is sent with FLASH priority to the White House and NMCC telling of a dire emergency requiring immediate action, such as an incoming nuclear assault.

Overhead—Nautical term for ceiling.

Ow-Sow—Pronunciation of ASWSOW, antisubmarine warfare standoff weapon.

P.A. Circuit One—Shipwide Public Address announcing system.

P.A. Circuit Two—Similar to P.A. Circuit One, except that it only announces in the engineering spaces.

P.A. Circuit Seven—Speaker announcing system used between the Conn, Maneuvering, the bridge, and the torpedo room.

Passive Sonar—Most common mode of employment of most submarine sonar systems. Sonar system is used only to *listen*, not to ping out active sonar beams, since pinging gives away a covert submarine's presence. Use of passive sonar makes it difficult to determine a contact's range, course, and speed (solution). TMA is the means of obtaining a solution when using passive sonar.

Patrol Quiet—Ship system's lineup to ensure maximum quiet while allowing normal creature comforts such as cooking and movie watching. Maintenance on equipment is allowed, if it does not involve banging on the hull. Noisy operations are permitted only with the captain's permission, such as reactor coolant discharge, steam generator blowdowns, etc.

PD (Periscope Depth)—An operation in which a ship comes shallow enough to see with the periscope. Certain operations can be done only at periscope depth by decree of the Submarine Standard Operating Procedures manual. Such items include steam generator blowdown, shooting trash from the TDU, and blowing sanitary. Some things can only be done at PD, including radio reception of satellite broadcasts, reception of a NAVSAT pass, and ESM activities. Slows the ship down since high speeds can rip off the periscope. Dangerous operation since quiet surface ships can get close without being detected by sonar.

Pilot—A person who has detailed knowledge and experience of a port and approach waterways. Taken on prior to entering or exiting port to serve as an advisor to the captain. A mixed blessing for ship captains, since a pilot's mistake still gets the captain fired (the ship is the captain's ultimate responsibility, not the pilot's), while ignoring a pilot can also get a captain fired, especially if the ship runs aground.

Ping—An active sonar pulse.

PLA—People's Liberation Army. The Chinese military, composing both the army and navy.

Polymer Injection—The injection of a polymer into the boundary layer of a submarine at the nosecone. The slippery liquid reduces the skin friction of the ship, reducing the drag. The result is the ability to dramatically increase ship's top speed for short periods of time. Ideal for torpedo evasion.

Poopy Suit—Underway uniform worn by American submariners. Usually cotton coveralls. Origin unknown, but probably refers to frequent occurrence of showers and laundry service being curtailed when rigged for ultraquiet or when the evaporator is broken, causing the coveralls to stink.

Position One (Pos One)—Furthest forward console of the firecontrol system. Usually set up with the captain's and XO's guess solution to the contact, or shows the geographic display for a God's eye view of the sea.

Position Two (Pos Two)—Firecontrol console between Pos One and the Firing Panel. Usually set up to the Line-of-Sight mode so that the Pos Two officer can come up with his own independent firecontrol solution under the XO's supervision.

Position Three (Pos Three)—Furthest aft console of the firecontrol system. Usually set up to program torpedo tubes and weapons.

Power Range—Nuclear power level above the intermediate range. In the power range, steam can be produced by the reactor for propulsion.

PRC—People's Republic of China, the Communists.

Propulsor—Sophisticated screw that uses ducting and multistage water turbine blades for propulsion instead of a conventional screw. Similar to a water jet. Extremely quiet and nearly impossible to cavitate.

Disadvantage includes slow response and acceleration due to relatively low thrust compared to conventional screws.

Radar Intercept Officer (RIO)—Weapons officer
aboard a U.S. Navy fighter aircraft.

Range—Distance to a contact.

Reactor Compartment—Compartment housing the reactor, pressurizer, steam generators, and reactor
main coolant pumps. Access fore and aft is through
a shielded tunnel, since anyone inside the compartment when the reactor is critical would be dead
within a minute from the intense radiation.

Reactor Main Coolant Pumps—Massive pumps, each
consuming between 100 and 400 horsepower, that
force main coolant water through the reactor and
then to the steam generators. Three are in each
main coolant loop. Special design allows zero
leakage.

Reactor Plant Control Panel (RPCP)—Control panel
in the maneuvering room where the Reactor Operator controls the reactor.

Reduction Gear—The mechanism that converts the
high RPMs of the two main engines (propulsion
turbines) to the slow RPM of the screw. Solves the
problem of how to get two turbines to drive a single
screw. Also solves the problem of how to let the
main engines rotate at high RPM where they are
efficient while letting the screw rotate at the low
RPM where it is efficient. Unfortunately, the reduction gear is one of the noisiest pieces of equipment
aboard.

REM—Roentgen Equivalent Man. A unit of radiation
dosage that takes into account tissue damage due

to neutron radiation. Convenient since it allows gamma, alpha, and neutron radiation to be measured with the same units. 1000 rem will kill. 500 rem may kill. Yearly dose for submarine personnel is restricted to less than 25 to 100 millirem.

Rig For Black—Submarine term meaning "turn off the lights in the control room."

Rig For Dive—A detailed valve and switch lineup done in preparation to dive. Initially done by a dolphin-wearing enlisted man and checked by a dolphin-wearing officer.

Rig For Patrol Quiet—Ship systems lineup to ensure maximum quiet while allowing normal creature comforts such as cooking and movie watching. Maintenance on equipment is allowed, if it does not involve banging on the hull. Noisy operations are permitted only with the captain's permission, such as reactor coolant discharge, steam generator blow-downs, etc.

Rig For Ultraquiet—Ship systems lineup done in a tactical situation such as a close trailing OP or in wartime. Only the quietest equipment is running. Offwatch personnel are required to be in bed. The galley, showers, laundry, movies, and maintenance of equipment are all prohibited to minimize noise. Hard-soled shoes are prohibited. Lights are shifted to red to remind the crew of the need for silence. The ship is eerily quiet, as if run by ghosts.

Rig For White—Submarine term meaning "turn on the lights in the control room."

RO (Reactor Operator)—Nuclear-trained enlisted man who mans the Reactor Plant Control Panel and reports to the EOOW.

RPG—Rocket-propelled grenade.

Run-To-Enable—Initial torpedo run taking it away from own ship. During the run-to-enable, the warhead is not armed and the sonar is not operational. When the run-to-enable is complete, the weapon activates the active or passive sonar and swims the search pattern. The warhead is not armed until it has a detect on the target.

Sail—Conning tower. Named because, unlike the conning towers of World War II diesel boats, which were misshapen and asymmetrical, modern nuclear submarine conning towers are smooth fins with square profiles when viewed from the side. Someone in the distant past called it a sail and the term became official.

SCRAM—An emergency shutdown of a nuclear reactor, done by driving control rods to the bottom of the core using springs. A term left over from the 1940s when primitive lab reactors had a single control rod suspended by a rope. An emergency shutdown would be done by cutting the rope and letting the rod drop by gravity. The safety man was called the Safety Control Rod Ax Man—hence SCRAM.

SCRAM Breaker—A circuit breaker that interrupts power to the latching electromagnets of the control rod drive mechanisms. When the breaker opens, electrical power to the electromagnets is shut off, the magnets lose their magnetism, and the latches of the rods open, allowing springs to drop the rods to the bottom of the core.

Scrambled Eggs—The gold branches of leaves sewn onto the brim of a senior officer's cap.

Scrubber—CO_2 scrubber. Atmospheric control equipment that rids the ship of carbon dioxide (from breathing, the diesel, and the CO burner) by blowing it over an amine bed.

SEAL—Sea/Air/Land commando.

Sea Trials—Post-construction shakedown cruise of a ship. Done to ensure the equipment lives up to specifications and is ready to perform its mission.

SECDEF—Secretary of Defense.

Section Tracking Team—A firecontrol team stationed to man the plots and firecontrol system when tracking a hostile contact for extended periods of time. Modified battlestations. So named because each watchsection (similar to a shift) has its own tracking team.

Ship Control Panel (SCP)—The console from which the ship's depth, course, and speed are controlled. This console resembles a 747 cockpit, with the Sternplanesman on one side, the Helmsman on the other, and the Diving Officer behind and between them.

Ship Control Team—The watchstanders manning the Ship Control Panel, including the Sternplanesman, the Helmsman, and the Diving Officer. Sometimes includes the Chief of the Watch, off to the port side at the Ballast Control Panel.

Shoot On Generated Bearing—Captain's order to shoot a torpedo based on the firecontrol solution's estimate of where a target should be, not on the last actual bearing from sonar. When ordered, the firecontrol team locks in the firecontrol solution to the target, and when the torpedo reports back, the captain is given one last chance to say either "Shoot" or "Check fire."

SITREP—Situation report, a high priority radio message to a high-level commander reporting the status of a contact or enemy.

Signal Ejector—A small torpedo tube used to eject flares (for signalling surface ships), communication buoys (which can transmit hours after the ship has cleared datum; also used for SUBSUNK buoys), and countermeasures (torpedo decoys).

SLAAM—Submarine-launched anti-air missile.

Snapshot—A quick reaction torpedo shot, usually done only when fired upon first.

Snorkel—A mast designed to bring air into the submarine so that the airbreathing diesel generator can use it for combustion when the reactor is scrammed.

Solution—A contact's range, course, and speed. A great mystery when using passive sonar. Determining the solution requires maneuvering own ship and doing calculations on the target's bearing rate. Can be obtained manually or with the firecontrol computer.

Sonobuoys—Small objects dropped from ASW aircraft that float on the surface and listen to the ocean below, then transmit that information up to the aircraft. A method of giving an aircraft sonar capability.

SPEC-OP—Special operation, usually top secret, and usually very hairy.

SPECWAR—Special warfare. Commando operations.

Spherical Array—A sphere in the nosecone of a submarine fitted with transducers over most of its surface to be able to hear in all directions (except the baffles). Useful since it not only tells the bearing to an incoming noise, but also its D/E (deflection/elevation). The D/E can give clues that the sound is relayed via bottom bounce or surface bounce, or even that a close contact is deeper or shallower than own ship.

Spin Up—Start the gyro and computer system of a weapon in preparation for launch.

Spook—A spy, either from Naval Intelligence, CIA, National Security Agency, or a nameless U.S. Navy organization that sends riders onboard to gather electronic intelligence when the ship is on a special OP.

SSN—A fast attack submarine. Literally stands for Submersible Ship Nuclear, although most crews agree it means Saturdays, Sundays, and Nights.

Steam Leak, Major—When one of the large steam pipes ruptures in the engineroom. Result is rapid cooking of engineering crew unless the leak is isolated using MS-1 or -2 valves. Steam leaks are also dangerous because they will overpower the reactor.

Steam Plant Control Panel (SPCP)—Console in the maneuvering room that monitors the steam plant. Has the large throttle wheel in front that controls the speed of the main engines. Manned by the throttleman.

Sternplanes—Horizontal control surfaces at the tail of a submarine. Similar to the elevator tail surfaces of an aircraft, the sternplanes cause the ship to rise or dive.

Sternplanesman—Enlisted watchstander in the Ship Control Party who controls the sternplanes at the Ship Control Panel.

Sustainer Engine—The jet engine of a cruise missile. It sustains continued flight.

Target One—The designation of a sonar, radar, ESM, or visual contact as a target to be fired upon or tracked.

Target Zig—A term used to describe a target's maneuver, either a turn, speed change, or both. Totally messes up a passive sonar firecontrol solution, requiring the ship to do more TMA to get a new solution. Note: the term "zig-zag" is never used in the modern submarine force.

TG's (Turbine Generators)—The two turbines aft that turn the ship's electrical generators and provide electrical power.

Throttle—The valves at the inlet of a steam turbine that determine how much steam flow the turbine will receive, and thus, the amount of power the turbine will produce (and its speed). Done at the Steam Plant Control Panel.

Throttleman—Nuclear-trained enlisted watchstander who monitors the steam plant at the Steam Plant Control Panel and positions the throttle based on the speed orders of the control room (which are transmitted by the engine order telegraph).

TMA (Target Motion Analysis)—Means of establishing a target solution using passive sonar. Own ship does maneuvers to generate speed first on one side of the line-of-sight, then on the other. Several maneuvers or legs can quickly find the target solution. Stealthy method of determining what the target is doing. The system is weak when the target is himself doing TMA. Result is a melee or PCO Waltz, where both submarines are maneuvering and neither knows what the other is doing. In worst case, submarines may need to shift to active sonar to determine range or clear datum until the target can be ambushed stealthily.

Towed Array—A passive sonar hydrophone array towed astern of a submarine on a cable up to several miles long. The array itself may be a thousand feet long. The array is used to detect narrowband tonals at extreme ranges.

Transient—A noise that is made by an enemy sub due to a temporary condition. Examples include dropped wrenches, boots clomping on deckplates, slamming hatches, boiler blowdowns, rattling checkvalves, etc.

Turbine—A mechanical rotating device with blades that converts the pressure energy, velocity energy, and internal (temperature) energy of a fluid steam (steam or combustion gases) into mechanical power.

Ultraquiet—Ship systems lineup done in a tactical situation such as a close trailing OP or in wartime. Only the quietest equipment is running. Offwatch personnel are required to be in bed. The galley, showers, laundry, movies, and maintenance of equipment are all prohibited to minimize noise. Hard soled shoes are prohibited. Lights are shifted to red to remind the crew of the need for silence. The ship is eerily quiet, as if run by ghosts.

Unit—A torpedo launched by own ship. As opposed to a torpedo (after sonar calls "torpedo in the water") which is launched by a hostile submarine.

UWT (Underwater Telephone)—A sonar system using voice transmissions instead of tones or pulses, used for communication between two submarines that are fairly close.

VLS (Vertical Launch System)—New missile launch system on later *Los Angeles* class attack submarines, in which space in the forward group of ballast tanks has vertical torpedo tubes for launching Javelin cruise missiles. Allows torpedo room space to hold more torpedoes.

Wardroom—(1) Officer's messroom. Used also as a conference room, briefing room, reconstruction room, junior officer's office, movie screening room, and place to converse, (2) The group of officers assigned to a ship.

Warshot—A weapon that is used to sink an enemy ship or inflict damage on a target, as opposed to an exercise shot.

Watch/Watchstation—A watch is an eight-hour shift during which a group of men at specific stations run the submarine. A watchstation is a person's station or assignment during the watch. Example: helmsman, Diving Officer, Chief of the Watch, Throttleman, etc.

Watchsection—A collection of watchstanders who run the submarine for an eight-hour shift called a watch.

Waterfall—A display of broadband sonar with bearing on the horizontal and time on the vertical. Broadband noise traces fall down the screen, looking like a waterfall.

XO (Executive Officer)—Officer who is second in command of a nuclear submarine, responsible to the captain for the administrative functioning of the ship. At battlestations, the XO coordinates the firecontrol team and makes recommendations to the captain.

Zig—A term used to describe a target's maneuver, either a turn, speed change, or both. Totally messes up a passive sonar firecontrol solution, requiring the ship to do more TMA to get a new solution. Note: the term "zig-zag" is never used in the modern submarine force.

Zulu—Same as Greenwich Mean Time.